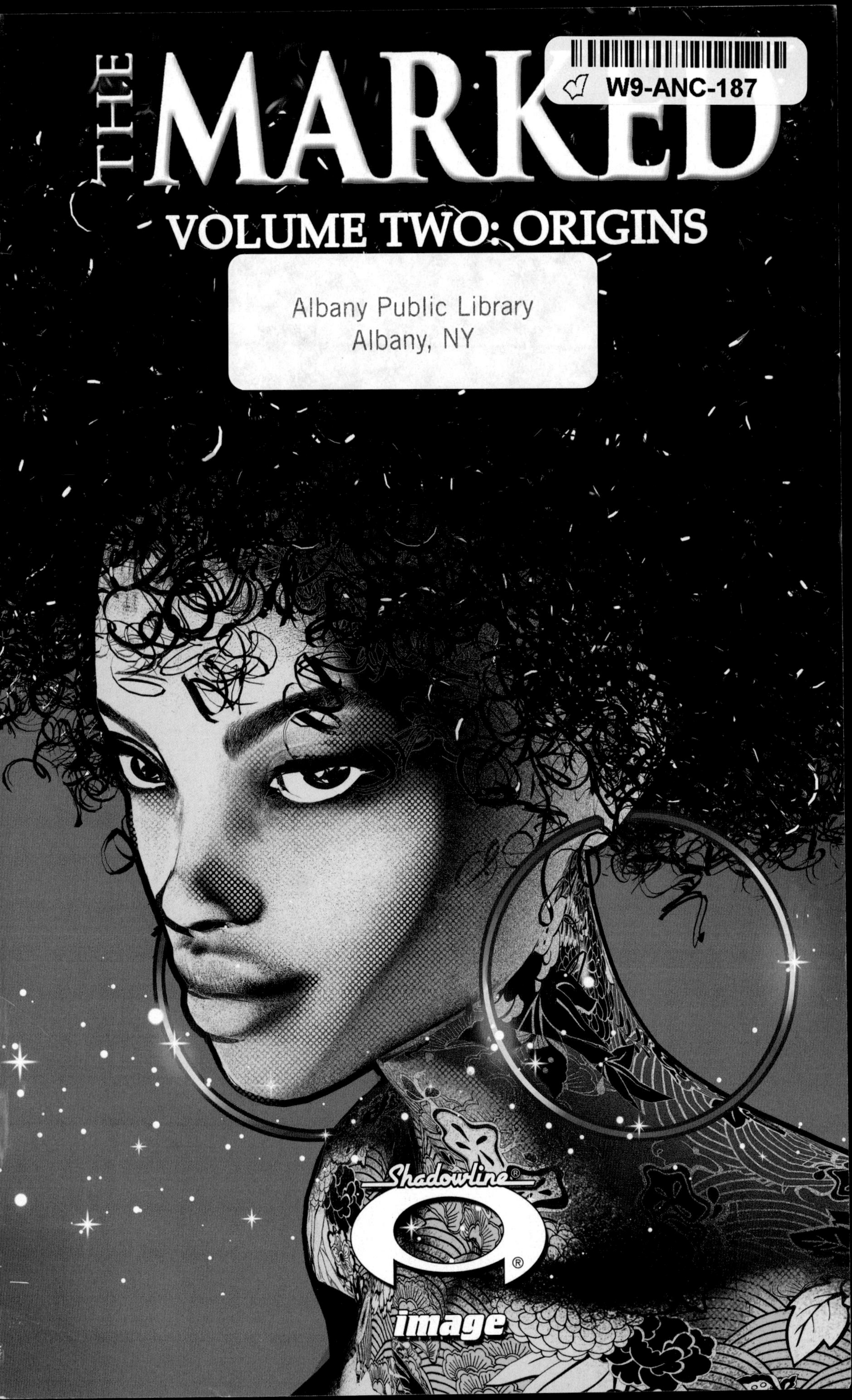
THE MARKED
VOLUME TWO: ORIGINS
Shadowline
image

First printing: January 2021

ISBN: 978-1-5343-1673-7

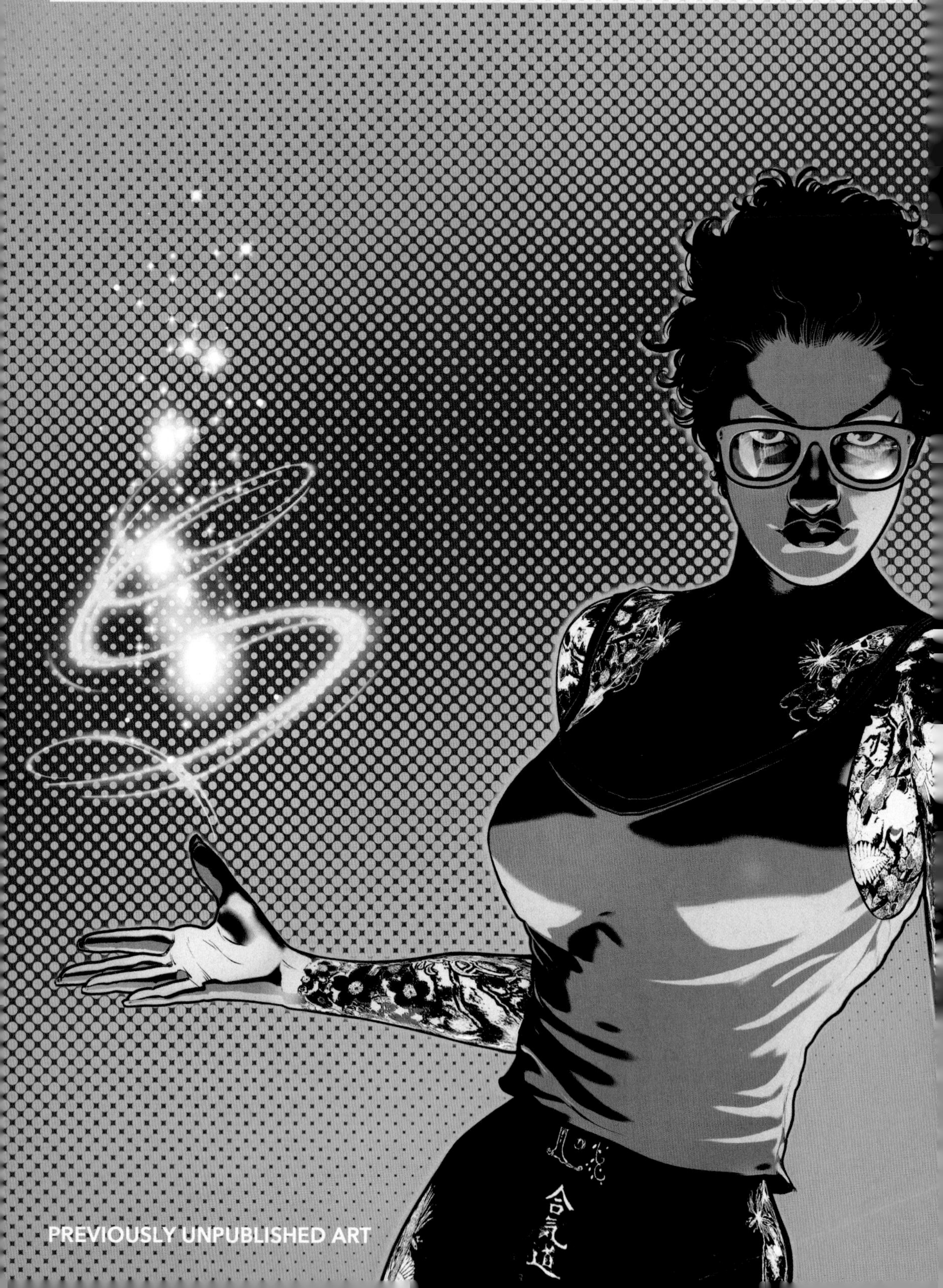
合気道

PREVIOUSLY UNPUBLISHED ART

IMAGE COMICS PRESENTS

THE MARKED ™

FOR

STORY
BRIAN HABERLIN
(CHAPTERS 6–10)

DAVID HINE
(CHAPTERS 6 & 7)

ART
BRIAN HABERLIN

COLORS
GEIRROD VAN DYKE

LETTERS
FRANCIS TAKENAGA

LEAD DEVELOPER
DAVID PENTZ

PRODUCTION
HANNAH WALL

IMAGE COMICS, INC.

Todd McFarlane: President
Jim Valentino: Vice President
Marc Silvestri: Chief Executive Officer
Erik Larsen: Chief Financial Officer
Robert Kirkman: Chief Operating Officer

Eric Stephenson: Publisher / Chief Creative Officer
Shanna Matuszak: Editorial Coordinator
Marla Eizik: Talent Liaison
Nicole Lapalme: Controller
Leanna Caunter: Accounting Analyst
Sue Korpela: Accounting & HR Manager
Jeff Boison: Director of Sales & Publishing Planning
Dirk Wood: Director of International Sales & Licensing
Alex Cox: Director of Direct Market & Specialty Sales
Chloe Ramos-Peterson: Book Market
& Library Sales Manager
Emilio Bautista: Digital Sales Coordinator
Kat Salazar: Director of PR & Marketing
Drew Fitzgerald: Marketing Content Associate
Heather Doornink: Production Director
Drew Gill: Art Director
Hilary DiLoreto: Print Manager
Tricia Ramos: Traffic Manager
Erika Schnatz: Senior Production Artist
Ryan Brewer: Production Artist
Deanna Phelps: Production Artist

IMAGECOMICS.COM

A
Shadowline ®
PRODUCTION

MELANIE HACKETT
EDITOR

MARC LOMBARDI
COMMUNICATIONS

JIM VALENTINO
PUBLISHER

PREVIOUSLY UNPUBLISHED ART

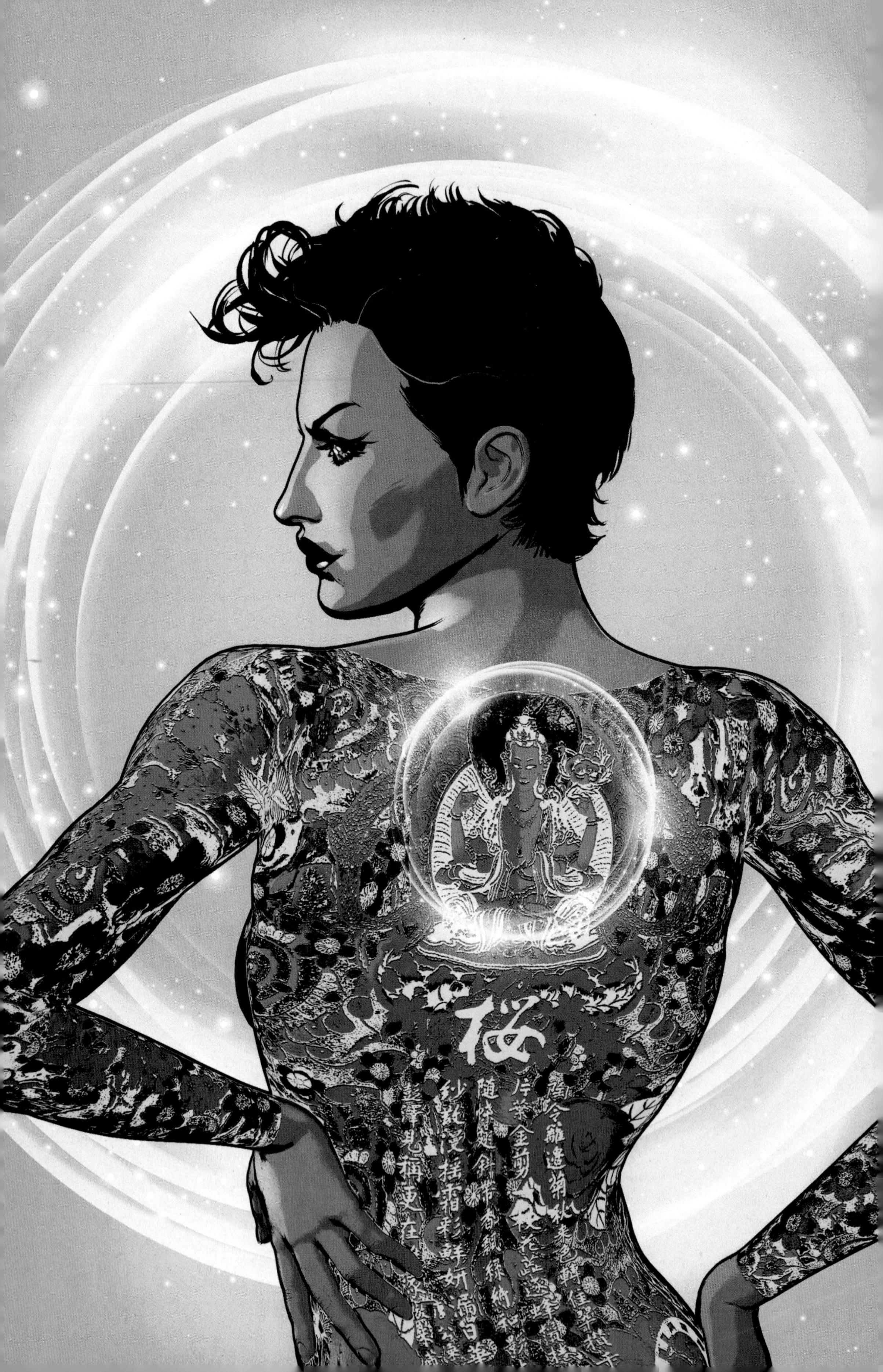
桜

CHAPTER SIX

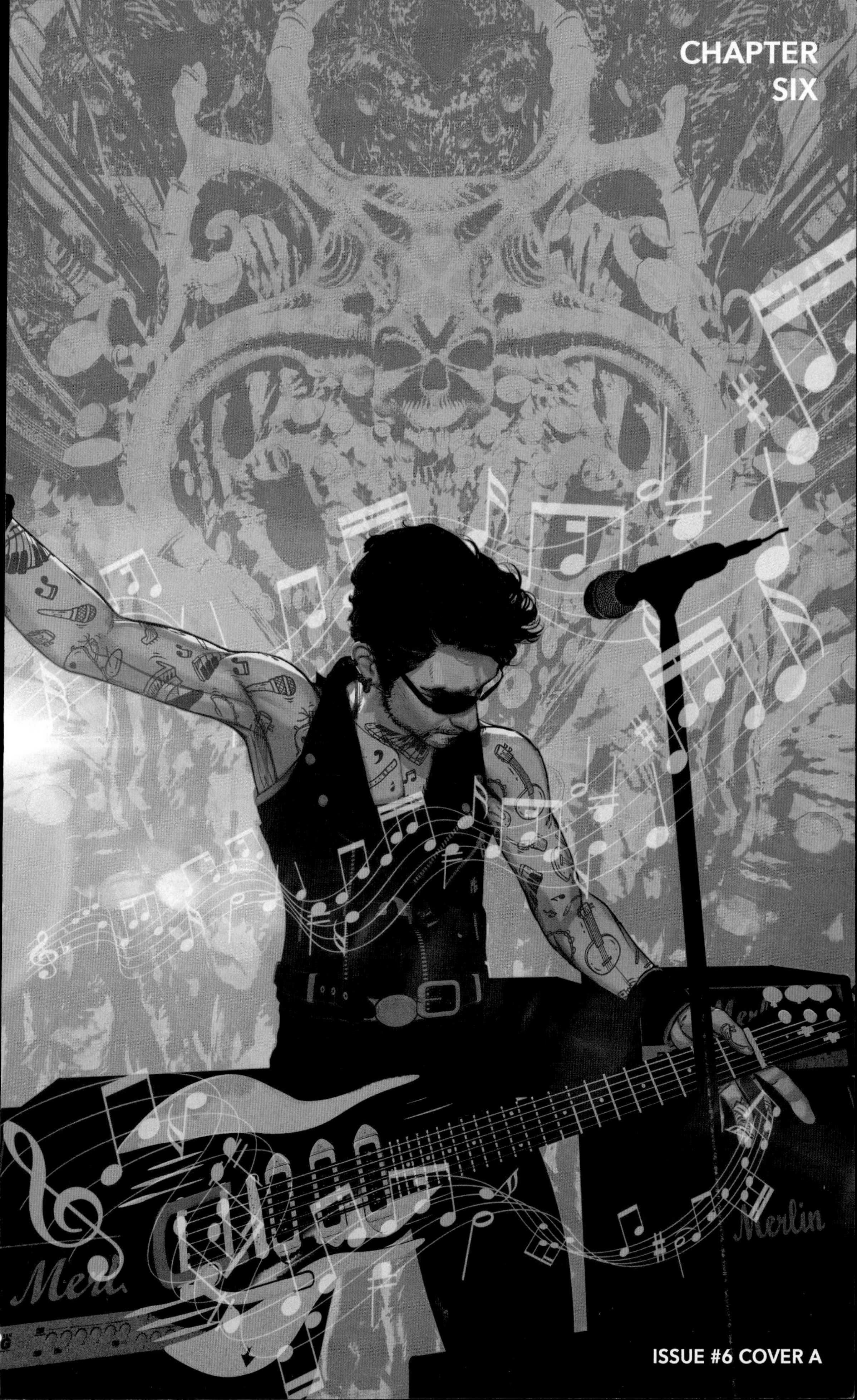
Merlin

ISSUE #6 COVER A

ISSUE #6 COVER B

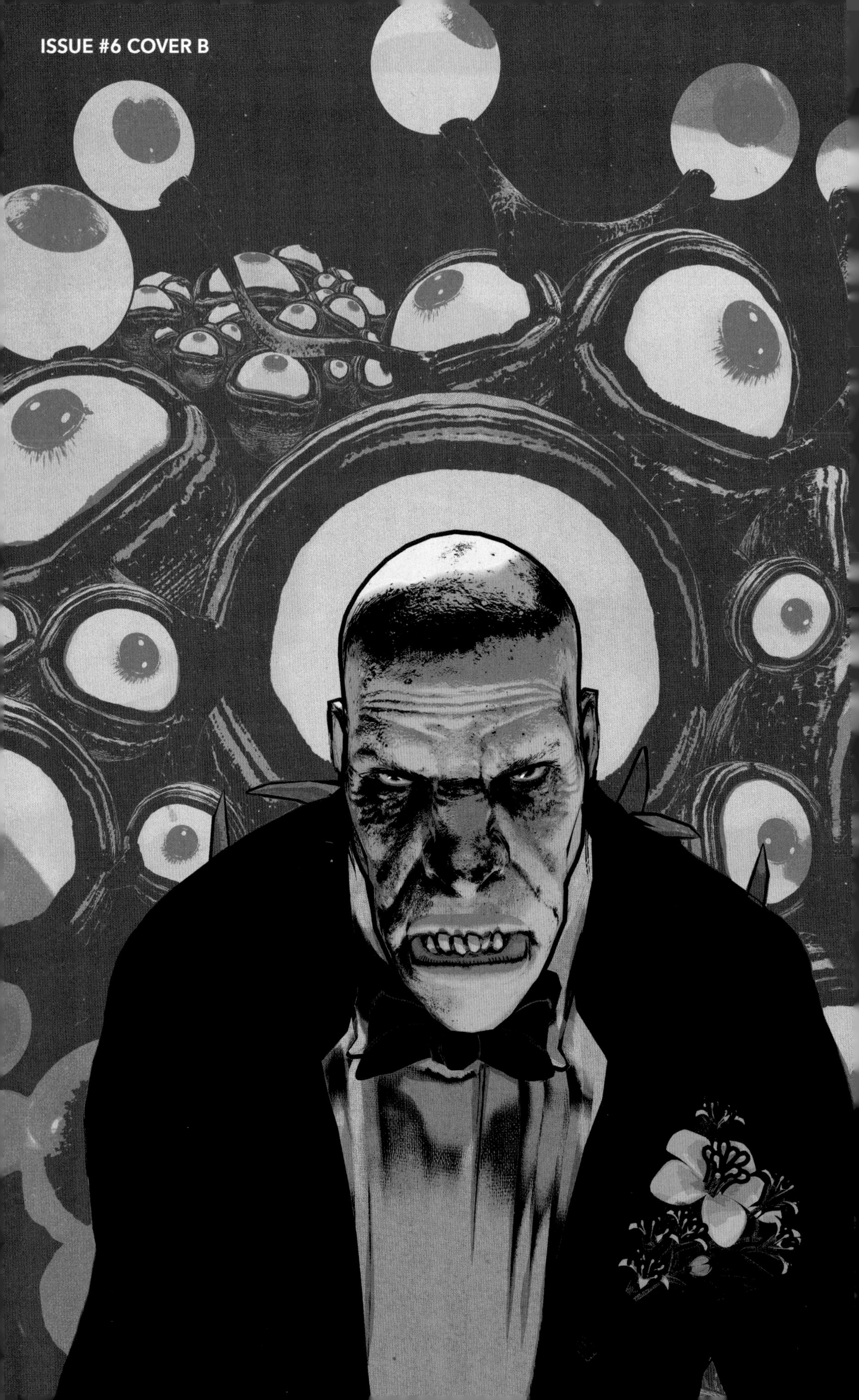

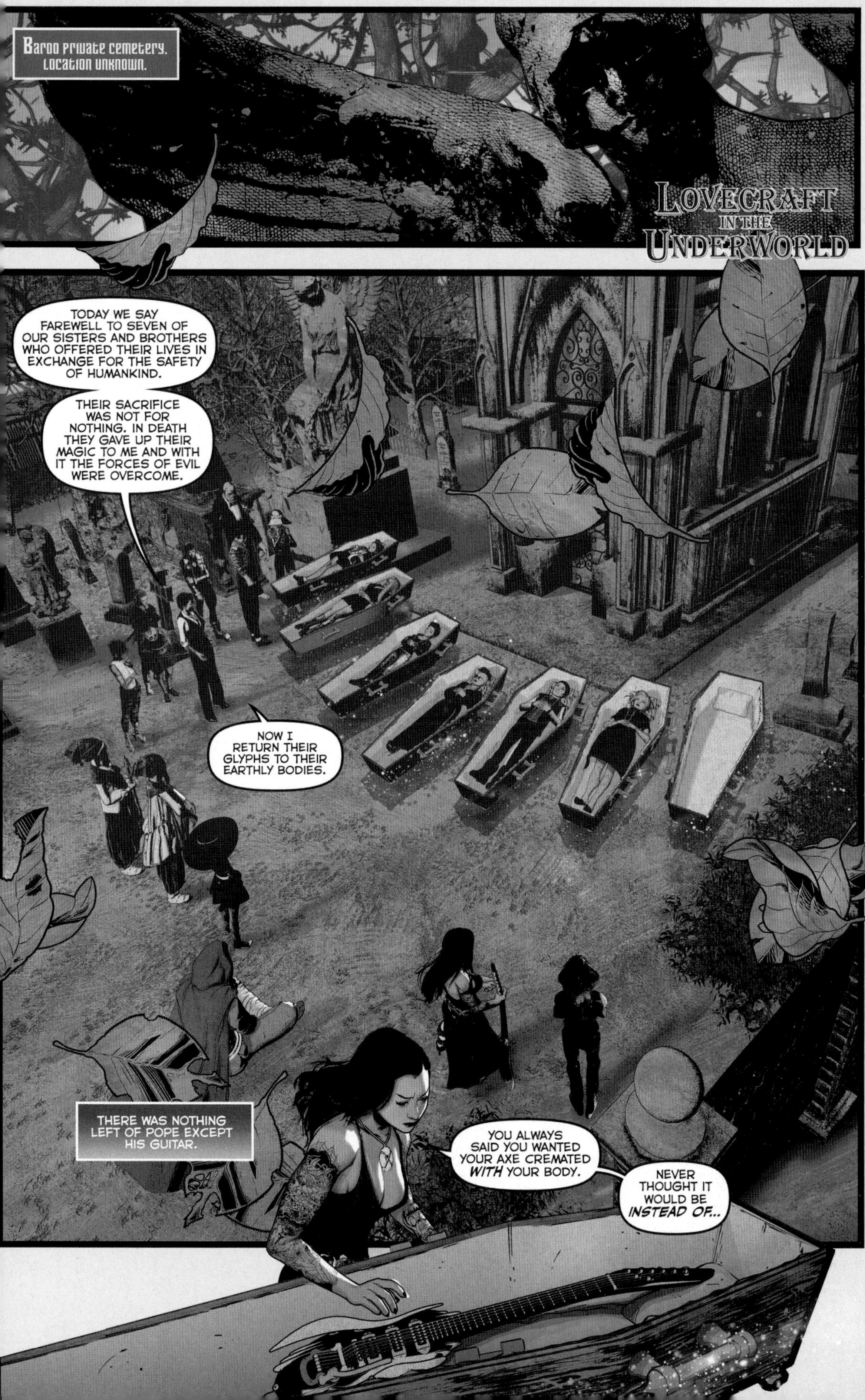
Baroo private cemetery. Location unknown.
LOVECRAFT IN THE UNDERWORLD
TODAY WE SAY FAREWELL TO SEVEN OF OUR SISTERS AND BROTHERS WHO OFFERED THEIR LIVES IN EXCHANGE FOR THE SAFETY OF HUMANKIND.
THEIR SACRIFICE WAS NOT FOR NOTHING. IN DEATH THEY GAVE UP THEIR MAGIC TO ME AND WITH IT THE FORCES OF EVIL WERE OVERCOME.
NOW I RETURN THEIR GLYPHS TO THEIR EARTHLY BODIES.
THERE WAS NOTHING LEFT OF POPE EXCEPT HIS GUITAR.
YOU ALWAYS SAID YOU WANTED YOUR AXE CREMATED *WITH* YOUR BODY.
NEVER THOUGHT IT WOULD BE *INSTEAD OF*...

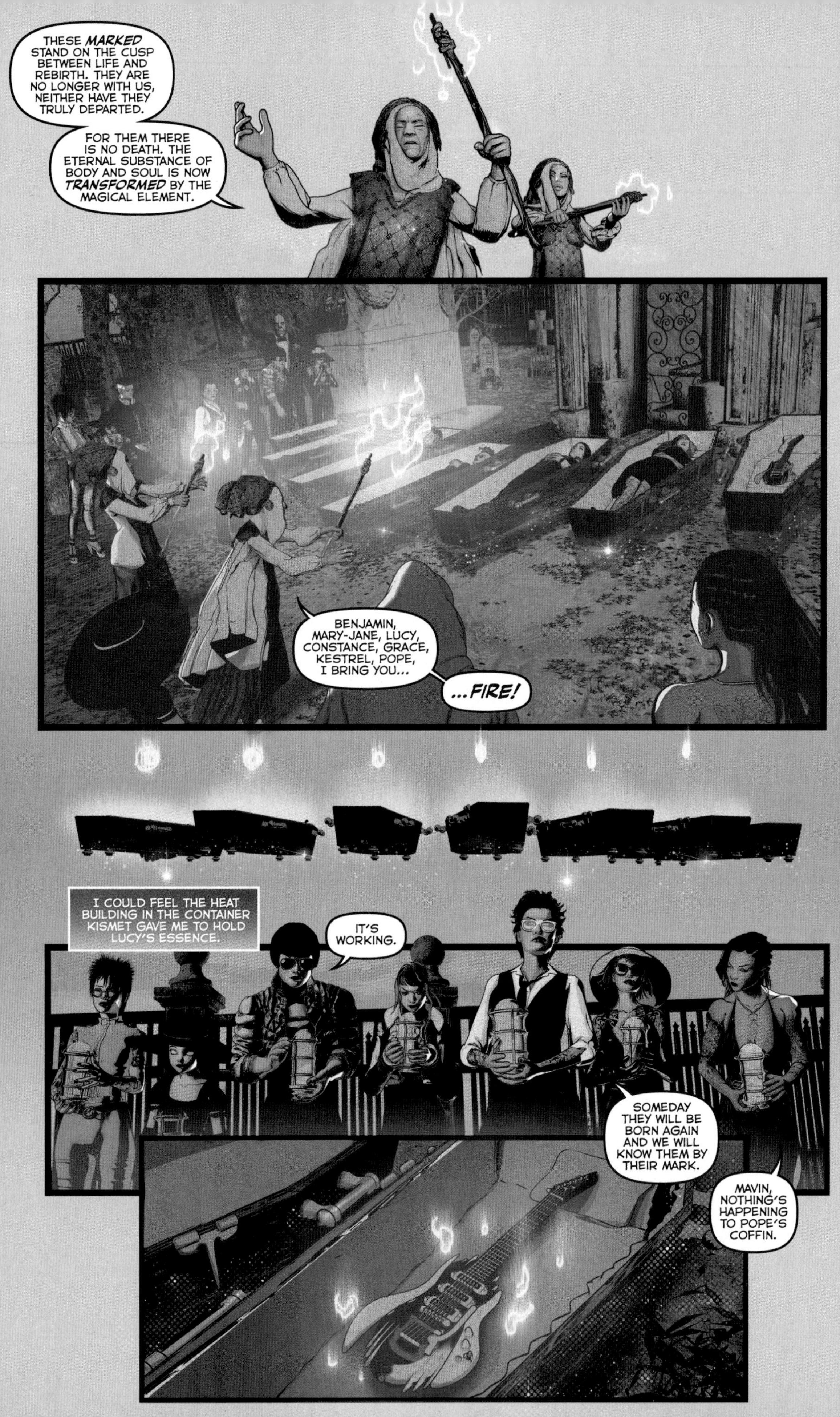

THESE MARKED STAND ON THE CUSP BETWEEN LIFE AND REBIRTH. THEY ARE NO LONGER WITH US, NEITHER HAVE THEY TRULY DEPARTED.
FOR THEM THERE IS NO DEATH. THE ETERNAL SUBSTANCE OF BODY AND SOUL IS NOW TRANSFORMED BY THE MAGICAL ELEMENT.
BENJAMIN, MARY-JANE, LUCY, CONSTANCE, GRACE, KESTREL, POPE, I BRING YOU...
...FIRE!
I COULD FEEL THE HEAT BUILDING IN THE CONTAINER KISMET GAVE ME TO HOLD LUCY'S ESSENCE.
IT'S WORKING.
SOMEDAY THEY WILL BE BORN AGAIN AND WE WILL KNOW THEM BY THEIR MARK.
MAVIN, NOTHING'S HAPPENING TO POPE'S COFFIN.

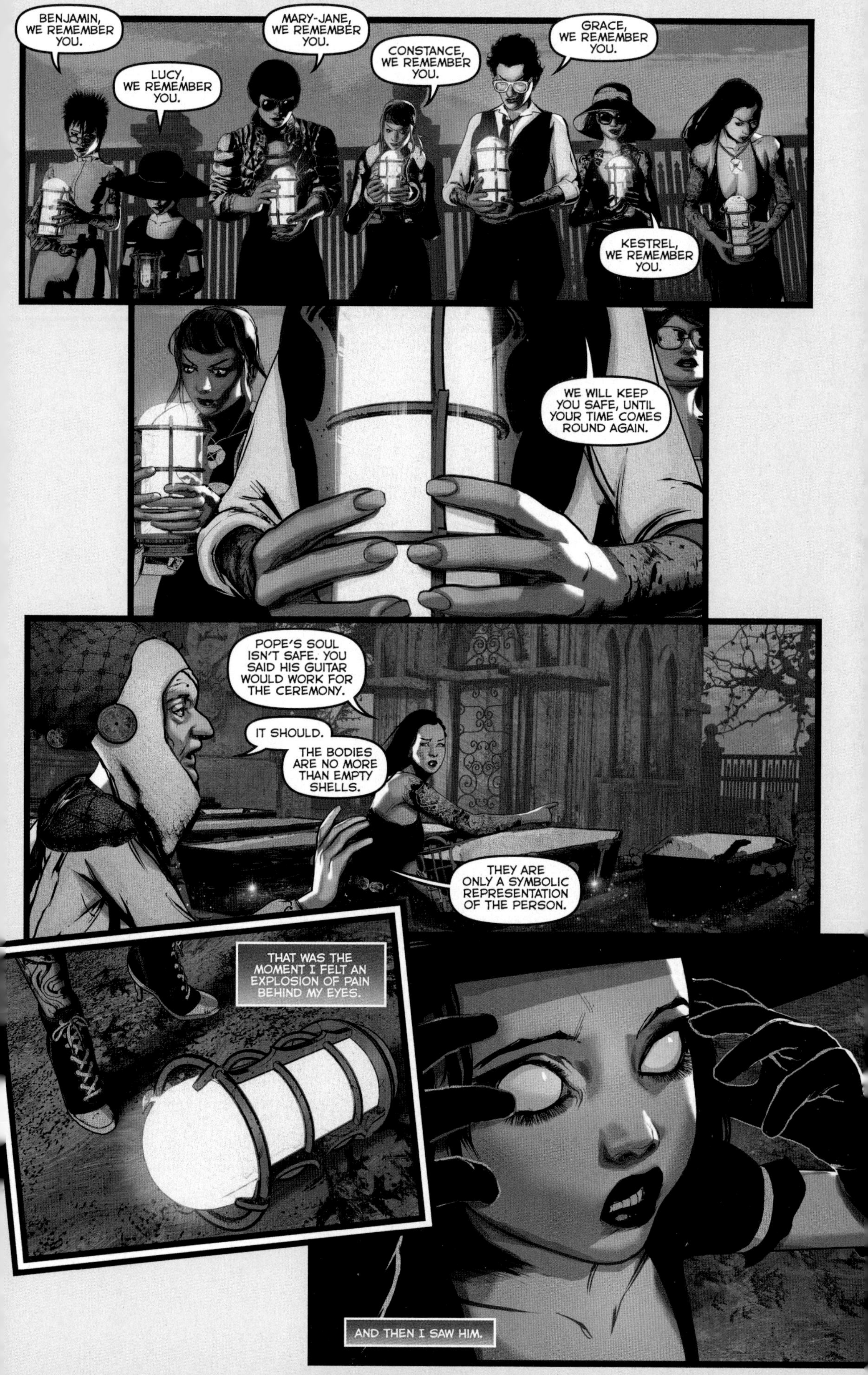
BENJAMIN, WE REMEMBER YOU.
LUCY, WE REMEMBER YOU.
MARY-JANE, WE REMEMBER YOU.
CONSTANCE, WE REMEMBER YOU.
GRACE, WE REMEMBER YOU.
KESTREL, WE REMEMBER YOU.
WE WILL KEEP YOU SAFE, UNTIL YOUR TIME COMES ROUND AGAIN.
POPE'S SOUL ISN'T SAFE. YOU SAID HIS GUITAR WOULD WORK FOR THE CEREMONY.
IT SHOULD.
THE BODIES ARE NO MORE THAN EMPTY SHELLS.
THEY ARE ONLY A SYMBOLIC REPRESENTATION OF THE PERSON.
THAT WAS THE MOMENT I FELT AN EXPLOSION OF PAIN BEHIND MY EYES.
AND THEN I SAW HIM.

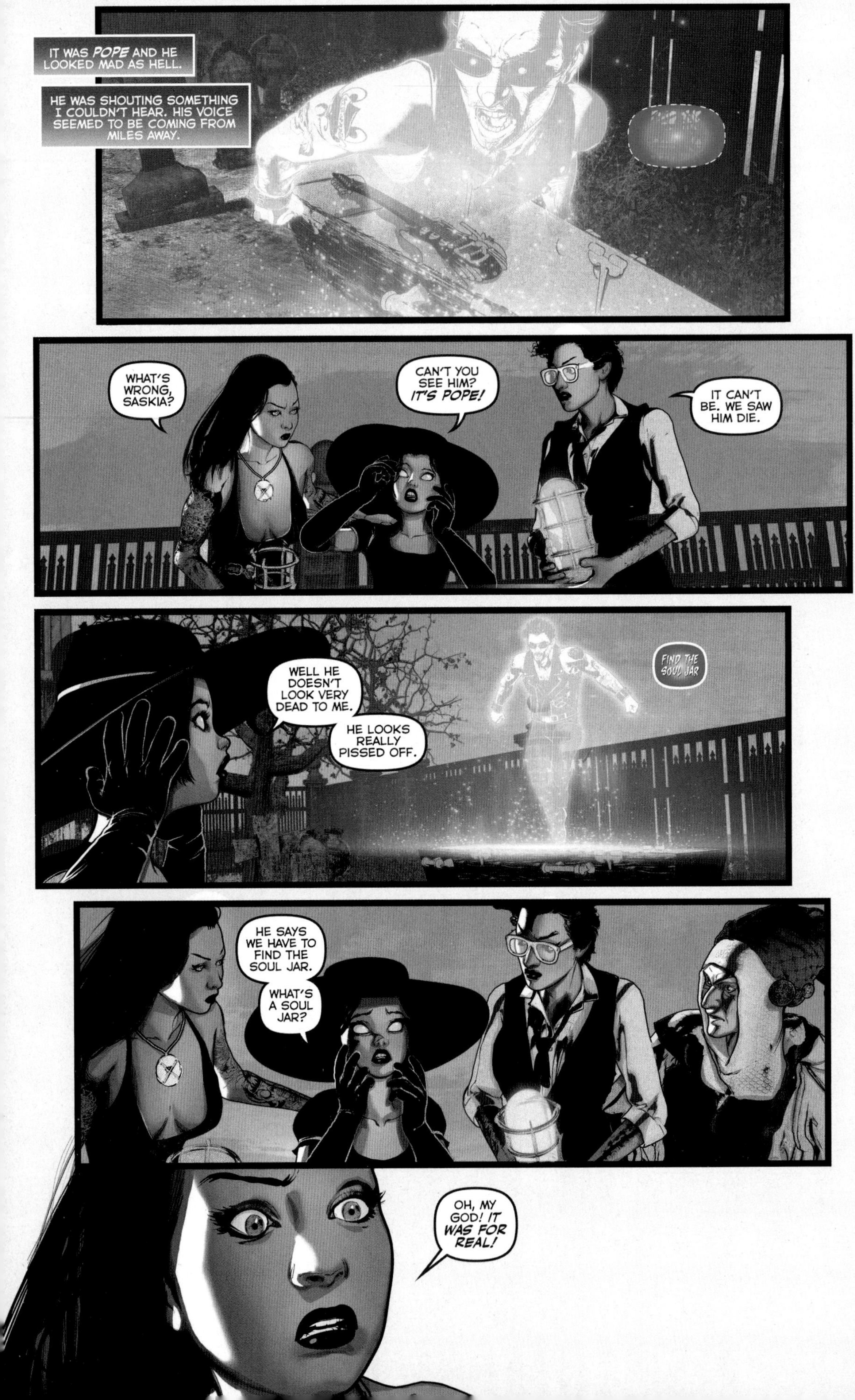
IT WAS POPE AND HE LOOKED MAD AS HELL.
HE WAS SHOUTING SOMETHING I COULDN'T HEAR. HIS VOICE SEEMED TO BE COMING FROM MILES AWAY.
WHAT'S WRONG, SASKIA?
CAN'T YOU SEE HIM? IT'S POPE!
IT CAN'T BE. WE SAW HIM DIE.
WELL HE DOESN'T LOOK VERY DEAD TO ME.
HE LOOKS REALLY PISSED OFF.
FIND THE SOUL JAR
HE SAYS WE HAVE TO FIND THE SOUL JAR.
WHAT'S A SOUL JAR?
OH, MY GOD! IT WAS FOR REAL!

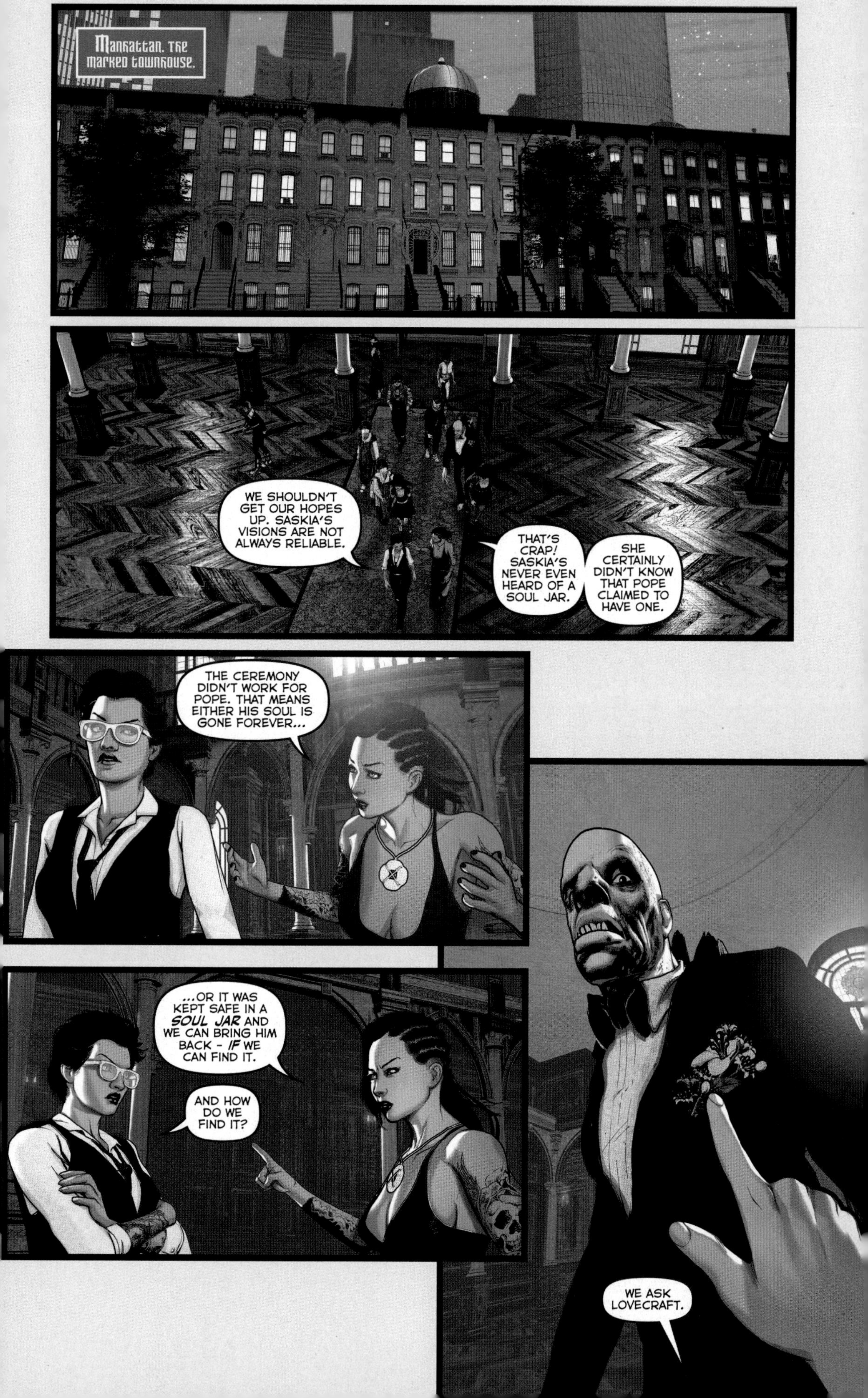
Manhattan. The marked townhouse.
WE SHOULDN'T GET OUR HOPES UP. SASKIA'S VISIONS ARE NOT ALWAYS RELIABLE.
THAT'S CRAP! SASKIA'S NEVER EVEN HEARD OF A SOUL JAR.
SHE CERTAINLY DIDN'T KNOW THAT POPE CLAIMED TO HAVE ONE.
THE CEREMONY DIDN'T WORK FOR POPE. THAT MEANS EITHER HIS SOUL IS GONE FOREVER...
...OR IT WAS KEPT SAFE IN A SOUL JAR AND WE CAN BRING HIM BACK - IF WE CAN FIND IT.
AND HOW DO WE FIND IT?
WE ASK LOVECRAFT.

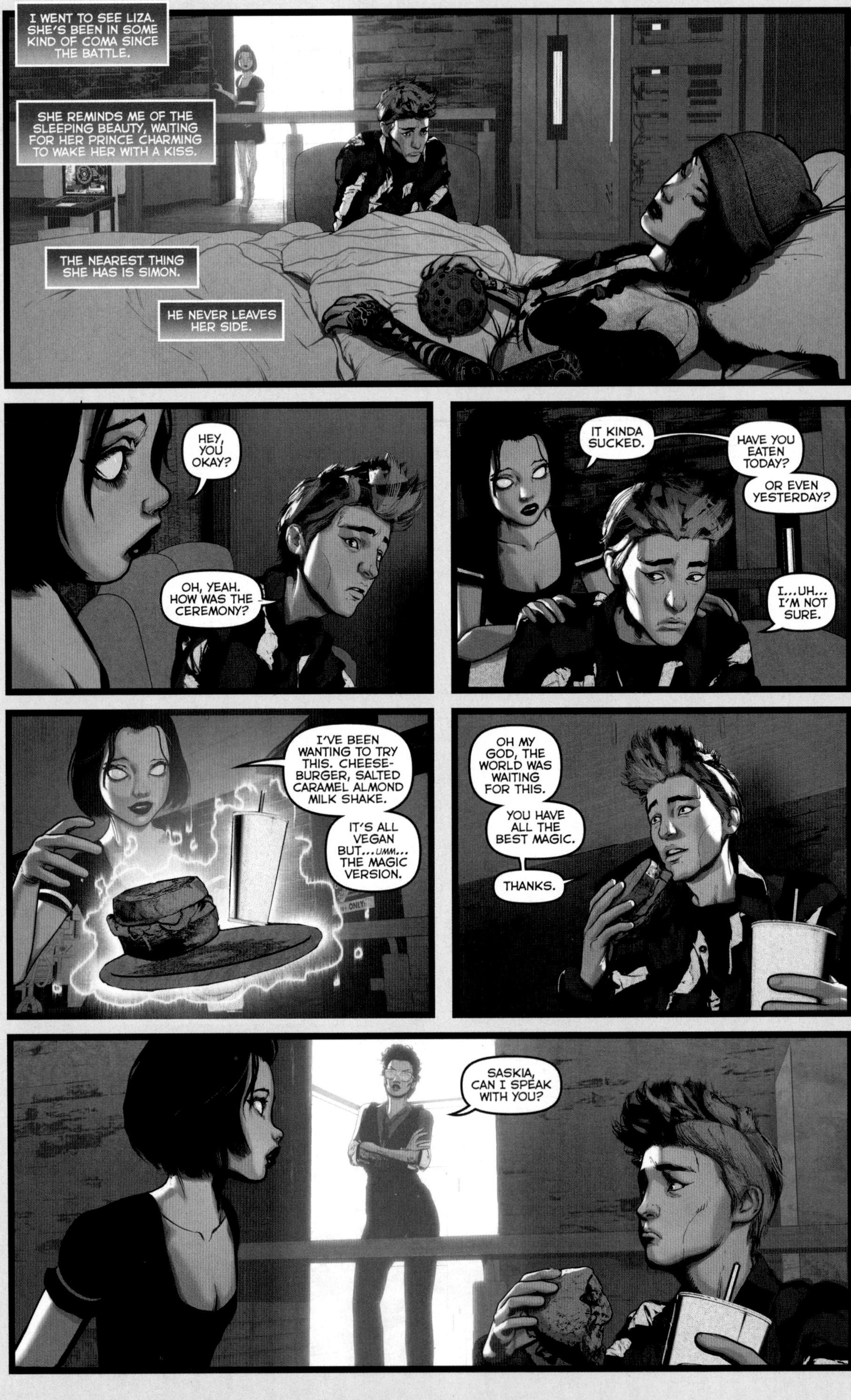
I WENT TO SEE LIZA. SHE'S BEEN IN SOME KIND OF COMA SINCE THE BATTLE.
SHE REMINDS ME OF THE SLEEPING BEAUTY, WAITING FOR HER PRINCE CHARMING TO WAKE HER WITH A KISS.
THE NEAREST THING SHE HAS IS SIMON.
HE NEVER LEAVES HER SIDE.
HEY, YOU OKAY?
OH, YEAH. HOW WAS THE CEREMONY?
IT KINDA SUCKED.
HAVE YOU EATEN TODAY?
OR EVEN YESTERDAY?
I...UH... I'M NOT SURE.
I'VE BEEN WANTING TO TRY THIS. CHEESE-BURGER, SALTED CARAMEL ALMOND MILK SHAKE.
IT'S ALL VEGAN BUT...UMM... THE MAGIC VERSION.
OH MY GOD, THE WORLD WAS WAITING FOR THIS.
YOU HAVE ALL THE BEST MAGIC.
THANKS.
SASKIA, CAN I SPEAK WITH YOU?

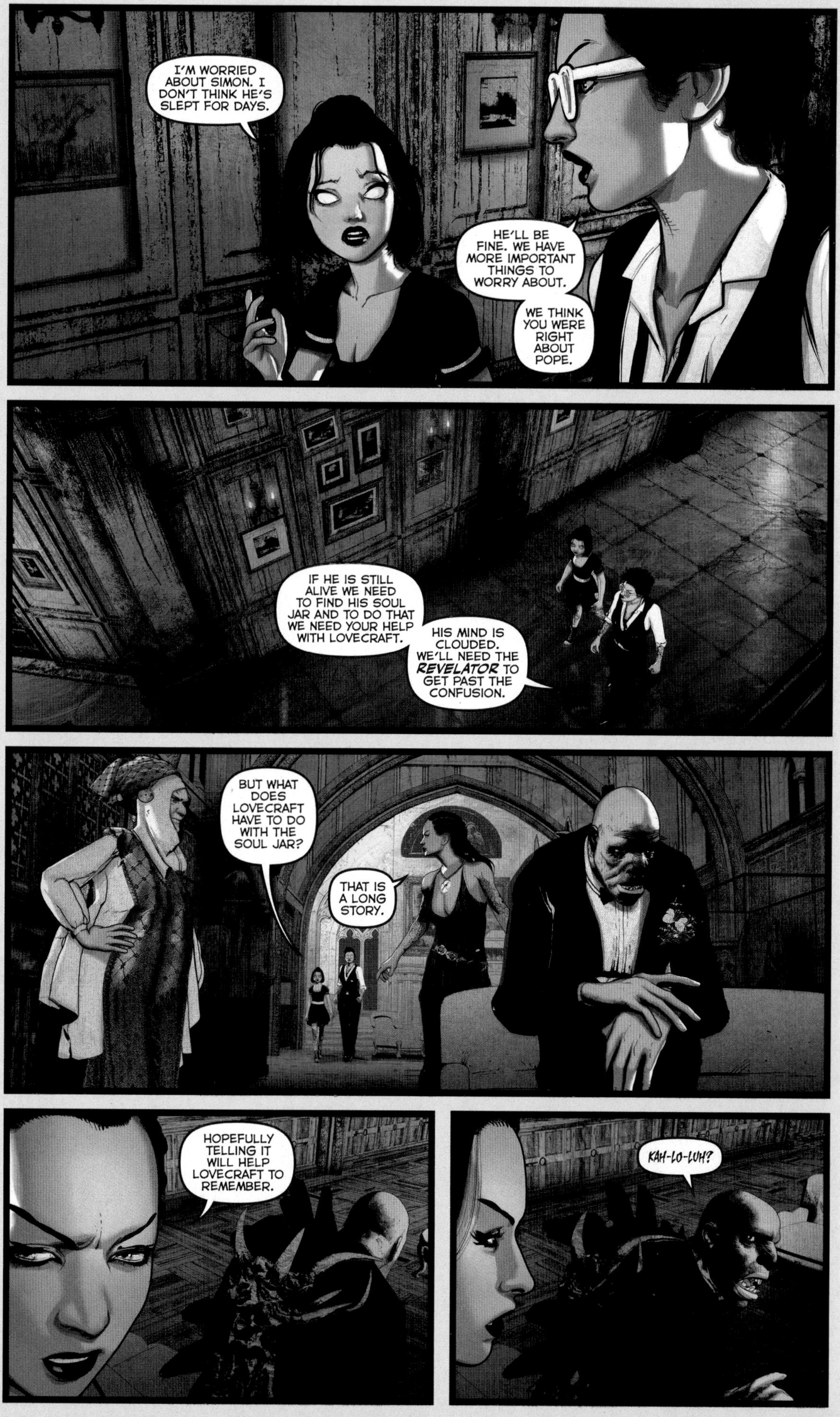
I'M WORRIED ABOUT SIMON. I DON'T THINK HE'S SLEPT FOR DAYS.
HE'LL BE FINE. WE HAVE MORE IMPORTANT THINGS TO WORRY ABOUT.
WE THINK YOU WERE RIGHT ABOUT POPE.
IF HE IS STILL ALIVE WE NEED TO FIND HIS SOUL JAR AND TO DO THAT WE NEED YOUR HELP WITH LOVECRAFT.
HIS MIND IS CLOUDED. WE'LL NEED THE REVELATOR TO GET PAST THE CONFUSION.
BUT WHAT DOES LOVECRAFT HAVE TO DO WITH THE SOUL JAR?
THAT IS A LONG STORY.
HOPEFULLY TELLING IT WILL HELP LOVECRAFT TO REMEMBER.
KAH-LO-LUH?

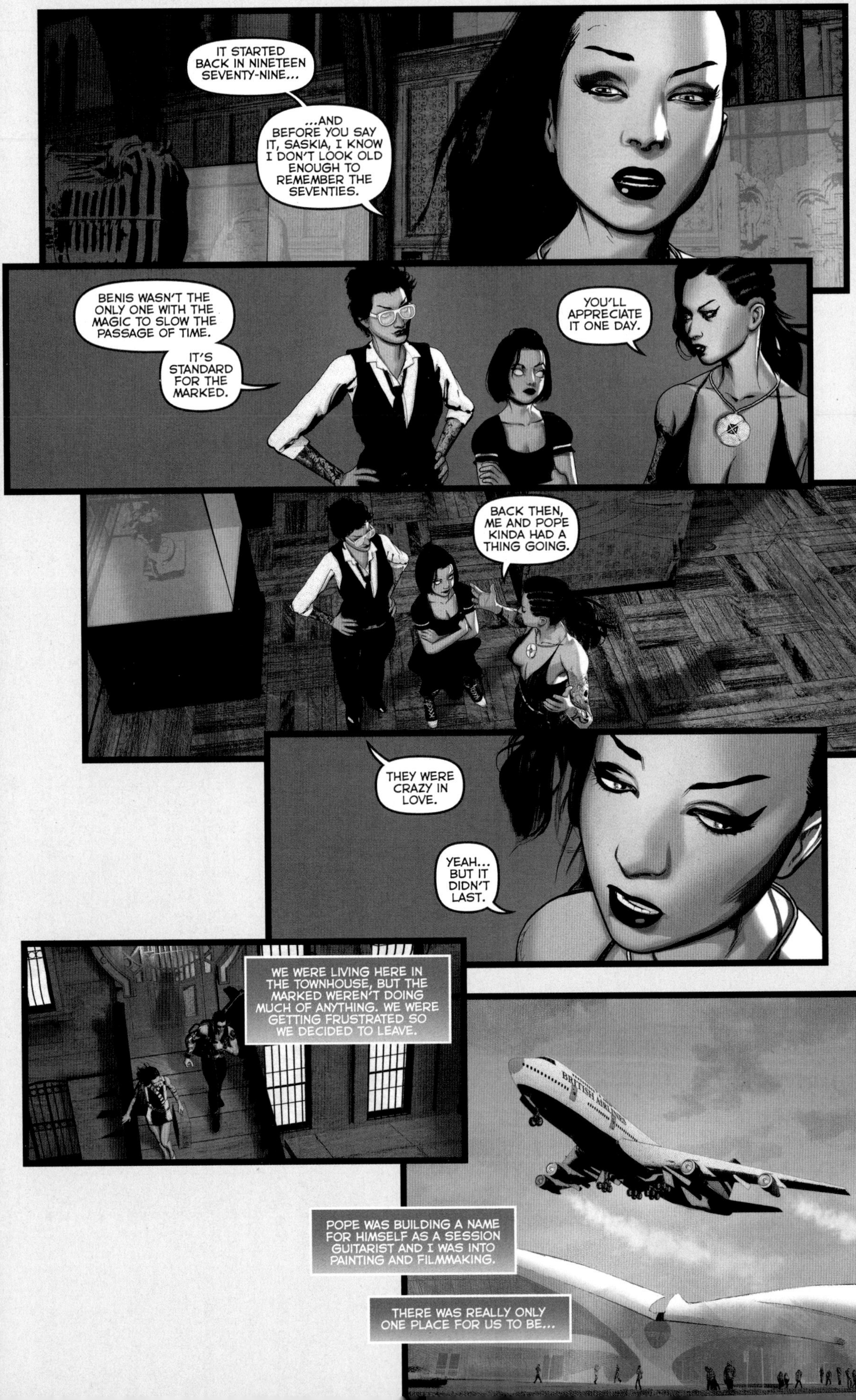
IT STARTED BACK IN NINETEEN SEVENTY-NINE...
...AND BEFORE YOU SAY IT, SASKIA, I KNOW I DON'T LOOK OLD ENOUGH TO REMEMBER THE SEVENTIES.
BENIS WASN'T THE ONLY ONE WITH THE MAGIC TO SLOW THE PASSAGE OF TIME.
IT'S STANDARD FOR THE MARKED.
YOU'LL APPRECIATE IT ONE DAY.
BACK THEN, ME AND POPE KINDA HAD A THING GOING.
THEY WERE CRAZY IN LOVE.
YEAH... BUT IT DIDN'T LAST.
WE WERE LIVING HERE IN THE TOWNHOUSE, BUT THE MARKED WEREN'T DOING MUCH OF ANYTHING. WE WERE GETTING FRUSTRATED SO WE DECIDED TO LEAVE.
BRITISH AIRWAYS
POPE WAS BUILDING A NAME FOR HIMSELF AS A SESSION GUITARIST AND I WAS INTO PAINTING AND FILMMAKING.
THERE WAS REALLY ONLY ONE PLACE FOR US TO BE...

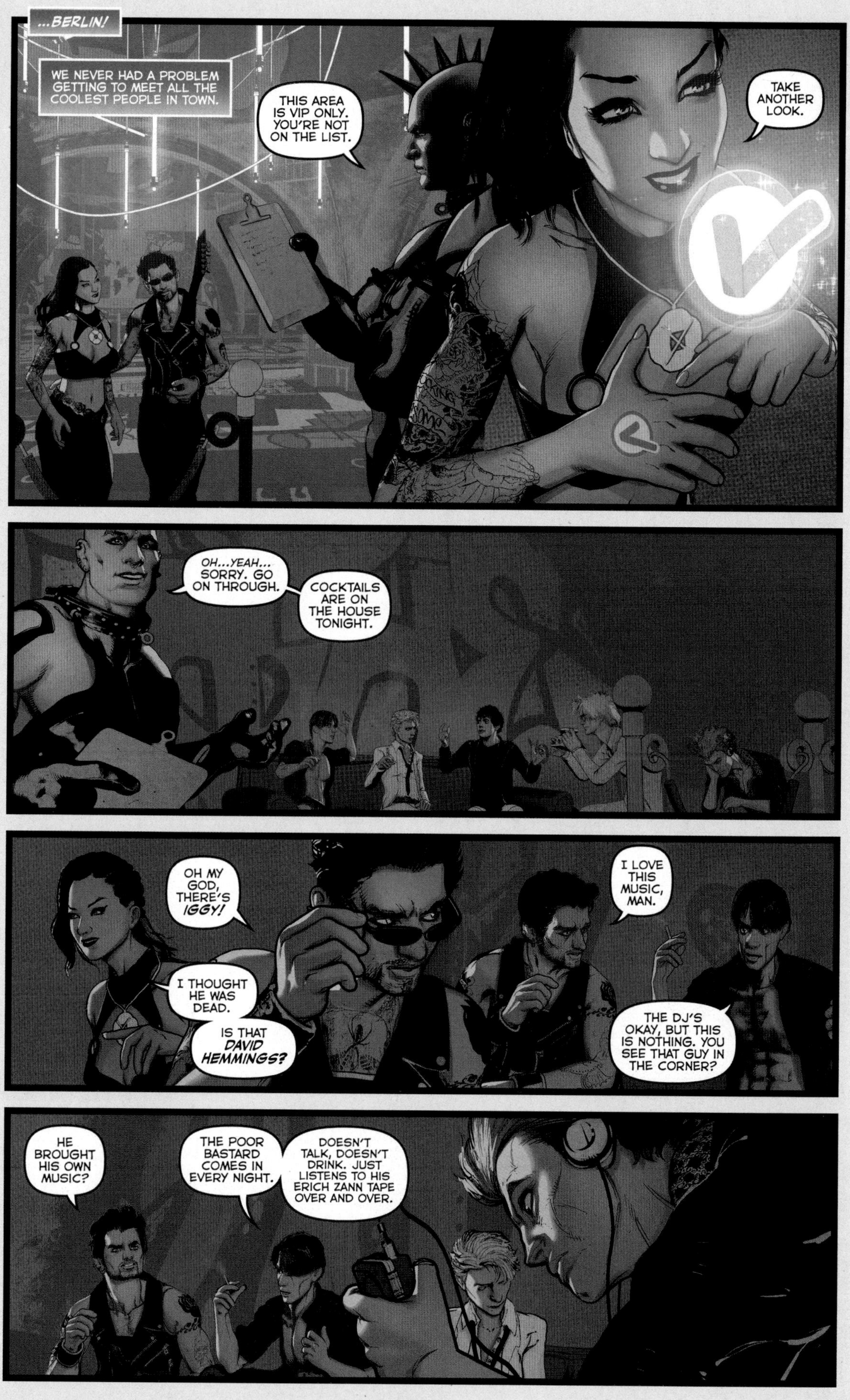
...BERLIN!
WE NEVER HAD A PROBLEM GETTING TO MEET ALL THE COOLEST PEOPLE IN TOWN.
THIS AREA IS VIP ONLY. YOU'RE NOT ON THE LIST.
TAKE ANOTHER LOOK.
OH...YEAH... SORRY. GO ON THROUGH.
COCKTAILS ARE ON THE HOUSE TONIGHT.
OH MY GOD, THERE'S IGGY!
I THOUGHT HE WAS DEAD.
IS THAT DAVID HEMMINGS?
I LOVE THIS MUSIC, MAN.
THE DJ'S OKAY, BUT THIS IS NOTHING. YOU SEE THAT GUY IN THE CORNER?
HE BROUGHT HIS OWN MUSIC?
THE POOR BASTARD COMES IN EVERY NIGHT.
DOESN'T TALK, DOESN'T DRINK. JUST LISTENS TO HIS ERICH ZANN TAPE OVER AND OVER.

"THE MUSIC OF ERICH ZANN." IT'S A STORY BY H.P. LOVECRAFT.

THEY SAY IT DOES ONE OF TWO THINGS. IF YOU'RE TALENTED IT CAN INSPIRE YOU TO GREATNESS.

ERICH ZANN? HE PLAY WITH THE STONES?

WHAT'S THE OTHER?

IF YOU DON'T HAVE WHAT IT TAKES, IT'LL DRIVE YOU INSANE.

SO DID YOU EVER LISTEN TO IT?

ME? I PLAY ROCK 'N' ROLL.

LIFE IS MY INSPIRATION.

HE LISTENED TO IT...

...ONCE...

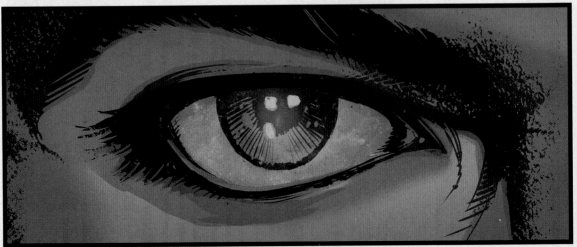

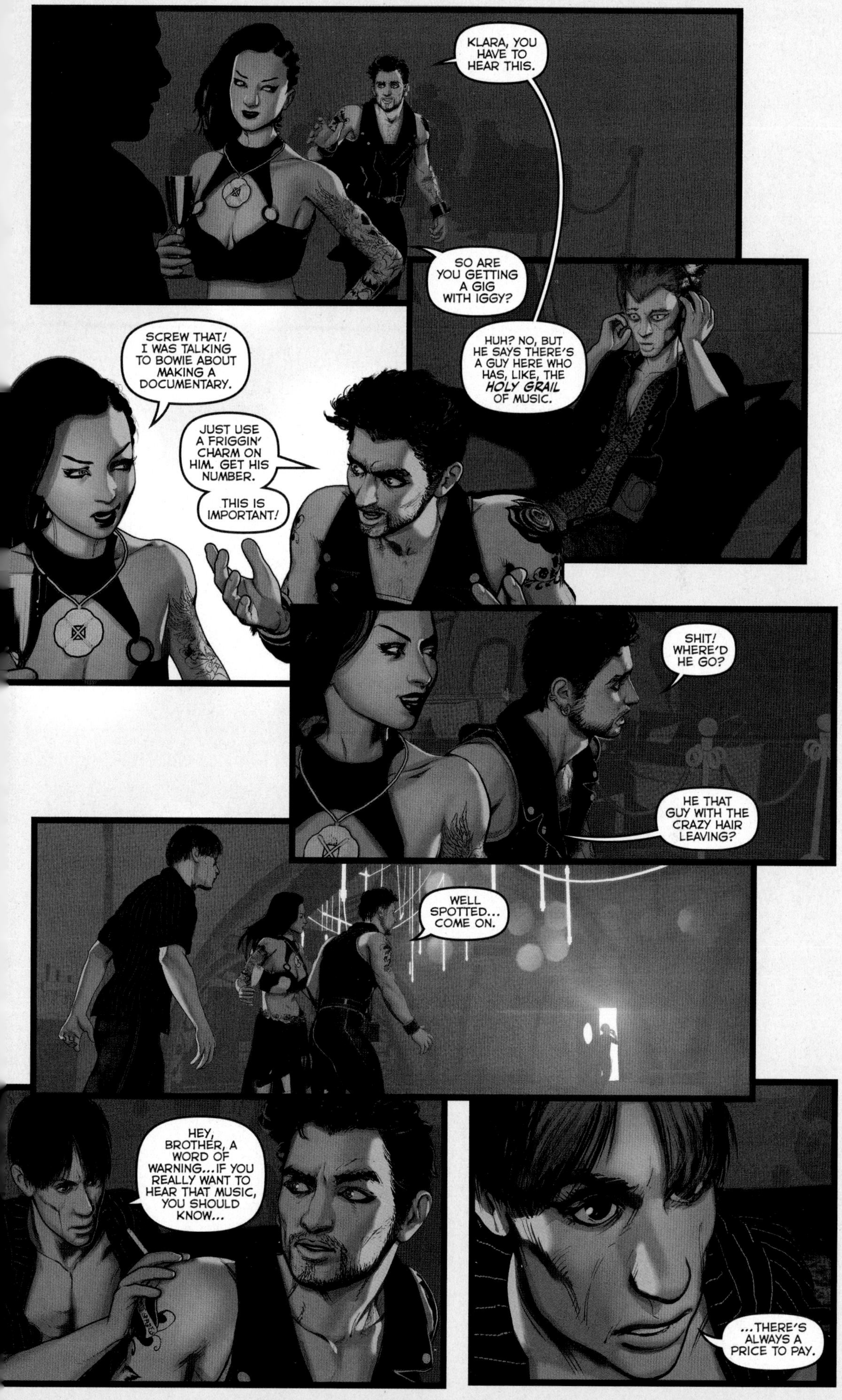
KLARA, YOU HAVE TO HEAR THIS.
SO ARE YOU GETTING A GIG WITH IGGY?
HUH? NO, BUT HE SAYS THERE'S A GUY HERE WHO HAS, LIKE, THE *HOLY GRAIL* OF MUSIC.
SCREW THAT! I WAS TALKING TO BOWIE ABOUT MAKING A DOCUMENTARY.
JUST USE A FRIGGIN' CHARM ON HIM. GET HIS NUMBER.
THIS IS IMPORTANT!
SHIT! WHERE'D HE GO?
HE THAT GUY WITH THE CRAZY HAIR LEAVING?
WELL SPOTTED... COME ON.
HEY, BROTHER, A WORD OF WARNING...IF YOU REALLY WANT TO HEAR THAT MUSIC, YOU SHOULD KNOW...
...THERE'S ALWAYS A PRICE TO PAY.

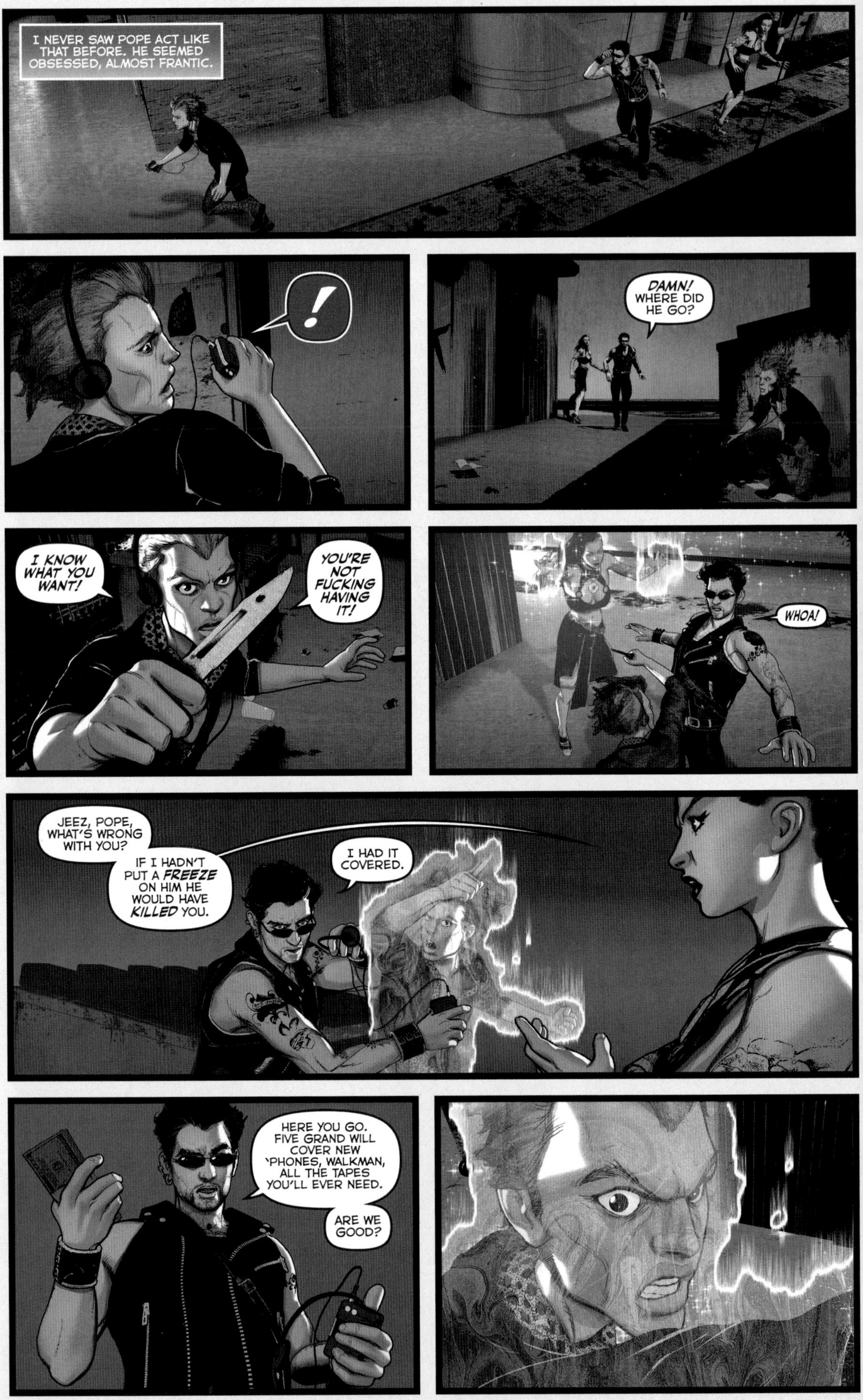

I NEVER SAW POPE ACT LIKE THAT BEFORE. HE SEEMED OBSESSED, ALMOST FRANTIC.
!
DAMN! WHERE DID HE GO?
I KNOW WHAT YOU WANT!
YOU'RE NOT FUCKING HAVING IT!
WHOA!
JEEZ, POPE, WHAT'S WRONG WITH YOU?
IF I HADN'T PUT A FREEZE ON HIM HE WOULD HAVE KILLED YOU.
I HAD IT COVERED.
HERE YOU GO. FIVE GRAND WILL COVER NEW 'PHONES, WALKMAN, ALL THE TAPES YOU'LL EVER NEED.
ARE WE GOOD?

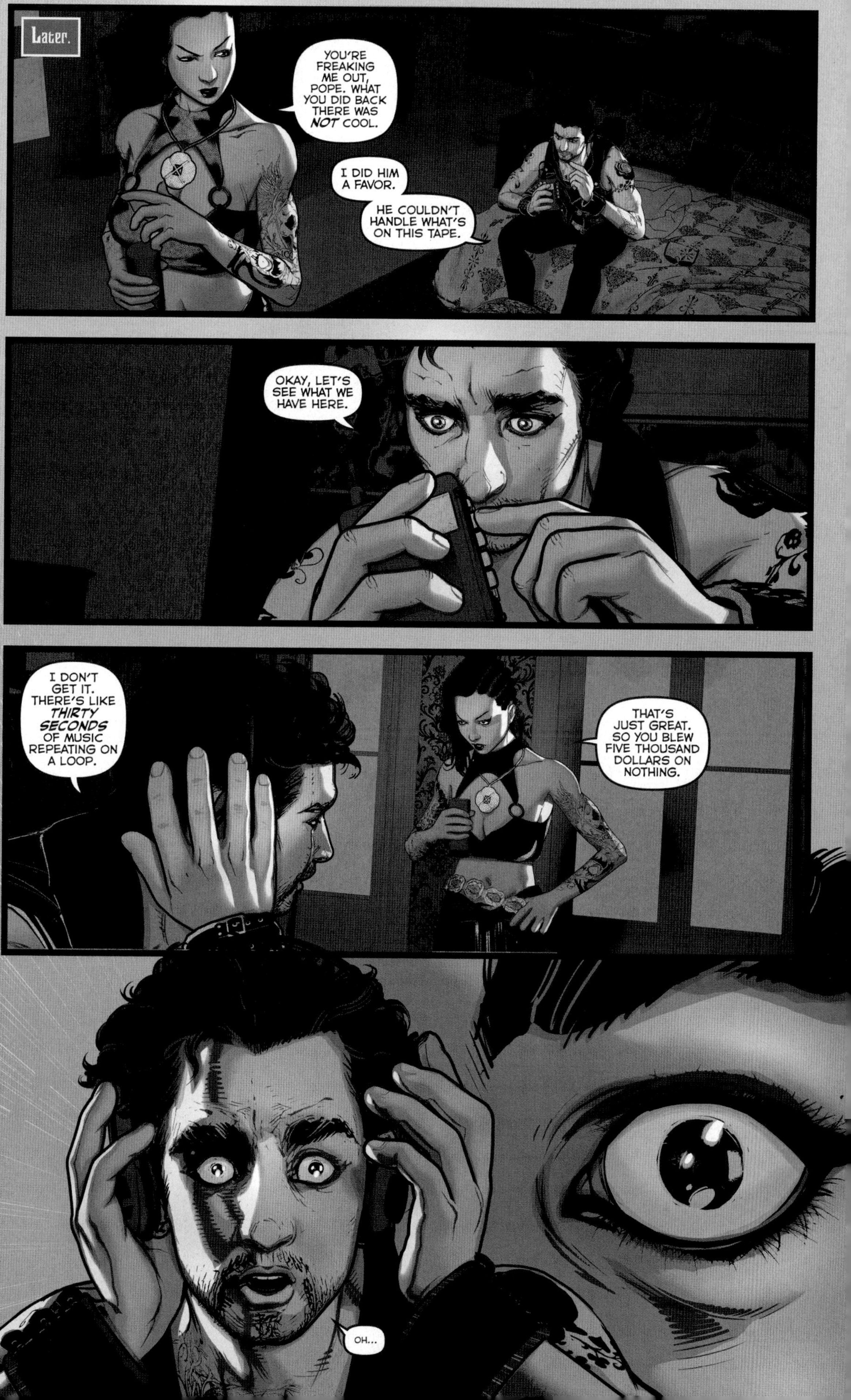
Later.
YOU'RE FREAKING ME OUT, POPE. WHAT YOU DID BACK THERE WAS NOT COOL.
I DID HIM A FAVOR.
HE COULDN'T HANDLE WHAT'S ON THIS TAPE.
OKAY, LET'S SEE WHAT WE HAVE HERE.
I DON'T GET IT. THERE'S LIKE THIRTY SECONDS OF MUSIC REPEATING ON A LOOP.
THAT'S JUST GREAT. SO YOU BLEW FIVE THOUSAND DOLLARS ON NOTHING.
OH...

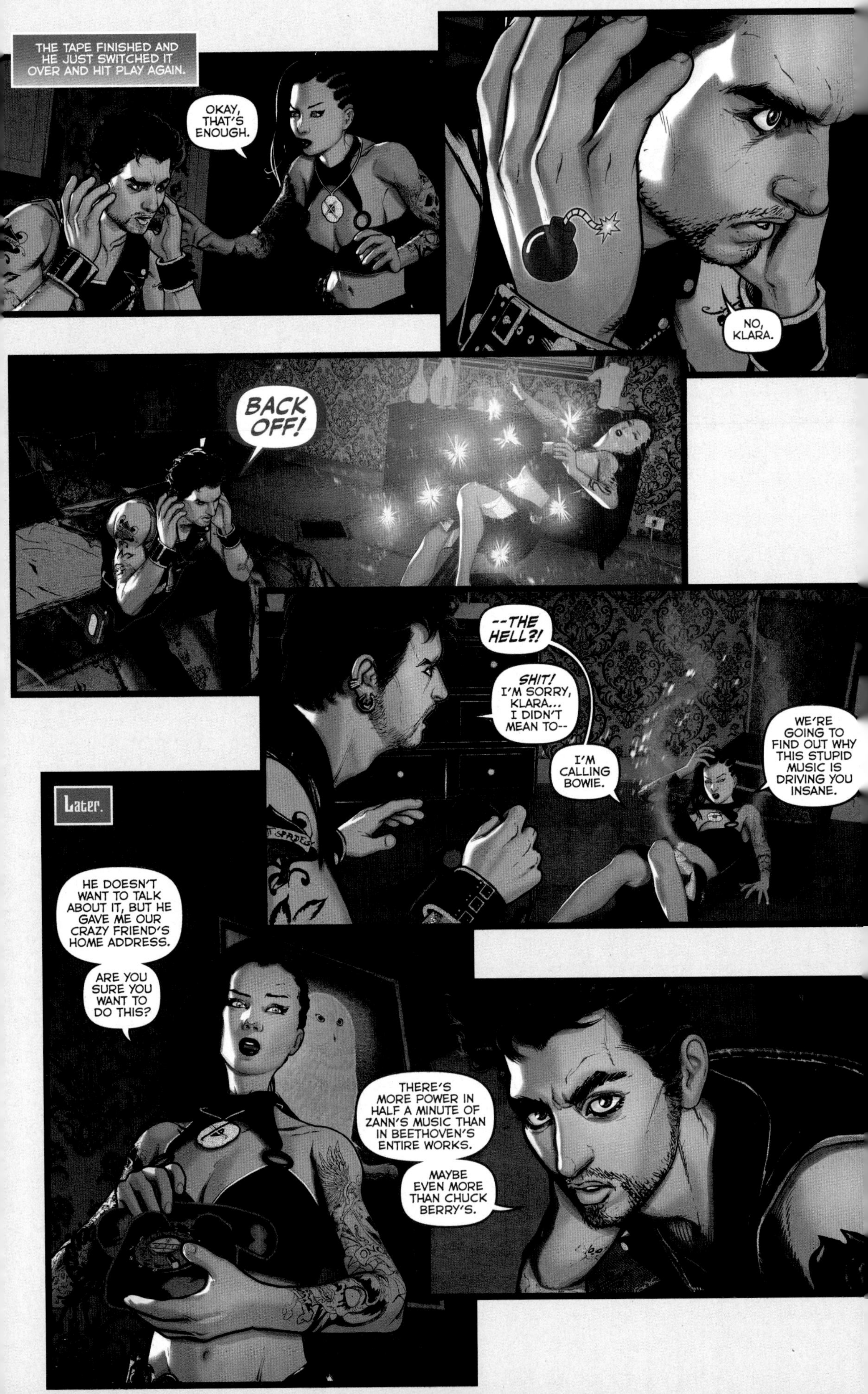
THE TAPE FINISHED AND HE JUST SWITCHED IT OVER AND HIT PLAY AGAIN.
OKAY, THAT'S ENOUGH.
NO, KLARA.
BACK OFF!
--THE HELL?!
SHIT! I'M SORRY, KLARA... I DIDN'T MEAN TO--
I'M CALLING BOWIE.
WE'RE GOING TO FIND OUT WHY THIS STUPID MUSIC IS DRIVING YOU INSANE.
Later.
HE DOESN'T WANT TO TALK ABOUT IT, BUT HE GAVE ME OUR CRAZY FRIEND'S HOME ADDRESS.
ARE YOU SURE YOU WANT TO DO THIS?
THERE'S MORE POWER IN HALF A MINUTE OF ZANN'S MUSIC THAN IN BEETHOVEN'S ENTIRE WORKS.
MAYBE EVEN MORE THAN CHUCK BERRY'S.

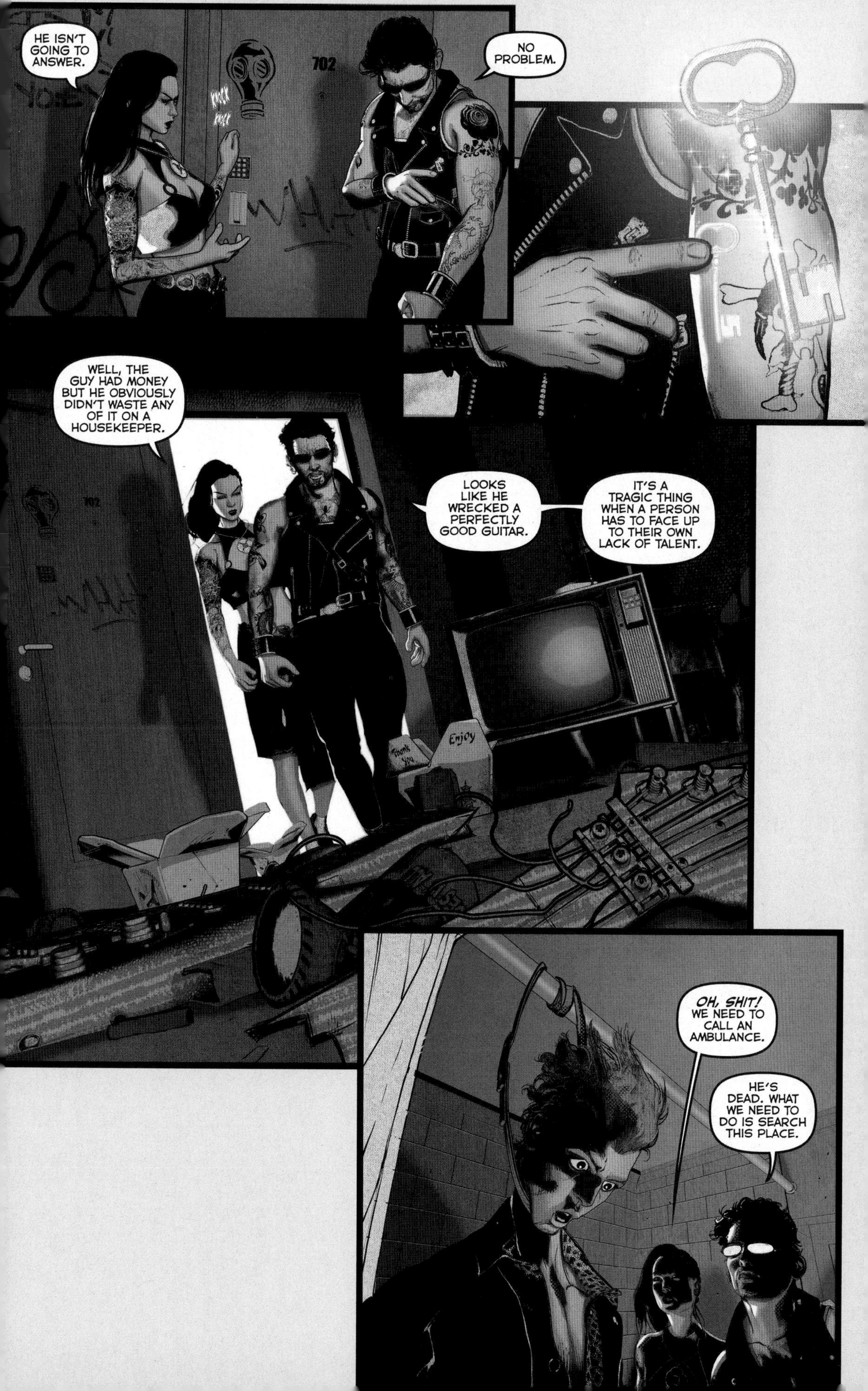
HE ISN'T GOING TO ANSWER.
KNOCK KNOCK
NO PROBLEM.
WELL, THE GUY HAD MONEY BUT HE OBVIOUSLY DIDN'T WASTE ANY OF IT ON A HOUSEKEEPER.
LOOKS LIKE HE WRECKED A PERFECTLY GOOD GUITAR.
IT'S A TRAGIC THING WHEN A PERSON HAS TO FACE UP TO THEIR OWN LACK OF TALENT.
OH, SHIT! WE NEED TO CALL AN AMBULANCE.
HE'S DEAD. WHAT WE NEED TO DO IS SEARCH THIS PLACE.

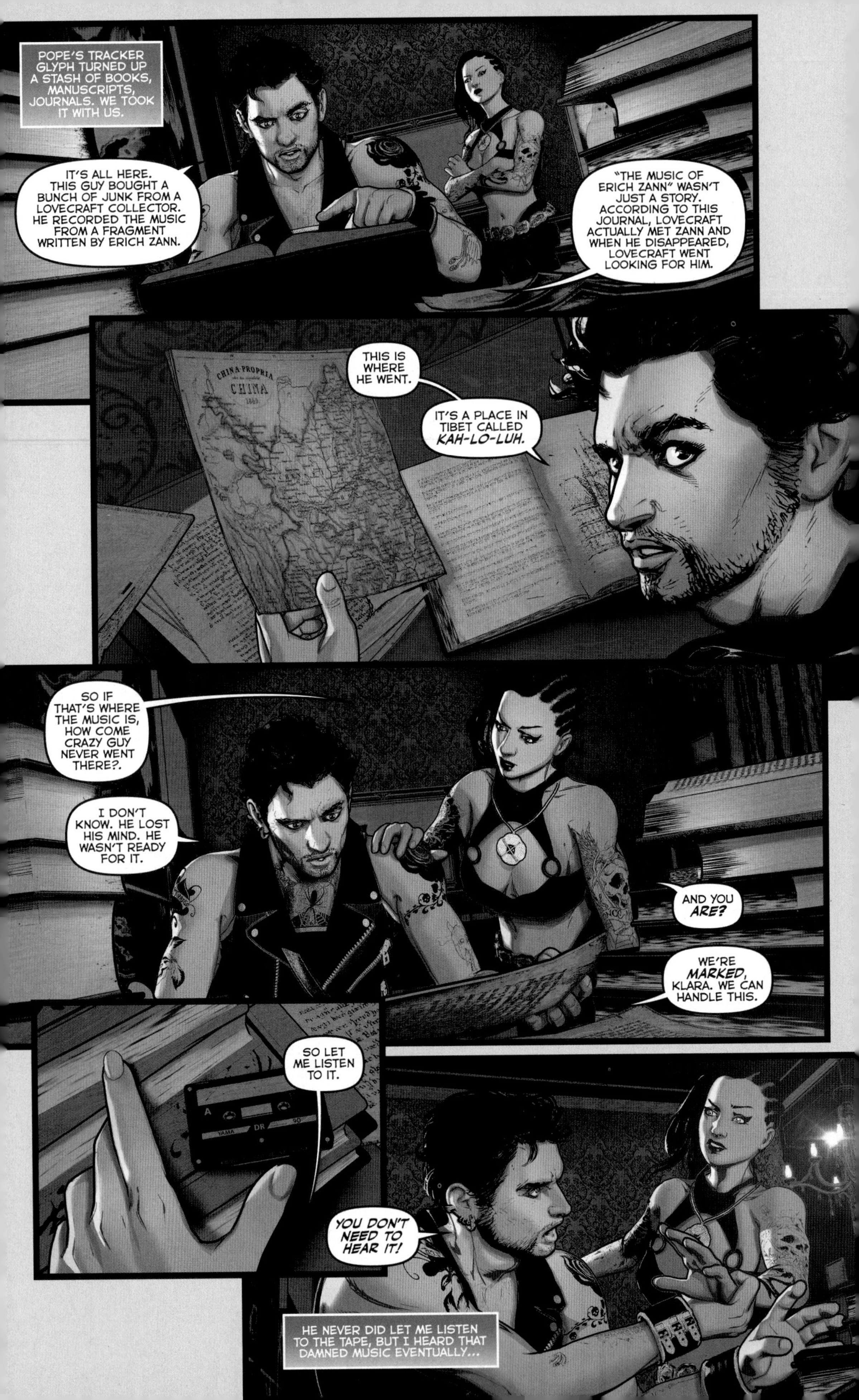
POPE'S TRACKER GLYPH TURNED UP A STASH OF BOOKS, MANUSCRIPTS, JOURNALS. WE TOOK IT WITH US.
IT'S ALL HERE. THIS GUY BOUGHT A BUNCH OF JUNK FROM A LOVECRAFT COLLECTOR. HE RECORDED THE MUSIC FROM A FRAGMENT WRITTEN BY ERICH ZANN.
"THE MUSIC OF ERICH ZANN" WASN'T JUST A STORY. ACCORDING TO THIS JOURNAL, LOVECRAFT ACTUALLY MET ZANN AND WHEN HE DISAPPEARED, LOVECRAFT WENT LOOKING FOR HIM.
CHINA·PROPRIA
CHINA
THIS IS WHERE HE WENT.
IT'S A PLACE IN TIBET CALLED *KAH-LO-LUH*.
SO IF THAT'S WHERE THE MUSIC IS, HOW COME CRAZY GUY NEVER WENT THERE?.
I DON'T KNOW. HE LOST HIS MIND. HE WASN'T READY FOR IT.
AND YOU *ARE?*
WE'RE *MARKED*, KLARA. WE CAN HANDLE THIS.
SO LET ME LISTEN TO IT.
YOU DON'T NEED TO HEAR IT!
HE NEVER DID LET ME LISTEN TO THE TAPE, BUT I HEARD THAT DAMNED MUSIC EVENTUALLY...

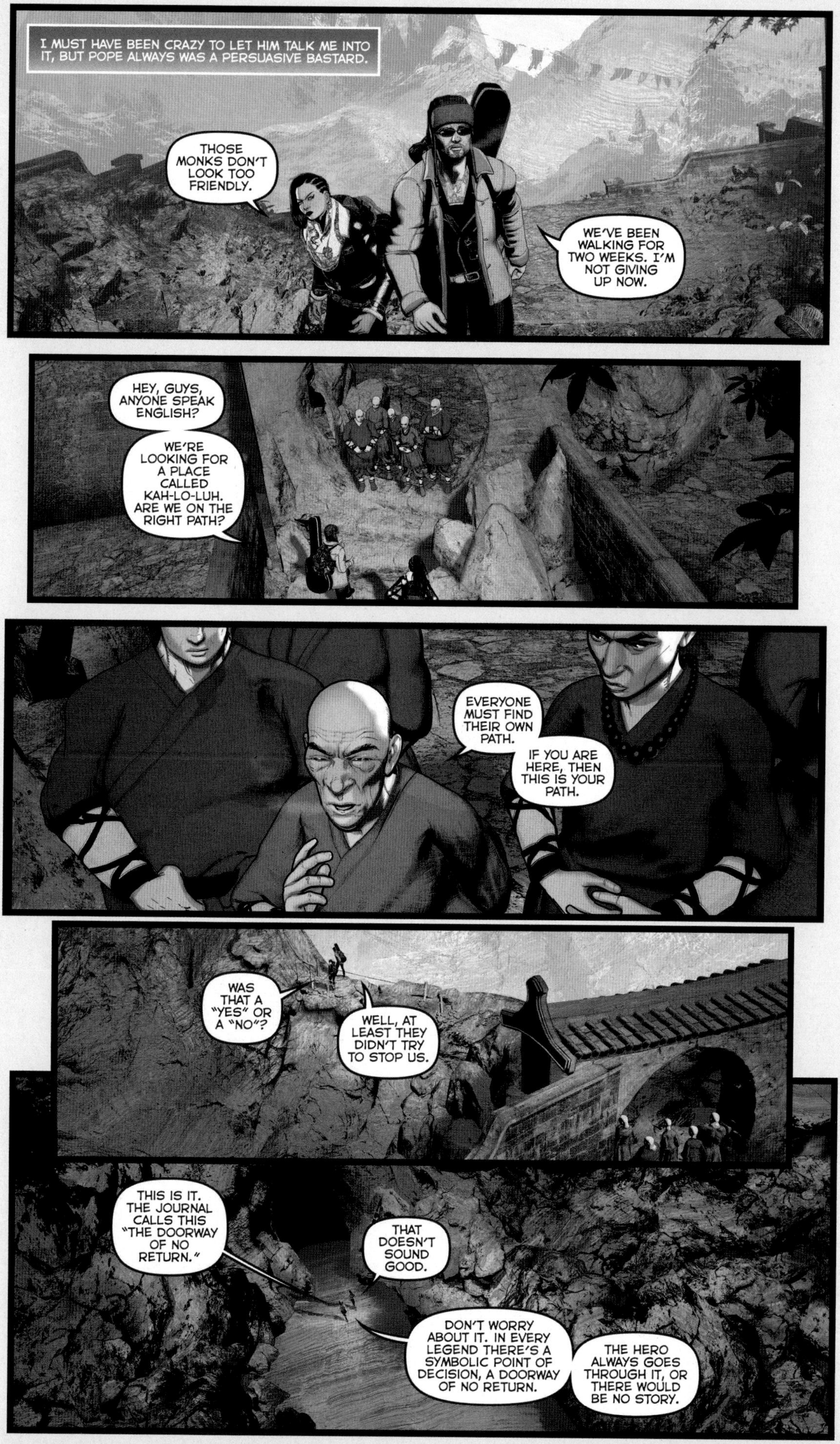
I MUST HAVE BEEN CRAZY TO LET HIM TALK ME INTO IT, BUT POPE ALWAYS WAS A PERSUASIVE BASTARD.
THOSE MONKS DON'T LOOK TOO FRIENDLY.
WE'VE BEEN WALKING FOR TWO WEEKS. I'M NOT GIVING UP NOW.
HEY, GUYS, ANYONE SPEAK ENGLISH?
WE'RE LOOKING FOR A PLACE CALLED KAH-LO-LUH. ARE WE ON THE RIGHT PATH?
EVERYONE MUST FIND THEIR OWN PATH.
IF YOU ARE HERE, THEN THIS IS YOUR PATH.
WAS THAT A "YES" OR A "NO"?
WELL, AT LEAST THEY DIDN'T TRY TO STOP US.
THIS IS IT. THE JOURNAL CALLS THIS "THE DOORWAY OF NO RETURN."
THAT DOESN'T SOUND GOOD.
DON'T WORRY ABOUT IT. IN EVERY LEGEND THERE'S A SYMBOLIC POINT OF DECISION, A DOORWAY OF NO RETURN.
THE HERO ALWAYS GOES THROUGH IT, OR THERE WOULD BE NO STORY.

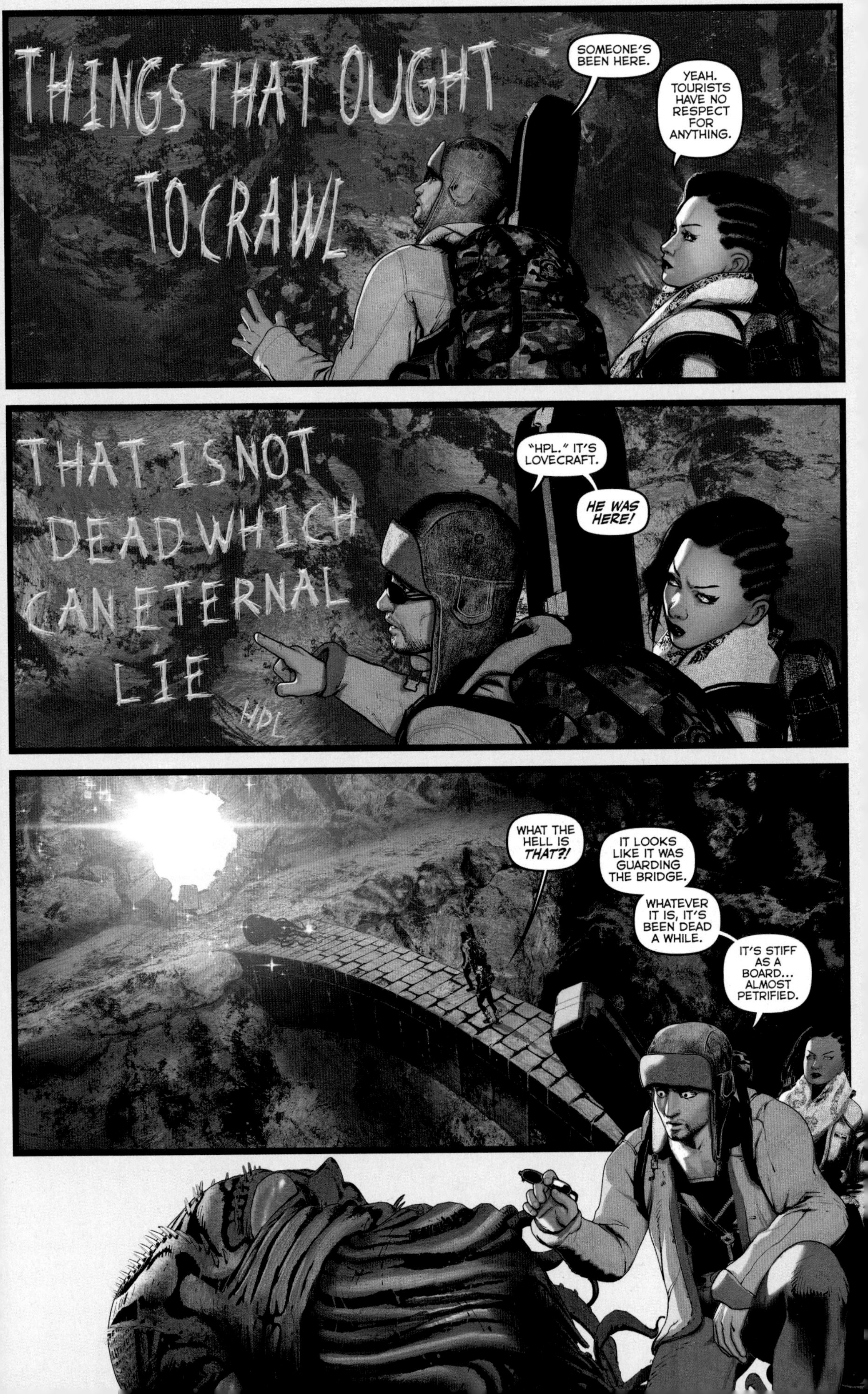
THINGS THAT OUGHT TO CRAWL
SOMEONE'S BEEN HERE.
YEAH. TOURISTS HAVE NO RESPECT FOR ANYTHING.
THAT IS NOT DEAD WHICH CAN ETERNAL LIE
HPL
"HPL." IT'S LOVECRAFT.
HE WAS HERE!
WHAT THE HELL IS THAT?!
IT LOOKS LIKE IT WAS GUARDING THE BRIDGE.
WHATEVER IT IS, IT'S BEEN DEAD A WHILE.
IT'S STIFF AS A BOARD... ALMOST PETRIFIED.

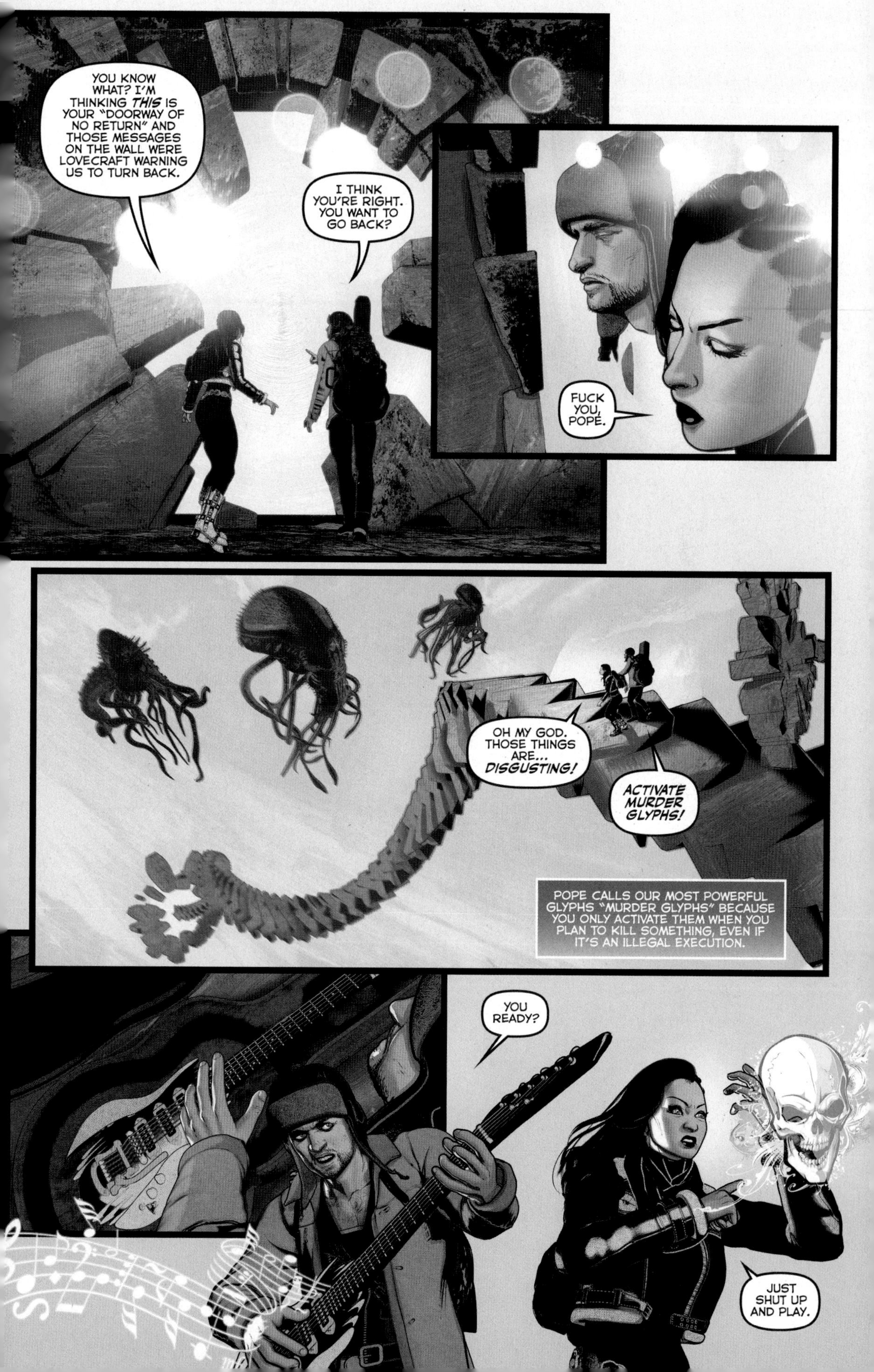

YOU KNOW WHAT? I'M THINKING THIS IS YOUR "DOORWAY OF NO RETURN" AND THOSE MESSAGES ON THE WALL WERE LOVECRAFT WARNING US TO TURN BACK.
I THINK YOU'RE RIGHT. YOU WANT TO GO BACK?
FUCK YOU, POPE.
OH MY GOD. THOSE THINGS ARE... DISGUSTING!
ACTIVATE MURDER GLYPHS!
POPE CALLS OUR MOST POWERFUL GLYPHS "MURDER GLYPHS" BECAUSE YOU ONLY ACTIVATE THEM WHEN YOU PLAN TO KILL SOMETHING, EVEN IF IT'S AN ILLEGAL EXECUTION.
YOU READY?
JUST SHUT UP AND PLAY.

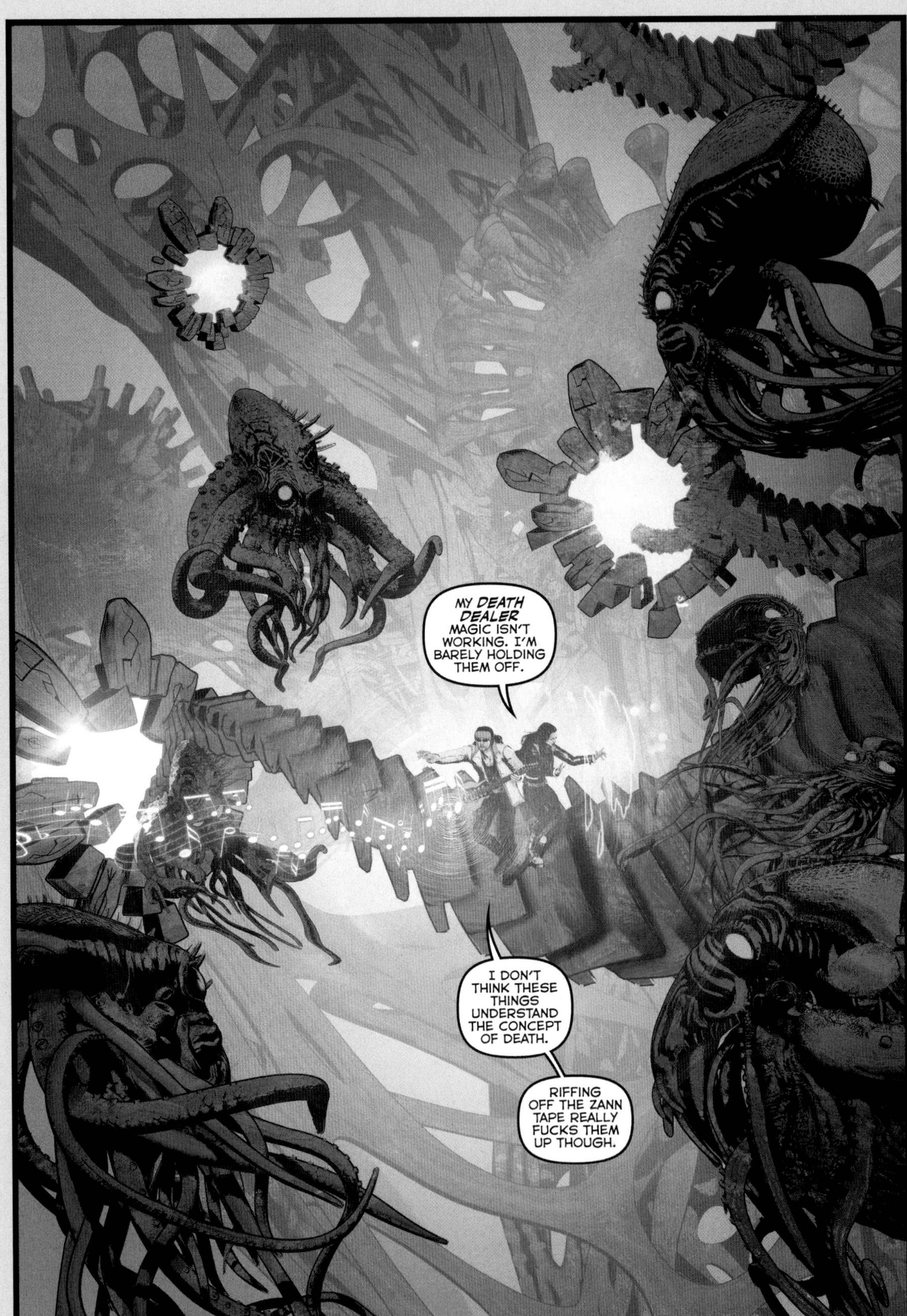
MY DEATH DEALER MAGIC ISN'T WORKING. I'M BARELY HOLDING THEM OFF.
I DON'T THINK THESE THINGS UNDERSTAND THE CONCEPT OF DEATH.
RIFFING OFF THE ZANN TAPE REALLY FUCKS THEM UP THOUGH.

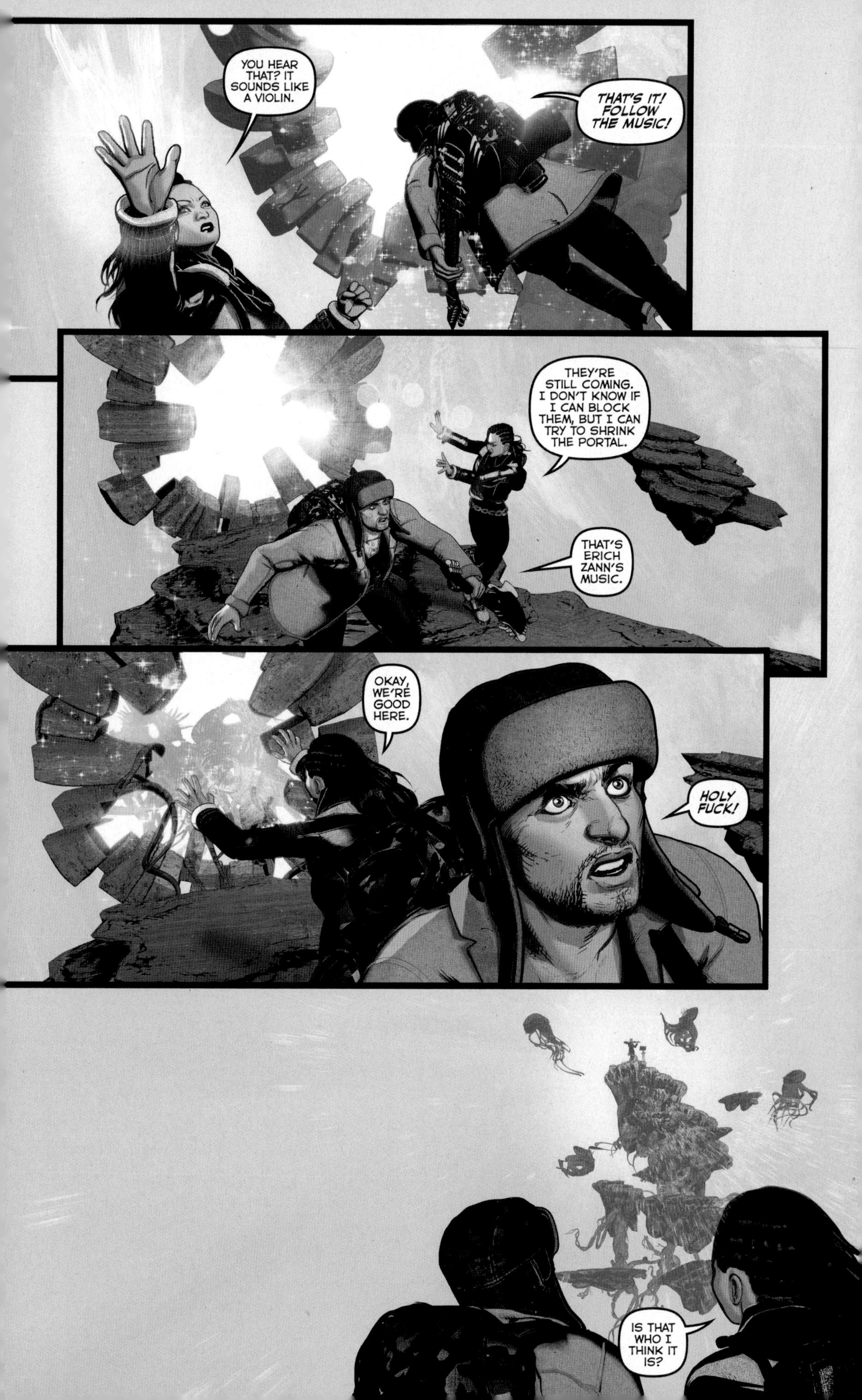
YOU HEAR THAT? IT SOUNDS LIKE A VIOLIN.
THAT'S IT! FOLLOW THE MUSIC!
THEY'RE STILL COMING. I DON'T KNOW IF I CAN BLOCK THEM, BUT I CAN TRY TO SHRINK THE PORTAL.
THAT'S ERICH ZANN'S MUSIC.
OKAY, WE'RE GOOD HERE.
HOLY FUCK!
IS THAT WHO I THINK IT IS?

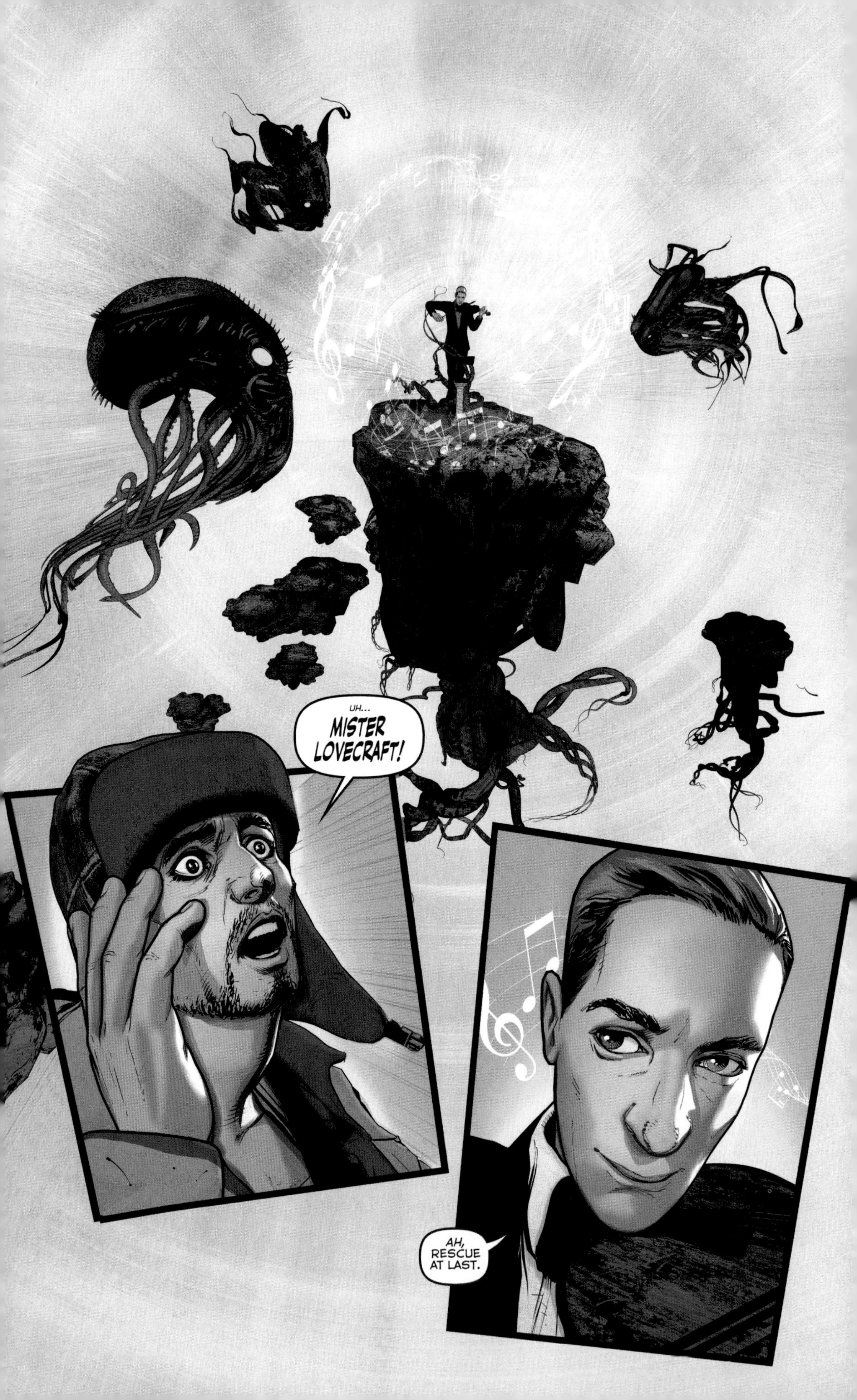
UH...
MISTER LOVECRAFT!
AH, RESCUE AT LAST.

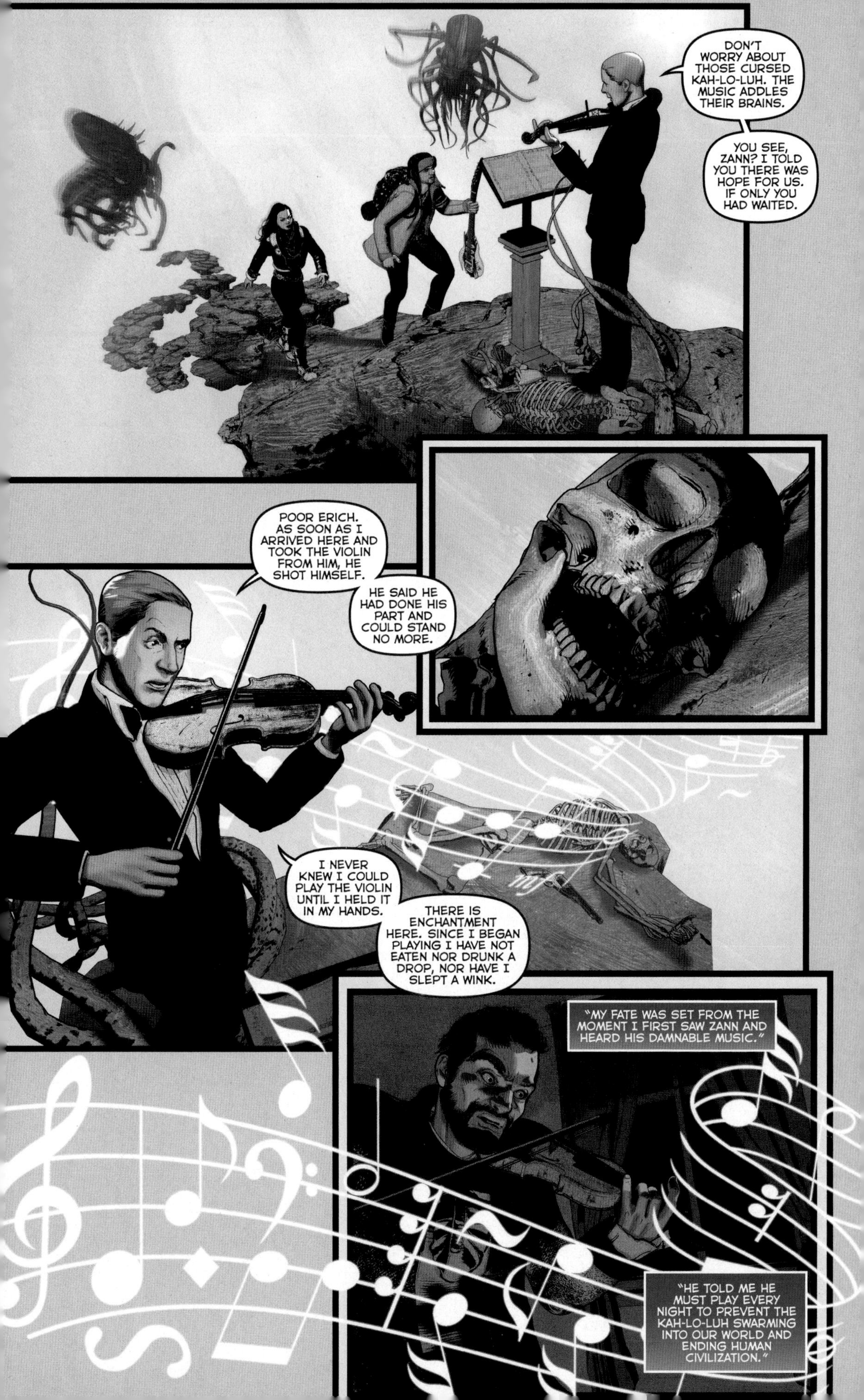
DON'T WORRY ABOUT THOSE CURSED KAH-LO-LUH. THE MUSIC ADDLES THEIR BRAINS.
YOU SEE, ZANN? I TOLD YOU THERE WAS HOPE FOR US. IF ONLY YOU HAD WAITED.
POOR ERICH. AS SOON AS I ARRIVED HERE AND TOOK THE VIOLIN FROM HIM, HE SHOT HIMSELF.
HE SAID HE HAD DONE HIS PART AND COULD STAND NO MORE.
I NEVER KNEW I COULD PLAY THE VIOLIN UNTIL I HELD IT IN MY HANDS.
THERE IS ENCHANTMENT HERE. SINCE I BEGAN PLAYING I HAVE NOT EATEN NOR DRUNK A DROP, NOR HAVE I SLEPT A WINK.
"MY FATE WAS SET FROM THE MOMENT I FIRST SAW ZANN AND HEARD HIS DAMNABLE MUSIC."
"HE TOLD ME HE MUST PLAY EVERY NIGHT TO PREVENT THE KAH-LO-LUH SWARMING INTO OUR WORLD AND ENDING HUMAN CIVILIZATION."

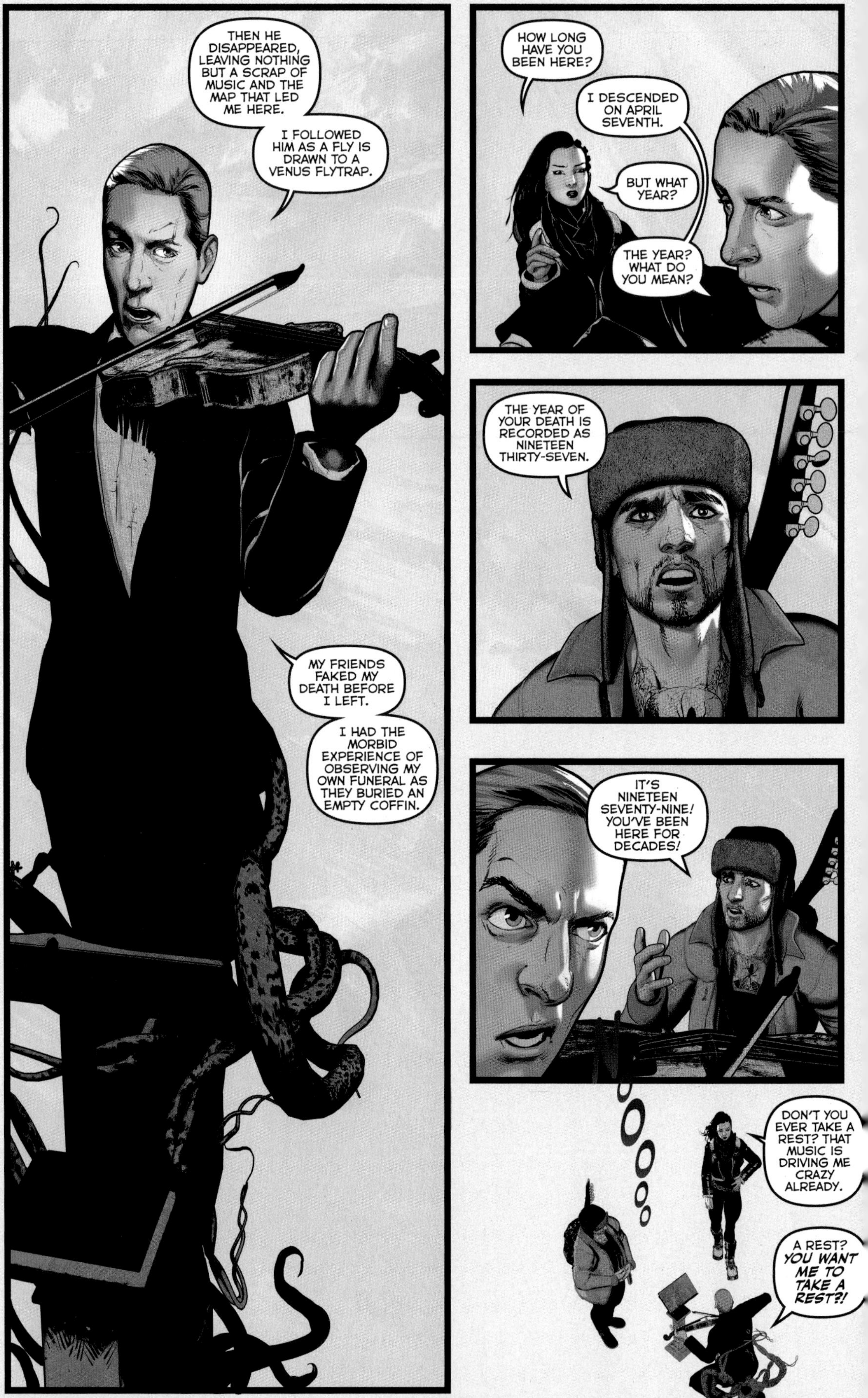
THEN HE DISAPPEARED, LEAVING NOTHING BUT A SCRAP OF MUSIC AND THE MAP THAT LED ME HERE.
I FOLLOWED HIM AS A FLY IS DRAWN TO A VENUS FLYTRAP.
MY FRIENDS FAKED MY DEATH BEFORE I LEFT.
I HAD THE MORBID EXPERIENCE OF OBSERVING MY OWN FUNERAL AS THEY BURIED AN EMPTY COFFIN.
HOW LONG HAVE YOU BEEN HERE?
I DESCENDED ON APRIL SEVENTH.
BUT WHAT YEAR?
THE YEAR? WHAT DO YOU MEAN?
THE YEAR OF YOUR DEATH IS RECORDED AS NINETEEN THIRTY-SEVEN.
IT'S NINETEEN SEVENTY-NINE! YOU'VE BEEN HERE FOR DECADES!
DON'T YOU EVER TAKE A REST? THAT MUSIC IS DRIVING ME CRAZY ALREADY.
A REST? *YOU WANT ME TO TAKE A REST?!*

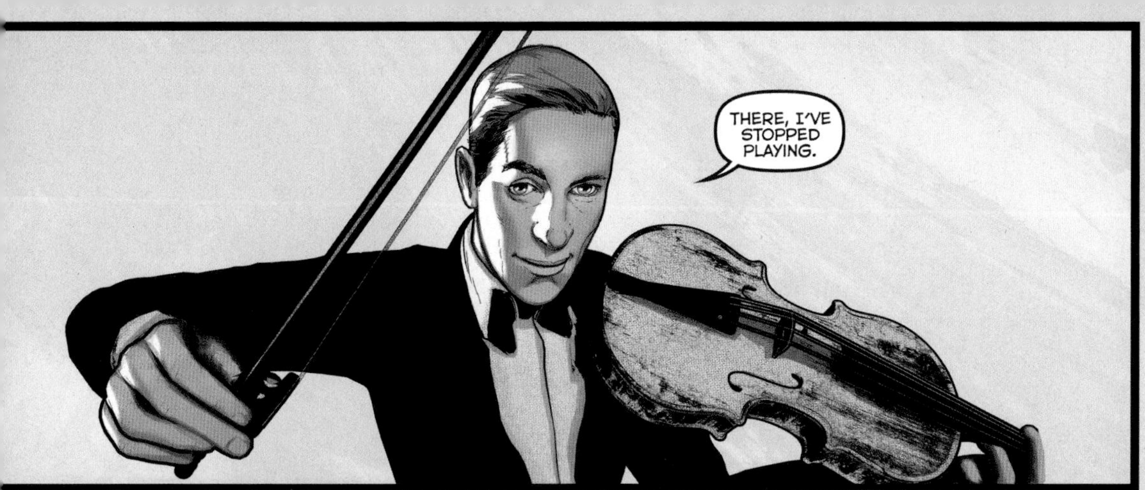
THERE, I'VE STOPPED PLAYING.

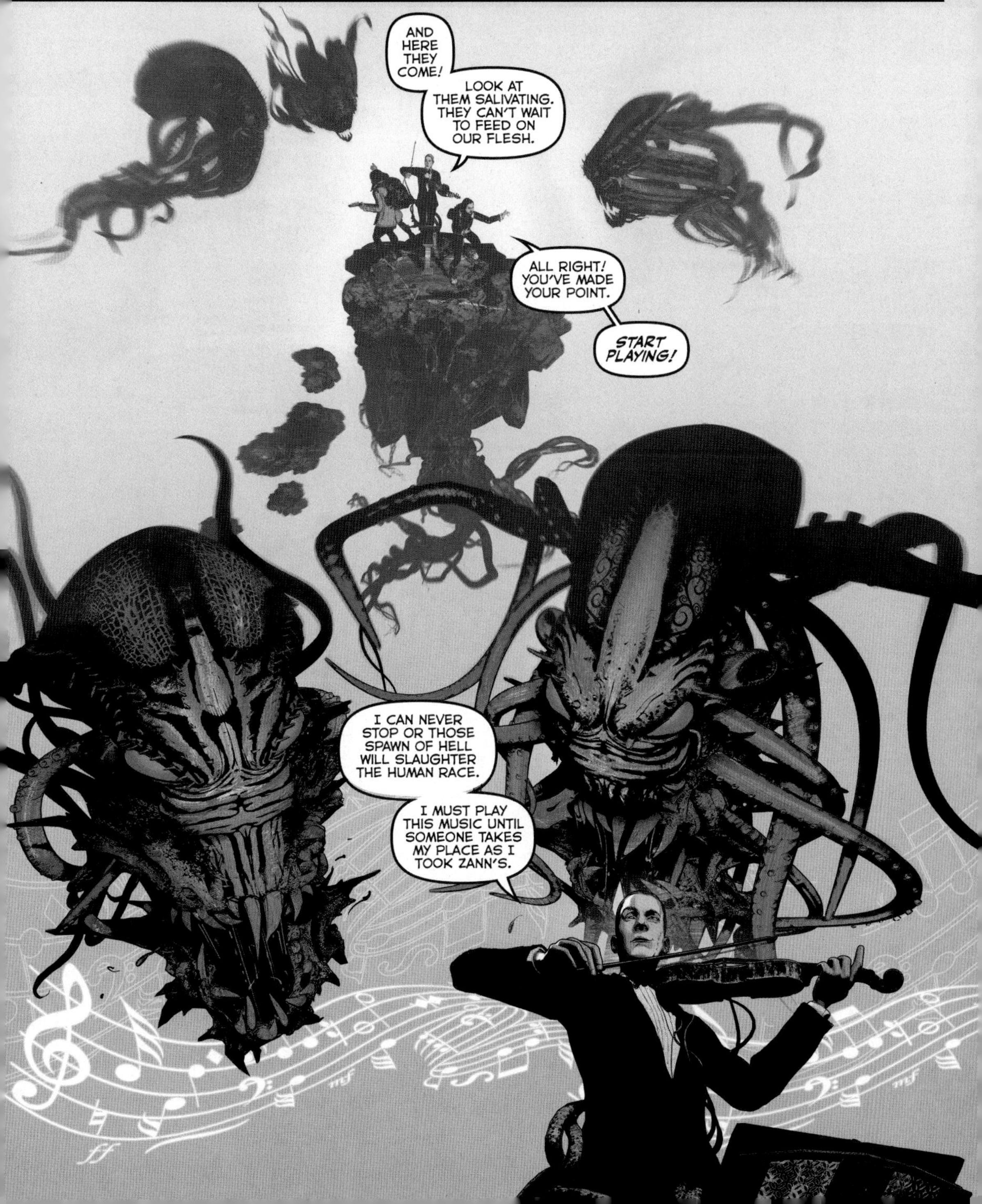
AND HERE THEY COME!
LOOK AT THEM SALIVATING. THEY CAN'T WAIT TO FEED ON OUR FLESH.
ALL RIGHT! YOU'VE MADE YOUR POINT.
START PLAYING!
I CAN NEVER STOP OR THOSE SPAWN OF HELL WILL SLAUGHTER THE HUMAN RACE.
I MUST PLAY THIS MUSIC UNTIL SOMEONE TAKES MY PLACE AS I TOOK ZANN'S.

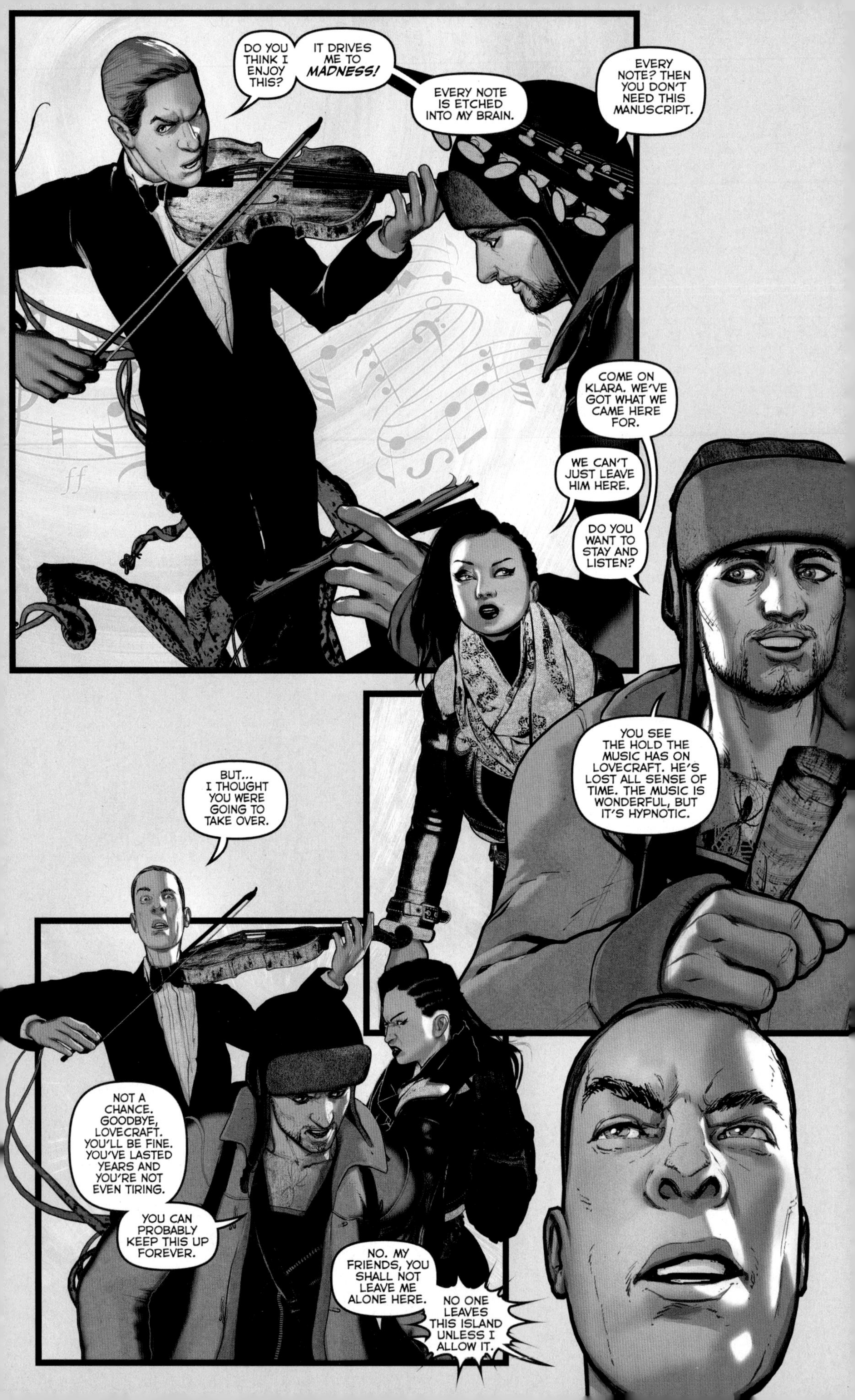
DO YOU THINK I ENJOY THIS?
IT DRIVES ME TO *MADNESS!*
EVERY NOTE IS ETCHED INTO MY BRAIN.
EVERY NOTE? THEN YOU DON'T NEED THIS MANUSCRIPT.
COME ON KLARA. WE'VE GOT WHAT WE CAME HERE FOR.
WE CAN'T JUST LEAVE HIM HERE.
DO YOU WANT TO STAY AND LISTEN?
YOU SEE THE HOLD THE MUSIC HAS ON LOVECRAFT. HE'S LOST ALL SENSE OF TIME. THE MUSIC IS WONDERFUL, BUT IT'S HYPNOTIC.
BUT... I THOUGHT YOU WERE GOING TO TAKE OVER.
NOT A CHANCE. GOODBYE, LOVECRAFT. YOU'LL BE FINE. YOU'VE LASTED YEARS AND YOU'RE NOT EVEN TIRING.
YOU CAN PROBABLY KEEP THIS UP FOREVER.
NO. MY FRIENDS, YOU SHALL NOT LEAVE ME ALONE HERE.
NO ONE LEAVES THIS ISLAND UNLESS I ALLOW IT.

CHAPTER SEVEN

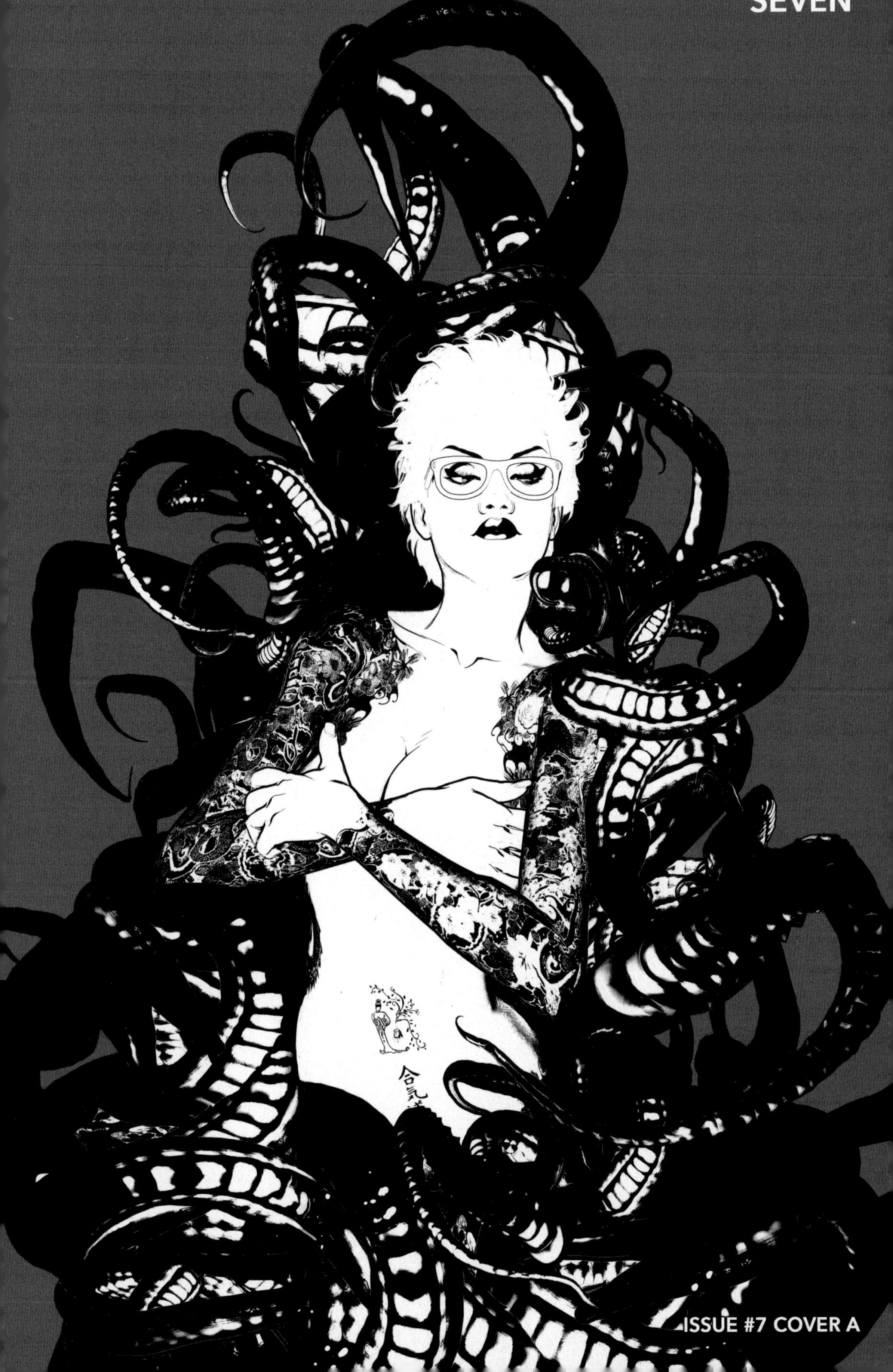

ISSUE #7 COVER A

ISSUE #7 COVER B

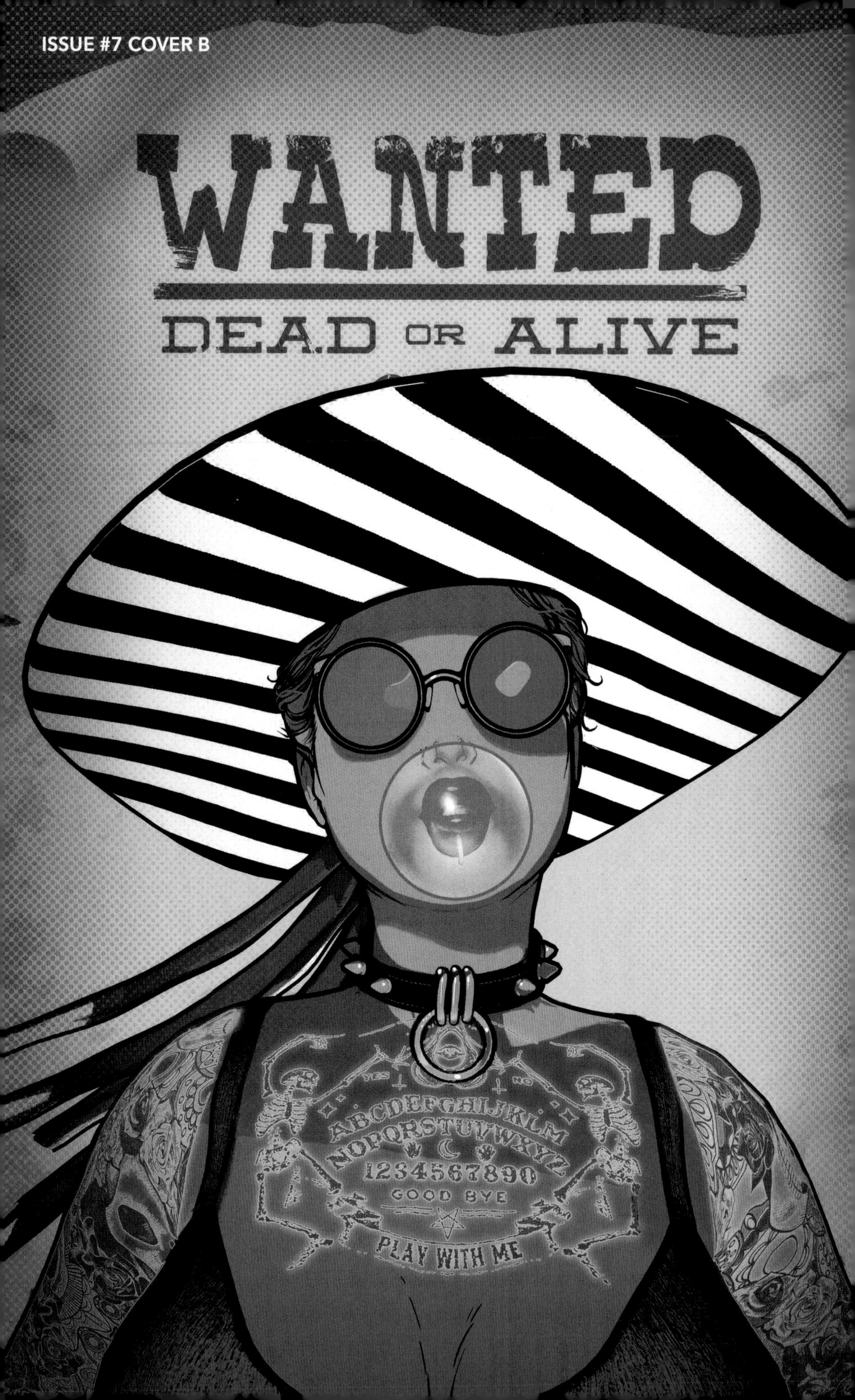
WANTED
DEAD OR ALIVE
YES
NO
ABCDEFGHIJKLM
NOPQRSTUVWXYZ
1234567890
GOOD BYE
PLAY WITH ME

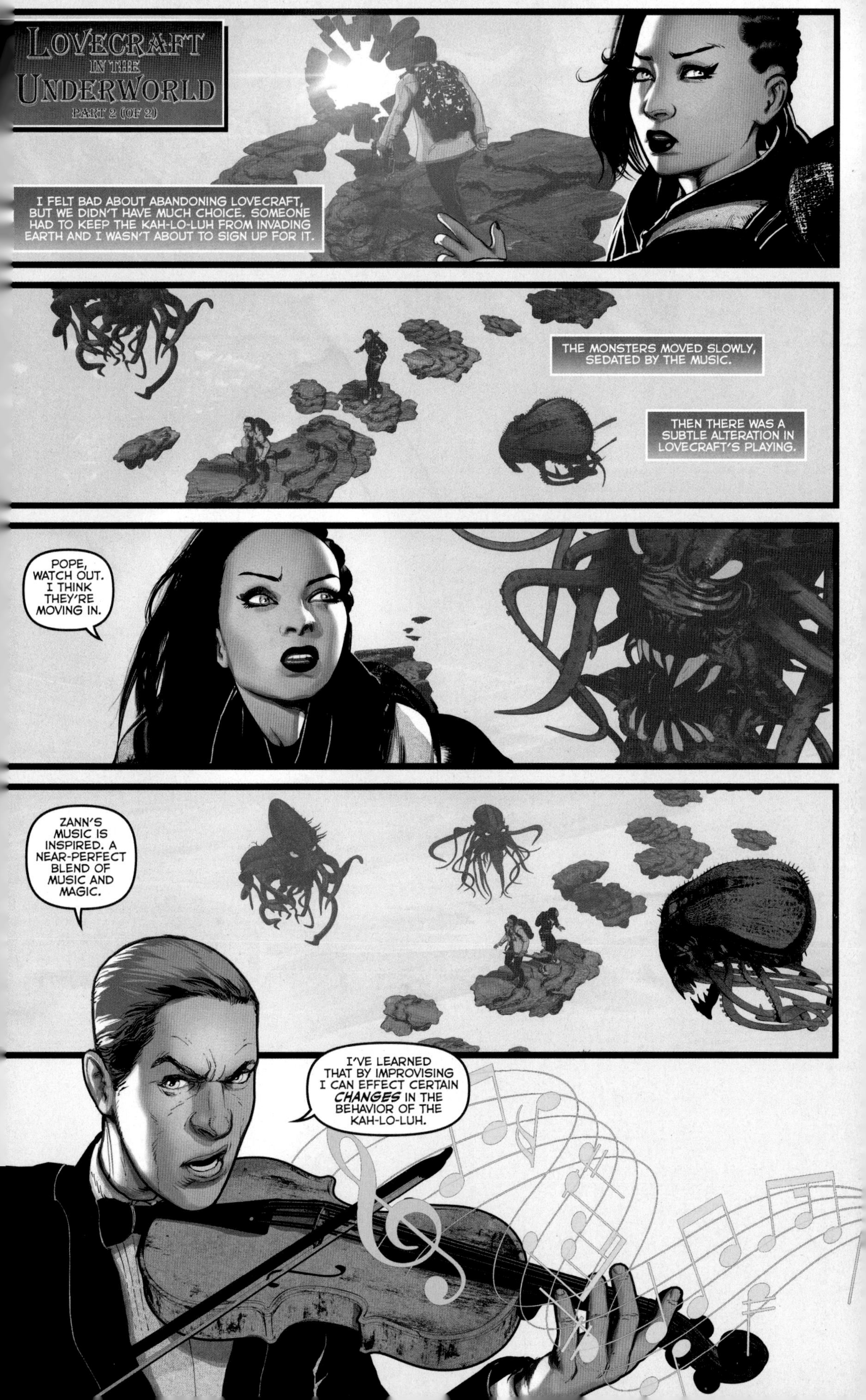
LOVECRAFT IN THE UNDERWORLD
PART 2 (OF 2)
I FELT BAD ABOUT ABANDONING LOVECRAFT, BUT WE DIDN'T HAVE MUCH CHOICE. SOMEONE HAD TO KEEP THE KAH-LO-LUH FROM INVADING EARTH AND I WASN'T ABOUT TO SIGN UP FOR IT.
THE MONSTERS MOVED SLOWLY, SEDATED BY THE MUSIC.
THEN THERE WAS A SUBTLE ALTERATION IN LOVECRAFT'S PLAYING.
POPE, WATCH OUT. I THINK THEY'RE MOVING IN.
ZANN'S MUSIC IS INSPIRED. A NEAR-PERFECT BLEND OF MUSIC AND MAGIC.
I'VE LEARNED THAT BY IMPROVISING I CAN EFFECT CERTAIN CHANGES IN THE BEHAVIOR OF THE KAH-LO-LUH.

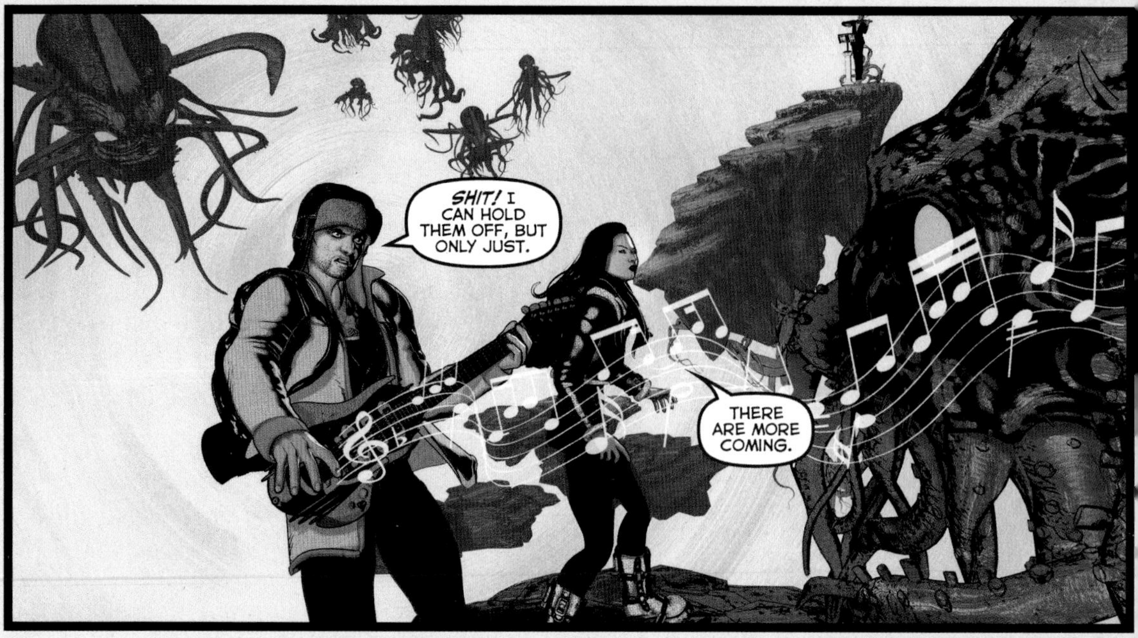
SHIT! I CAN HOLD THEM OFF, BUT ONLY JUST.
THERE ARE MORE COMING.

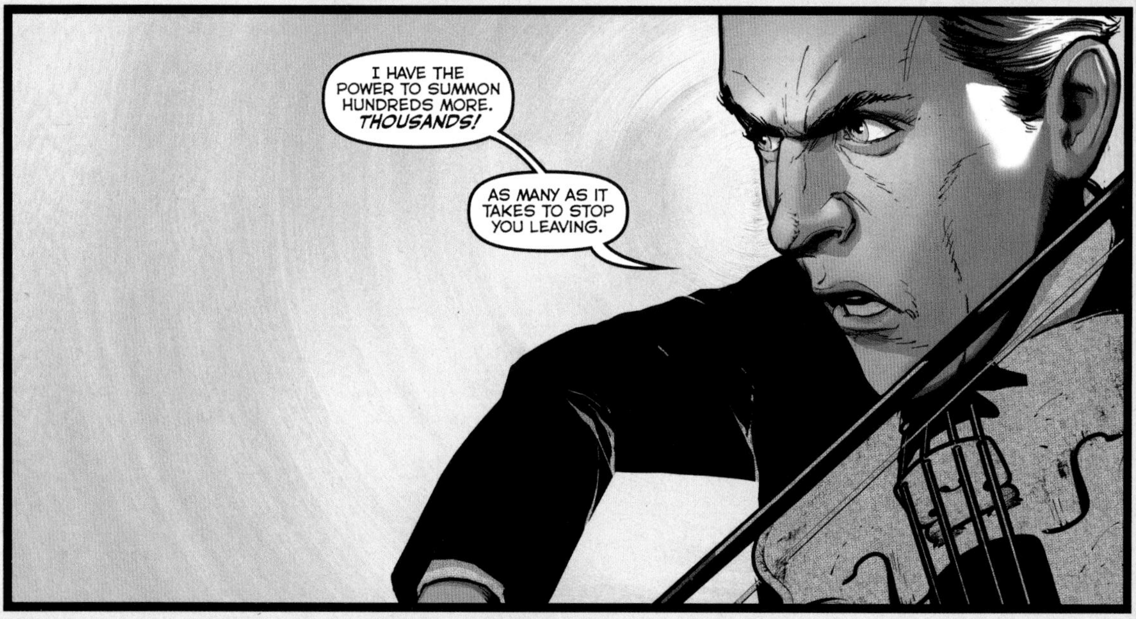
I HAVE THE POWER TO SUMMON HUNDREDS MORE. THOUSANDS!
AS MANY AS IT TAKES TO STOP YOU LEAVING.

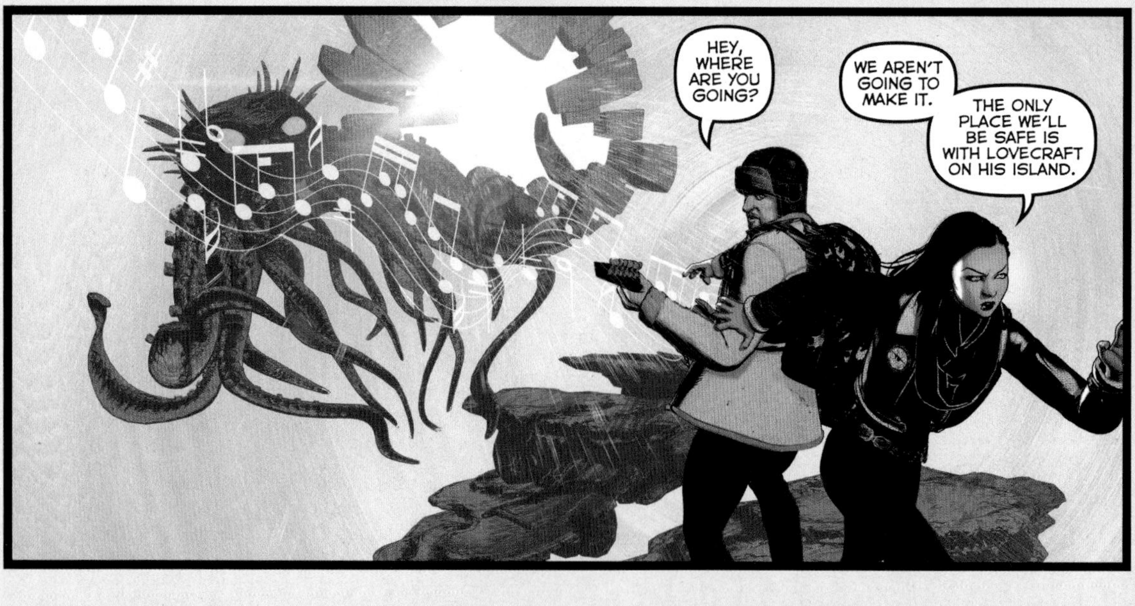
HEY, WHERE ARE YOU GOING?
WE AREN'T GOING TO MAKE IT.
THE ONLY PLACE WE'LL BE SAFE IS WITH LOVECRAFT ON HIS ISLAND.

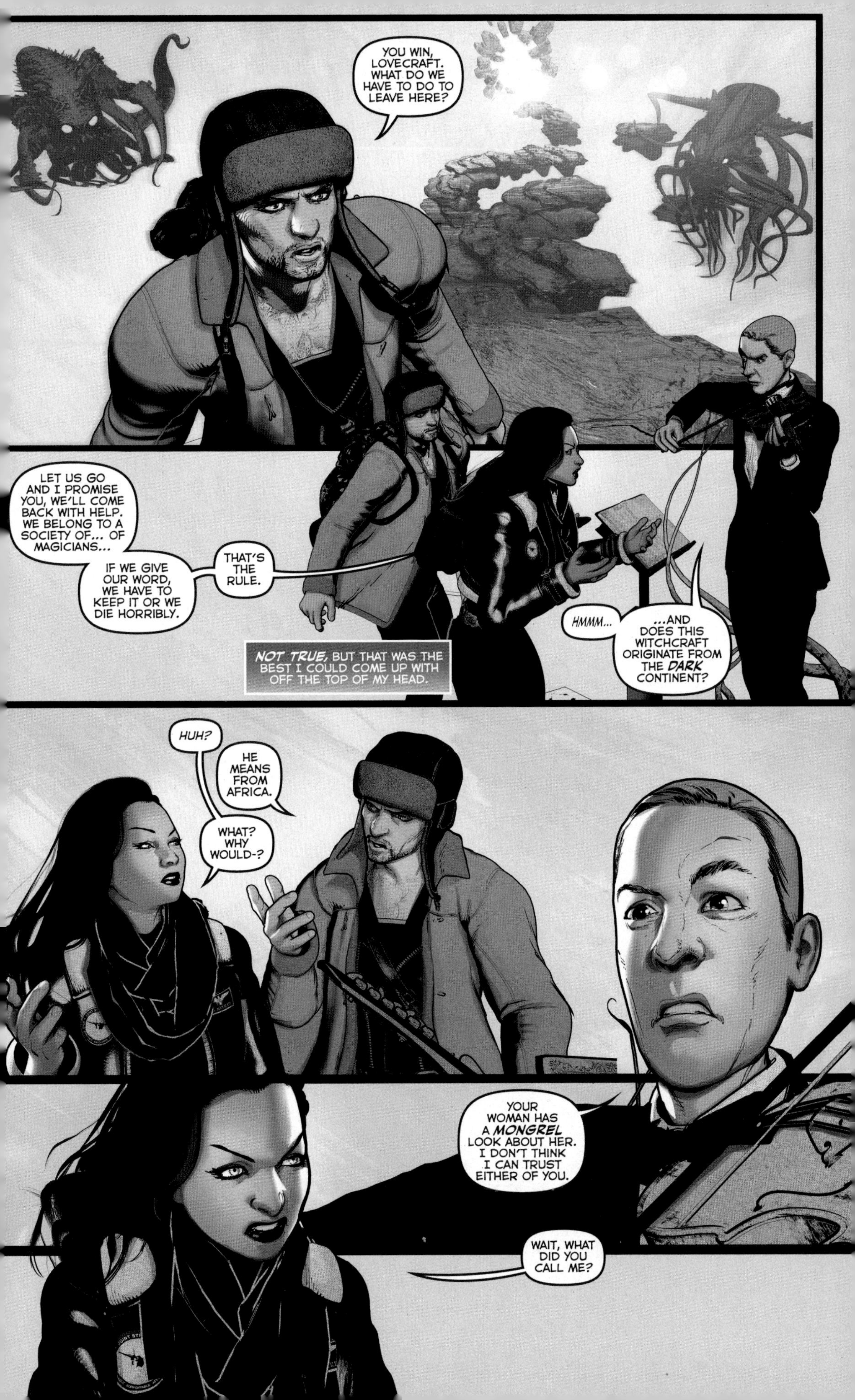
YOU WIN, LOVECRAFT. WHAT DO WE HAVE TO DO TO LEAVE HERE?
LET US GO AND I PROMISE YOU, WE'LL COME BACK WITH HELP. WE BELONG TO A SOCIETY OF... OF MAGICIANS...
IF WE GIVE OUR WORD, WE HAVE TO KEEP IT OR WE DIE HORRIBLY.
THAT'S THE RULE.
NOT TRUE, BUT THAT WAS THE BEST I COULD COME UP WITH OFF THE TOP OF MY HEAD.
HMMM...
...AND DOES THIS WITCHCRAFT ORIGINATE FROM THE DARK CONTINENT?
HUH?
HE MEANS FROM AFRICA.
WHAT? WHY WOULD-?
YOUR WOMAN HAS A MONGREL LOOK ABOUT HER. I DON'T THINK I CAN TRUST EITHER OF YOU.
WAIT, WHAT DID YOU CALL ME?

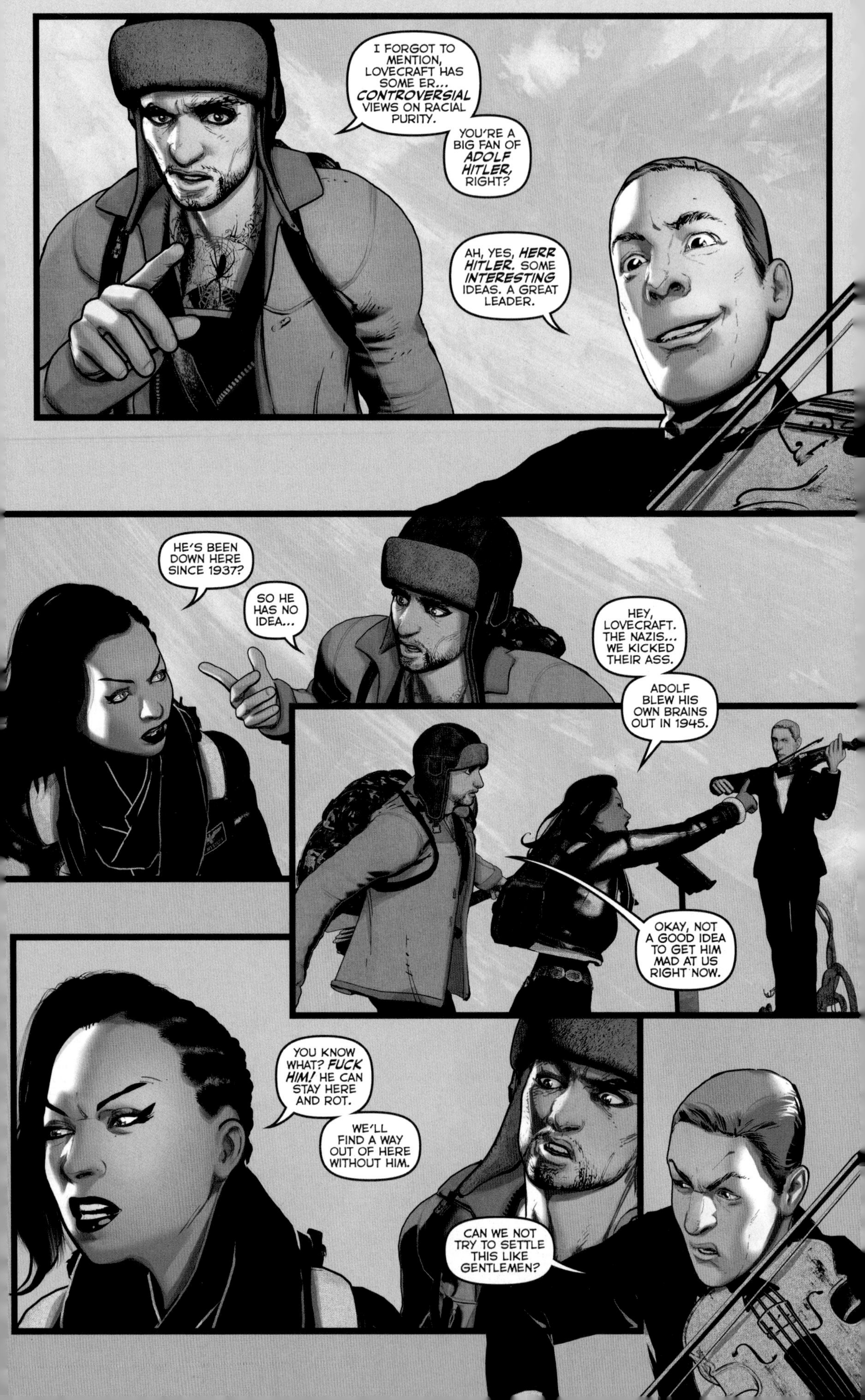
I FORGOT TO MENTION, LOVECRAFT HAS SOME ER... *CONTROVERSIAL* VIEWS ON RACIAL PURITY.
YOU'RE A BIG FAN OF *ADOLF HITLER,* RIGHT?
AH, YES, *HERR HITLER.* SOME *INTERESTING* IDEAS. A GREAT LEADER.
HE'S BEEN DOWN HERE SINCE 1937?
SO HE HAS NO IDEA...
HEY, LOVECRAFT. THE NAZIS... WE KICKED THEIR ASS.
ADOLF BLEW HIS OWN BRAINS OUT IN 1945.
OKAY, NOT A GOOD IDEA TO GET HIM MAD AT US RIGHT NOW.
YOU KNOW WHAT? *FUCK HIM!* HE CAN STAY HERE AND ROT.
WE'LL FIND A WAY OUT OF HERE WITHOUT HIM.
CAN WE NOT TRY TO SETTLE THIS LIKE GENTLEMEN?

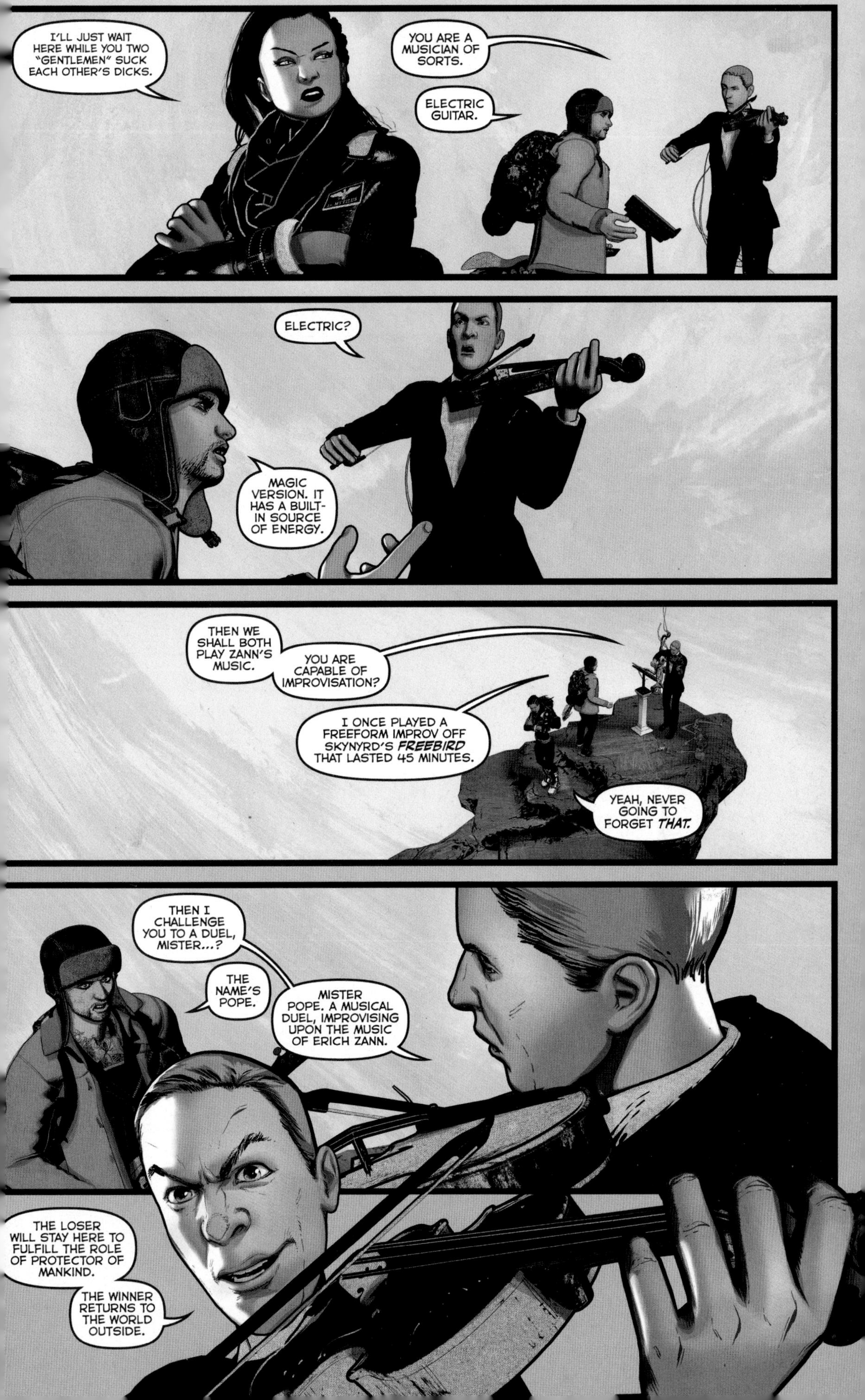
I'LL JUST WAIT HERE WHILE YOU TWO "GENTLEMEN" SUCK EACH OTHER'S DICKS.
YOU ARE A MUSICIAN OF SORTS.
ELECTRIC GUITAR.
ELECTRIC?
MAGIC VERSION. IT HAS A BUILT-IN SOURCE OF ENERGY.
THEN WE SHALL BOTH PLAY ZANN'S MUSIC.
YOU ARE CAPABLE OF IMPROVISATION?
I ONCE PLAYED A FREEFORM IMPROV OFF SKYNYRD'S *FREEBIRD* THAT LASTED 45 MINUTES.
YEAH, NEVER GOING TO FORGET *THAT.*
THEN I CHALLENGE YOU TO A DUEL, MISTER...?
THE NAME'S POPE.
MISTER POPE. A MUSICAL DUEL, IMPROVISING UPON THE MUSIC OF ERICH ZANN.
THE LOSER WILL STAY HERE TO FULFILL THE ROLE OF PROTECTOR OF MANKIND.
THE WINNER RETURNS TO THE WORLD OUTSIDE.

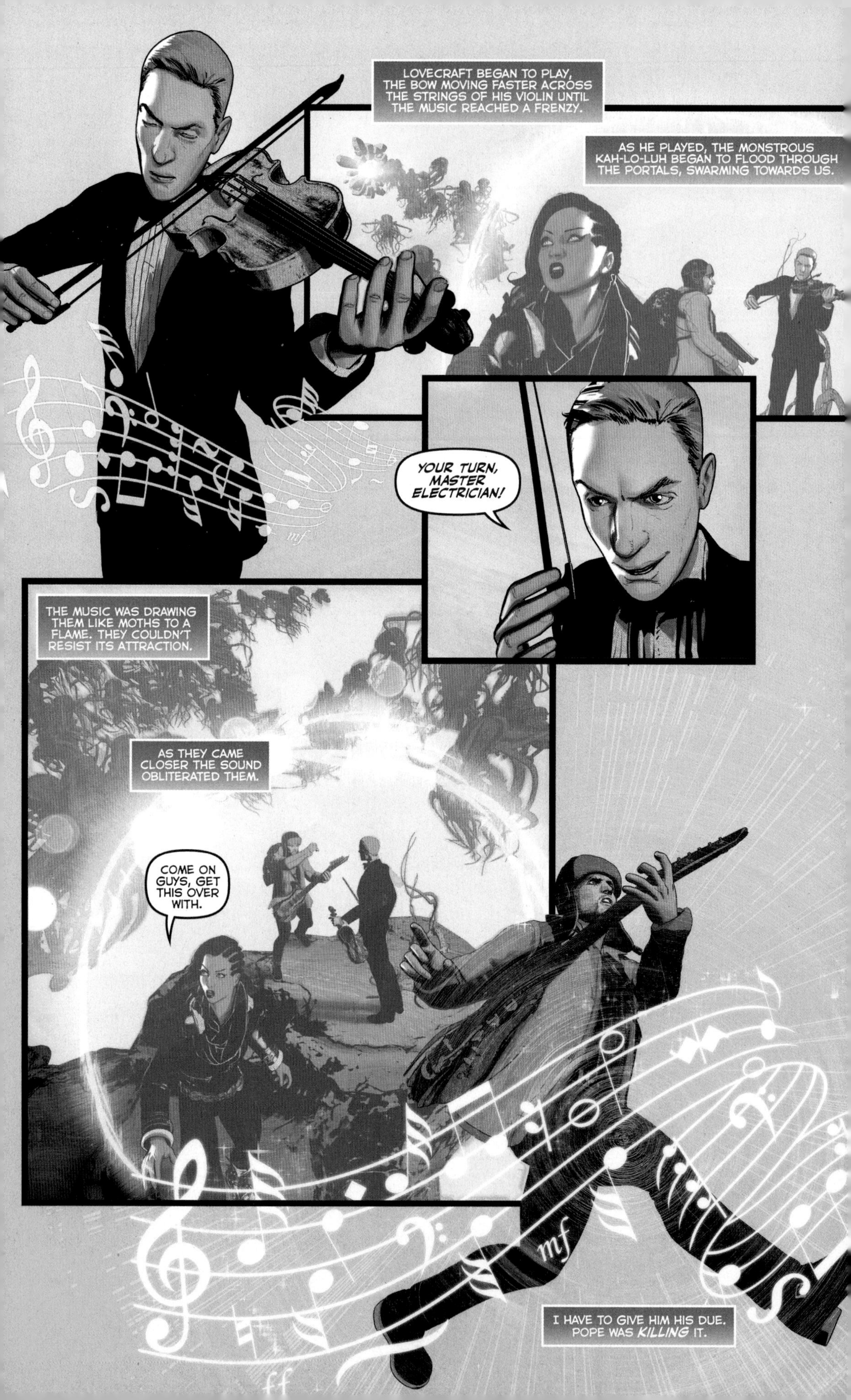
LOVECRAFT BEGAN TO PLAY, THE BOW MOVING FASTER ACROSS THE STRINGS OF HIS VIOLIN UNTIL THE MUSIC REACHED A FRENZY.
AS HE PLAYED, THE MONSTROUS KAH-LO-LUH BEGAN TO FLOOD THROUGH THE PORTALS, SWARMING TOWARDS US.
YOUR TURN, MASTER ELECTRICIAN!
THE MUSIC WAS DRAWING THEM LIKE MOTHS TO A FLAME. THEY COULDN'T RESIST ITS ATTRACTION.
AS THEY CAME CLOSER THE SOUND OBLITERATED THEM.
COME ON GUYS, GET THIS OVER WITH.
I HAVE TO GIVE HIM HIS DUE. POPE WAS *KILLING* IT.

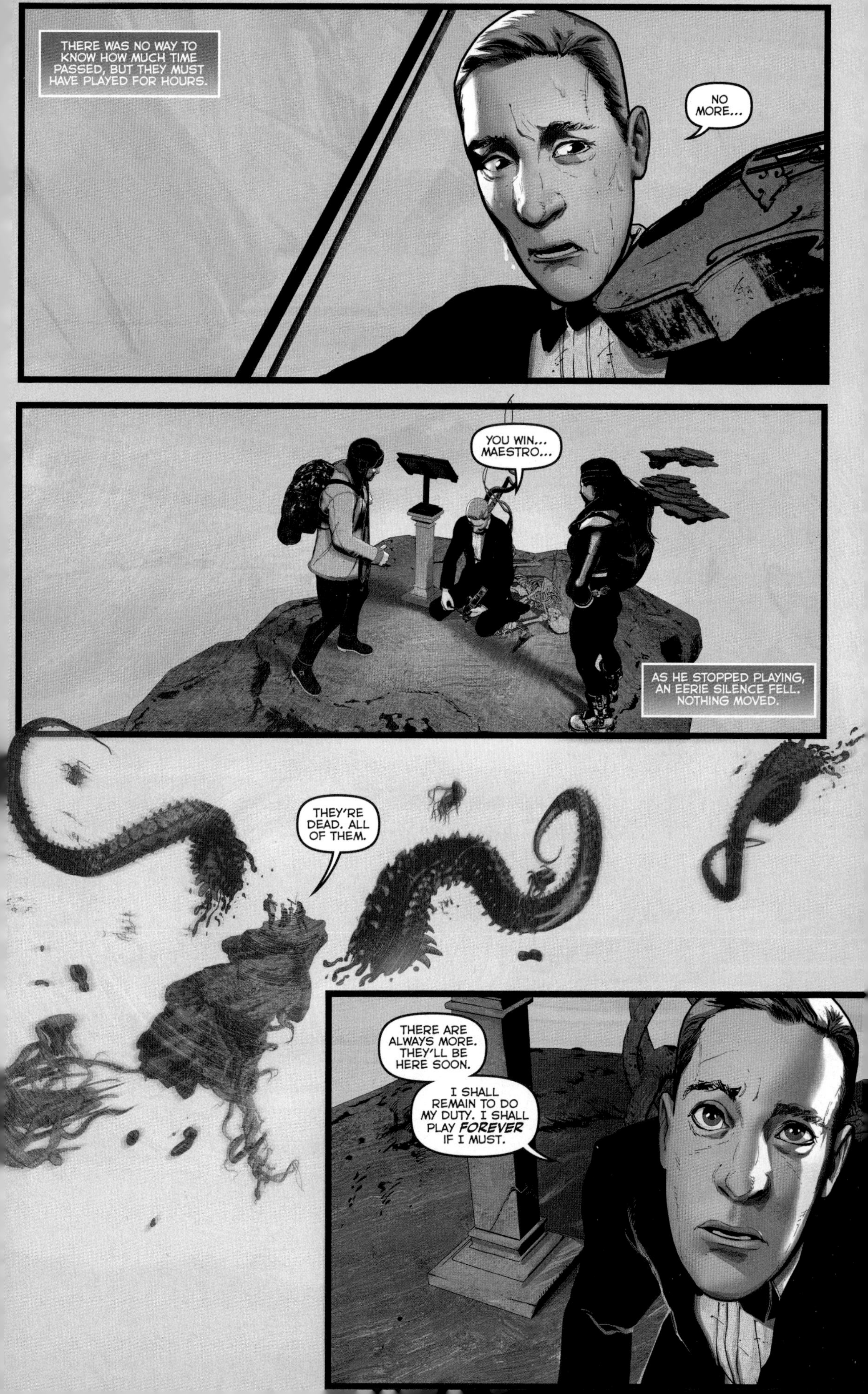
THERE WAS NO WAY TO KNOW HOW MUCH TIME PASSED, BUT THEY MUST HAVE PLAYED FOR HOURS.
NO MORE...
YOU WIN... MAESTRO...
AS HE STOPPED PLAYING, AN EERIE SILENCE FELL. NOTHING MOVED.
THEY'RE DEAD. ALL OF THEM.
THERE ARE ALWAYS MORE. THEY'LL BE HERE SOON.
I SHALL REMAIN TO DO MY DUTY. I SHALL PLAY *FOREVER* IF I MUST.

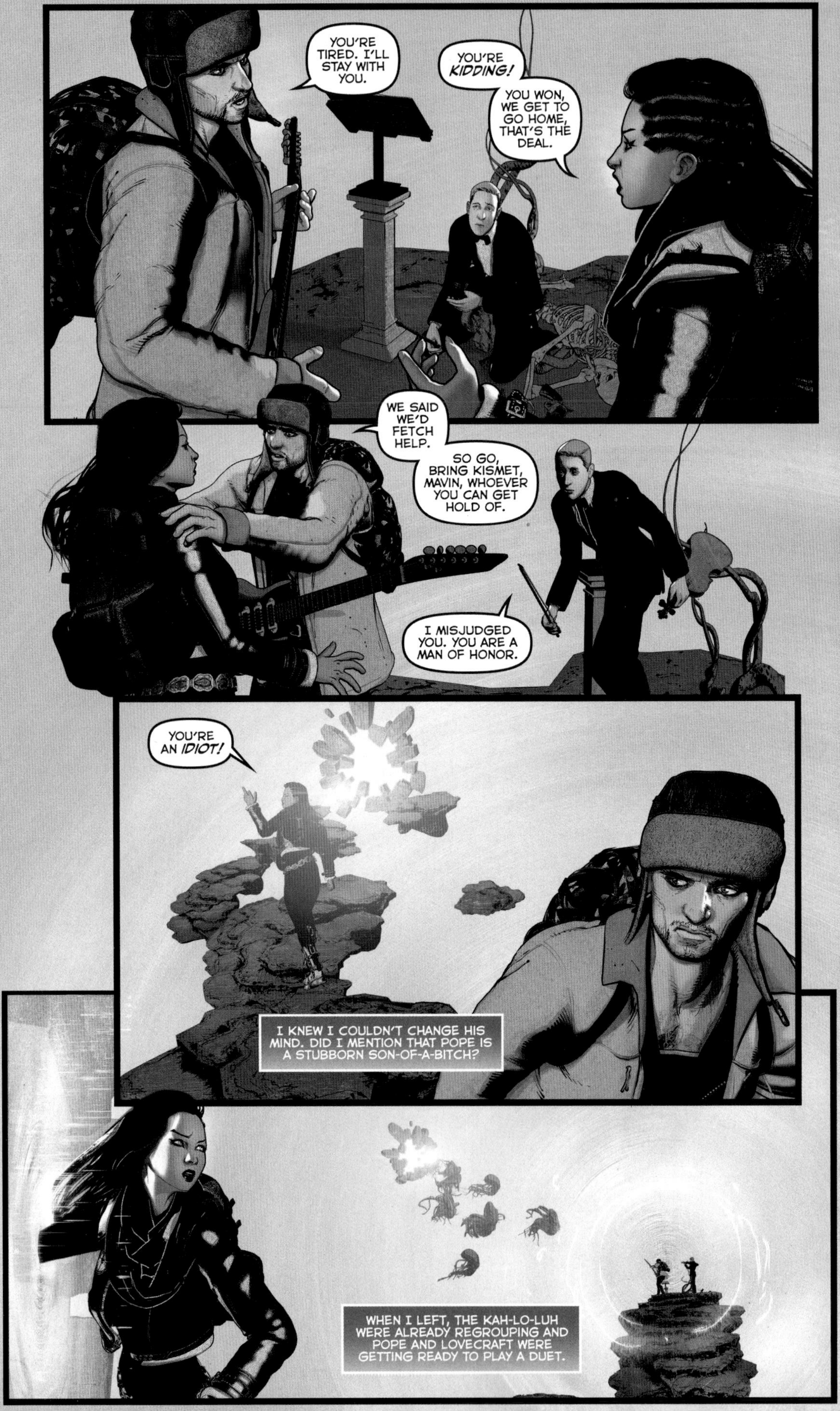
YOU'RE TIRED. I'LL STAY WITH YOU.
YOU'RE *KIDDING!*
YOU WON, WE GET TO GO HOME, THAT'S THE DEAL.
WE SAID WE'D FETCH HELP.
SO GO, BRING KISMET, MAVIN, WHOEVER YOU CAN GET HOLD OF.
I MISJUDGED YOU. YOU ARE A MAN OF HONOR.
YOU'RE AN *IDIOT!*
I KNEW I COULDN'T CHANGE HIS MIND. DID I MENTION THAT POPE IS A STUBBORN SON-OF-A-BITCH?
WHEN I LEFT, THE KAH-LO-LUH WERE ALREADY REGROUPING AND POPE AND LOVECRAFT WERE GETTING READY TO PLAY A DUET.

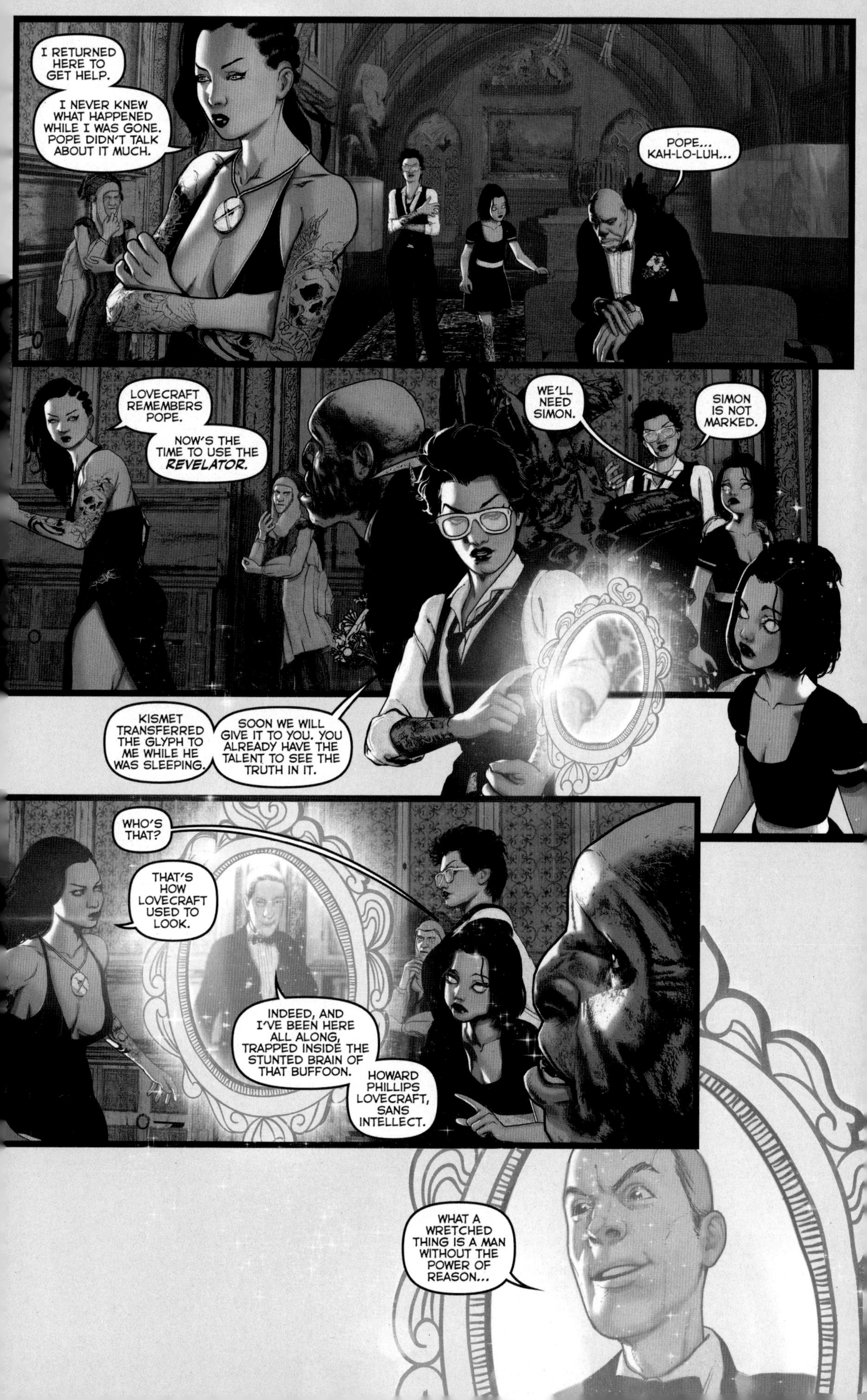

I RETURNED HERE TO GET HELP.
I NEVER KNEW WHAT HAPPENED WHILE I WAS GONE. POPE DIDN'T TALK ABOUT IT MUCH.
POPE... KAH-LO-LUH...
LOVECRAFT REMEMBERS POPE.
NOW'S THE TIME TO USE THE *REVELATOR.*
WE'LL NEED SIMON.
SIMON IS NOT MARKED.
KISMET TRANSFERRED THE GLYPH TO ME WHILE HE WAS SLEEPING.
SOON WE WILL GIVE IT TO YOU. YOU ALREADY HAVE THE TALENT TO SEE THE TRUTH IN IT.
WHO'S THAT?
THAT'S HOW LOVECRAFT USED TO LOOK.
INDEED, AND I'VE BEEN HERE ALL ALONG, TRAPPED INSIDE THE STUNTED BRAIN OF THAT BUFFOON.
HOWARD PHILLIPS LOVECRAFT, SANS INTELLECT.
WHAT A WRETCHED THING IS A MAN WITHOUT THE POWER OF REASON...

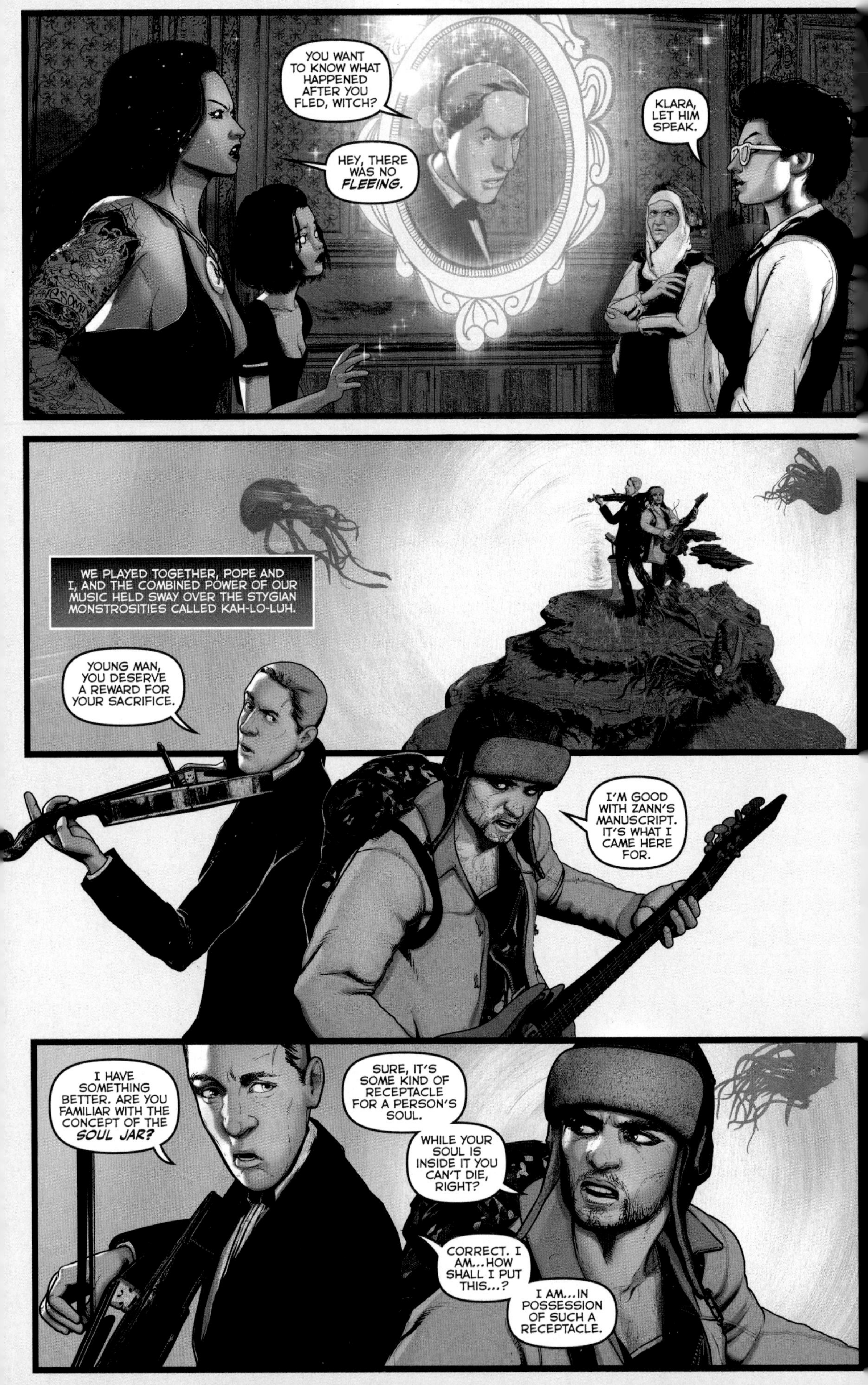

YOU WANT TO KNOW WHAT HAPPENED AFTER YOU FLED, WITCH?
HEY, THERE WAS NO *FLEEING.*
KLARA, LET HIM SPEAK.
WE PLAYED TOGETHER, POPE AND I, AND THE COMBINED POWER OF OUR MUSIC HELD SWAY OVER THE STYGIAN MONSTROSITIES CALLED KAH-LO-LUH.
YOUNG MAN, YOU DESERVE A REWARD FOR YOUR SACRIFICE.
I'M GOOD WITH ZANN'S MANUSCRIPT. IT'S WHAT I CAME HERE FOR.
I HAVE SOMETHING BETTER. ARE YOU FAMILIAR WITH THE CONCEPT OF THE *SOUL JAR?*
SURE, IT'S SOME KIND OF RECEPTACLE FOR A PERSON'S SOUL.
WHILE YOUR SOUL IS INSIDE IT YOU CAN'T DIE, RIGHT?
CORRECT. I AM...HOW SHALL I PUT THIS...?
I AM...IN POSSESSION OF SUCH A RECEPTACLE.

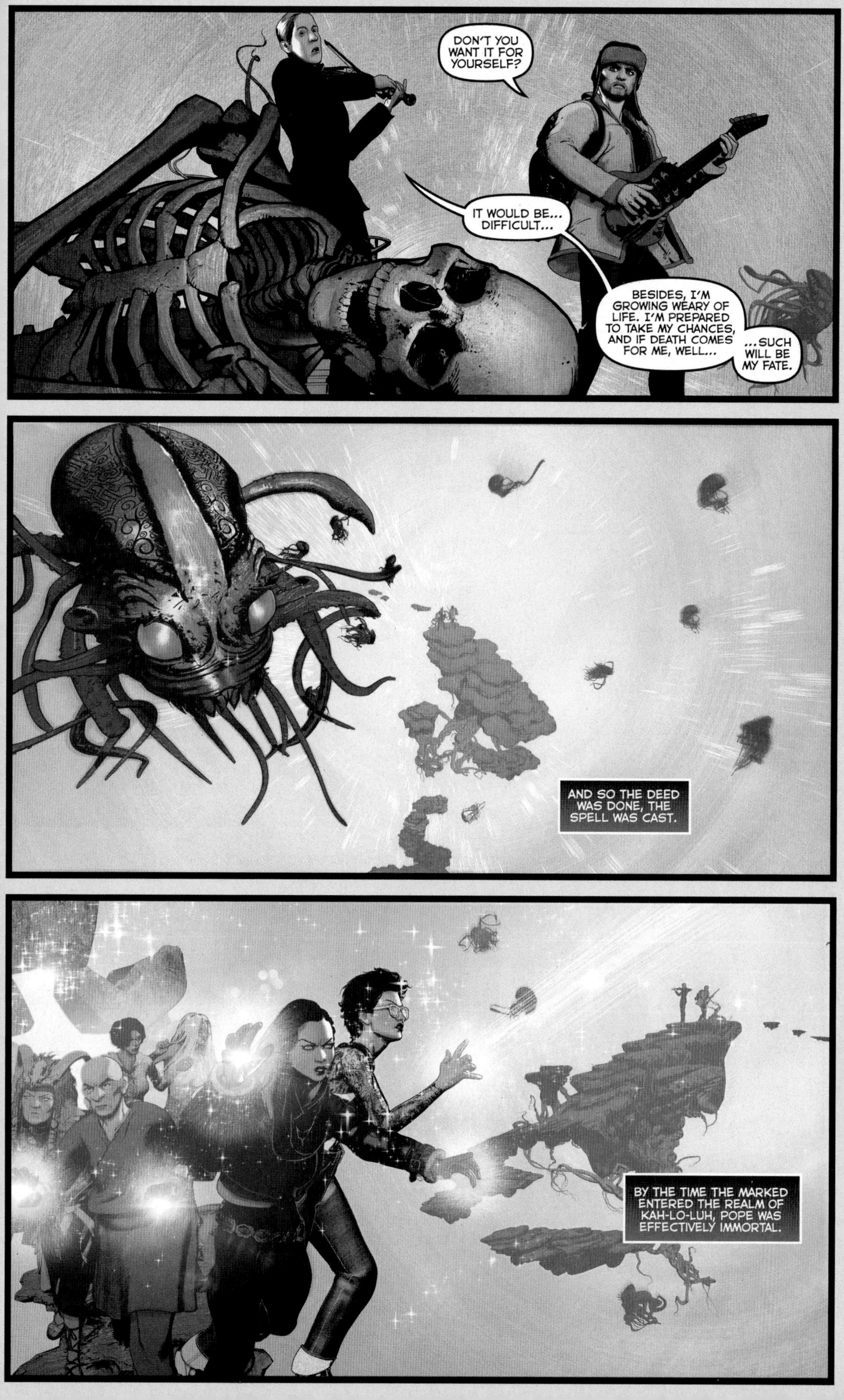
DON'T YOU WANT IT FOR YOURSELF?
IT WOULD BE... DIFFICULT...
BESIDES, I'M GROWING WEARY OF LIFE. I'M PREPARED TO TAKE MY CHANCES, AND IF DEATH COMES FOR ME, WELL...
...SUCH WILL BE MY FATE.
AND SO THE DEED WAS DONE, THE SPELL WAS CAST.
BY THE TIME THE MARKED ENTERED THE REALM OF KAH-LO-LUH, POPE WAS EFFECTIVELY IMMORTAL.

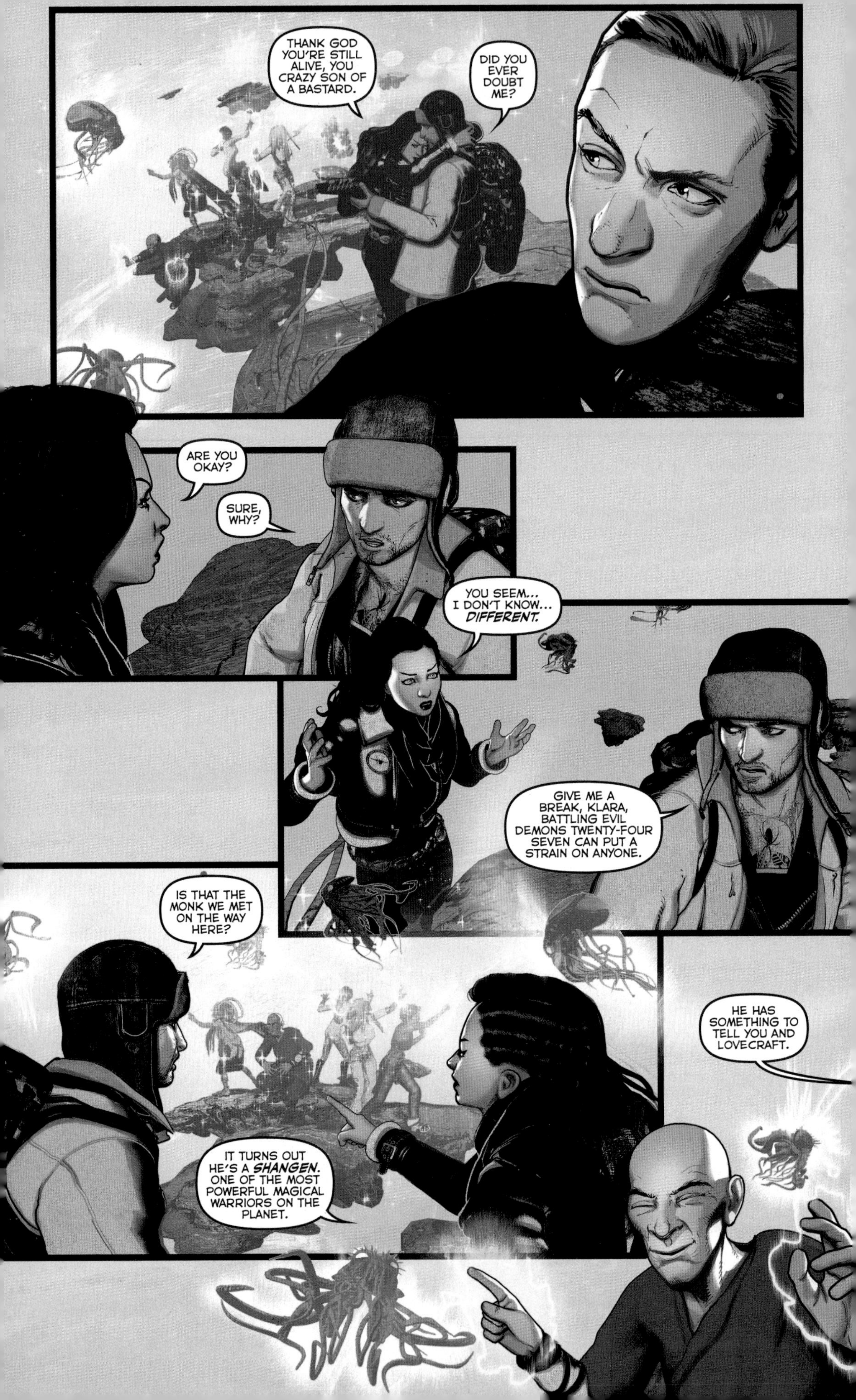
THANK GOD YOU'RE STILL ALIVE, YOU CRAZY SON OF A BASTARD.
DID YOU EVER DOUBT ME?
ARE YOU OKAY?
SURE, WHY?
YOU SEEM... I DON'T KNOW... *DIFFERENT.*
GIVE ME A BREAK, KLARA, BATTLING EVIL DEMONS TWENTY-FOUR SEVEN CAN PUT A STRAIN ON ANYONE.
IS THAT THE MONK WE MET ON THE WAY HERE?
IT TURNS OUT HE'S A *SHANGEN*. ONE OF THE MOST POWERFUL MAGICAL WARRIORS ON THE PLANET.
HE HAS SOMETHING TO TELL YOU AND LOVECRAFT.

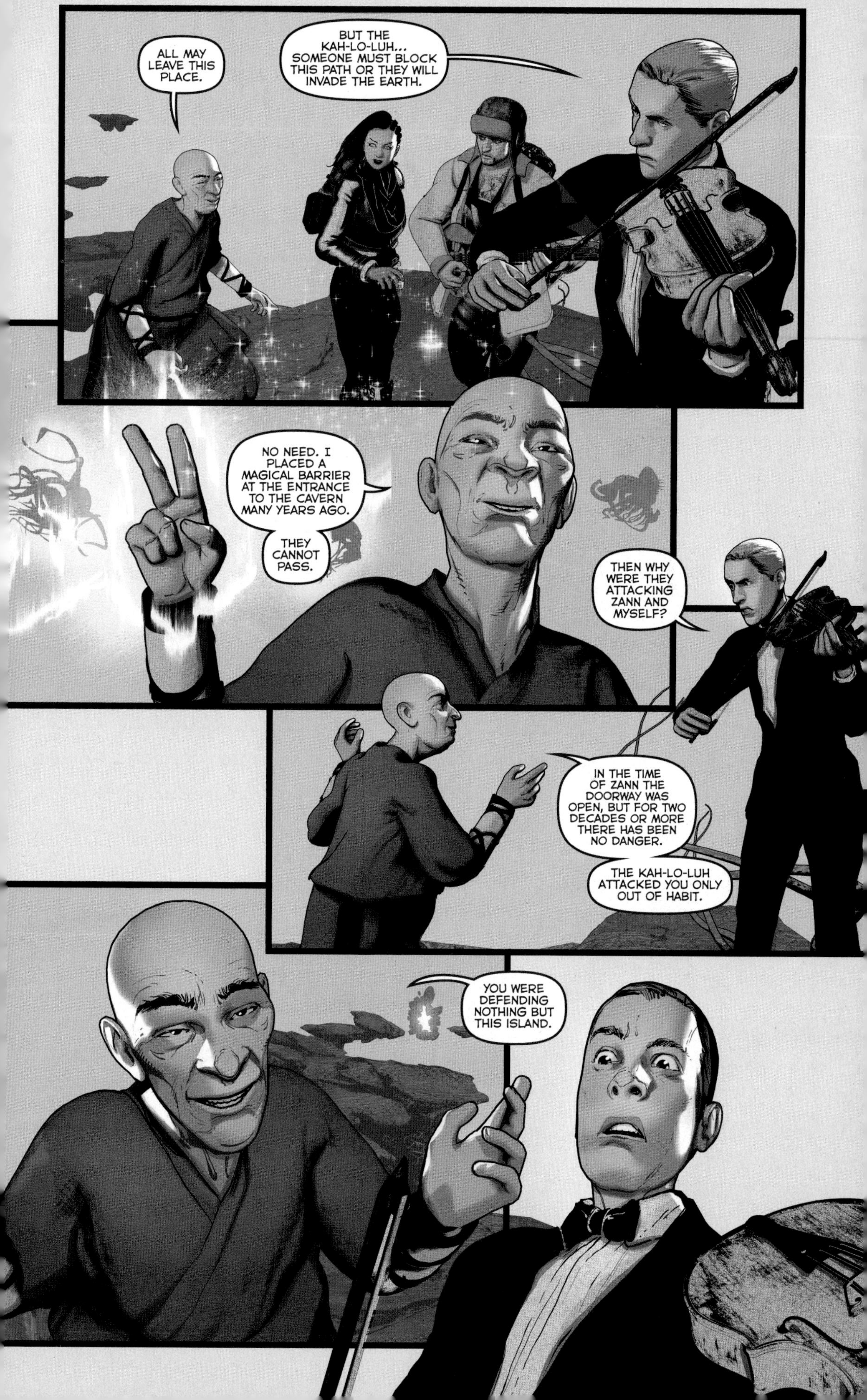
ALL MAY LEAVE THIS PLACE.
BUT THE KAH-LO-LUH... SOMEONE MUST BLOCK THIS PATH OR THEY WILL INVADE THE EARTH.
NO NEED. I PLACED A MAGICAL BARRIER AT THE ENTRANCE TO THE CAVERN MANY YEARS AGO.
THEY CANNOT PASS.
THEN WHY WERE THEY ATTACKING ZANN AND MYSELF?
IN THE TIME OF ZANN THE DOORWAY WAS OPEN, BUT FOR TWO DECADES OR MORE THERE HAS BEEN NO DANGER.
THE KAH-LO-LUH ATTACKED YOU ONLY OUT OF HABIT.
YOU WERE DEFENDING NOTHING BUT THIS ISLAND.

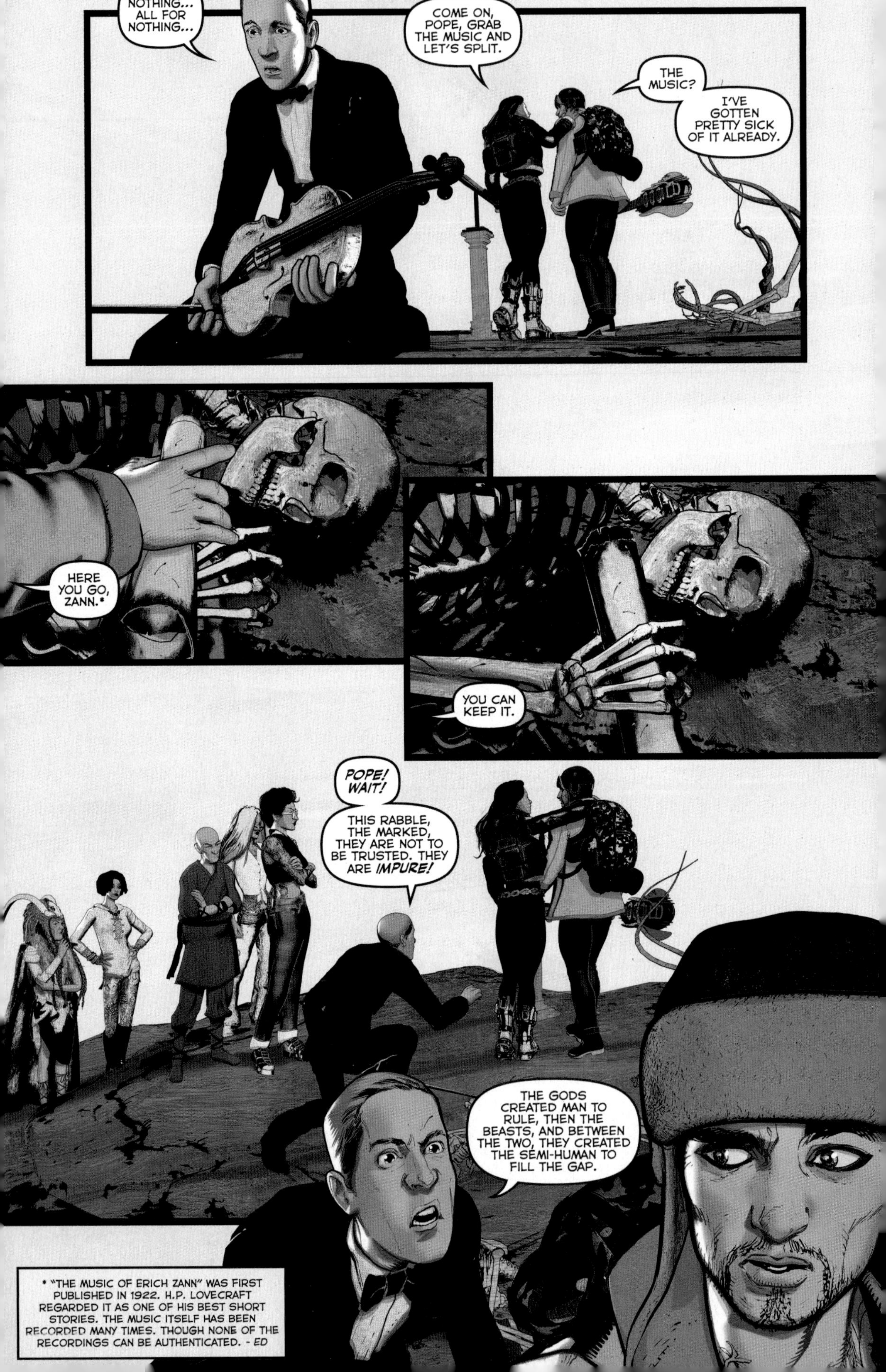
FOR NOTHING... ALL FOR NOTHING...
COME ON, POPE, GRAB THE MUSIC AND LET'S SPLIT.
THE MUSIC?
I'VE GOTTEN PRETTY SICK OF IT ALREADY.
HERE YOU GO, ZANN.*
YOU CAN KEEP IT.
POPE! WAIT!
THIS RABBLE, THE MARKED, THEY ARE NOT TO BE TRUSTED. THEY ARE *IMPURE!*
THE GODS CREATED MAN TO RULE, THEN THE BEASTS, AND BETWEEN THE TWO, THEY CREATED THE SEMI-HUMAN TO FILL THE GAP.
* "THE MUSIC OF ERICH ZANN" WAS FIRST PUBLISHED IN 1922. H.P. LOVECRAFT REGARDED IT AS ONE OF HIS BEST SHORT STORIES. THE MUSIC ITSELF HAS BEEN RECORDED MANY TIMES. THOUGH NONE OF THE RECORDINGS CAN BE AUTHENTICATED. - *ED*

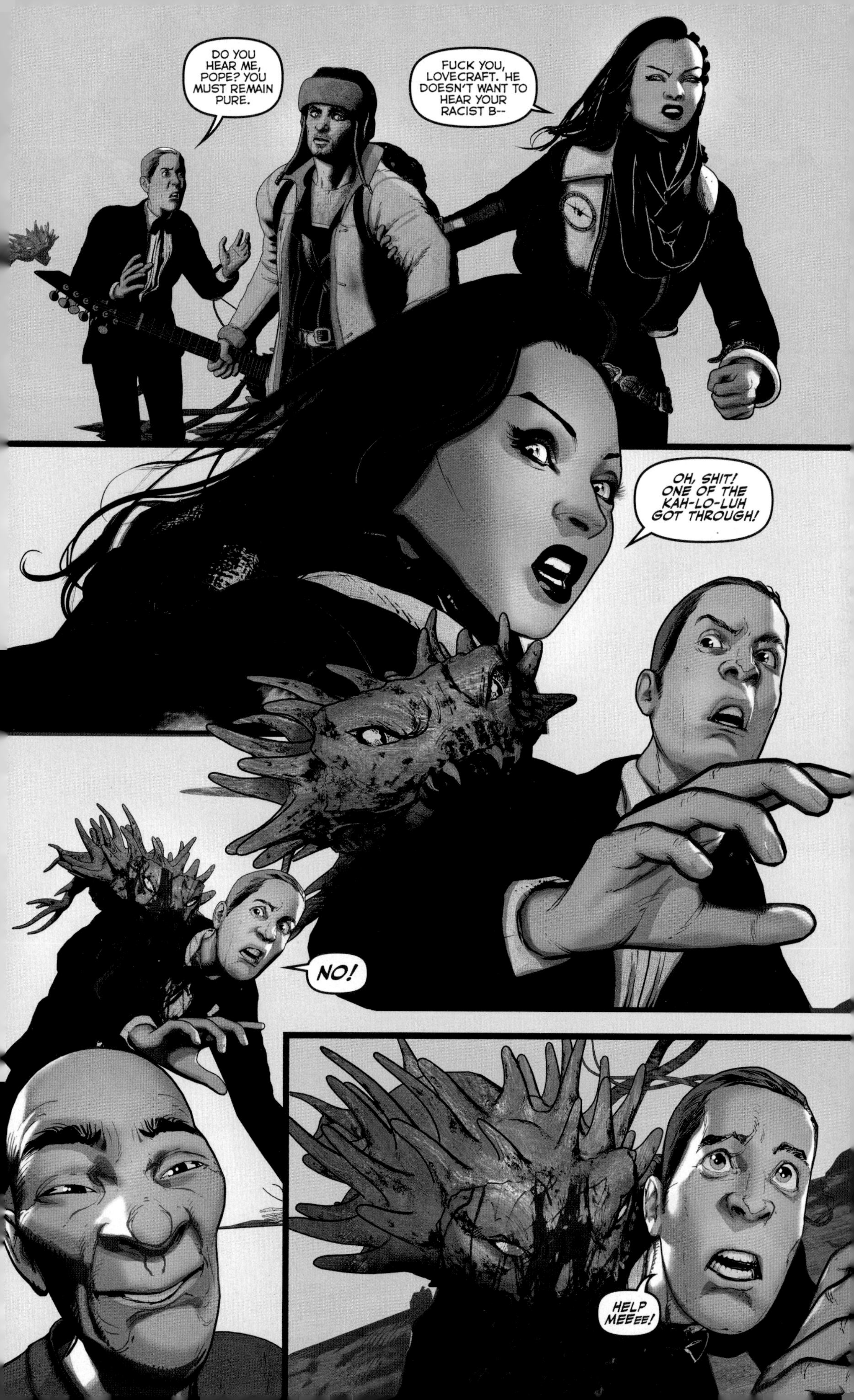
DO YOU HEAR ME, POPE? YOU MUST REMAIN PURE.
FUCK YOU, LOVECRAFT. HE DOESN'T WANT TO HEAR YOUR RACIST B--
OH, SHIT! ONE OF THE KAH-LO-LUH GOT THROUGH!
NO!
HELP MEEEE!

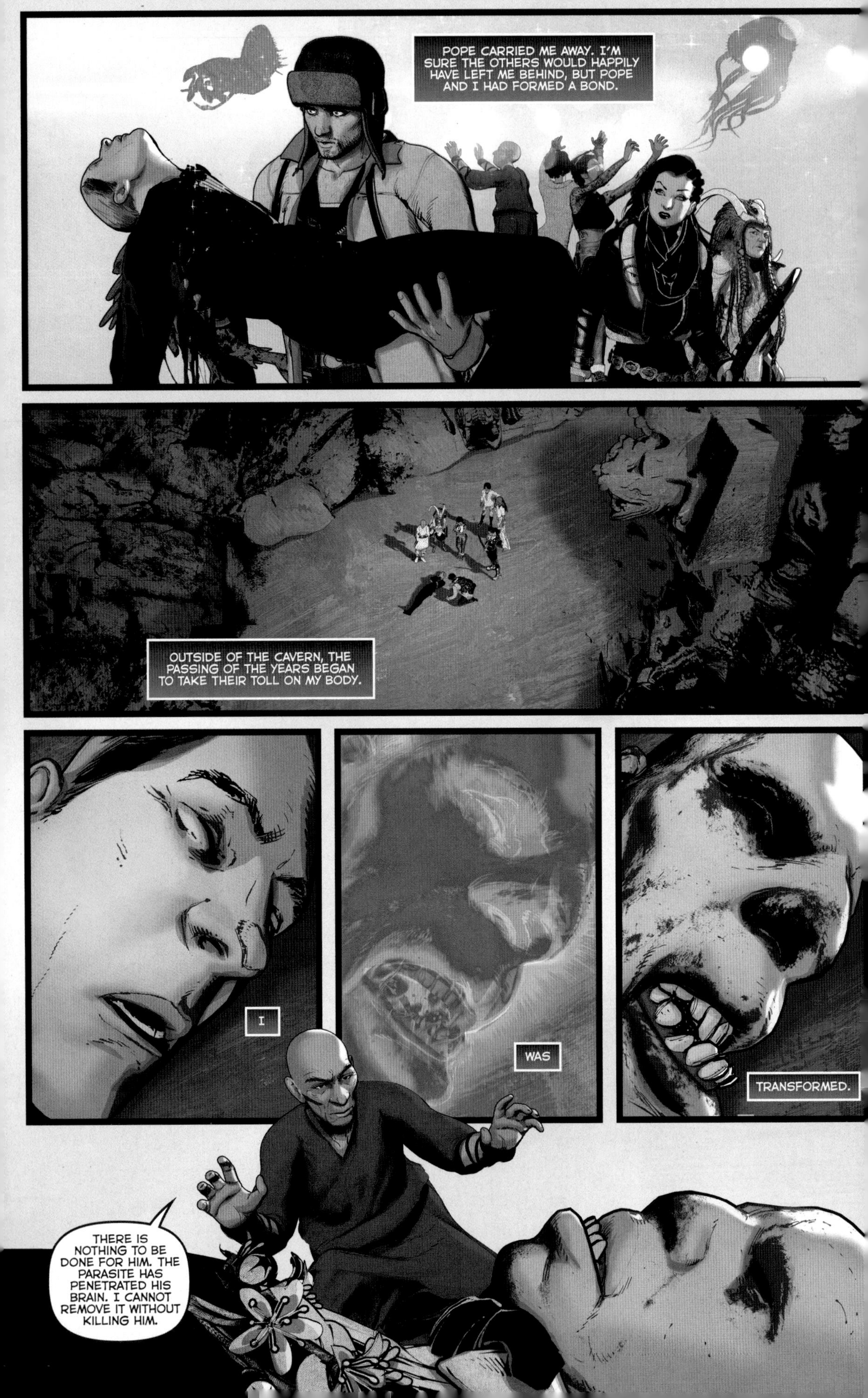
POPE CARRIED ME AWAY. I'M SURE THE OTHERS WOULD HAPPILY HAVE LEFT ME BEHIND, BUT POPE AND I HAD FORMED A BOND.
OUTSIDE OF THE CAVERN, THE PASSING OF THE YEARS BEGAN TO TAKE THEIR TOLL ON MY BODY.
I
WAS
TRANSFORMED.
THERE IS NOTHING TO BE DONE FOR HIM. THE PARASITE HAS PENETRATED HIS BRAIN. I CANNOT REMOVE IT WITHOUT KILLING HIM.

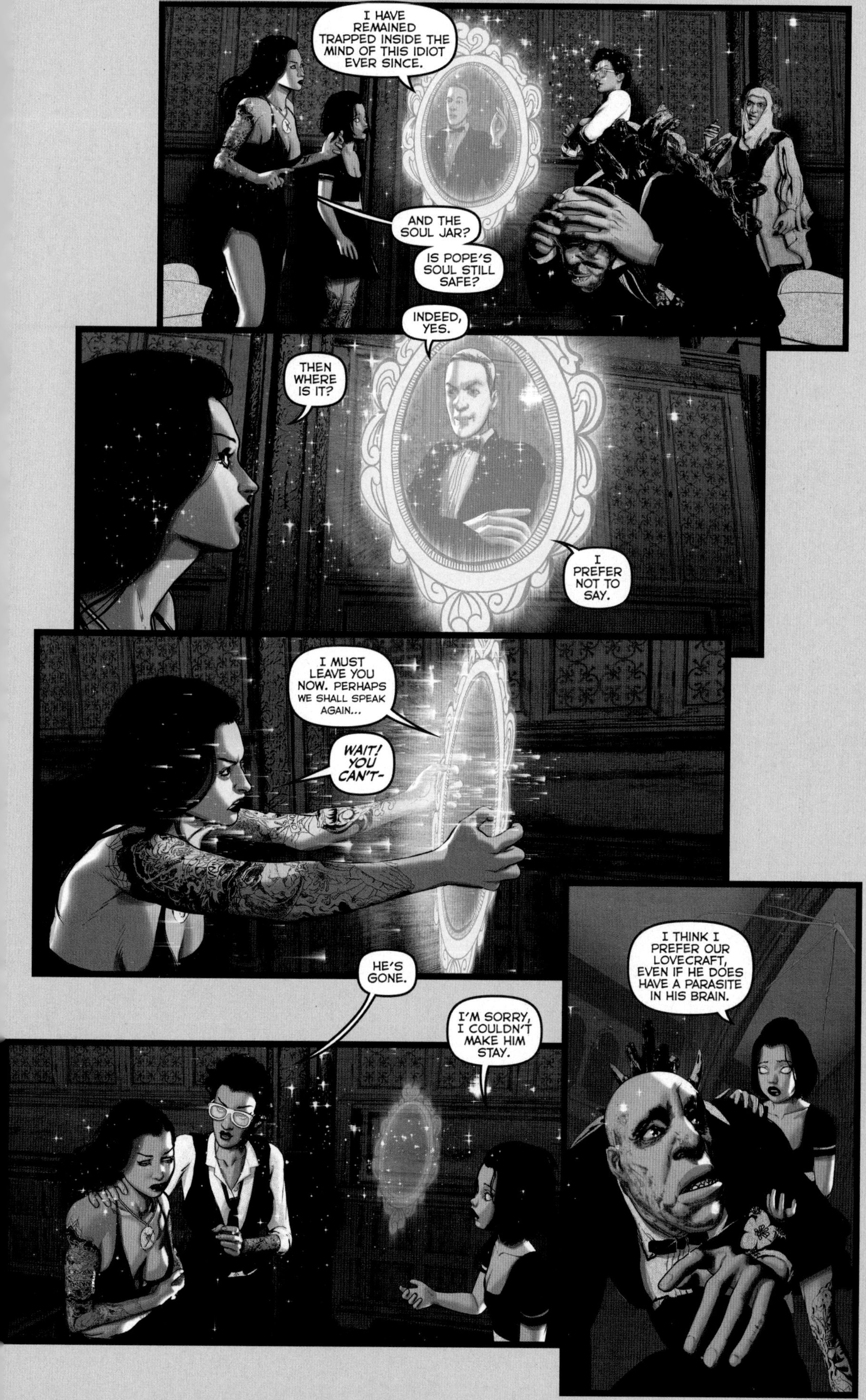
I HAVE REMAINED TRAPPED INSIDE THE MIND OF THIS IDIOT EVER SINCE.
AND THE SOUL JAR?
IS POPE'S SOUL STILL SAFE?
INDEED, YES.
THEN WHERE IS IT?
I PREFER NOT TO SAY.
I MUST LEAVE YOU NOW. PERHAPS WE SHALL SPEAK AGAIN...
WAIT! YOU CAN'T-
HE'S GONE.
I'M SORRY, I COULDN'T MAKE HIM STAY.
I THINK I PREFER OUR LOVECRAFT, EVEN IF HE DOES HAVE A PARASITE IN HIS BRAIN.

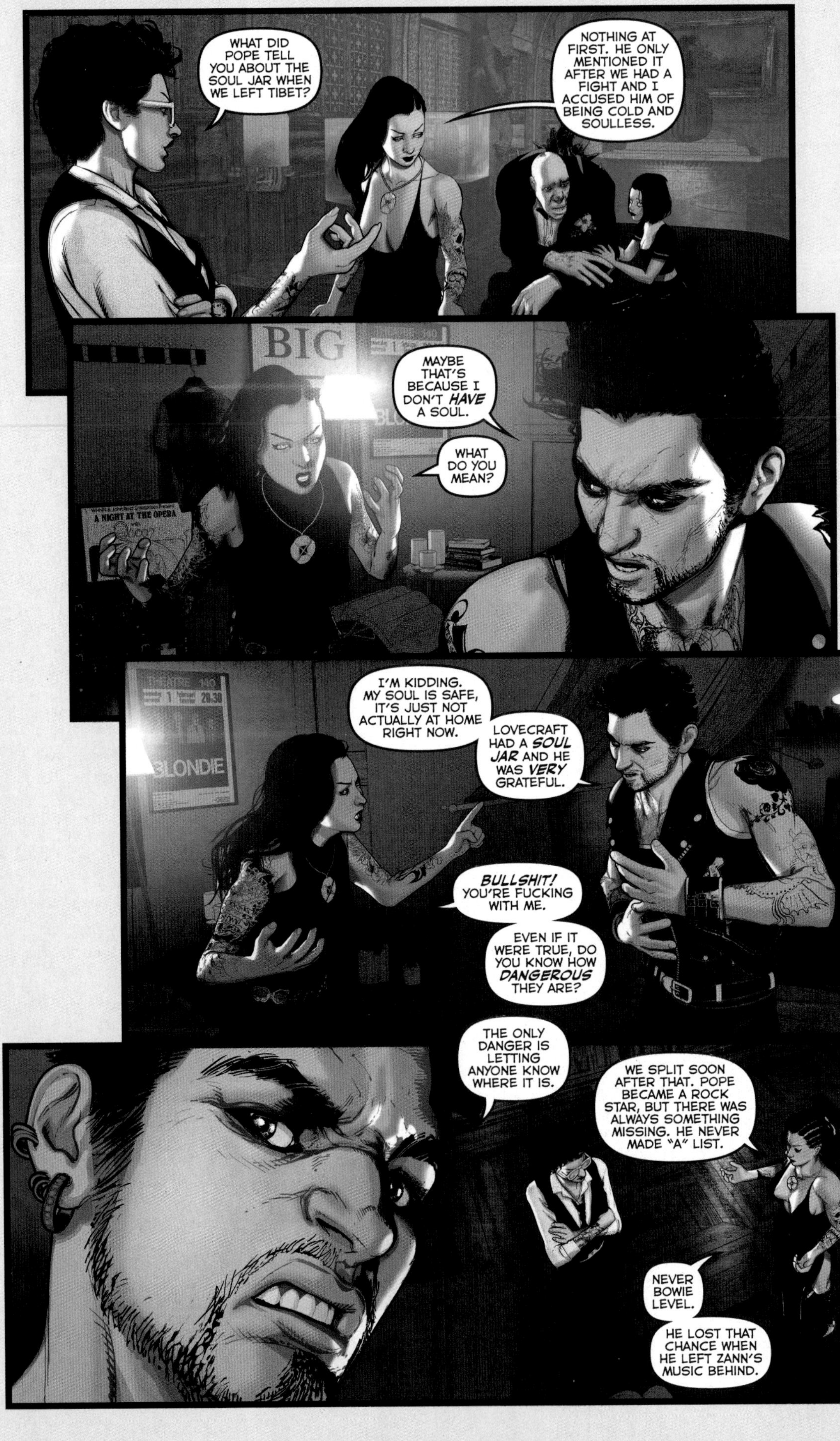
WHAT DID POPE TELL YOU ABOUT THE SOUL JAR WHEN WE LEFT TIBET?
NOTHING AT FIRST. HE ONLY MENTIONED IT AFTER WE HAD A FIGHT AND I ACCUSED HIM OF BEING COLD AND SOULLESS.
BIG
A NIGHT AT THE OPERA
MAYBE THAT'S BECAUSE I DON'T *HAVE* A SOUL.
WHAT DO YOU MEAN?
THEATRE 140
20:30
BLONDIE
I'M KIDDING. MY SOUL IS SAFE, IT'S JUST NOT ACTUALLY AT HOME RIGHT NOW.
LOVECRAFT HAD A *SOUL JAR* AND HE WAS *VERY* GRATEFUL.
BULLSHIT! YOU'RE FUCKING WITH ME.
EVEN IF IT WERE TRUE, DO YOU KNOW HOW *DANGEROUS* THEY ARE?
THE ONLY DANGER IS LETTING ANYONE KNOW WHERE IT IS.
WE SPLIT SOON AFTER THAT. POPE BECAME A ROCK STAR, BUT THERE WAS ALWAYS SOMETHING MISSING. HE NEVER MADE "A" LIST.
NEVER BOWIE LEVEL.
HE LOST THAT CHANCE WHEN HE LEFT ZANN'S MUSIC BEHIND.

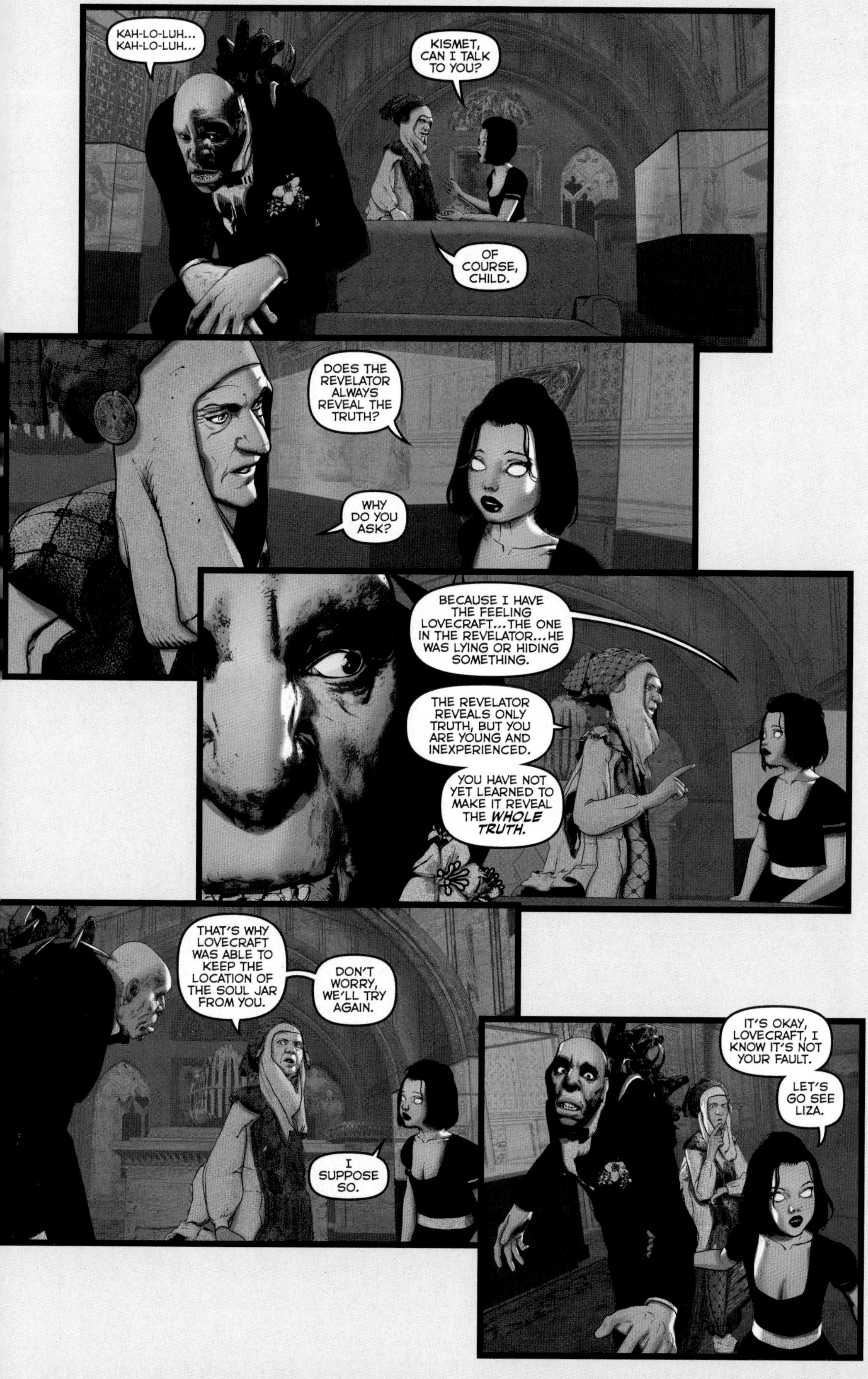
KAH-LO-LUH... KAH-LO-LUH...
KISMET, CAN I TALK TO YOU?
OF COURSE, CHILD.
DOES THE REVELATOR ALWAYS REVEAL THE TRUTH?
WHY DO YOU ASK?
BECAUSE I HAVE THE FEELING LOVECRAFT...THE ONE IN THE REVELATOR...HE WAS LYING OR HIDING SOMETHING.
THE REVELATOR REVEALS ONLY TRUTH, BUT YOU ARE YOUNG AND INEXPERIENCED.
YOU HAVE NOT YET LEARNED TO MAKE IT REVEAL THE *WHOLE TRUTH.*
THAT'S WHY LOVECRAFT WAS ABLE TO KEEP THE LOCATION OF THE SOUL JAR FROM YOU.
DON'T WORRY, WE'LL TRY AGAIN.
I SUPPOSE SO.
IT'S OKAY, LOVECRAFT, I KNOW IT'S NOT YOUR FAULT.
LET'S GO SEE LIZA.

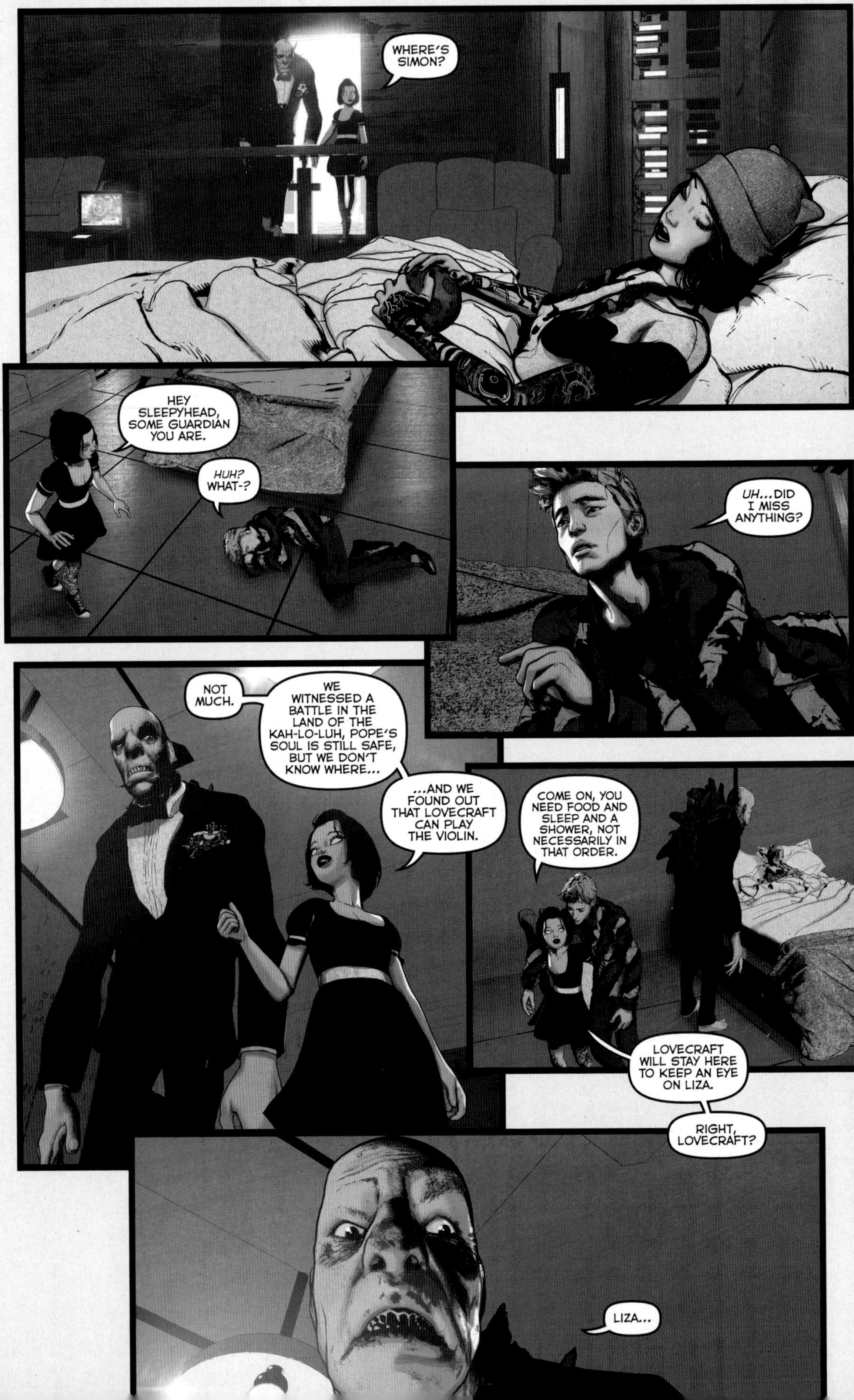
WHERE'S SIMON?
HEY SLEEPYHEAD, SOME GUARDIAN YOU ARE.
HUH? WHAT-?
UH...DID I MISS ANYTHING?
NOT MUCH.
WE WITNESSED A BATTLE IN THE LAND OF THE KAH-LO-LUH, POPE'S SOUL IS STILL SAFE, BUT WE DON'T KNOW WHERE...
...AND WE FOUND OUT THAT LOVECRAFT CAN PLAY THE VIOLIN.
COME ON, YOU NEED FOOD AND SLEEP AND A SHOWER, NOT NECESSARILY IN THAT ORDER.
LOVECRAFT WILL STAY HERE TO KEEP AN EYE ON LIZA.
RIGHT, LOVECRAFT?
LIZA...

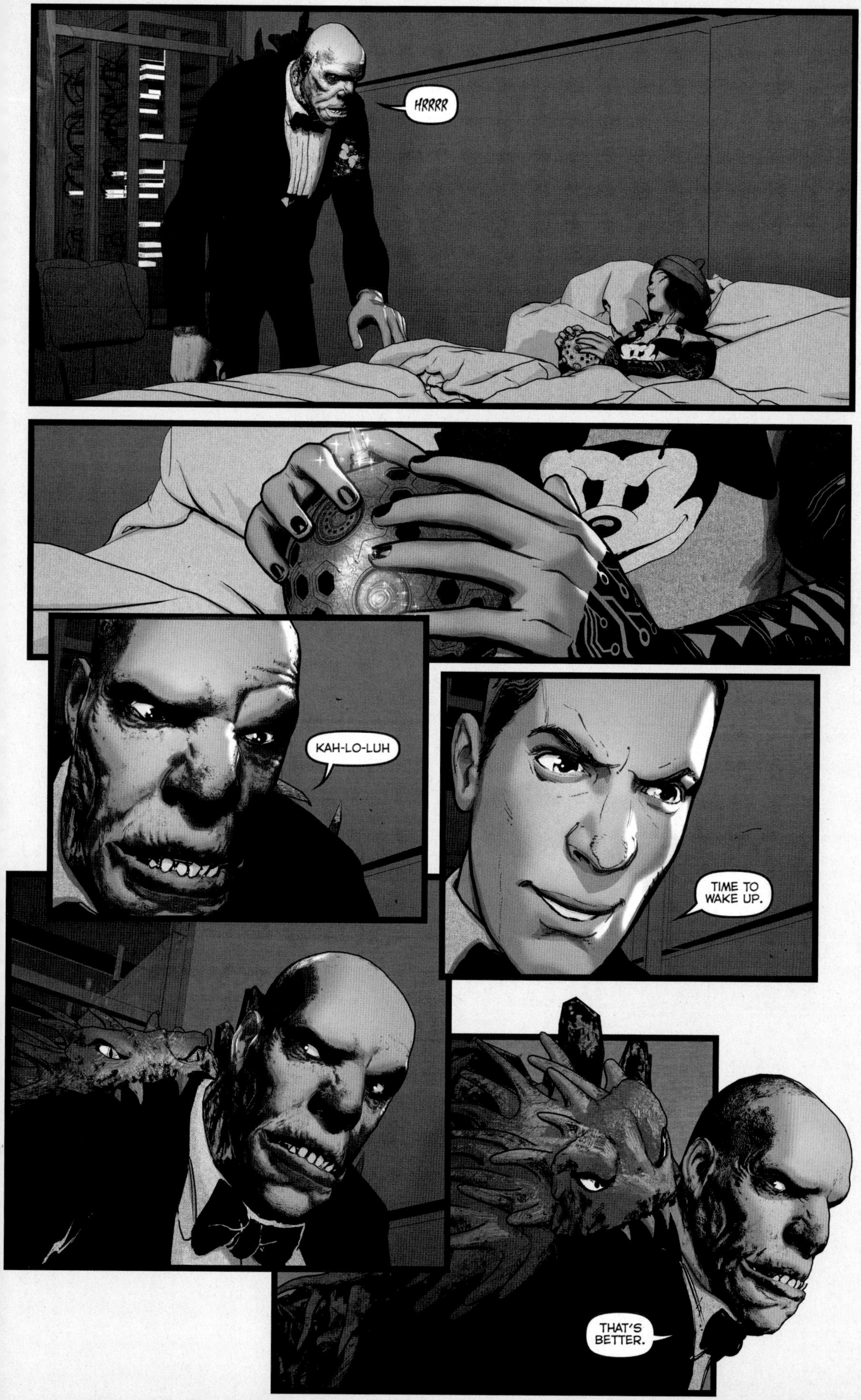
HRRRR
KAH-LO-LUH
TIME TO WAKE UP.
THAT'S BETTER.

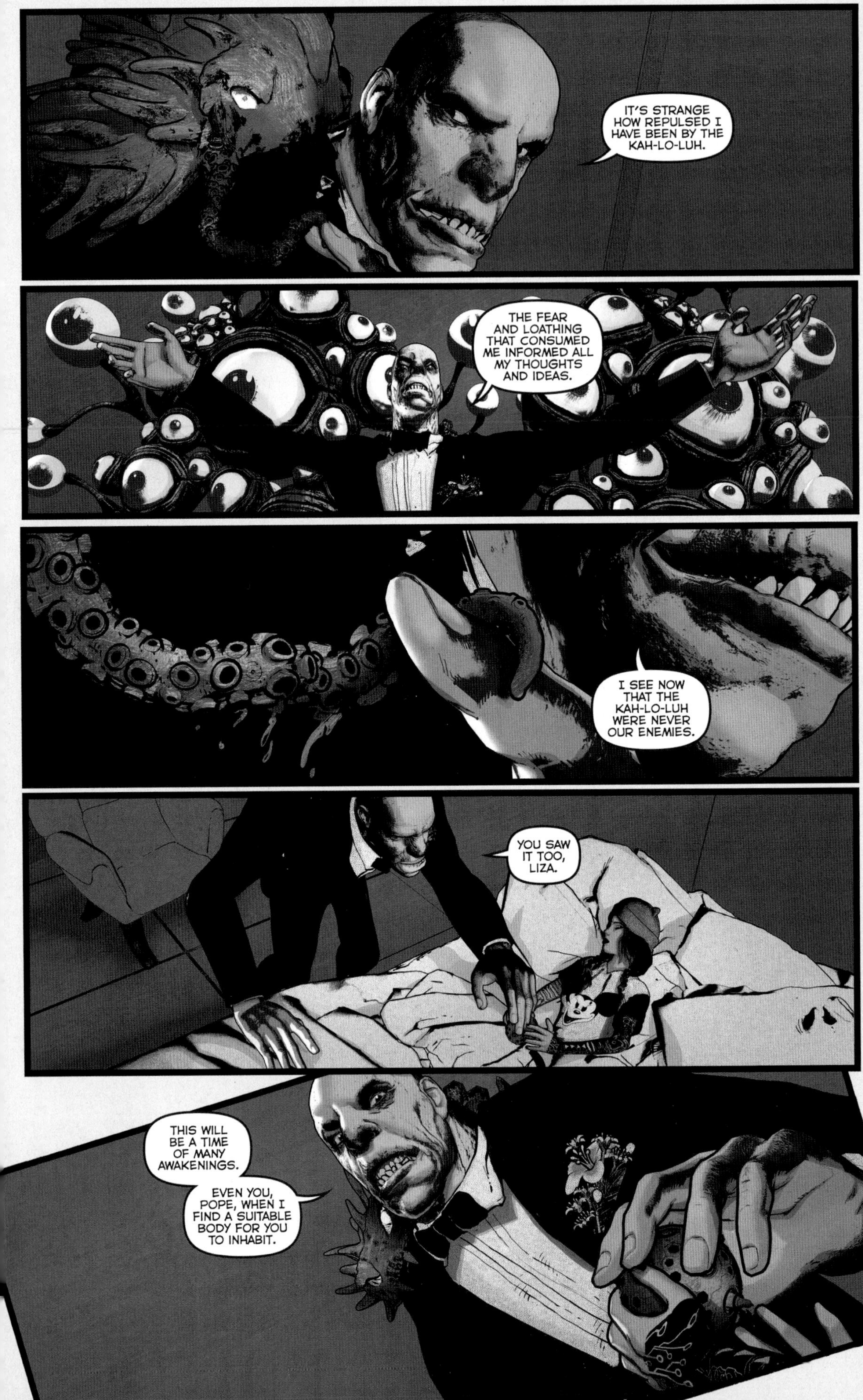
IT'S STRANGE HOW REPULSED I HAVE BEEN BY THE KAH-LO-LUH.
THE FEAR AND LOATHING THAT CONSUMED ME INFORMED ALL MY THOUGHTS AND IDEAS.
I SEE NOW THAT THE KAH-LO-LUH WERE NEVER OUR ENEMIES.
YOU SAW IT TOO, LIZA.
THIS WILL BE A TIME OF MANY AWAKENINGS.
EVEN YOU, POPE, WHEN I FIND A SUITABLE BODY FOR YOU TO INHABIT.

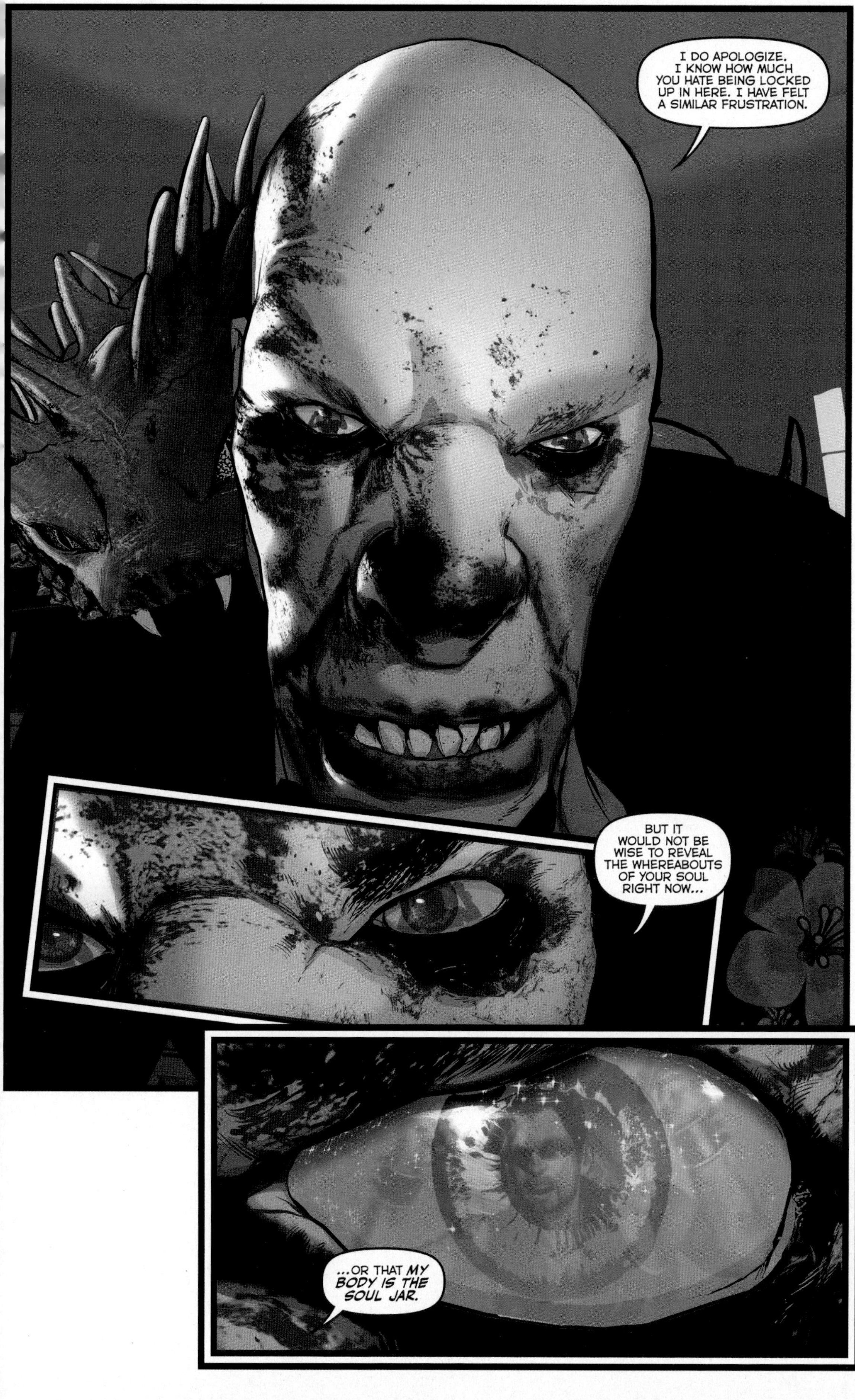
I DO APOLOGIZE. I KNOW HOW MUCH YOU HATE BEING LOCKED UP IN HERE. I HAVE FELT A SIMILAR FRUSTRATION.
BUT IT WOULD NOT BE WISE TO REVEAL THE WHEREABOUTS OF YOUR SOUL RIGHT NOW...
...OR THAT *MY BODY IS THE SOUL JAR.*

ISSUE #10 COVER C

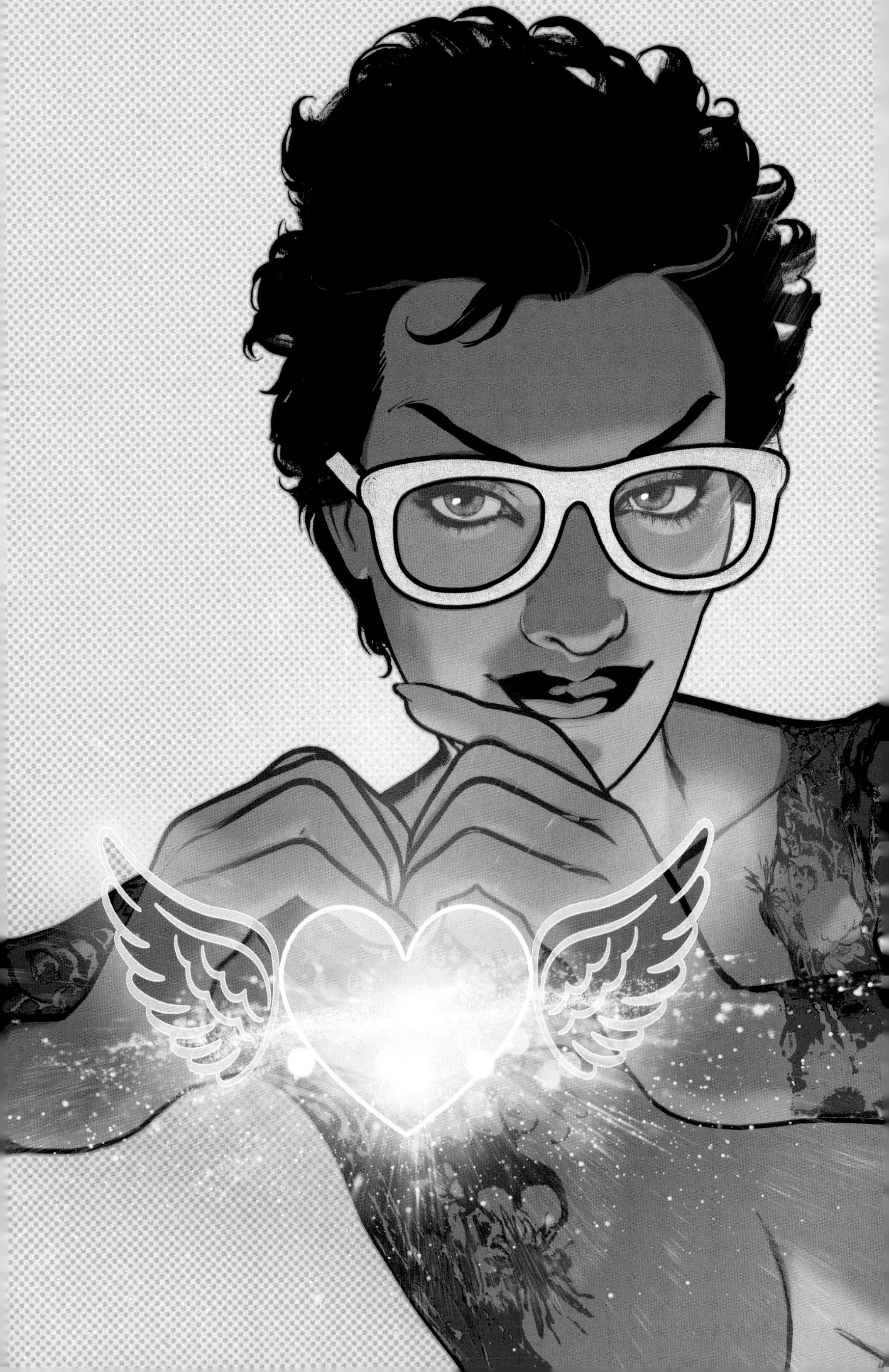

CHAPTER EIGHT

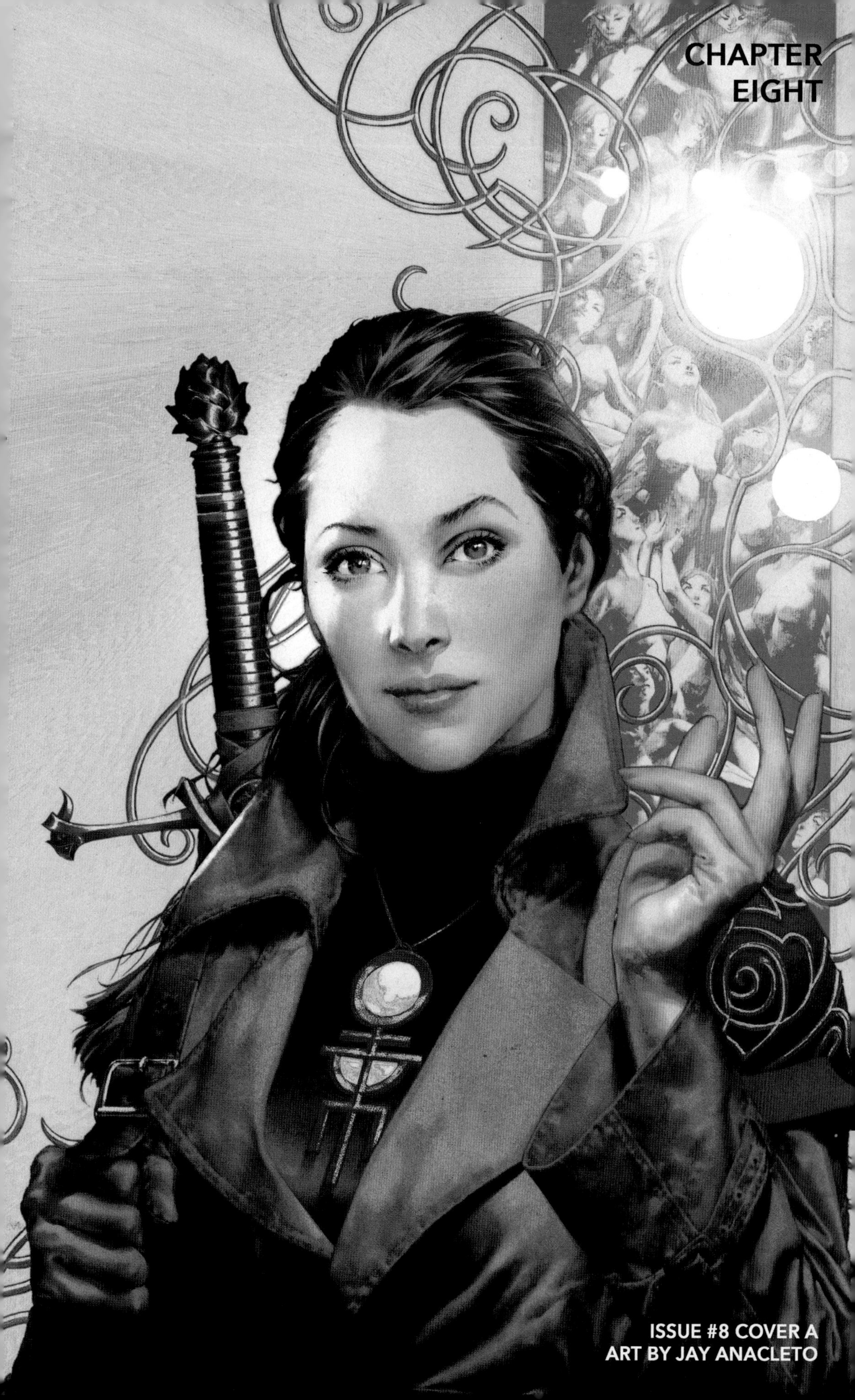

ISSUE #8 COVER A
ART BY JAY ANACLETO

ISSUE #8 COVER B

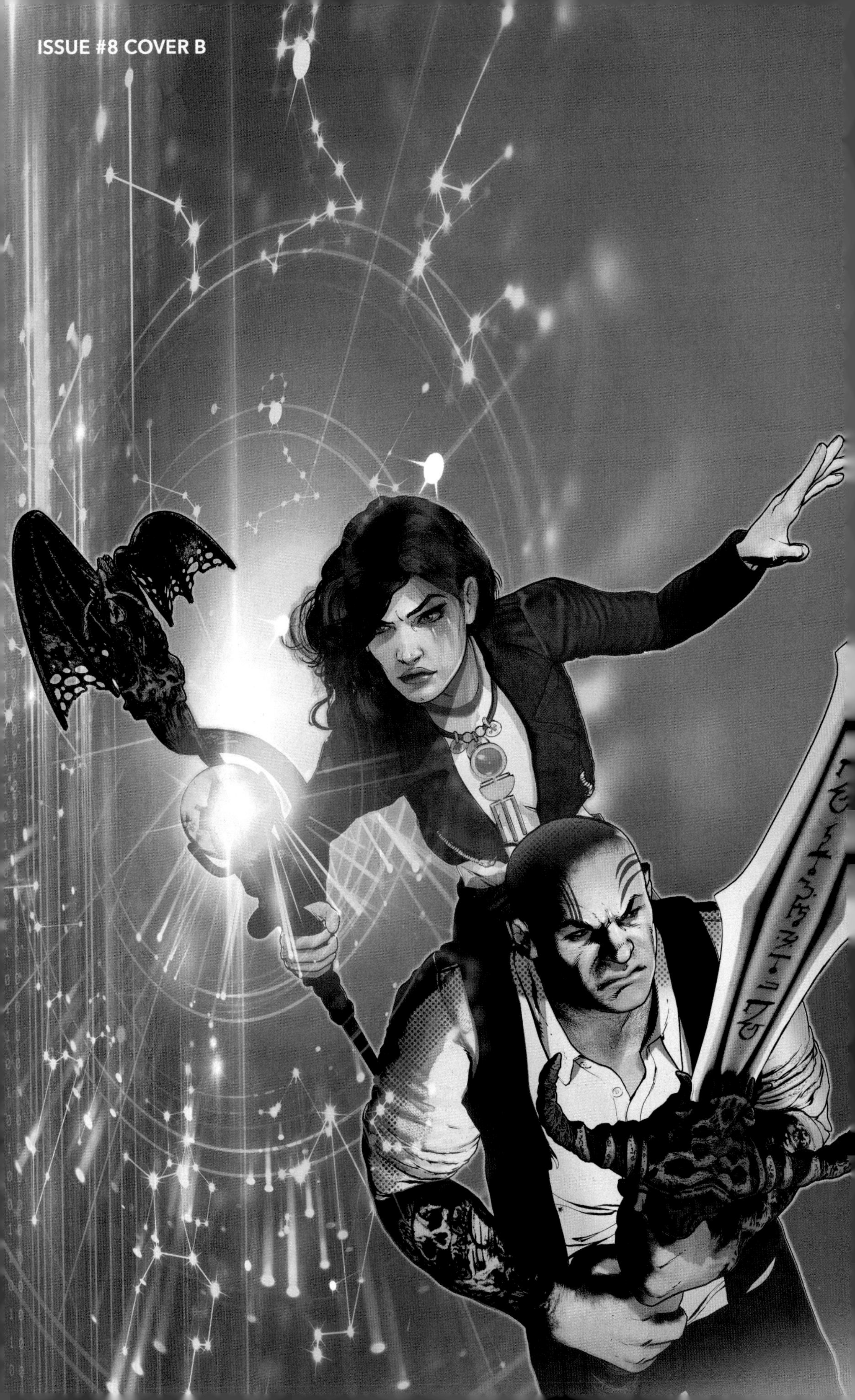

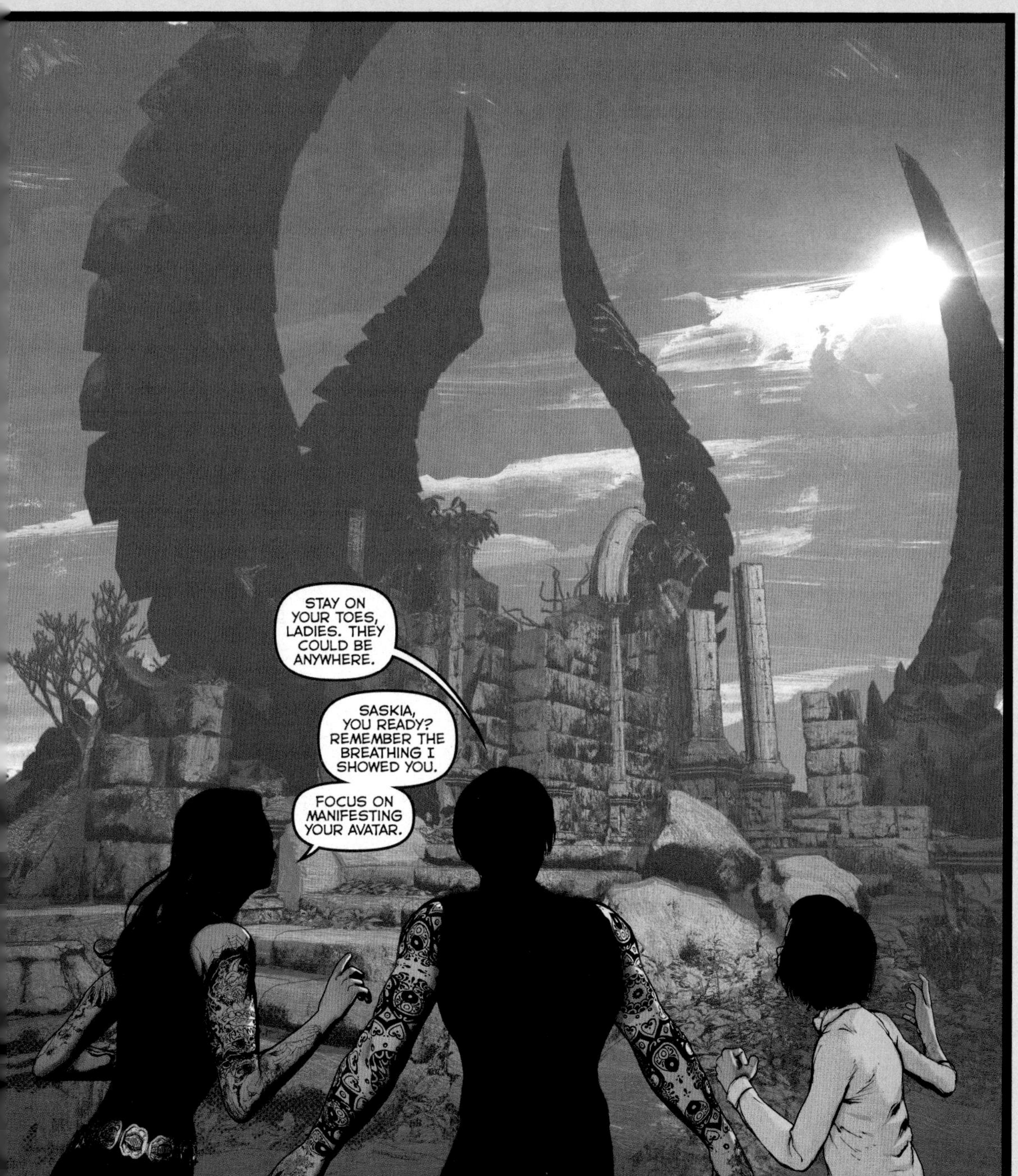
STAY ON YOUR TOES, LADIES. THEY COULD BE ANYWHERE.
SASKIA, YOU READY? REMEMBER THE BREATHING I SHOWED YOU.
FOCUS ON MANIFESTING YOUR AVATAR.

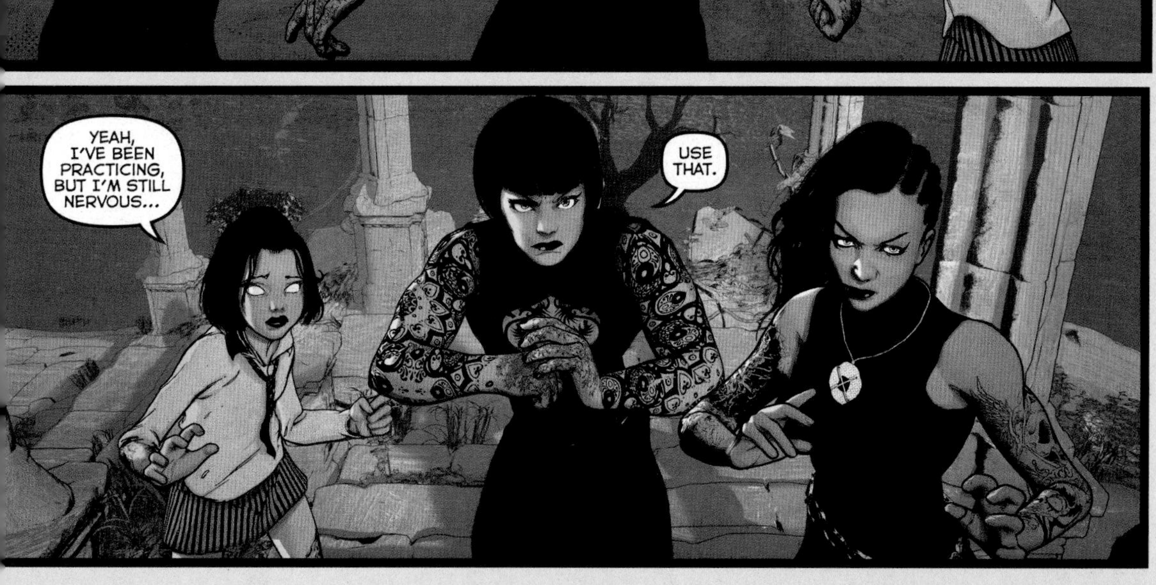
YEAH, I'VE BEEN PRACTICING, BUT I'M STILL NERVOUS...
USE THAT.

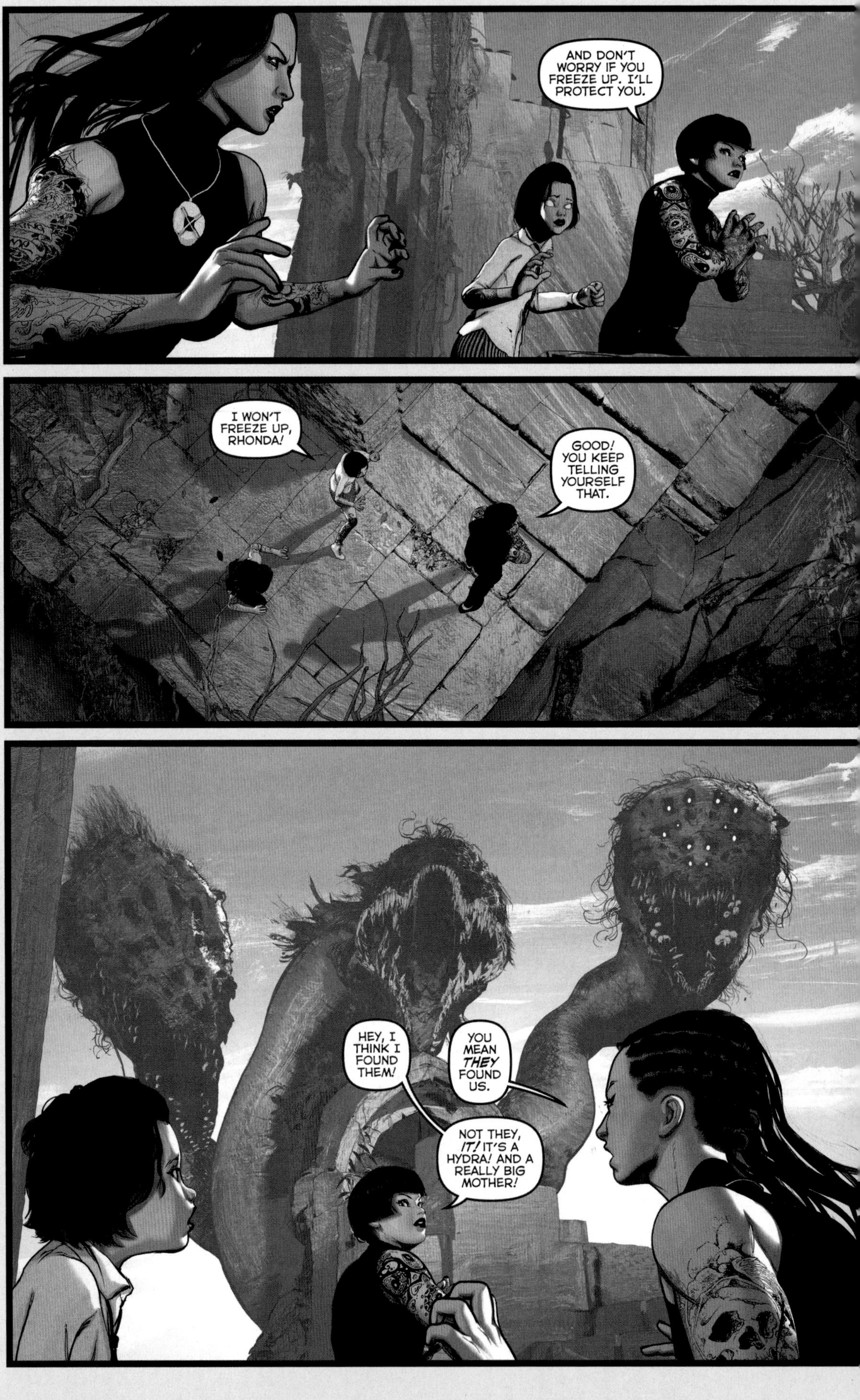
AND DON'T WORRY IF YOU FREEZE UP. I'LL PROTECT YOU.
I WON'T FREEZE UP, RHONDA!
GOOD! YOU KEEP TELLING YOURSELF THAT.
HEY, I THINK I FOUND THEM!
YOU MEAN THEY FOUND US.
NOT THEY, IT! IT'S A HYDRA! AND A REALLY BIG MOTHER!

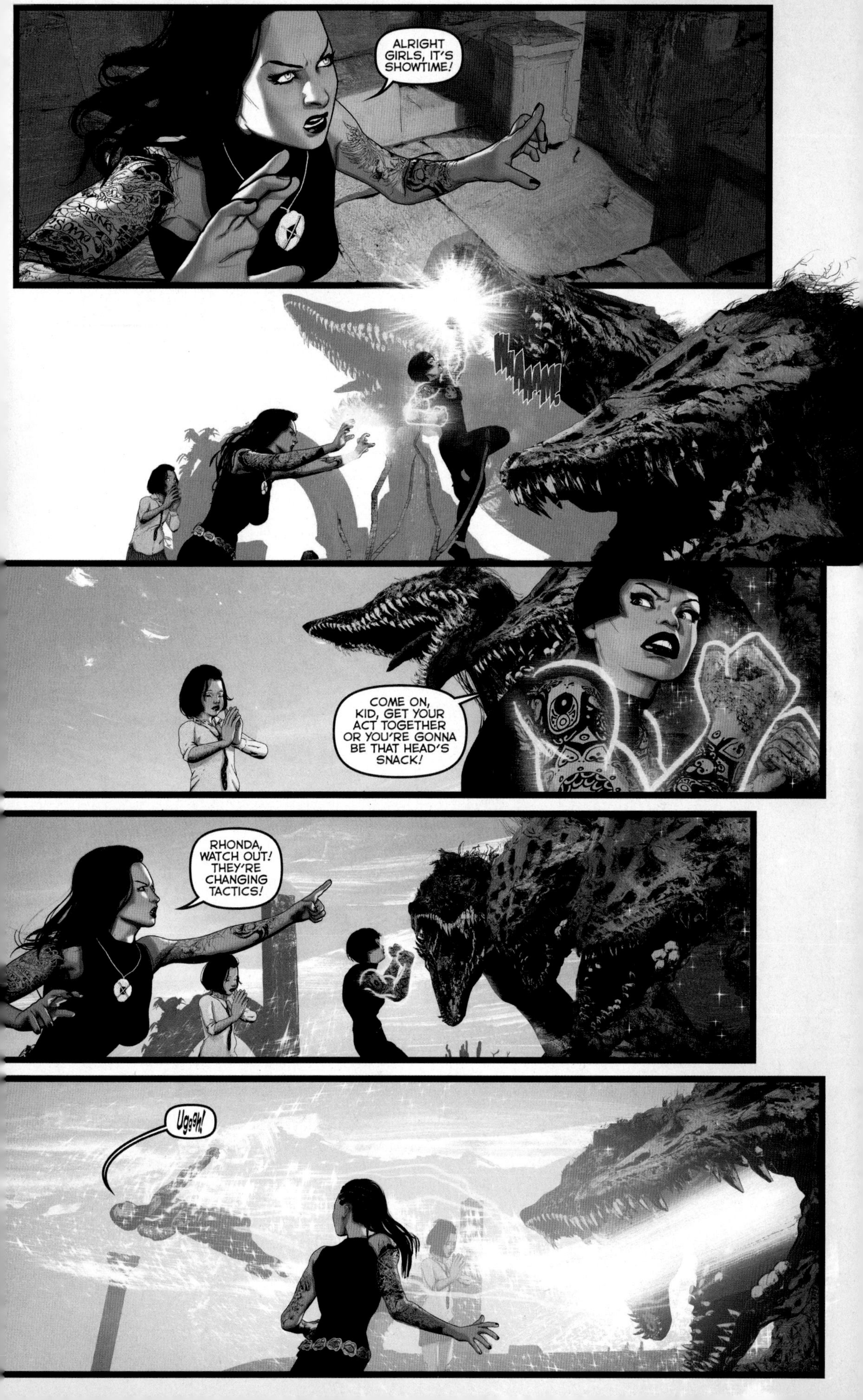
ALRIGHT GIRLS, IT'S SHOWTIME!
COME ON, KID, GET YOUR ACT TOGETHER OR YOU'RE GONNA BE THAT HEAD'S SNACK!
RHONDA, WATCH OUT! THEY'RE CHANGING TACTICS!
Ugggh!

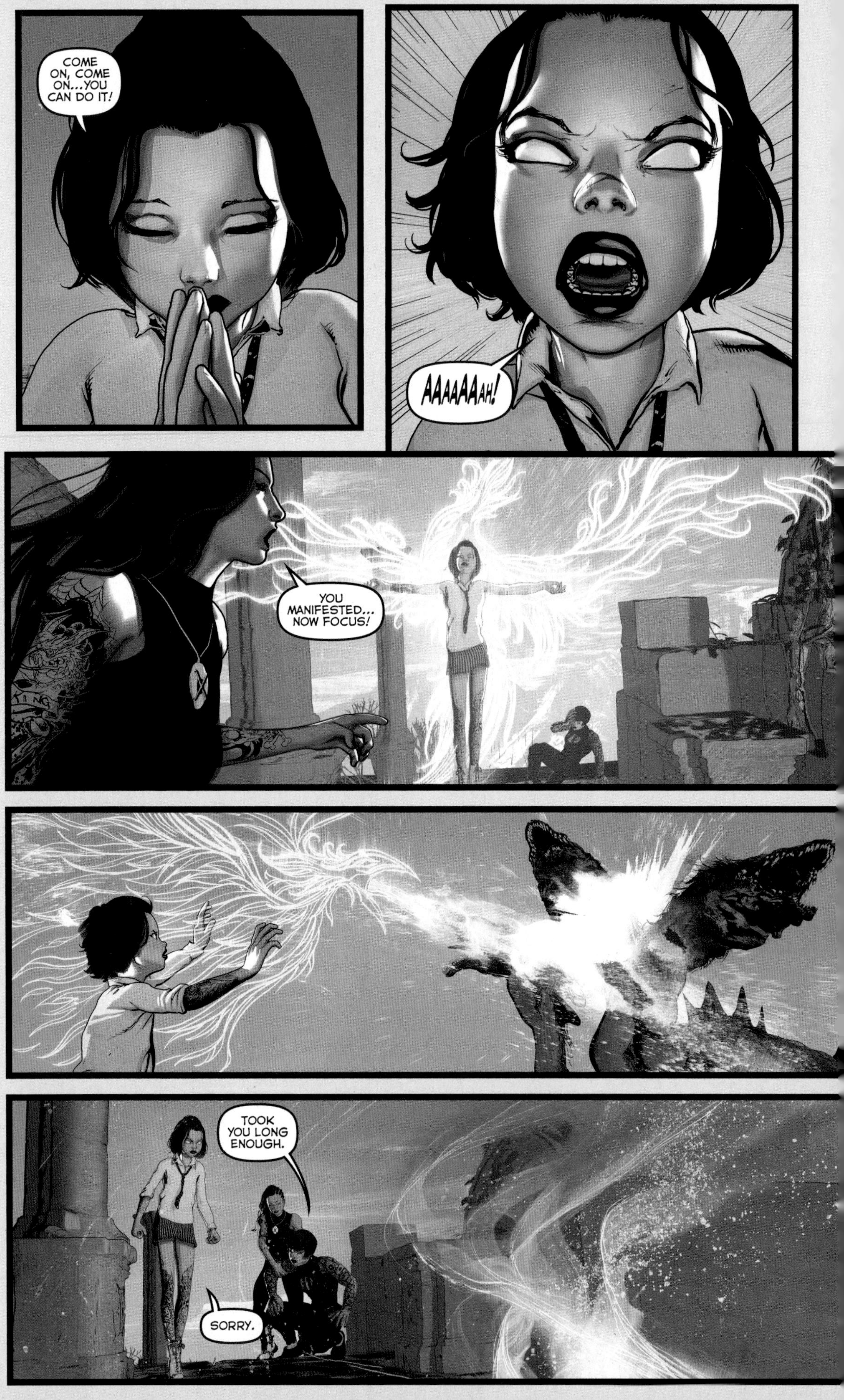
COME ON, COME ON...YOU CAN DO IT!
AAAAAAAH!
YOU MANIFESTED... NOW FOCUS!
TOOK YOU LONG ENOUGH.
SORRY.

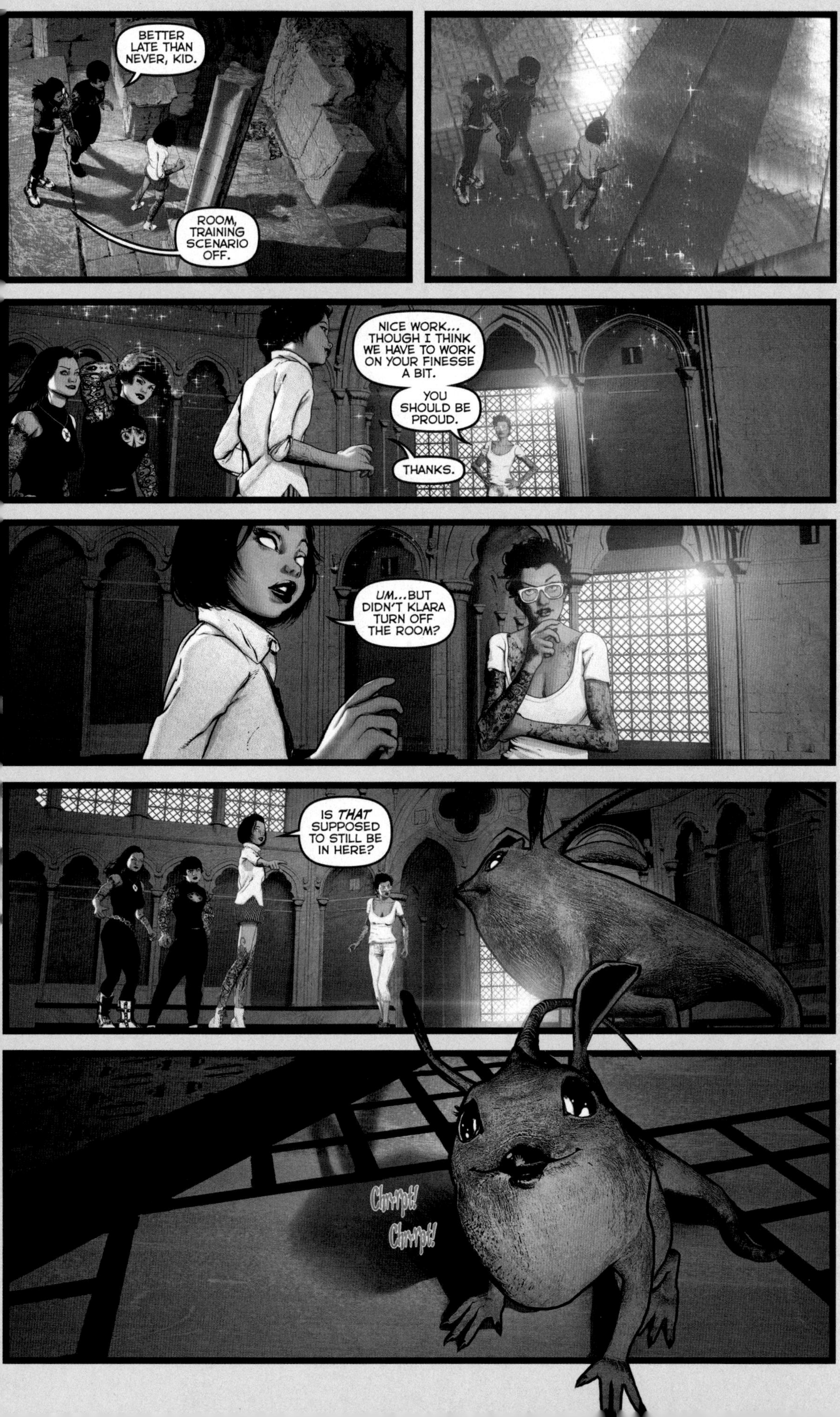
BETTER LATE THAN NEVER, KID.
ROOM, TRAINING SCENARIO OFF.
NICE WORK... THOUGH I THINK WE HAVE TO WORK ON YOUR FINESSE A BIT.
YOU SHOULD BE PROUD.
THANKS.
UM...BUT DIDN'T KLARA TURN OFF THE ROOM?
IS *THAT* SUPPOSED TO STILL BE IN HERE?
Chrrrpt!
Chrrrpt!

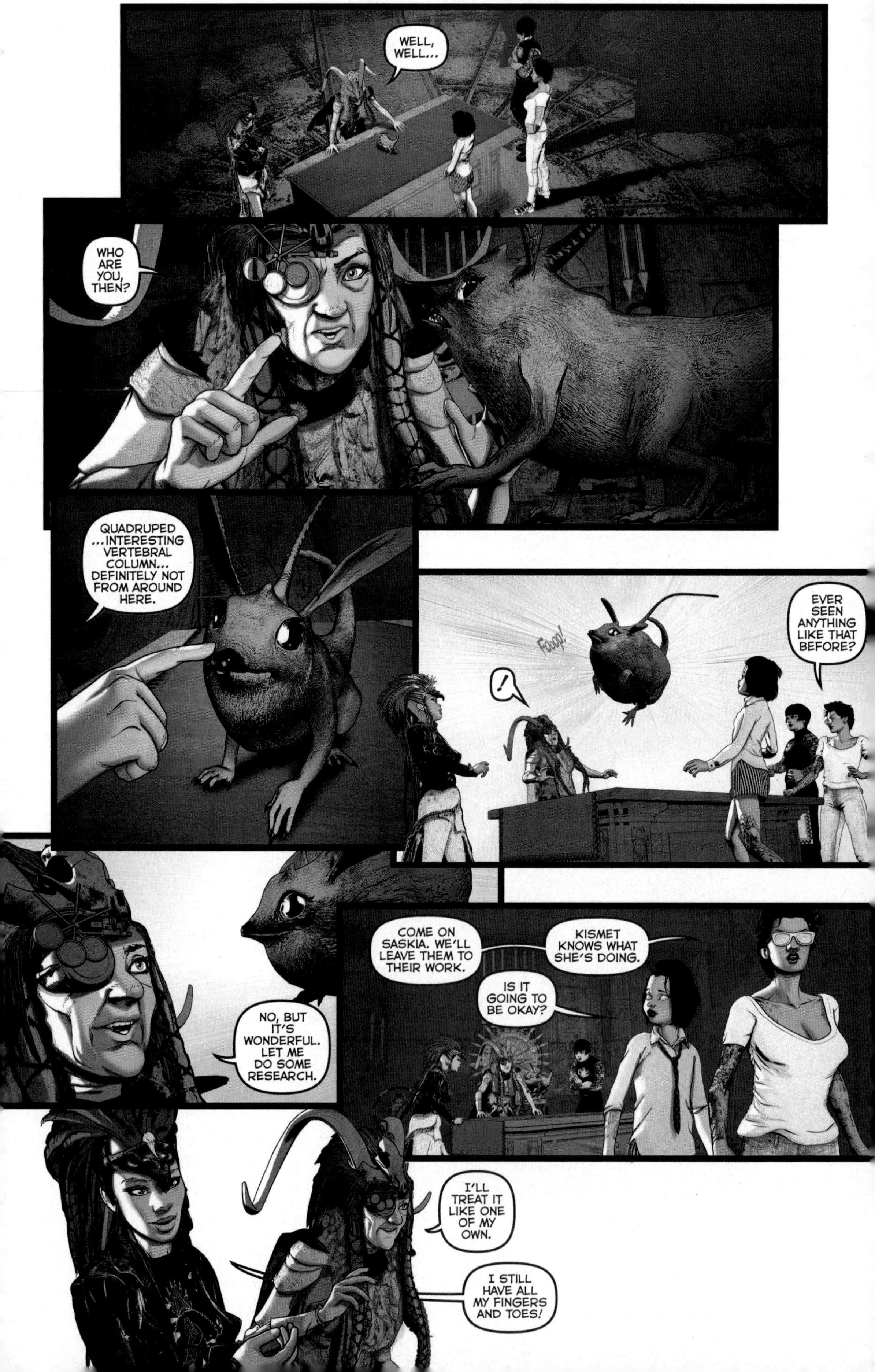
WELL, WELL...
WHO ARE YOU, THEN?
QUADRUPED ...INTERESTING VERTEBRAL COLUMN... DEFINITELY NOT FROM AROUND HERE.
FOOOP!
!
EVER SEEN ANYTHING LIKE THAT BEFORE?
NO, BUT IT'S WONDERFUL. LET ME DO SOME RESEARCH.
COME ON SASKIA. WE'LL LEAVE THEM TO THEIR WORK.
KISMET KNOWS WHAT SHE'S DOING.
IS IT GOING TO BE OKAY?
I'LL TREAT IT LIKE ONE OF MY OWN.
I STILL HAVE ALL MY FINGERS AND TOES!

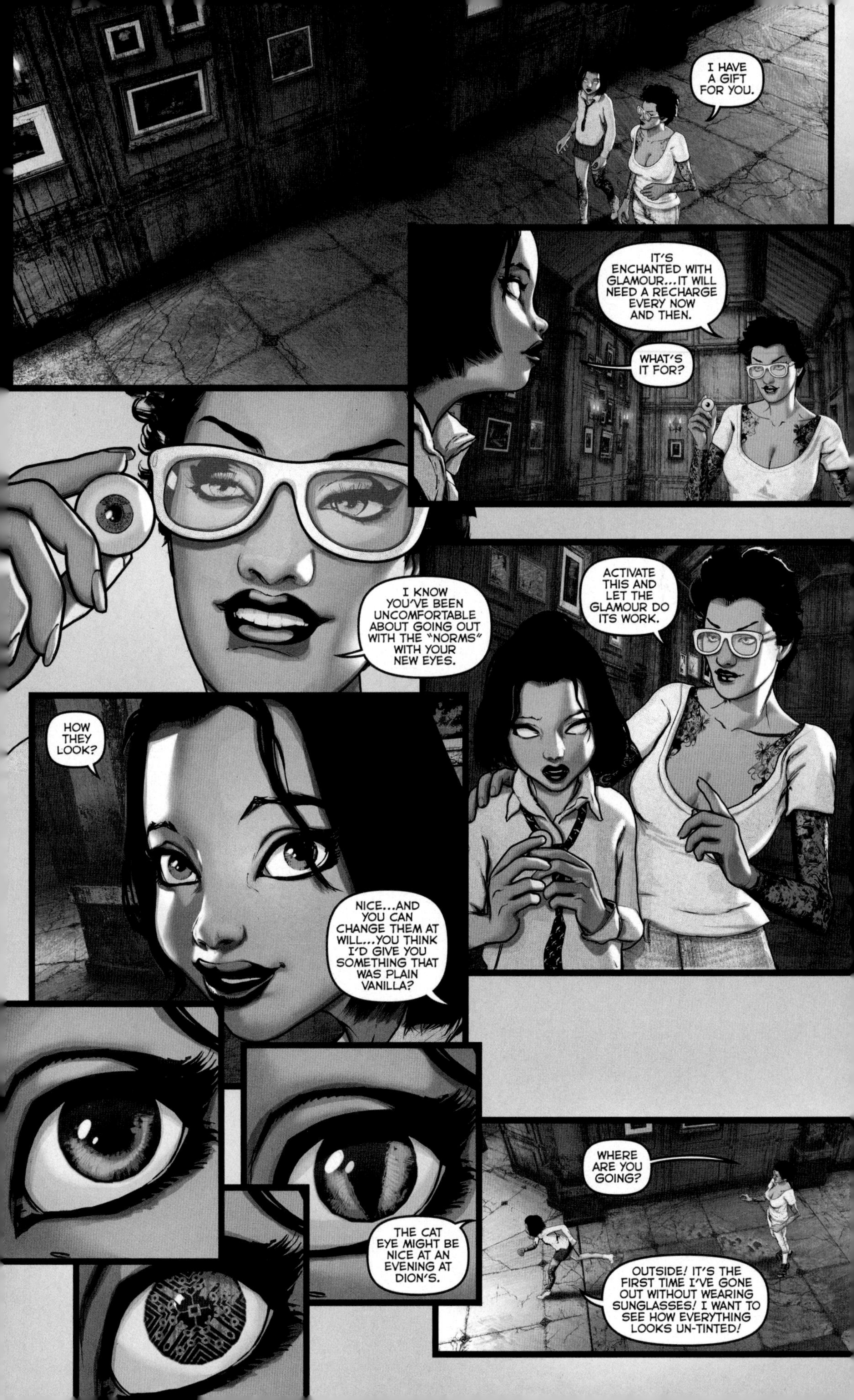
I HAVE A GIFT FOR YOU.
IT'S ENCHANTED WITH GLAMOUR...IT WILL NEED A RECHARGE EVERY NOW AND THEN.
WHAT'S IT FOR?
I KNOW YOU'VE BEEN UNCOMFORTABLE ABOUT GOING OUT WITH THE "NORMS" WITH YOUR NEW EYES.
ACTIVATE THIS AND LET THE GLAMOUR DO ITS WORK.
HOW THEY LOOK?
NICE...AND YOU CAN CHANGE THEM AT WILL...YOU THINK I'D GIVE YOU SOMETHING THAT WAS PLAIN VANILLA?
THE CAT EYE MIGHT BE NICE AT AN EVENING AT DION'S.
WHERE ARE YOU GOING?
OUTSIDE! IT'S THE FIRST TIME I'VE GONE OUT WITHOUT WEARING SUNGLASSES! I WANT TO SEE HOW EVERYTHING LOOKS UN-TINTED!

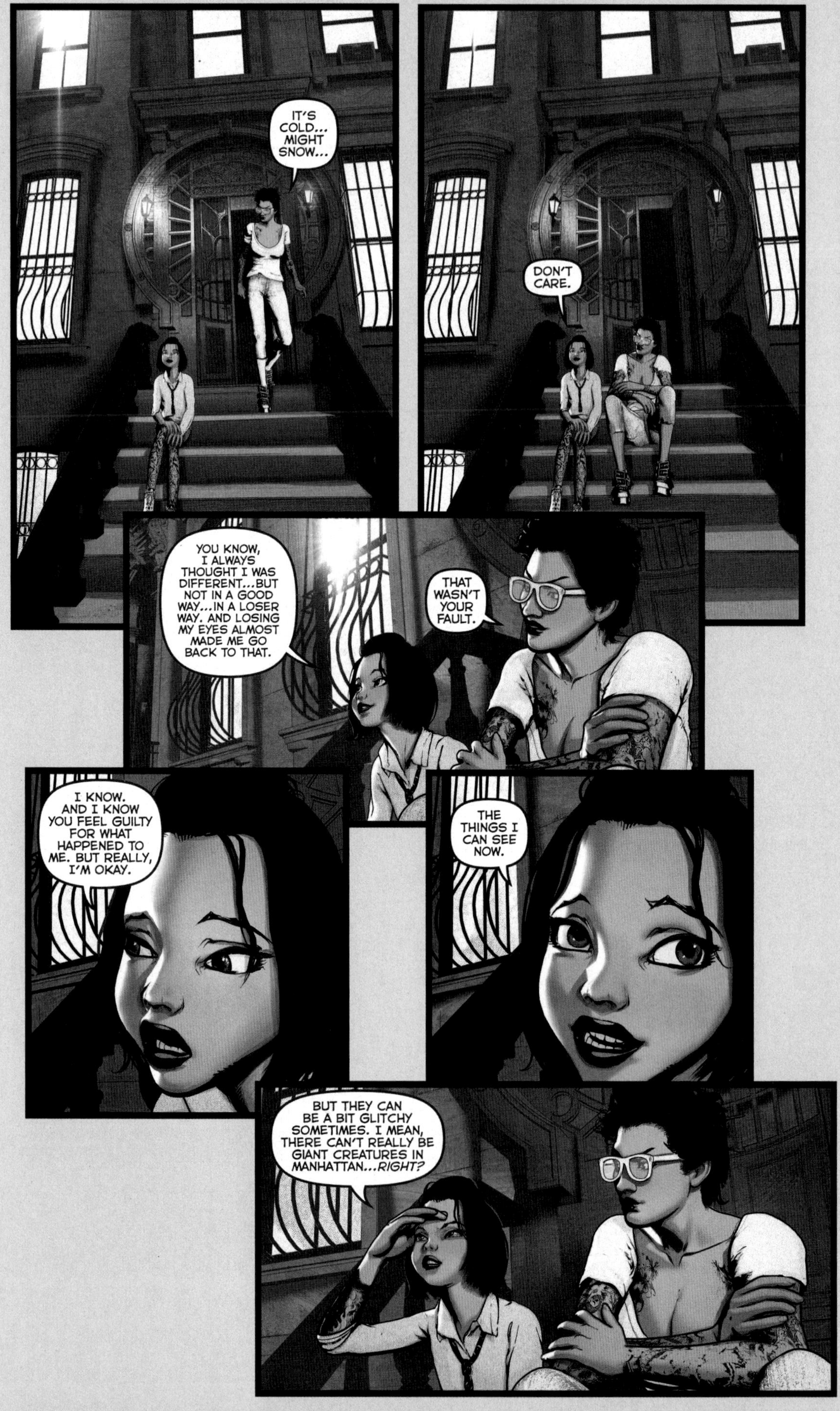
IT'S COLD... MIGHT SNOW...
DON'T CARE.
YOU KNOW, I ALWAYS THOUGHT I WAS DIFFERENT...BUT NOT IN A GOOD WAY...IN A LOSER WAY. AND LOSING MY EYES ALMOST MADE ME GO BACK TO THAT.
THAT WASN'T YOUR FAULT.
I KNOW. AND I KNOW YOU FEEL GUILTY FOR WHAT HAPPENED TO ME. BUT REALLY, I'M OKAY.
THE THINGS I CAN SEE NOW.
BUT THEY CAN BE A BIT GLITCHY SOMETIMES. I MEAN, THERE CAN'T REALLY BE GIANT CREATURES IN MANHATTAN...*RIGHT?*

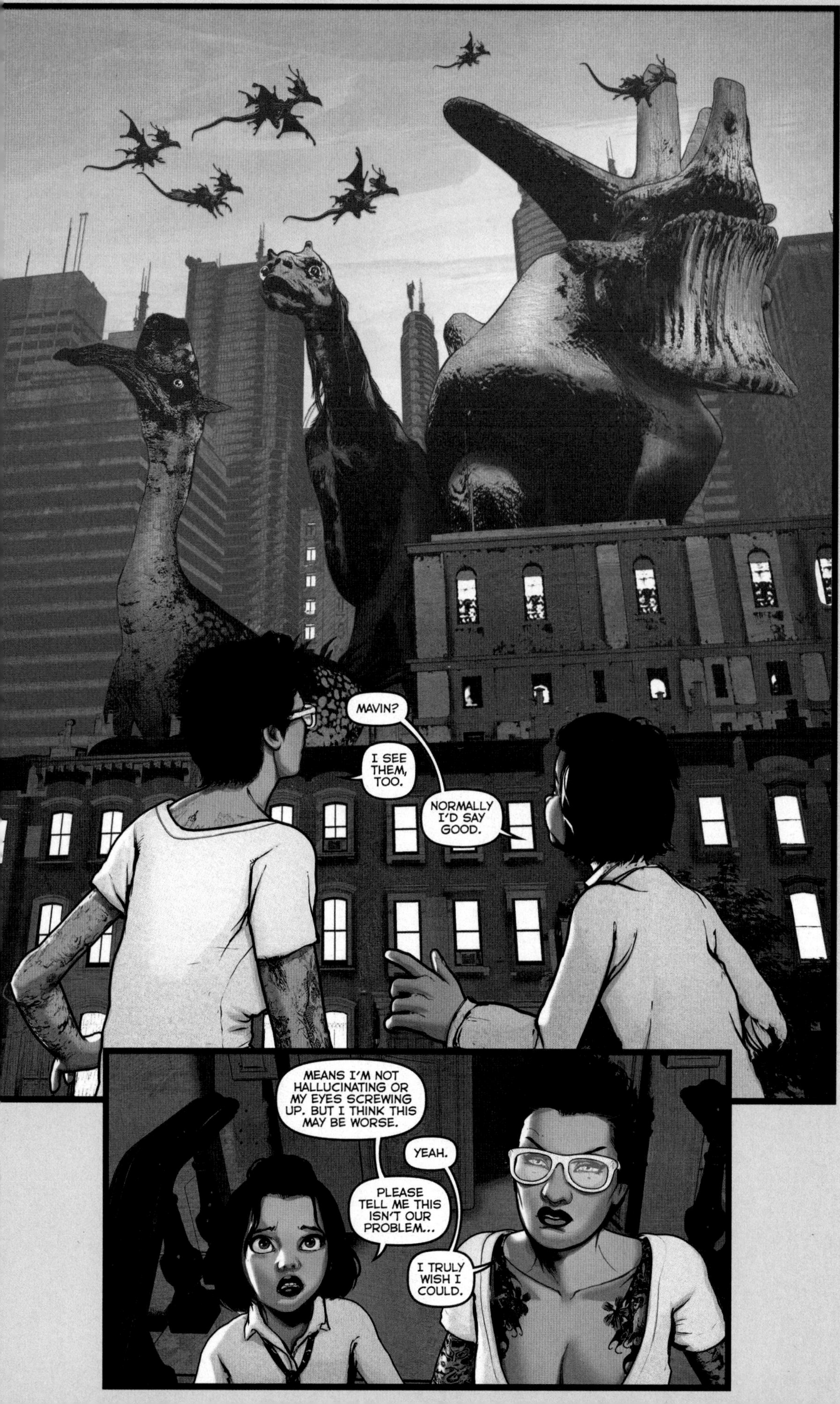
MAVIN?
I SEE THEM, TOO.
NORMALLY I'D SAY GOOD.
MEANS I'M NOT HALLUCINATING OR MY EYES SCREWING UP. BUT I THINK THIS MAY BE WORSE.
YEAH.
PLEASE TELL ME THIS ISN'T OUR PROBLEM...
I TRULY WISH I COULD.

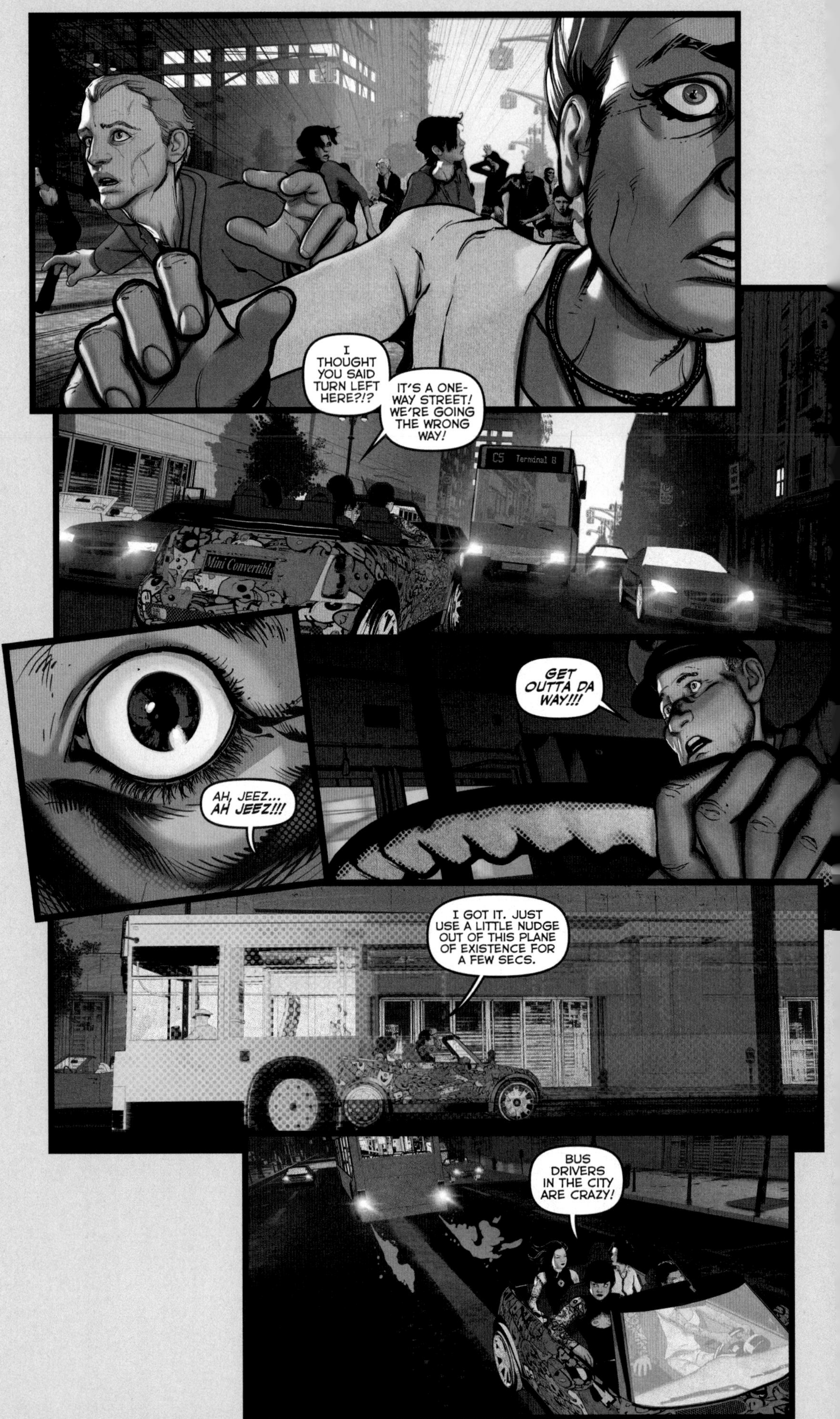
I THOUGHT YOU SAID TURN LEFT HERE?!?
IT'S A ONE-WAY STREET! WE'RE GOING THE WRONG WAY!
C5 Terminal B
Mini Convertible
GET OUTTA DA WAY!!!
AH, JEEZ... AH JEEZ!!!
I GOT IT. JUST USE A LITTLE NUDGE OUT OF THIS PLANE OF EXISTENCE FOR A FEW SECS.
BUS DRIVERS IN THE CITY ARE CRAZY!

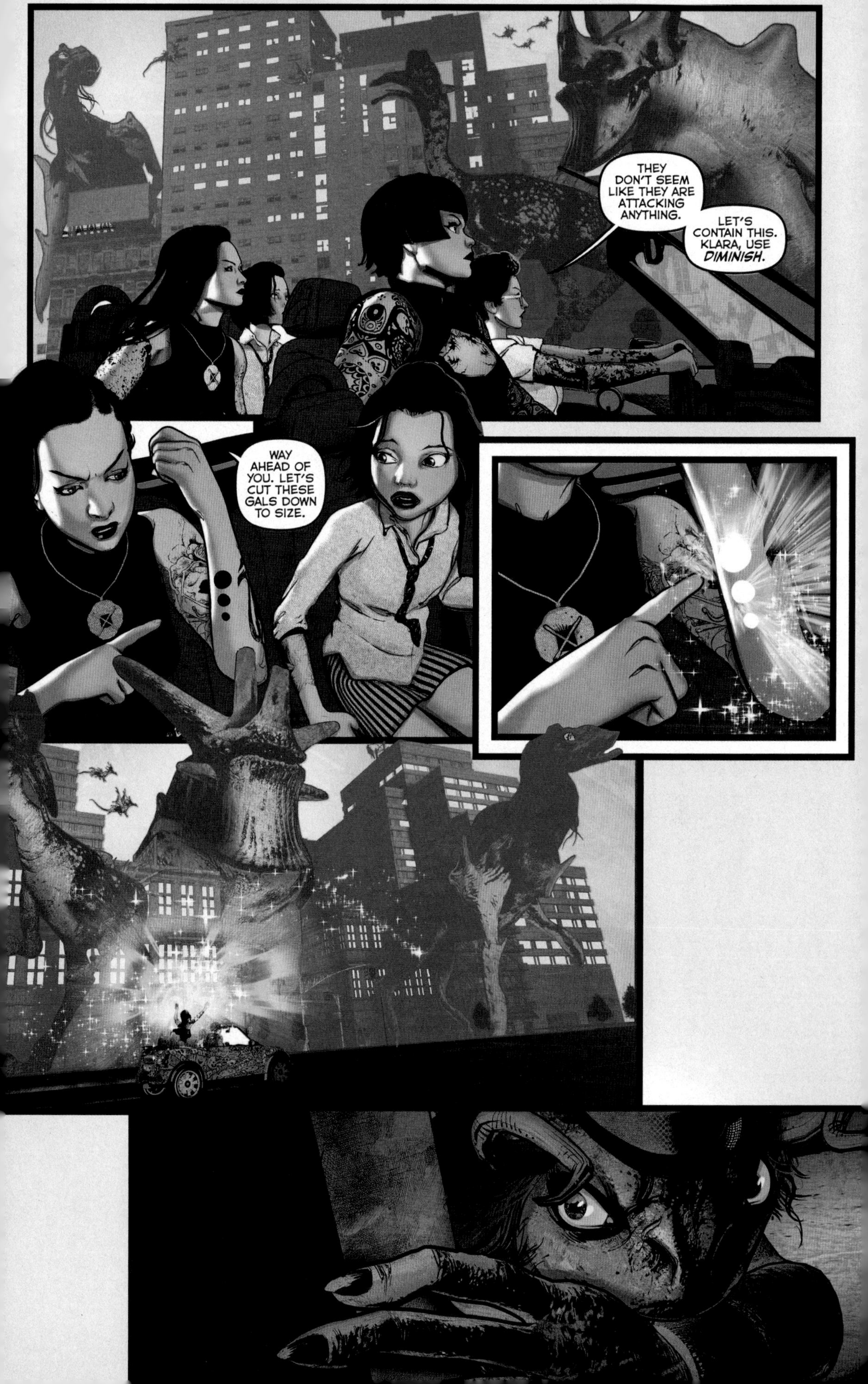
THEY DON'T SEEM LIKE THEY ARE ATTACKING ANYTHING.
LET'S CONTAIN THIS. KLARA, USE *DIMINISH*.
WAY AHEAD OF YOU. LET'S CUT THESE GALS DOWN TO SIZE.

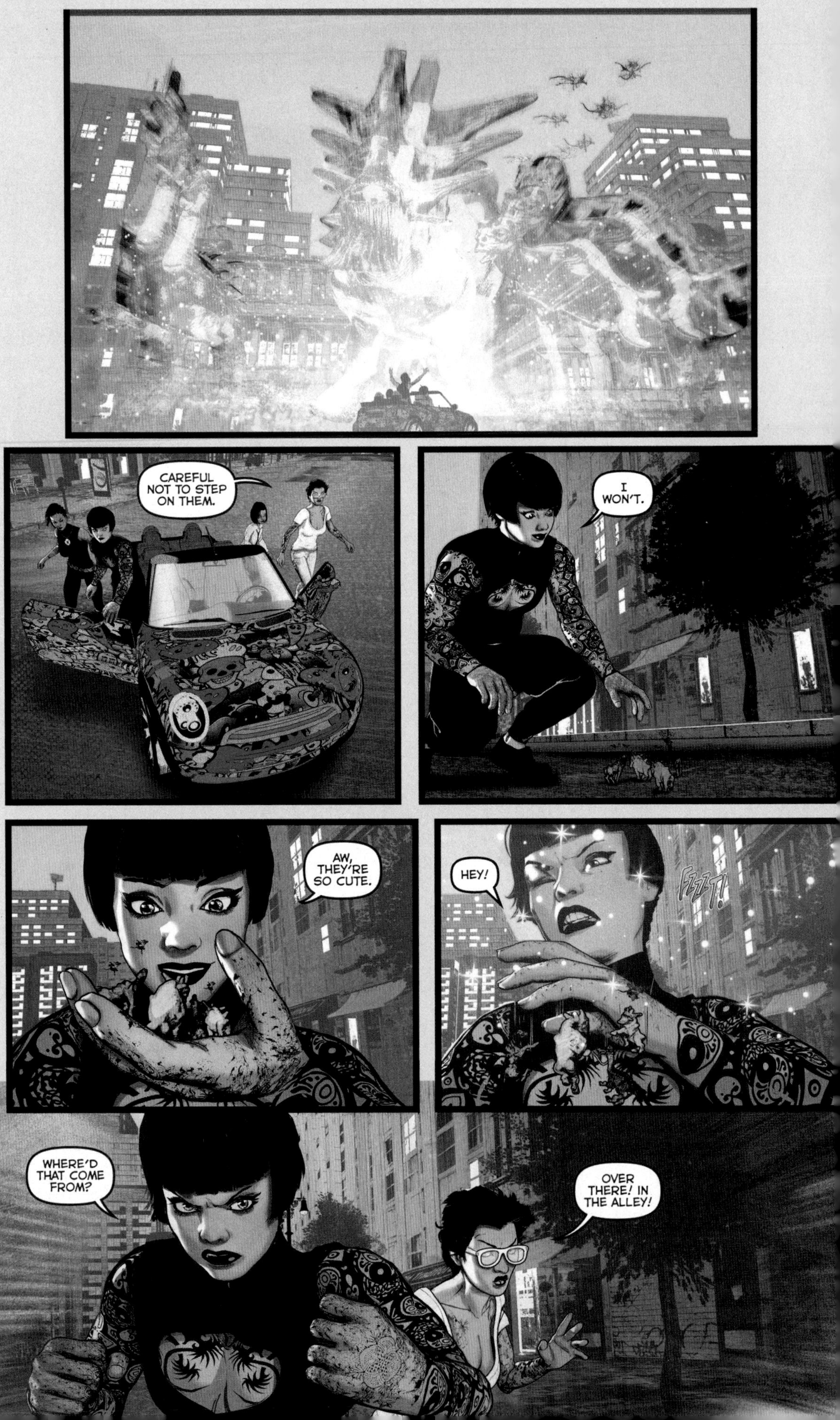
CAREFUL NOT TO STEP ON THEM.
I WON'T.
AW, THEY'RE SO CUTE.
HEY!
FZZZT!
WHERE'D THAT COME FROM?
OVER THERE! IN THE ALLEY!

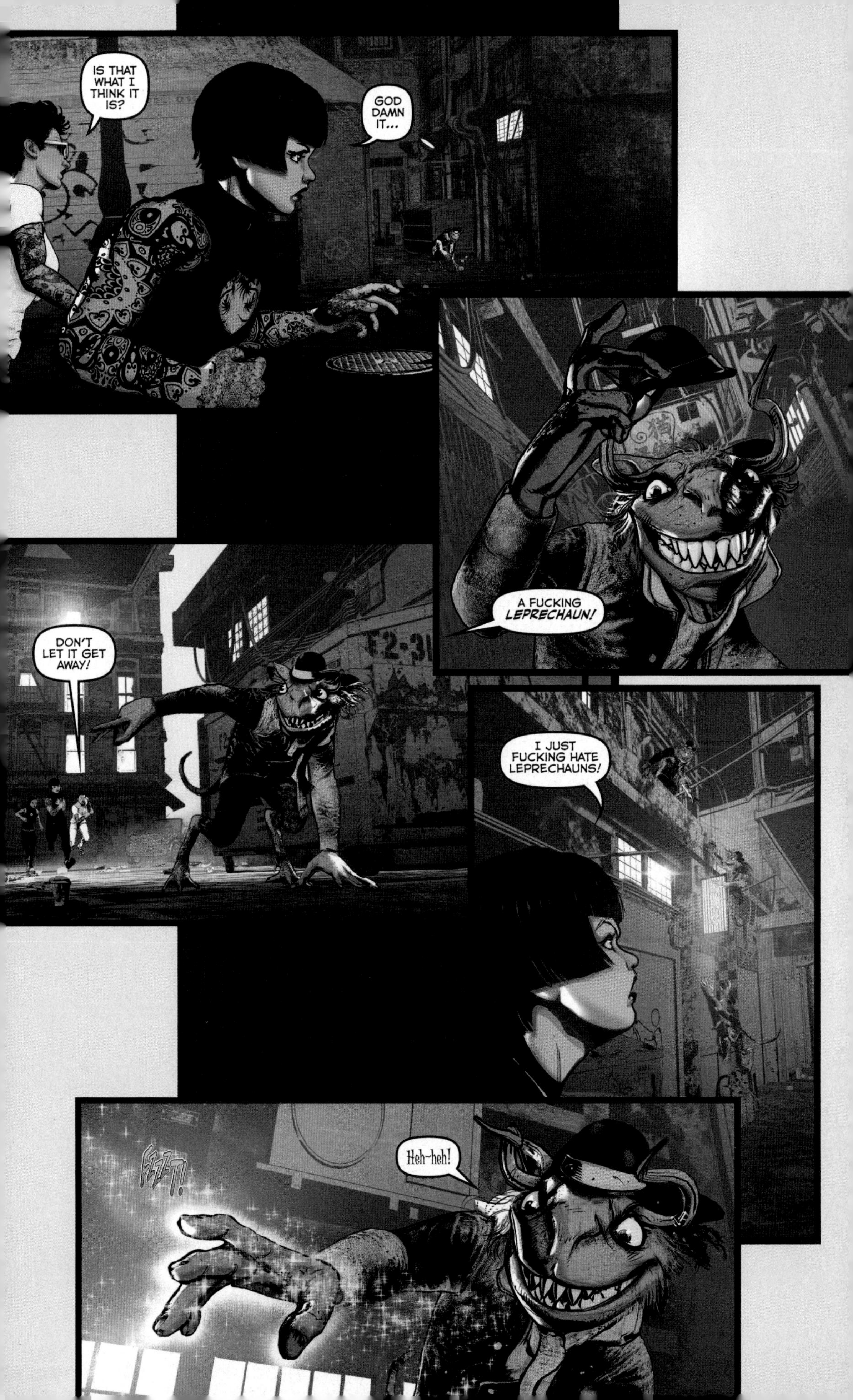
IS THAT WHAT I THINK IT IS?
GOD DAMN IT...
A FUCKING LEPRECHAUN!
DON'T LET IT GET AWAY!
I JUST FUCKING HATE LEPRECHAUNS!
FZZZT!
Heh-heh!

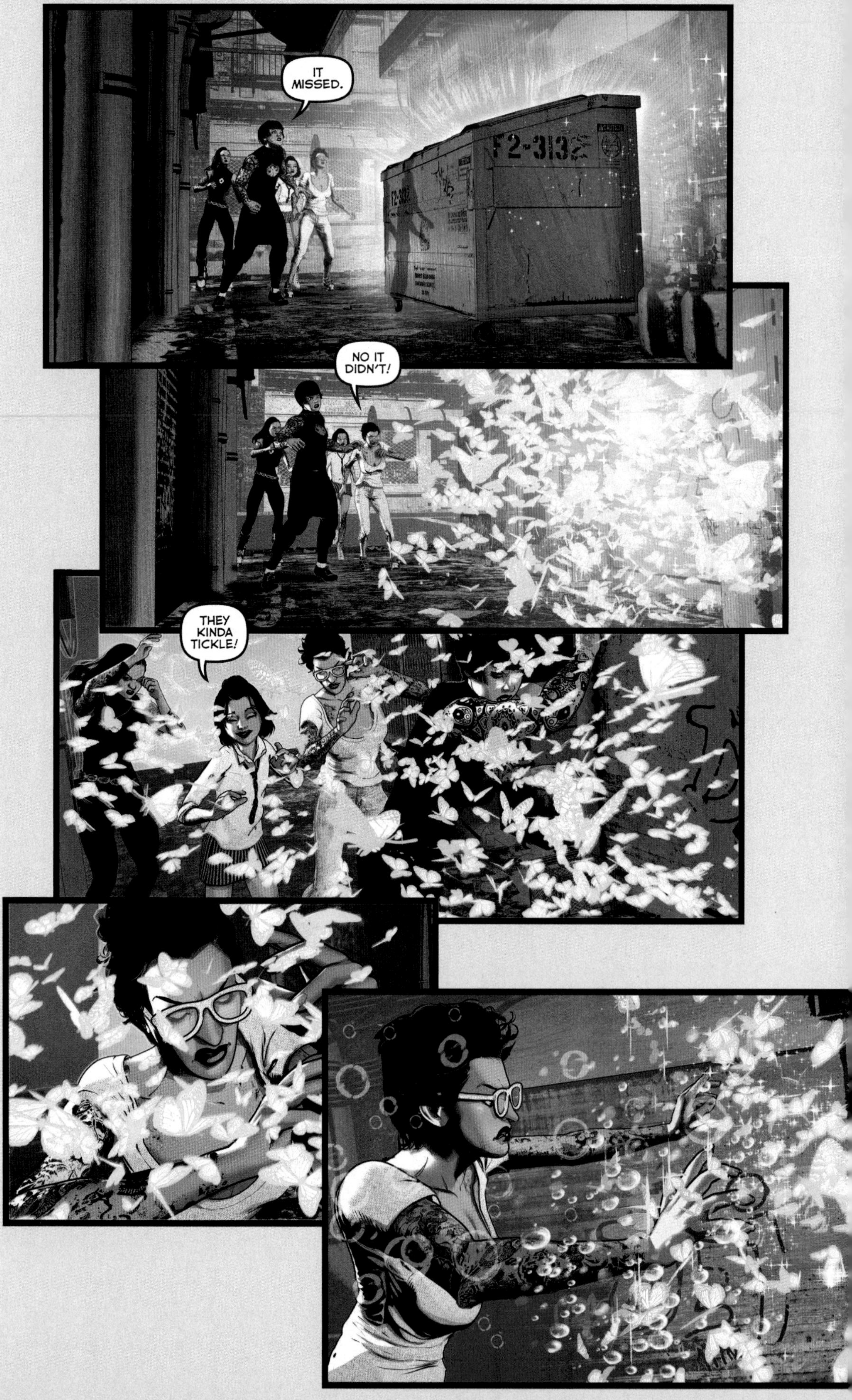
IT MISSED.
NO IT DIDN'T!
THEY KINDA TICKLE!

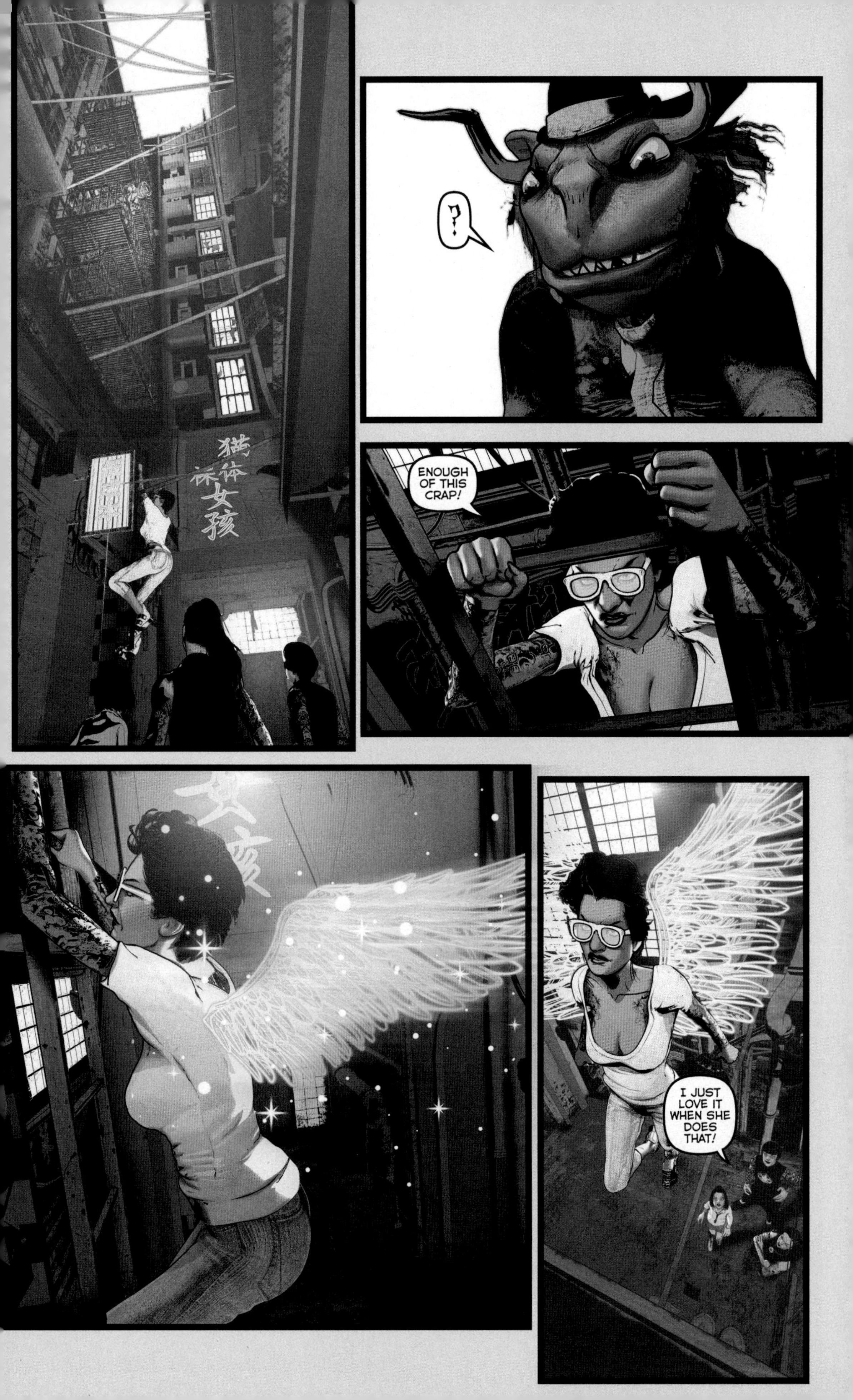
?!
ENOUGH OF THIS CRAP!
I JUST LOVE IT WHEN SHE DOES THAT!

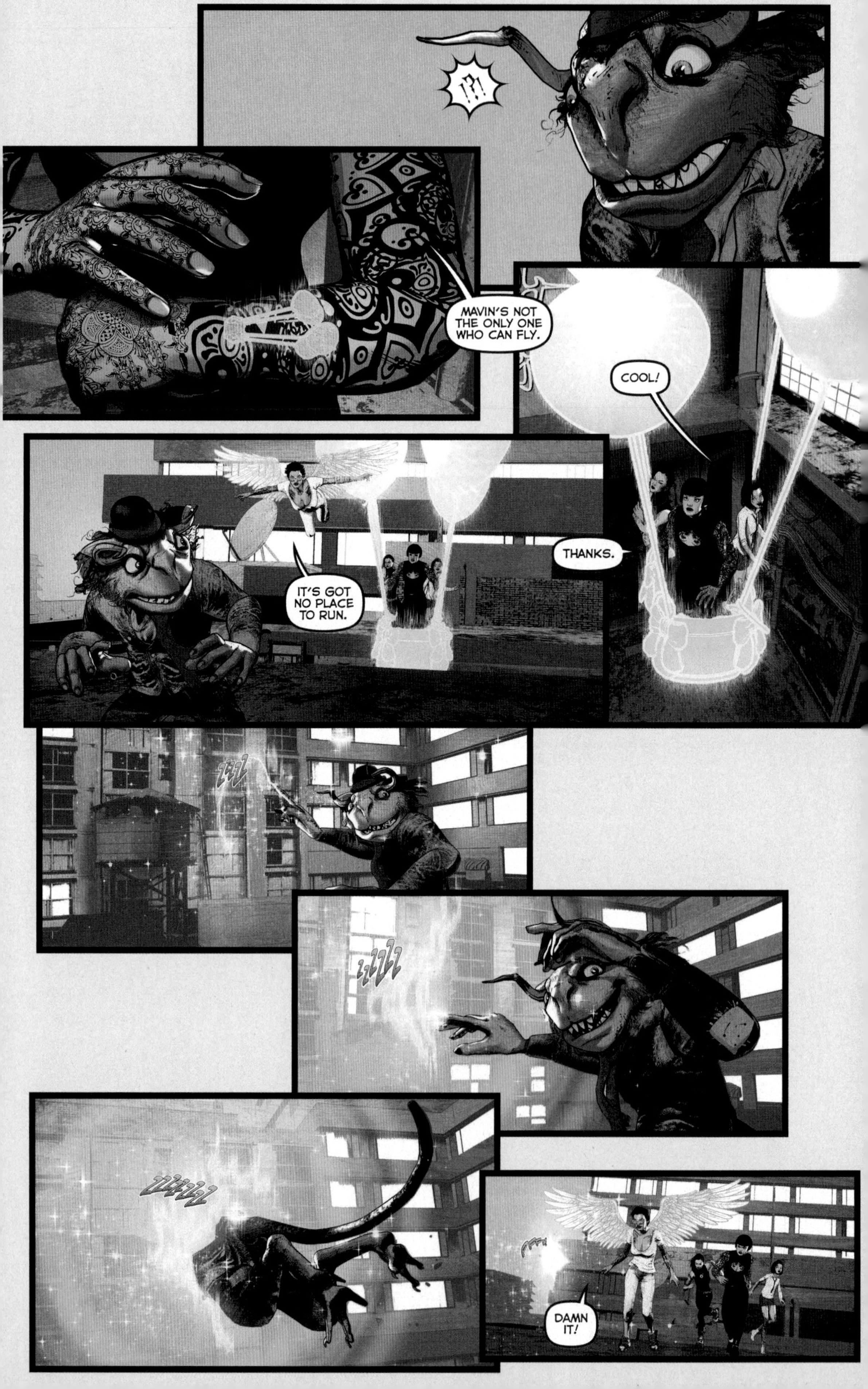
!?!
MAVIN'S NOT THE ONLY ONE WHO CAN FLY.
COOL!
THANKS.
IT'S GOT NO PLACE TO RUN.
ZZZ
ZZZZZ
ZZZZZZZ
DAMN IT!

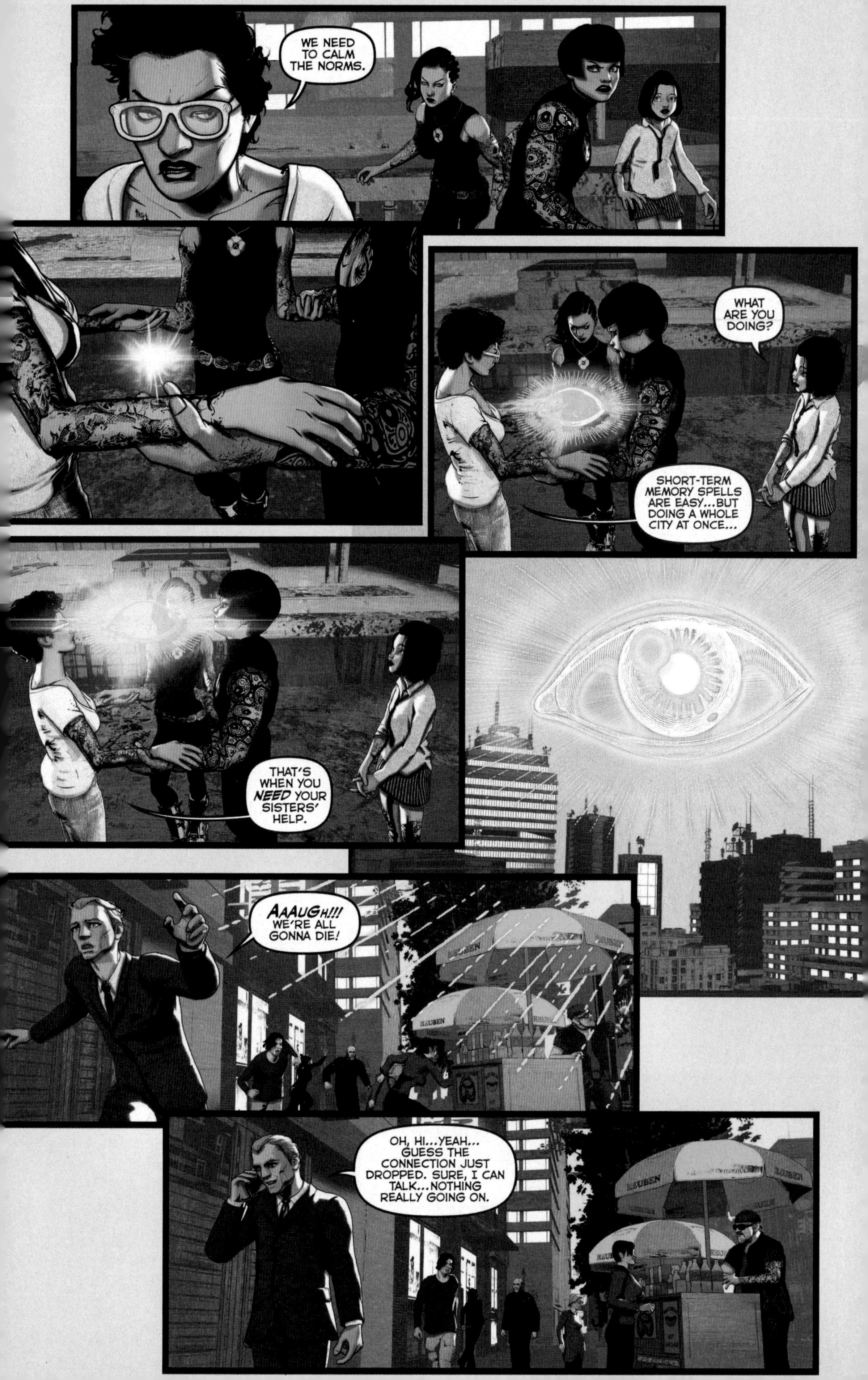
WE NEED TO CALM THE NORMS.
WHAT ARE YOU DOING?
SHORT-TERM MEMORY SPELLS ARE EASY...BUT DOING A WHOLE CITY AT ONCE...
THAT'S WHEN YOU *NEED* YOUR SISTERS' HELP.
AAAUGH!!! WE'RE ALL GONNA DIE!
OH, HI...YEAH... GUESS THE CONNECTION JUST DROPPED. SURE, I CAN TALK...NOTHING REALLY GOING ON.

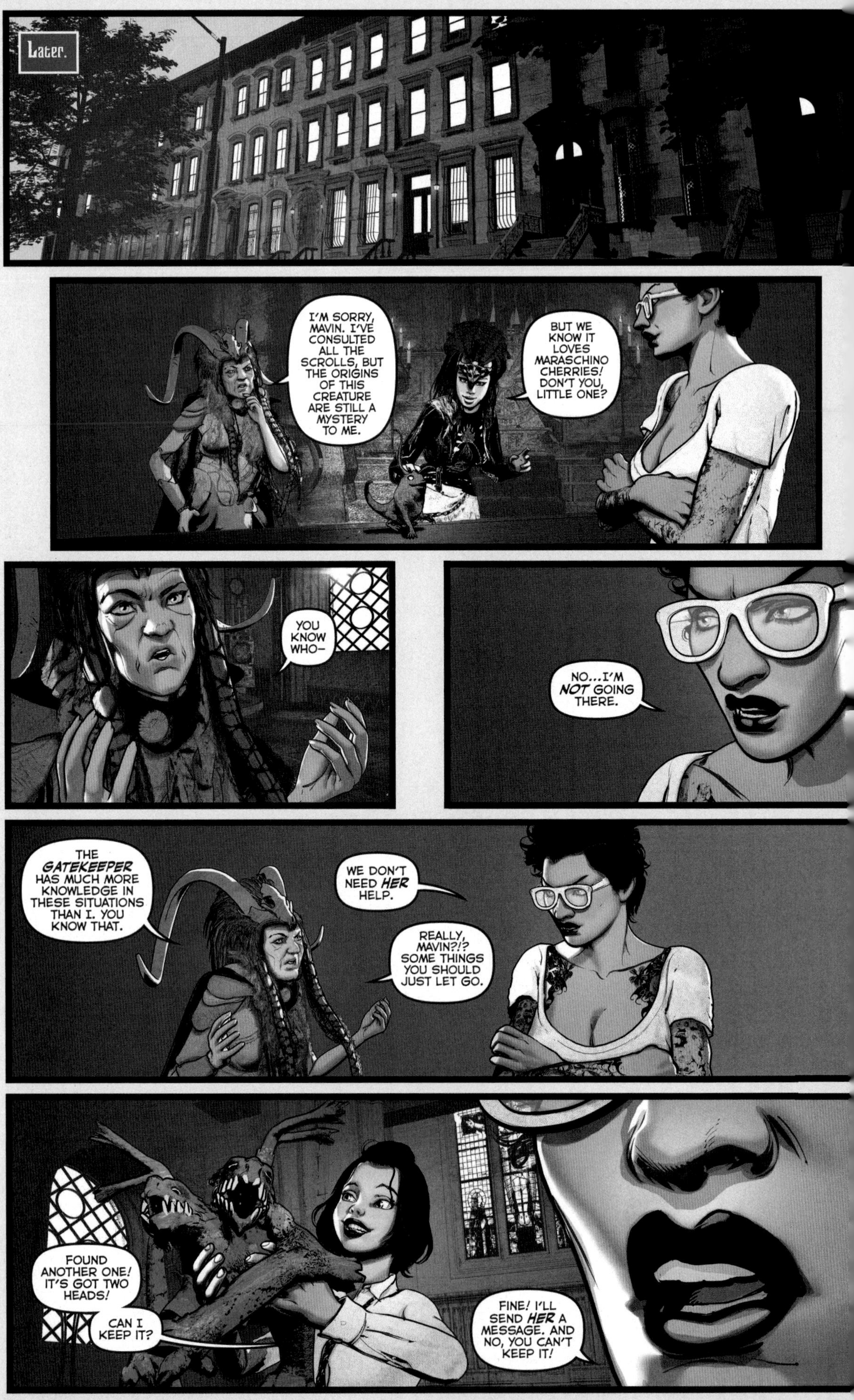
Later.
I'M SORRY, MAVIN. I'VE CONSULTED ALL THE SCROLLS, BUT THE ORIGINS OF THIS CREATURE ARE STILL A MYSTERY TO ME.
BUT WE KNOW IT LOVES MARASCHINO CHERRIES! DON'T YOU, LITTLE ONE?
YOU KNOW WHO–
NO...I'M NOT GOING THERE.
THE GATEKEEPER HAS MUCH MORE KNOWLEDGE IN THESE SITUATIONS THAN I. YOU KNOW THAT.
WE DON'T NEED HER HELP.
REALLY, MAVIN?!? SOME THINGS YOU SHOULD JUST LET GO.
FOUND ANOTHER ONE! IT'S GOT TWO HEADS!
CAN I KEEP IT?
FINE! I'LL SEND HER A MESSAGE. AND NO, YOU CAN'T KEEP IT!

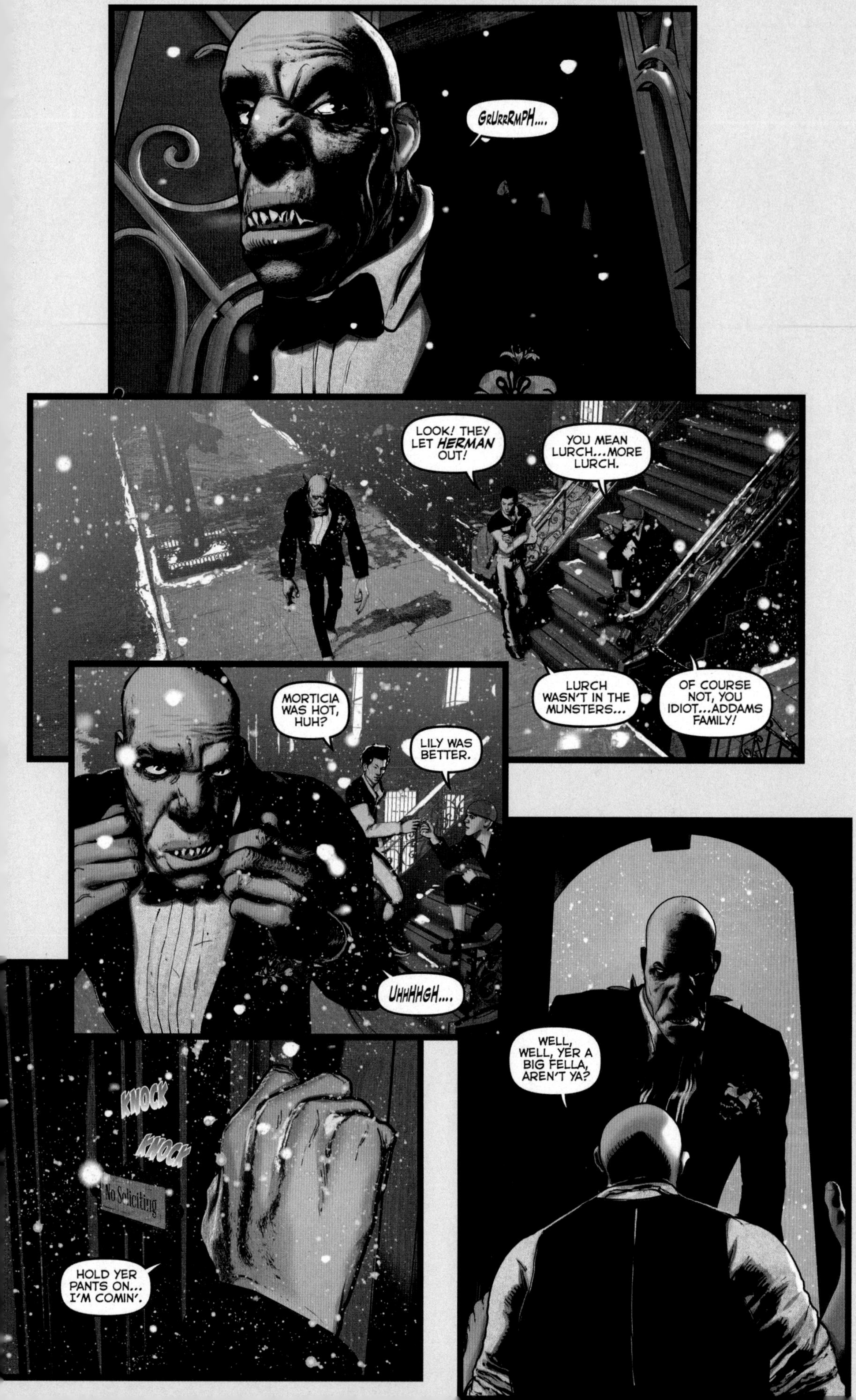
GRURRRMPH....
LOOK! THEY LET HERMAN OUT!
YOU MEAN LURCH...MORE LURCH.
LURCH WASN'T IN THE MUNSTERS...
OF COURSE NOT, YOU IDIOT...ADDAMS FAMILY!
MORTICIA WAS HOT, HUH?
LILY WAS BETTER.
UHHHHGH....
KNOCK
KNOCK
No Soliciting
HOLD YER PANTS ON... I'M COMIN'.
WELL, WELL, YER A BIG FELLA, AREN'T YA?

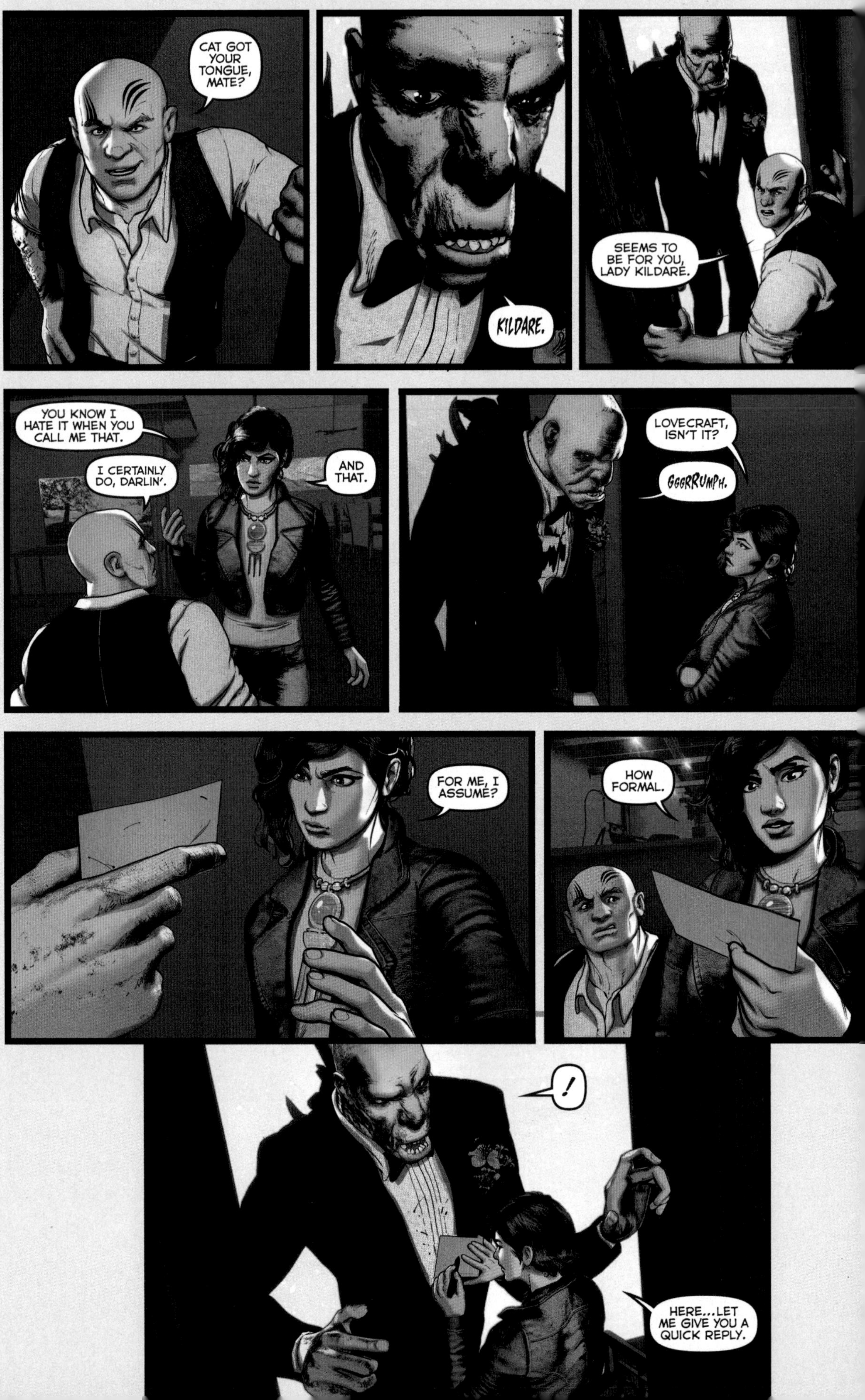
CAT GOT YOUR TONGUE, MATE?
KILDARE.
SEEMS TO BE FOR YOU, LADY KILDARE.
YOU KNOW I HATE IT WHEN YOU CALL ME THAT.
I CERTAINLY DO, DARLIN'.
AND THAT.
LOVECRAFT, ISN'T IT?
GGGRRUMPH.
FOR ME, I ASSUME?
HOW FORMAL.
!
HERE...LET ME GIVE YOU A QUICK REPLY.

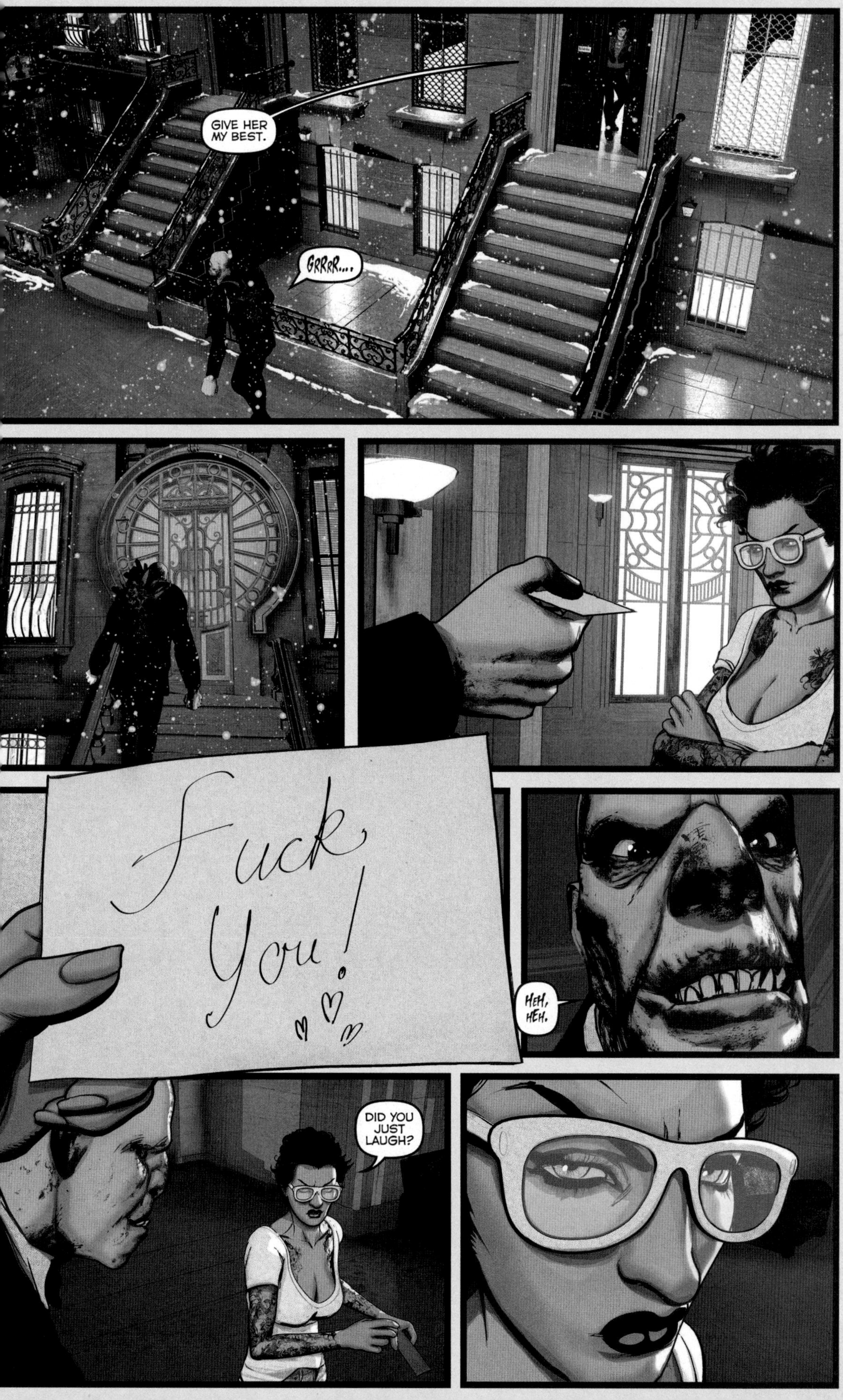
GIVE HER MY BEST.
GRRRR...
Fuck You!
HEH, HEH.
DID YOU JUST LAUGH?

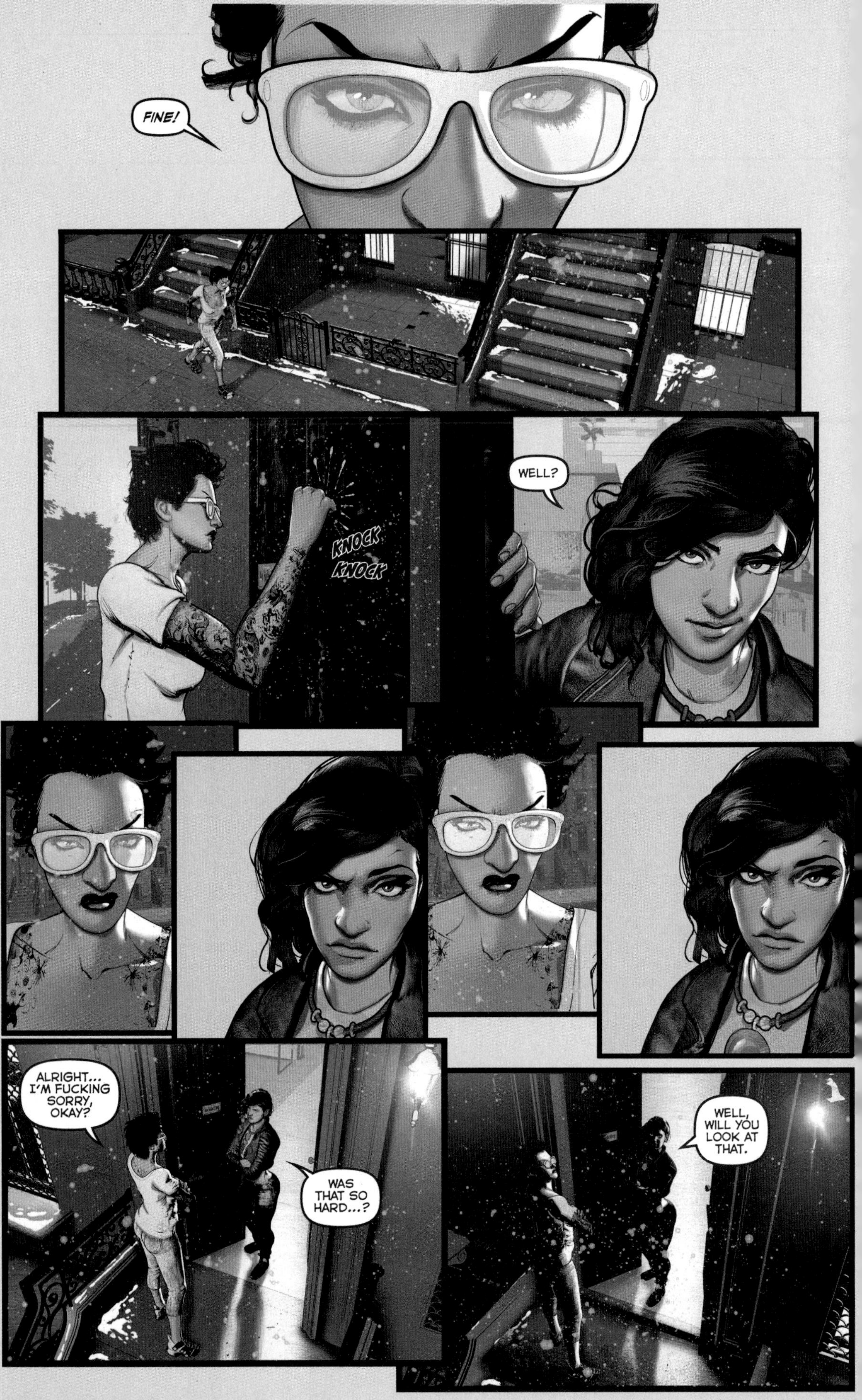
FINE!
KNOCK
KNOCK
WELL?
ALRIGHT... I'M FUCKING SORRY, OKAY?
WAS THAT SO HARD...?
WELL, WILL YOU LOOK AT THAT.

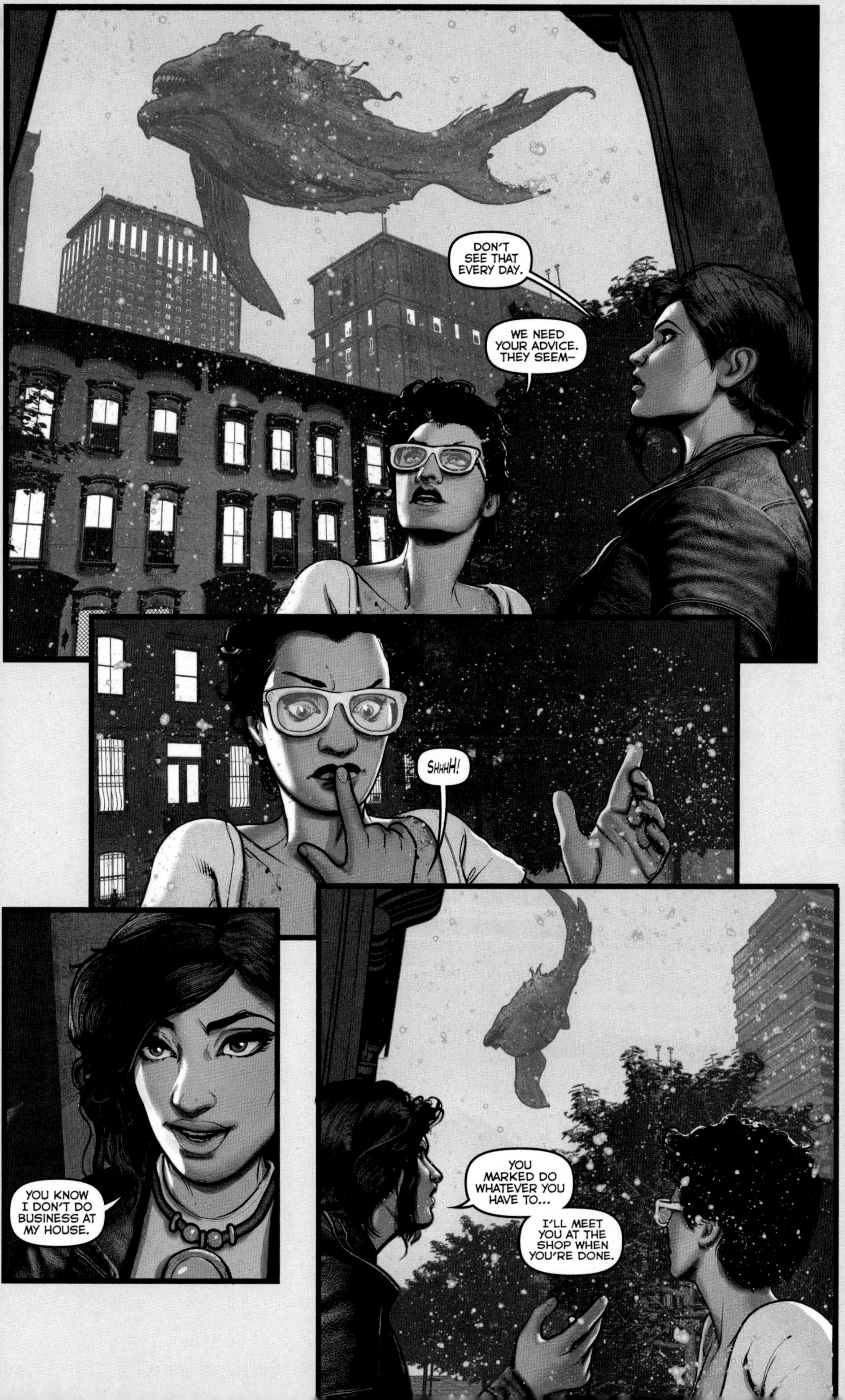
DON'T SEE THAT EVERY DAY.
WE NEED YOUR ADVICE. THEY SEEM–
SHHHH!
YOU KNOW I DON'T DO BUSINESS AT MY HOUSE.
YOU MARKED DO WHATEVER YOU HAVE TO...
I'LL MEET YOU AT THE SHOP WHEN YOU'RE DONE.

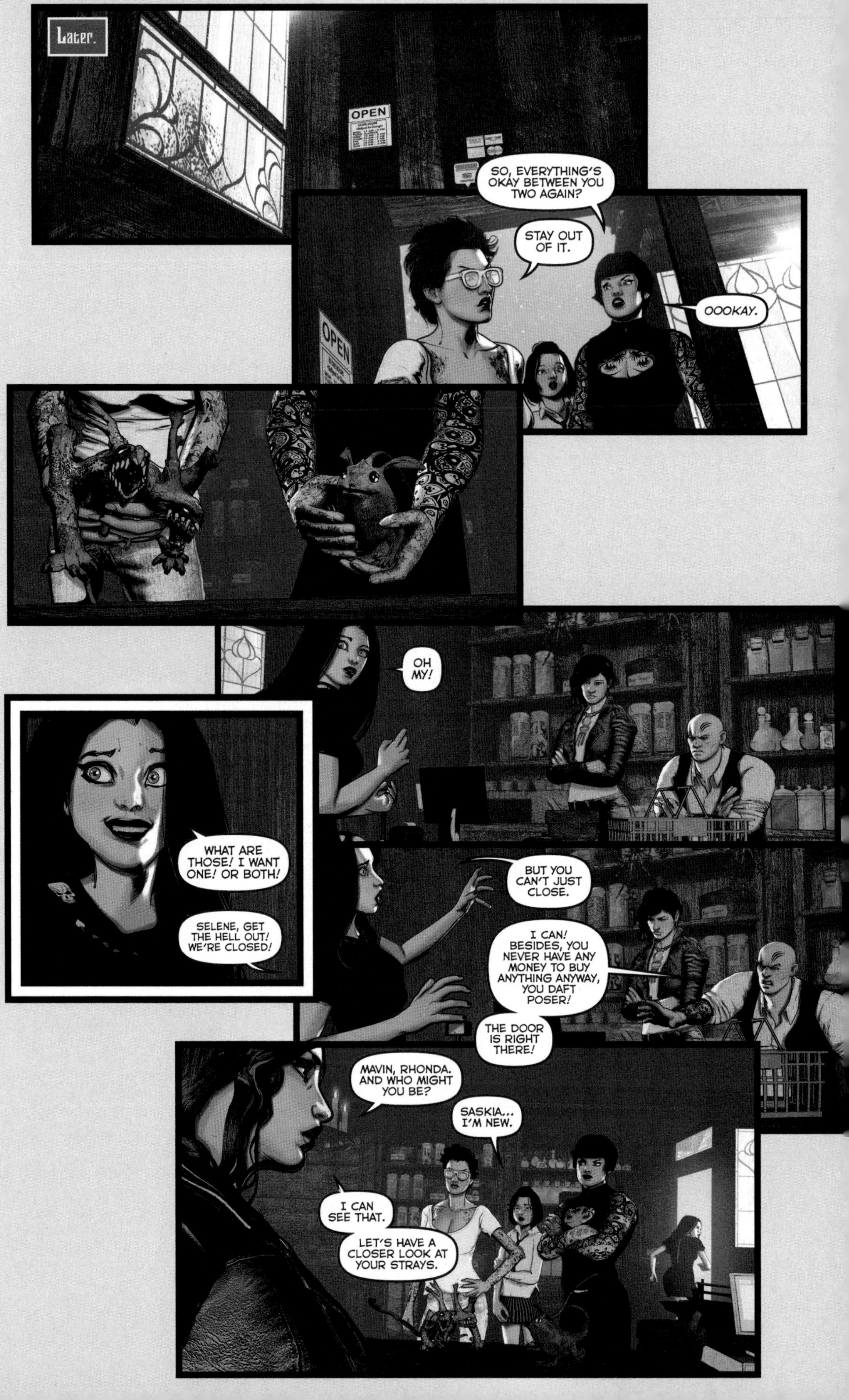
Later.
OPEN
SO, EVERYTHING'S OKAY BETWEEN YOU TWO AGAIN?
STAY OUT OF IT.
OOOKAY.
OPEN
OH MY!
WHAT ARE THOSE! I WANT ONE! OR BOTH!
SELENE, GET THE HELL OUT! WE'RE CLOSED!
BUT YOU CAN'T JUST CLOSE.
I CAN! BESIDES, YOU NEVER HAVE ANY MONEY TO BUY ANYTHING ANYWAY, YOU DAFT POSER!
THE DOOR IS RIGHT THERE!
MAVIN, RHONDA. AND WHO MIGHT YOU BE?
SASKIA... I'M NEW.
I CAN SEE THAT.
LET'S HAVE A CLOSER LOOK AT YOUR STRAYS.

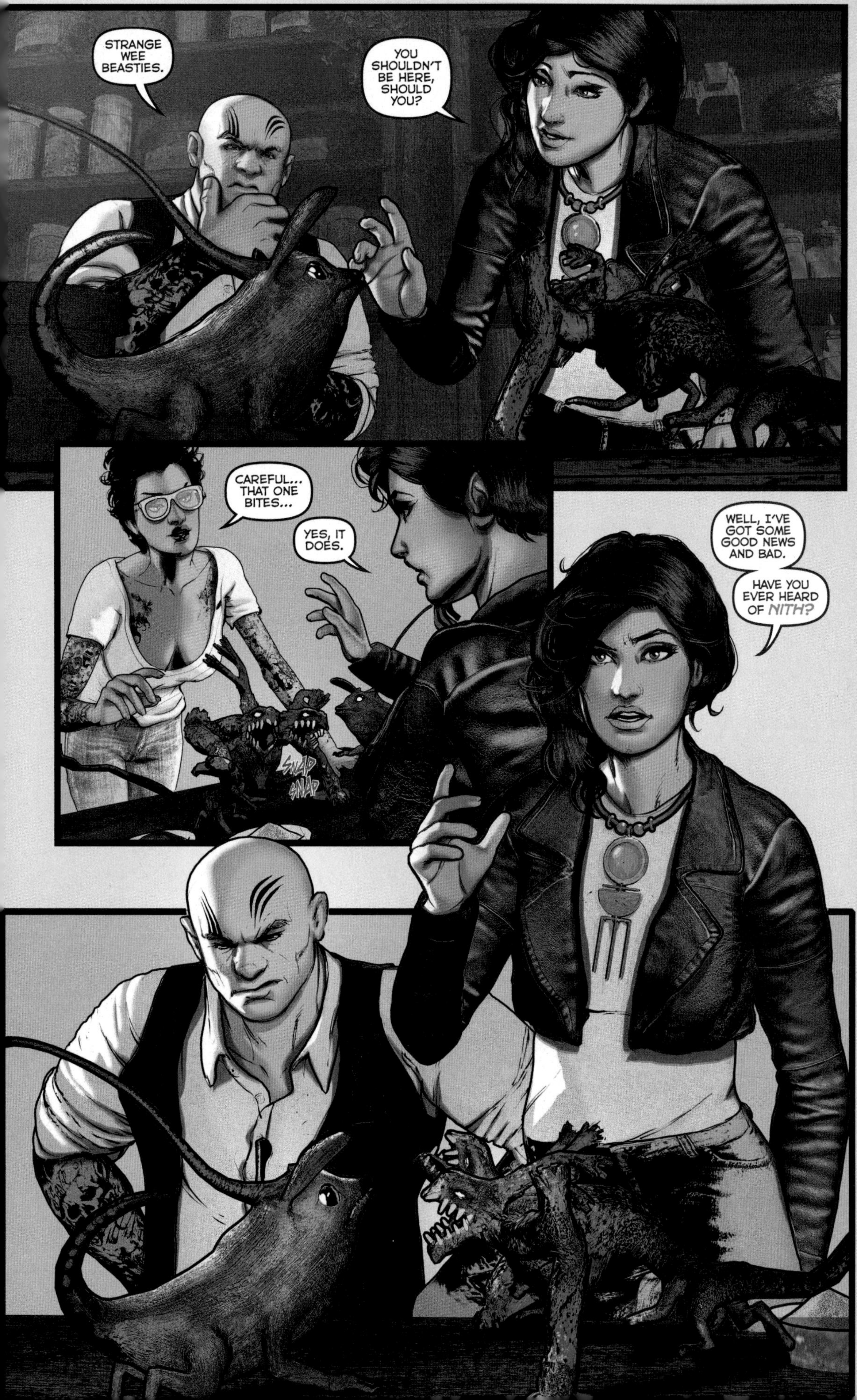
STRANGE WEE BEASTIES.
YOU SHOULDN'T BE HERE, SHOULD YOU?
CAREFUL... THAT ONE BITES...
YES, IT DOES.
SNAP SNAP
WELL, I'VE GOT SOME GOOD NEWS AND BAD.
HAVE YOU EVER HEARD OF NITH?

COVER ART FOR THIS VOLUME

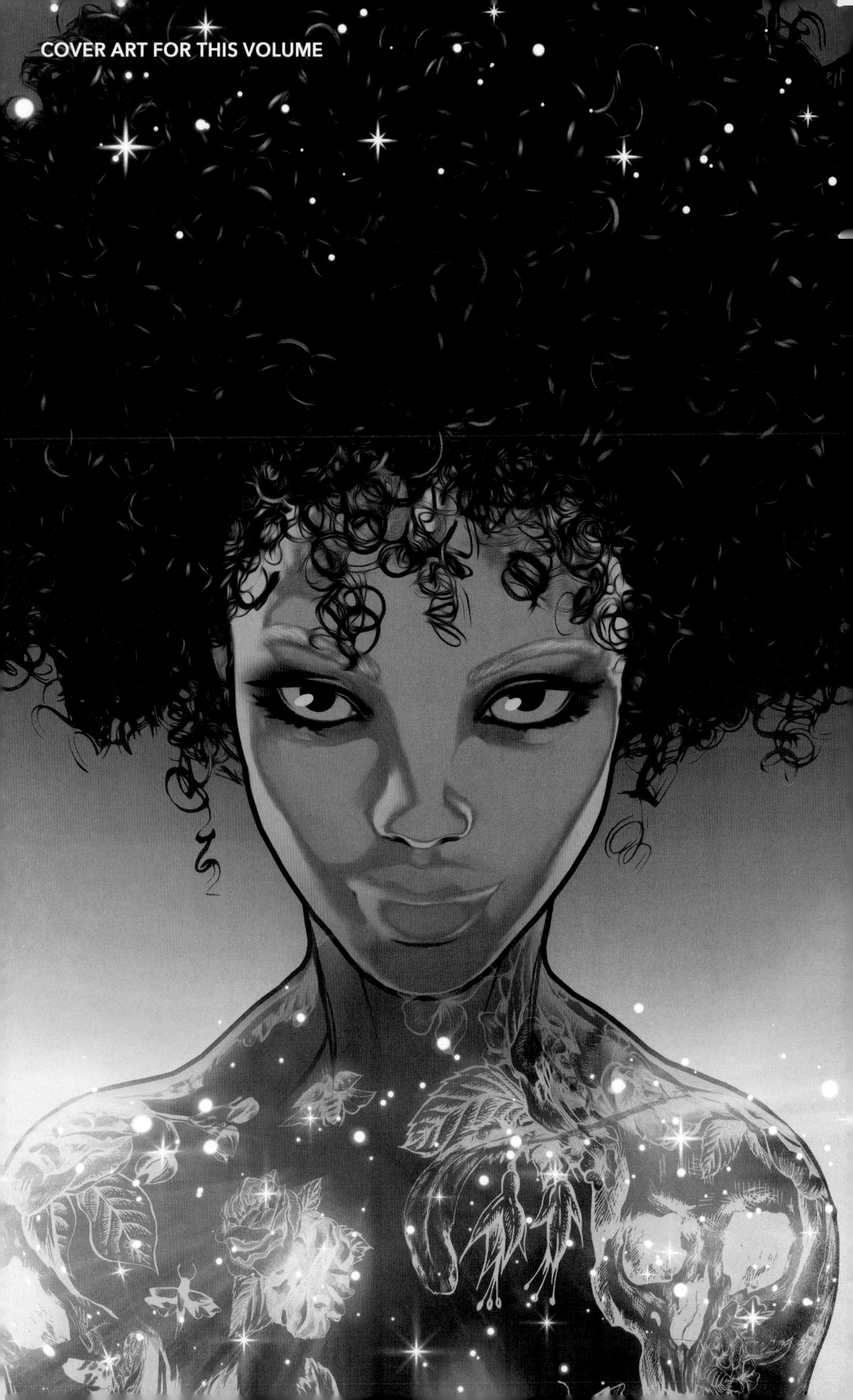

CHAPTER NINE

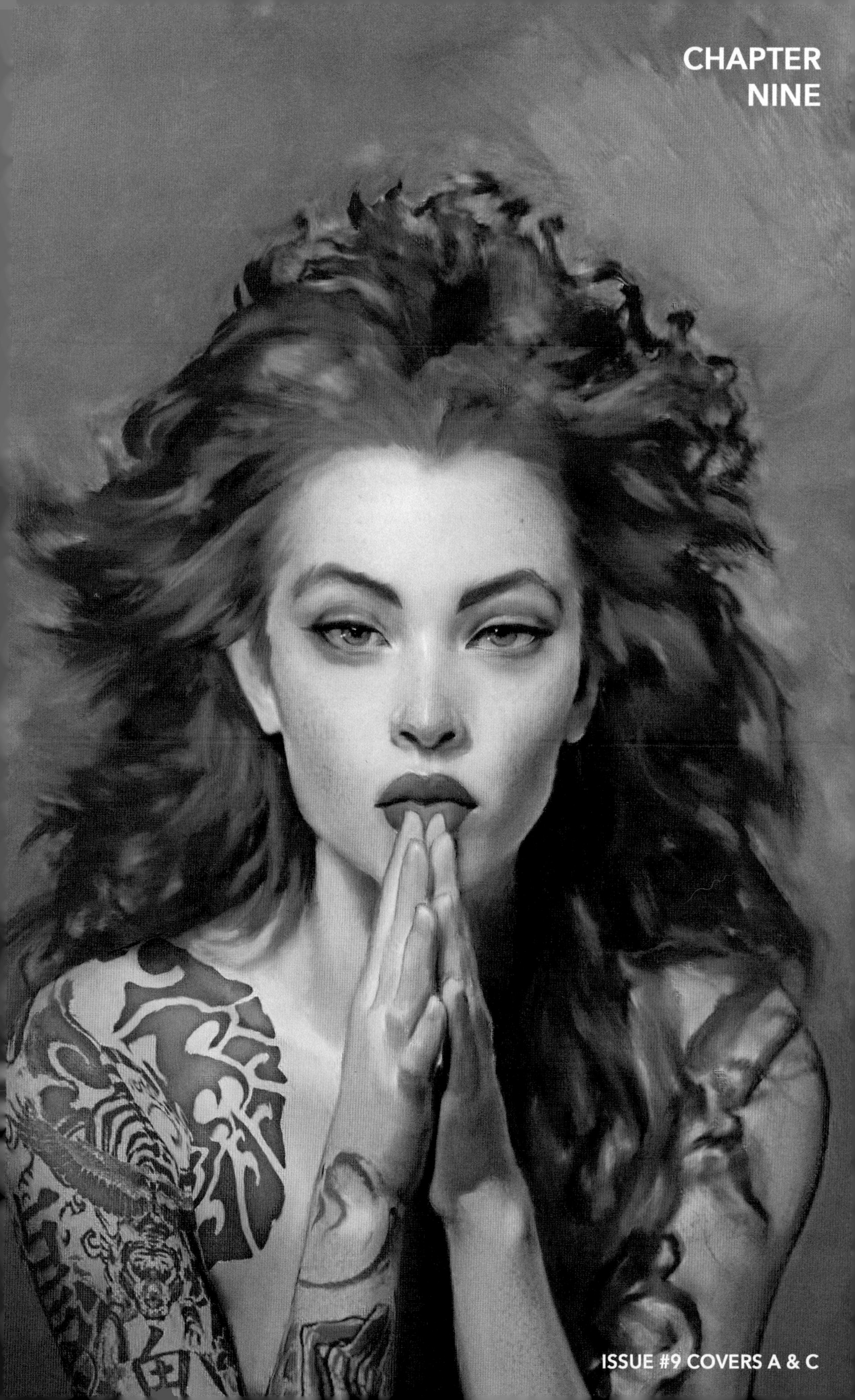

ISSUE #9 COVERS A & C

ISSUE #9 COVER B

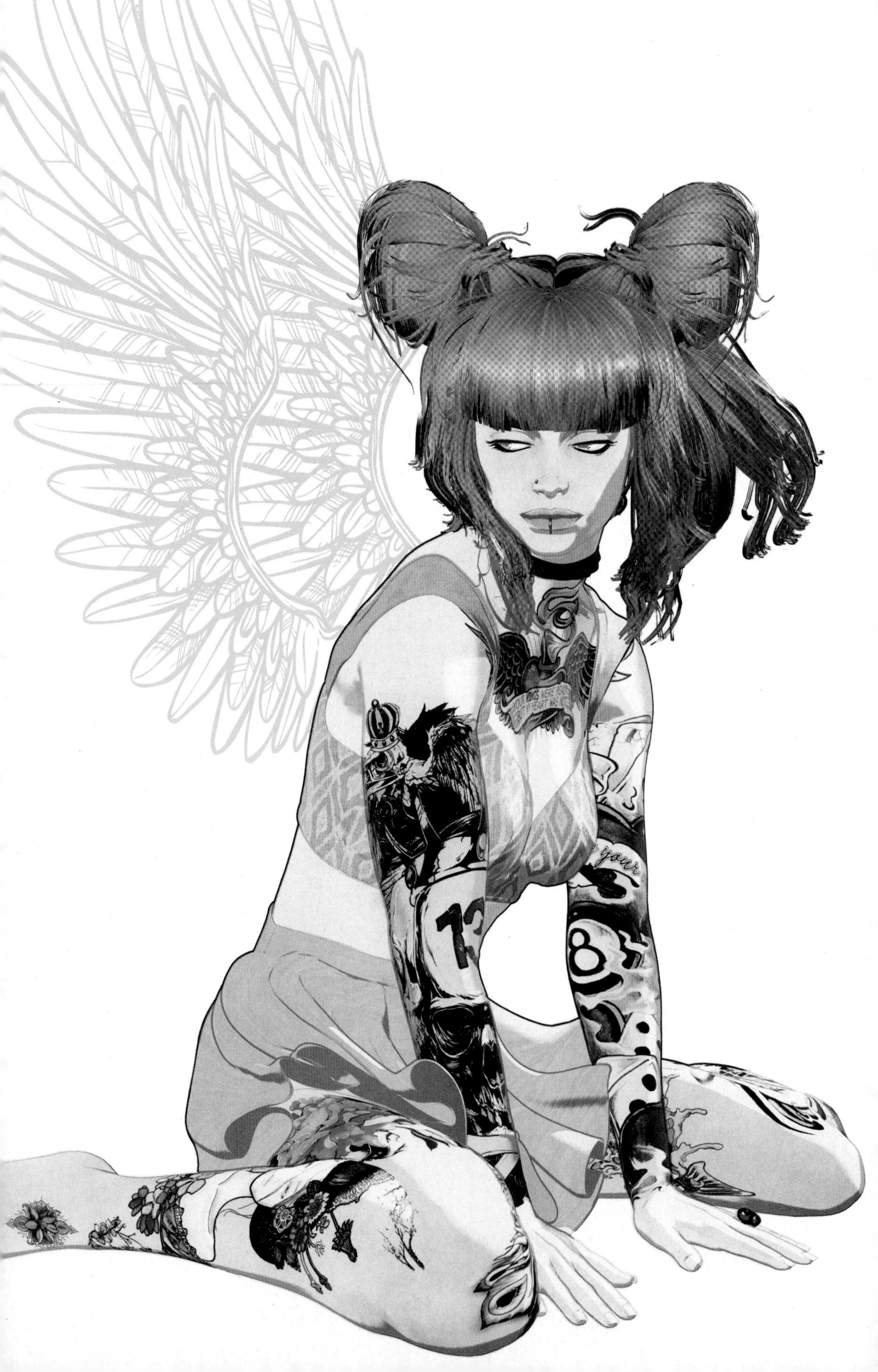

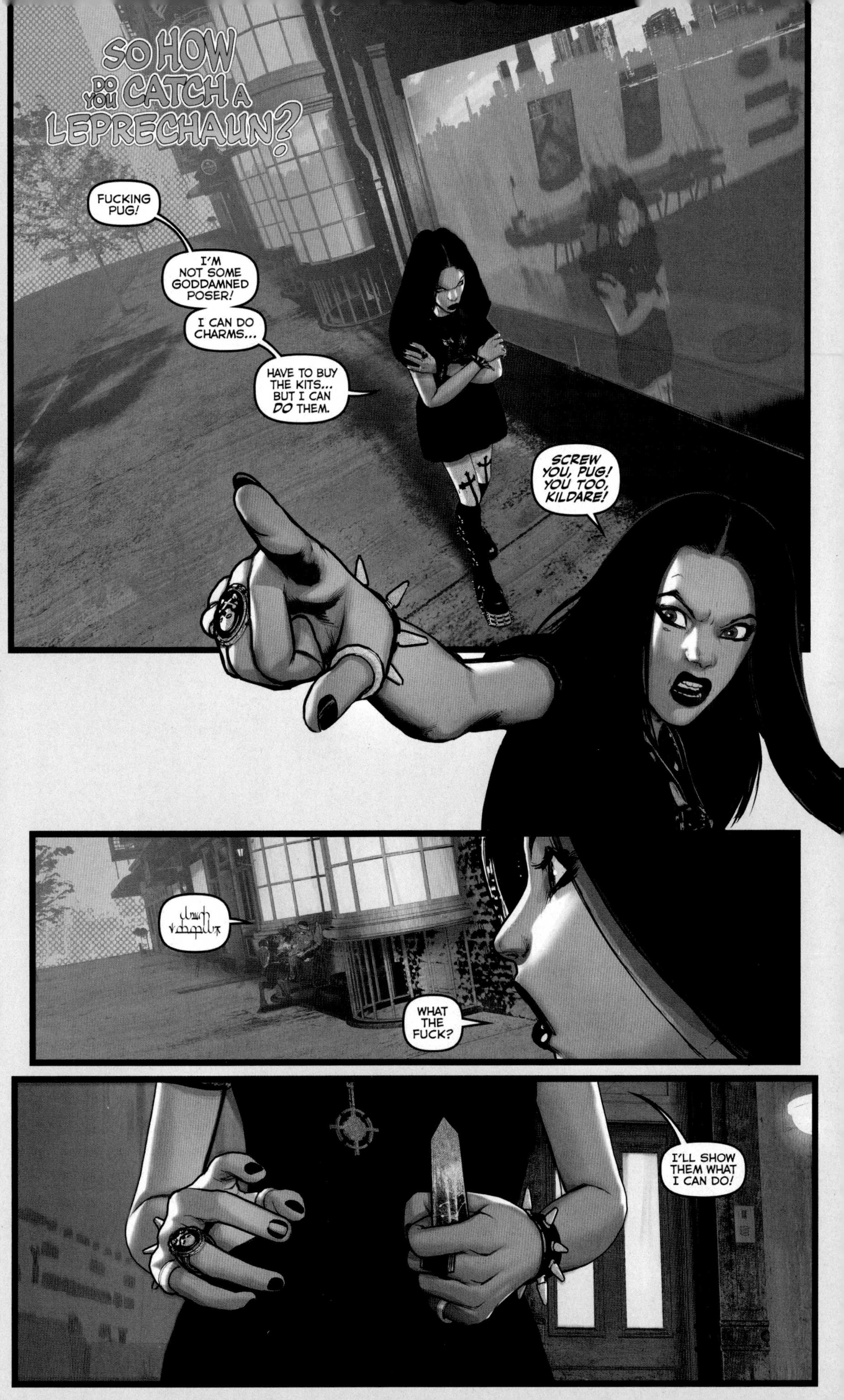
SO HOW DO YOU CATCH A LEPRECHAUN?
FUCKING PUG!
I'M NOT SOME GODDAMNED POSER!
I CAN DO CHARMS...
HAVE TO BUY THE KITS... BUT I CAN DO THEM.
SCREW YOU, PUG! YOU TOO, KILDARE!
WHAT THE FUCK?
I'LL SHOW THEM WHAT I CAN DO!

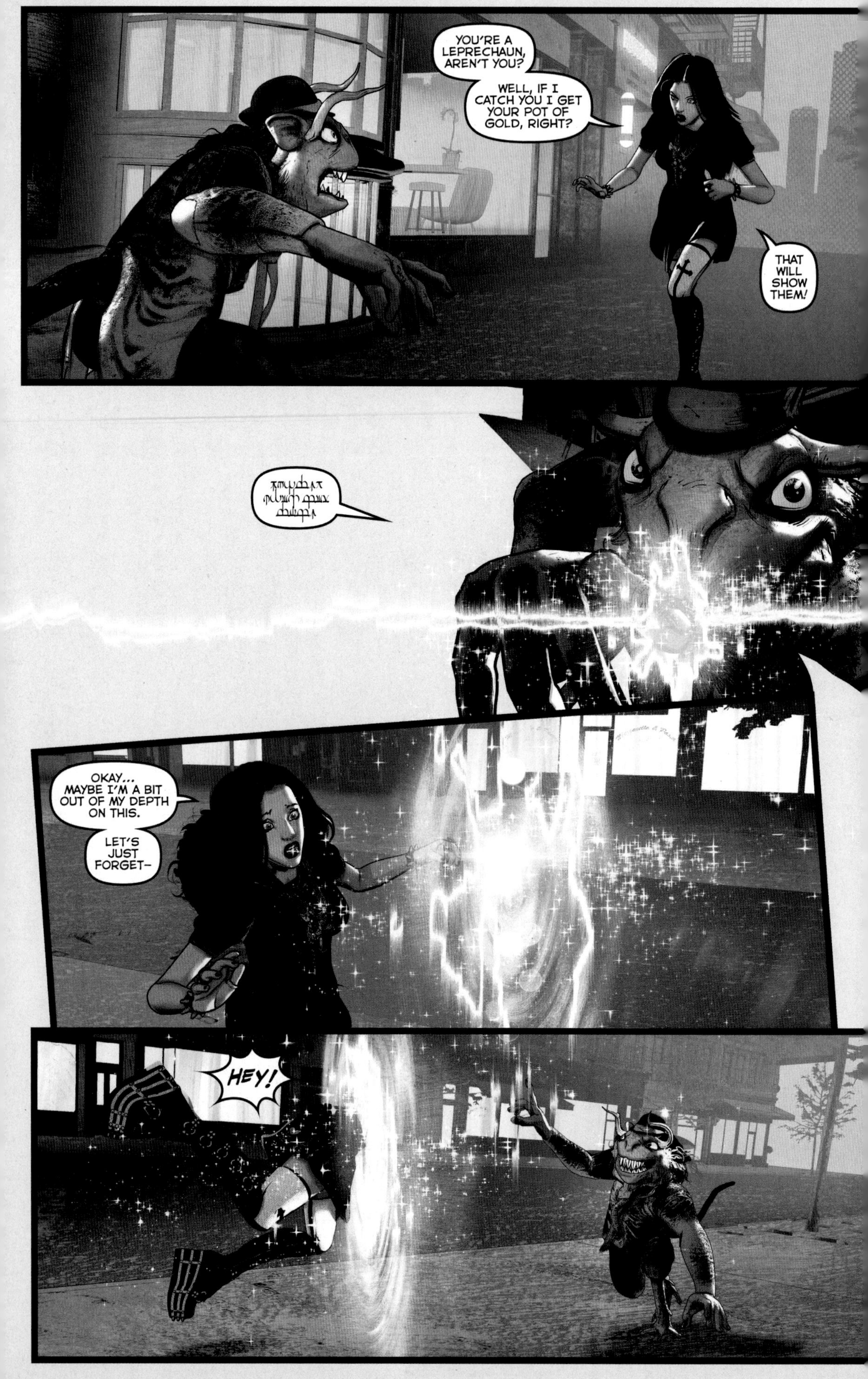
YOU'RE A LEPRECHAUN, AREN'T YOU?
WELL, IF I CATCH YOU I GET YOUR POT OF GOLD, RIGHT?
THAT WILL SHOW THEM!
OKAY... MAYBE I'M A BIT OUT OF MY DEPTH ON THIS.
LET'S JUST FORGET-
HEY!

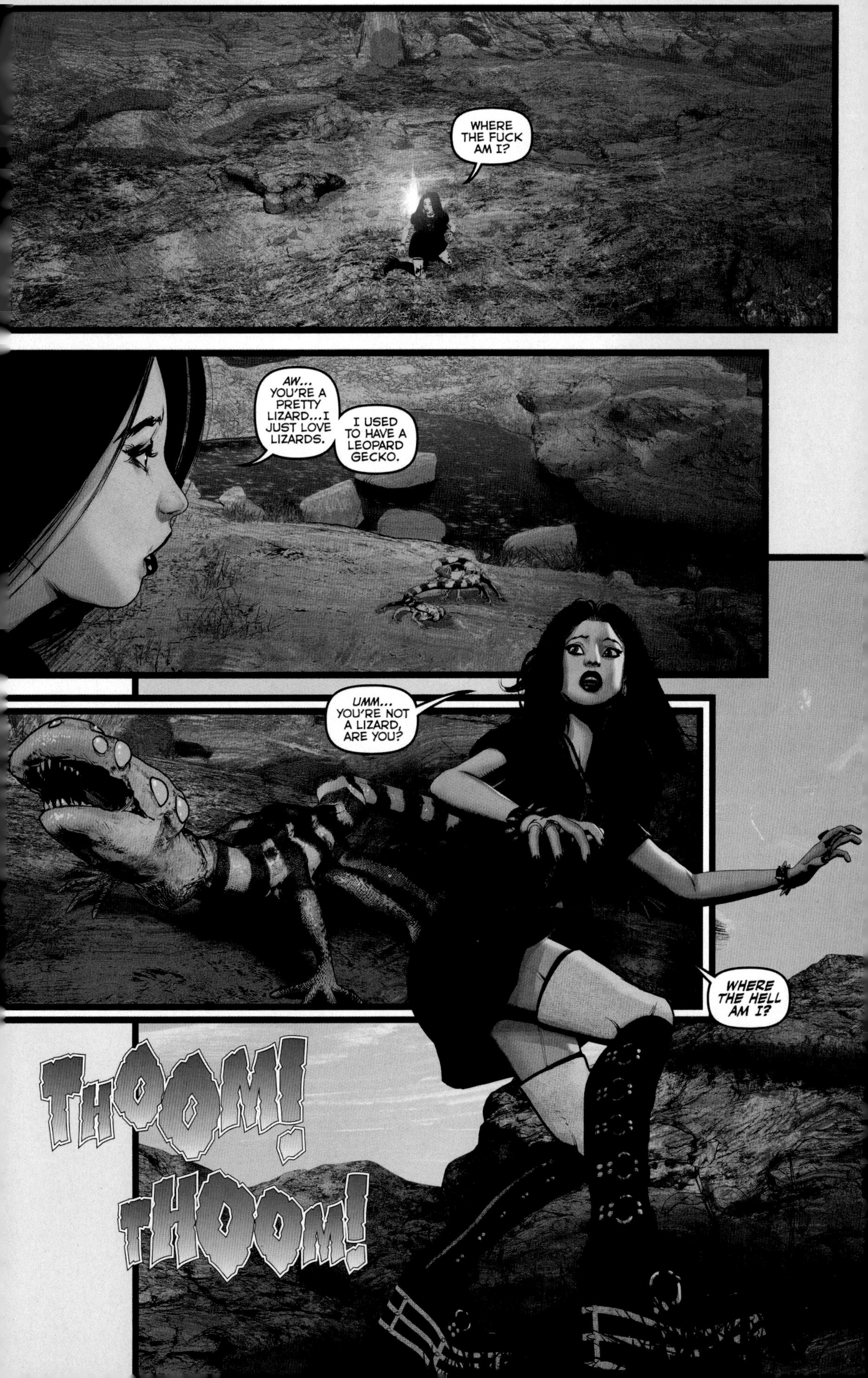
WHERE THE FUCK AM I?
AW... YOU'RE A PRETTY LIZARD...I JUST LOVE LIZARDS.
I USED TO HAVE A LEOPARD GECKO.
UMM... YOU'RE NOT A LIZARD, ARE YOU?
WHERE THE HELL AM I?
THOOM! THOOM!

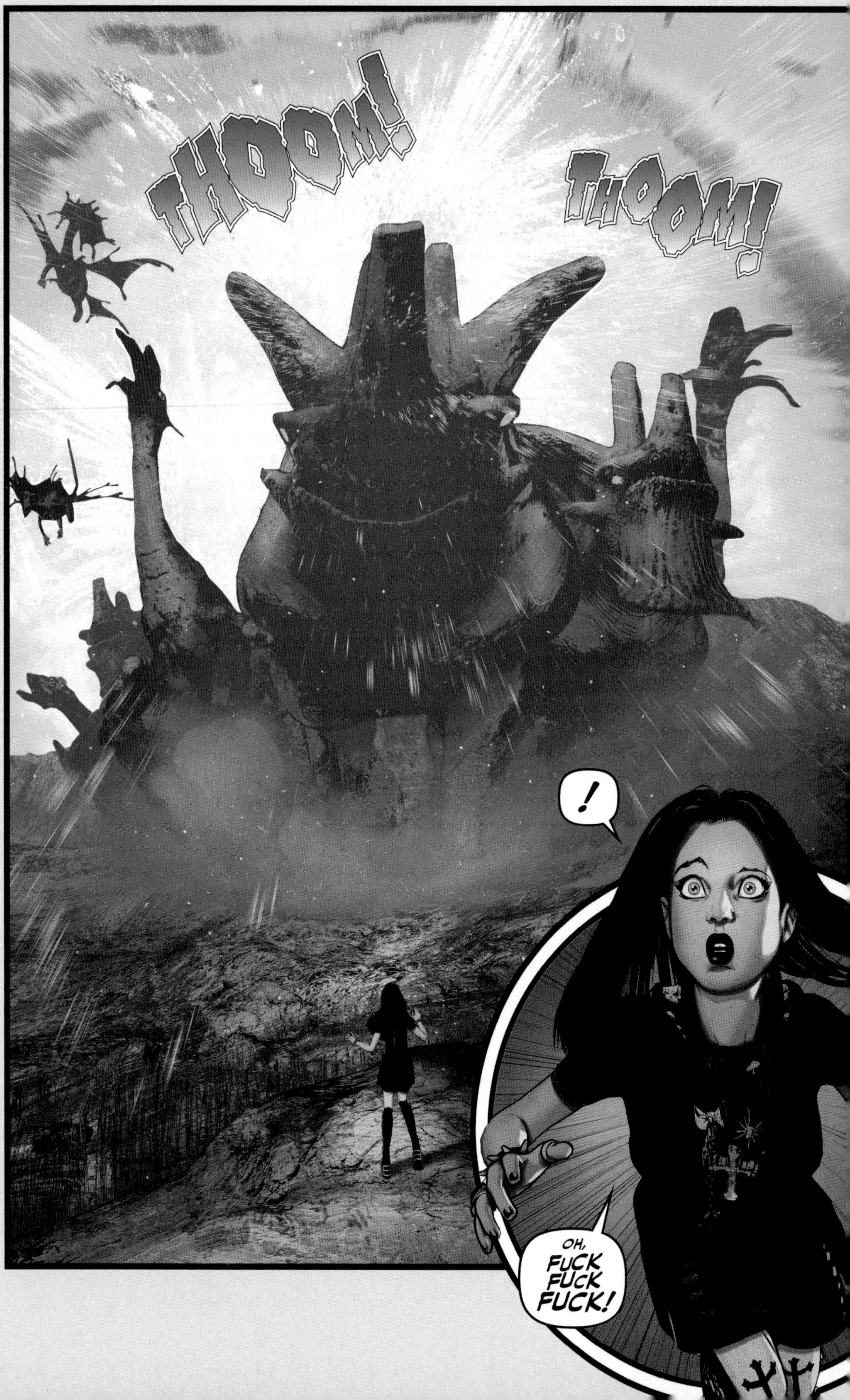
THOOM!
THOOM!
!
OH, FUCK FUCK FUCK!

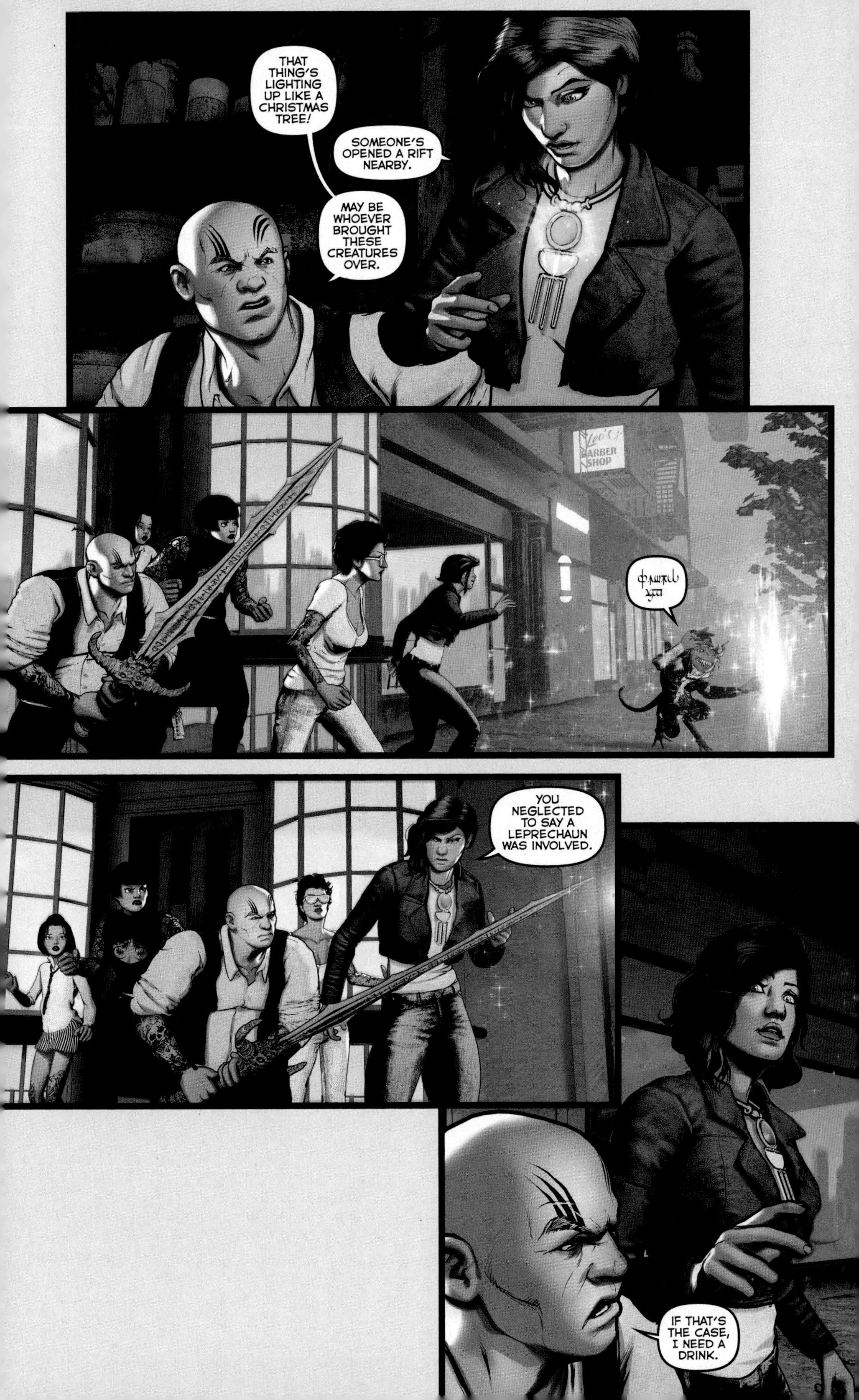
THAT THING'S LIGHTING UP LIKE A CHRISTMAS TREE!
SOMEONE'S OPENED A RIFT NEARBY.
MAY BE WHOEVER BROUGHT THESE CREATURES OVER.
LEE'S BARBER SHOP
YOU NEGLECTED TO SAY A LEPRECHAUN WAS INVOLVED.
IF THAT'S THE CASE, I NEED A DRINK.

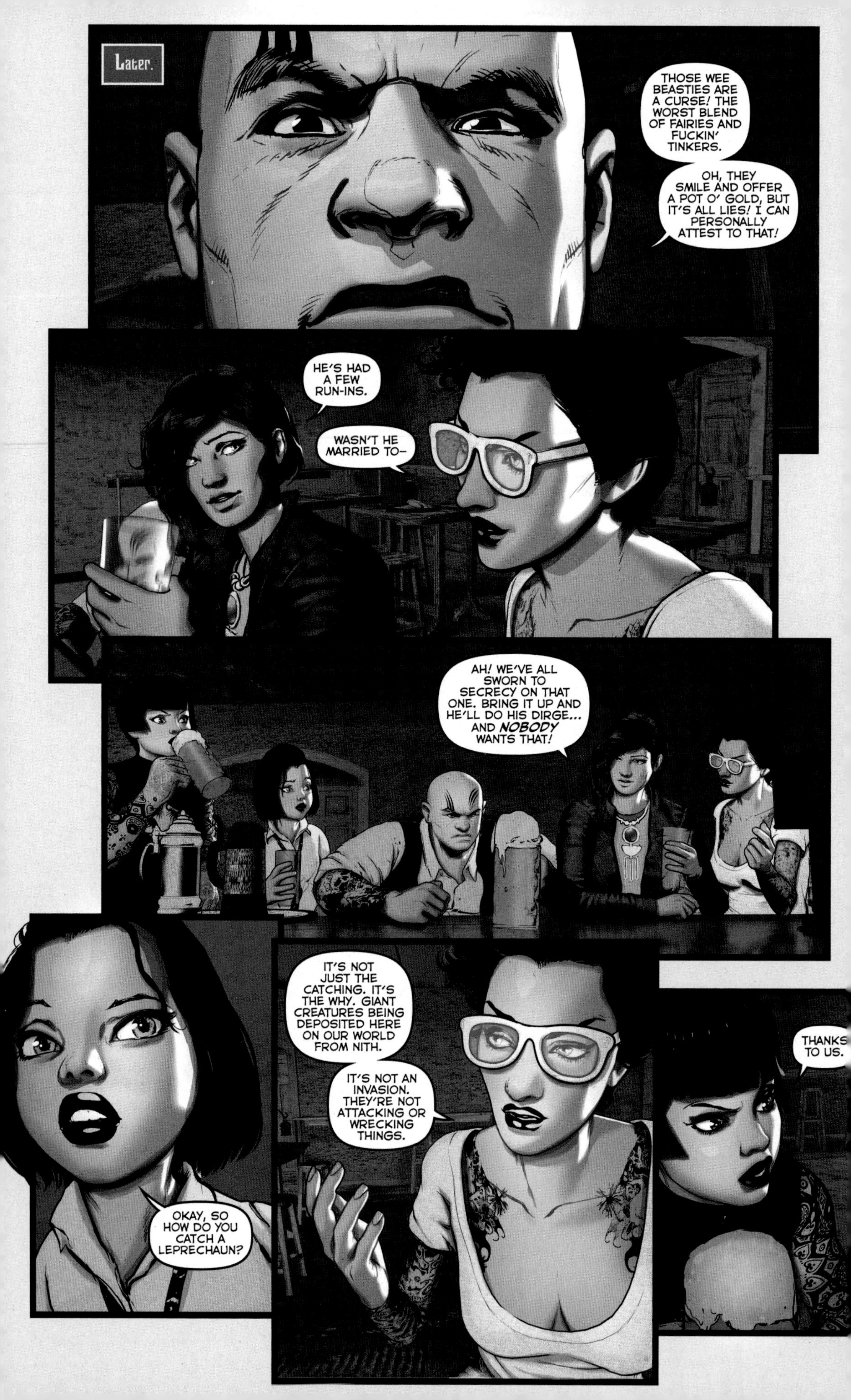
Later.
THOSE WEE BEASTIES ARE A CURSE! THE WORST BLEND OF FAIRIES AND FUCKIN' TINKERS.
OH, THEY SMILE AND OFFER A POT O' GOLD, BUT IT'S ALL LIES! I CAN PERSONALLY ATTEST TO THAT!
HE'S HAD A FEW RUN-INS.
WASN'T HE MARRIED TO–
AH! WE'VE ALL SWORN TO SECRECY ON THAT ONE. BRING IT UP AND HE'LL DO HIS DIRGE... AND *NOBODY* WANTS THAT!
OKAY, SO HOW DO YOU CATCH A LEPRECHAUN?
IT'S NOT JUST THE CATCHING. IT'S THE WHY. GIANT CREATURES BEING DEPOSITED HERE ON OUR WORLD FROM NITH.
IT'S NOT AN INVASION. THEY'RE NOT ATTACKING OR WRECKING THINGS.
THANKS TO US.

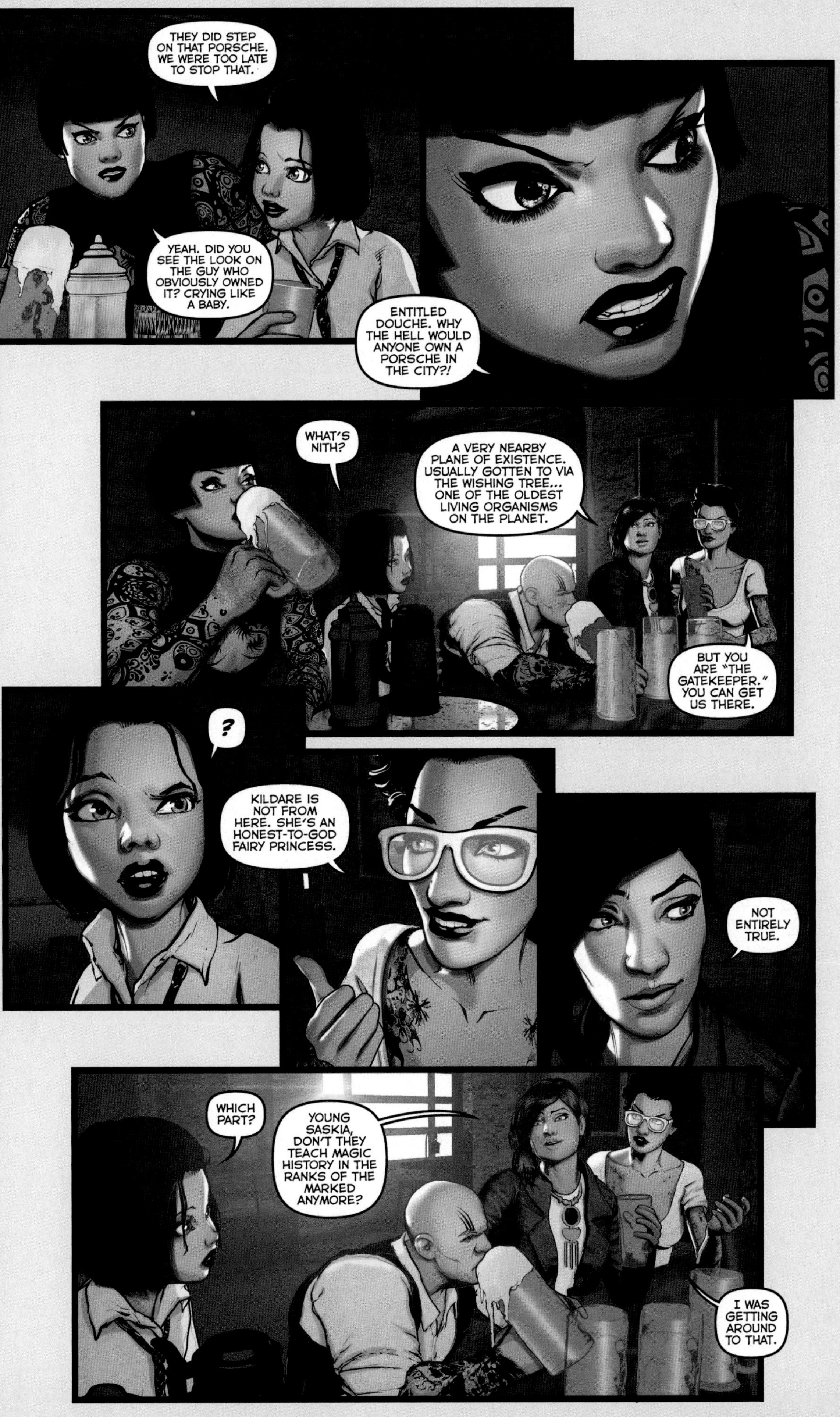
THEY DID STEP ON THAT PORSCHE. WE WERE TOO LATE TO STOP THAT.
YEAH. DID YOU SEE THE LOOK ON THE GUY WHO OBVIOUSLY OWNED IT? CRYING LIKE A BABY.
ENTITLED DOUCHE. WHY THE HELL WOULD ANYONE OWN A PORSCHE IN THE CITY?!
WHAT'S NITH?
A VERY NEARBY PLANE OF EXISTENCE. USUALLY GOTTEN TO VIA THE WISHING TREE... ONE OF THE OLDEST LIVING ORGANISMS ON THE PLANET.
BUT YOU ARE "THE GATEKEEPER." YOU CAN GET US THERE.
?
KILDARE IS NOT FROM HERE. SHE'S AN HONEST-TO-GOD FAIRY PRINCESS.
NOT ENTIRELY TRUE.
WHICH PART?
YOUNG SASKIA, DON'T THEY TEACH MAGIC HISTORY IN THE RANKS OF THE MARKED ANYMORE?
I WAS GETTING AROUND TO THAT.

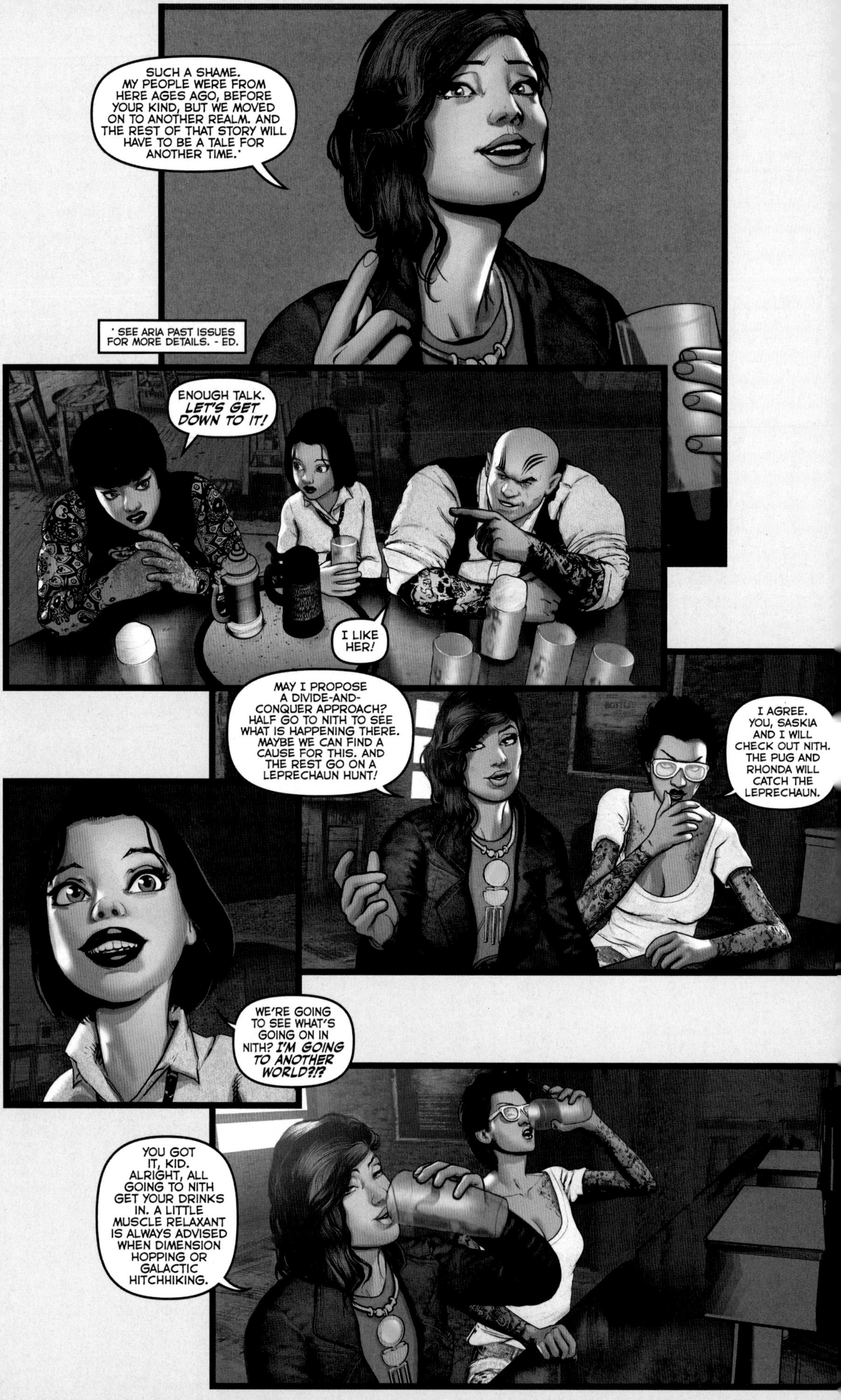
SUCH A SHAME. MY PEOPLE WERE FROM HERE AGES AGO, BEFORE YOUR KIND, BUT WE MOVED ON TO ANOTHER REALM. AND THE REST OF THAT STORY WILL HAVE TO BE A TALE FOR ANOTHER TIME.*
* SEE ARIA PAST ISSUES FOR MORE DETAILS. - ED.
ENOUGH TALK. LET'S GET DOWN TO IT!
I LIKE HER!
MAY I PROPOSE A DIVIDE-AND-CONQUER APPROACH? HALF GO TO NITH TO SEE WHAT IS HAPPENING THERE. MAYBE WE CAN FIND A CAUSE FOR THIS. AND THE REST GO ON A LEPRECHAUN HUNT!
I AGREE. YOU, SASKIA AND I WILL CHECK OUT NITH. THE PUG AND RHONDA WILL CATCH THE LEPRECHAUN.
WE'RE GOING TO SEE WHAT'S GOING ON IN NITH? I'M GOING TO ANOTHER WORLD?!?
YOU GOT IT, KID. ALRIGHT, ALL GOING TO NITH GET YOUR DRINKS IN. A LITTLE MUSCLE RELAXANT IS ALWAYS ADVISED WHEN DIMENSION HOPPING OR GALACTIC HITCHHIKING.

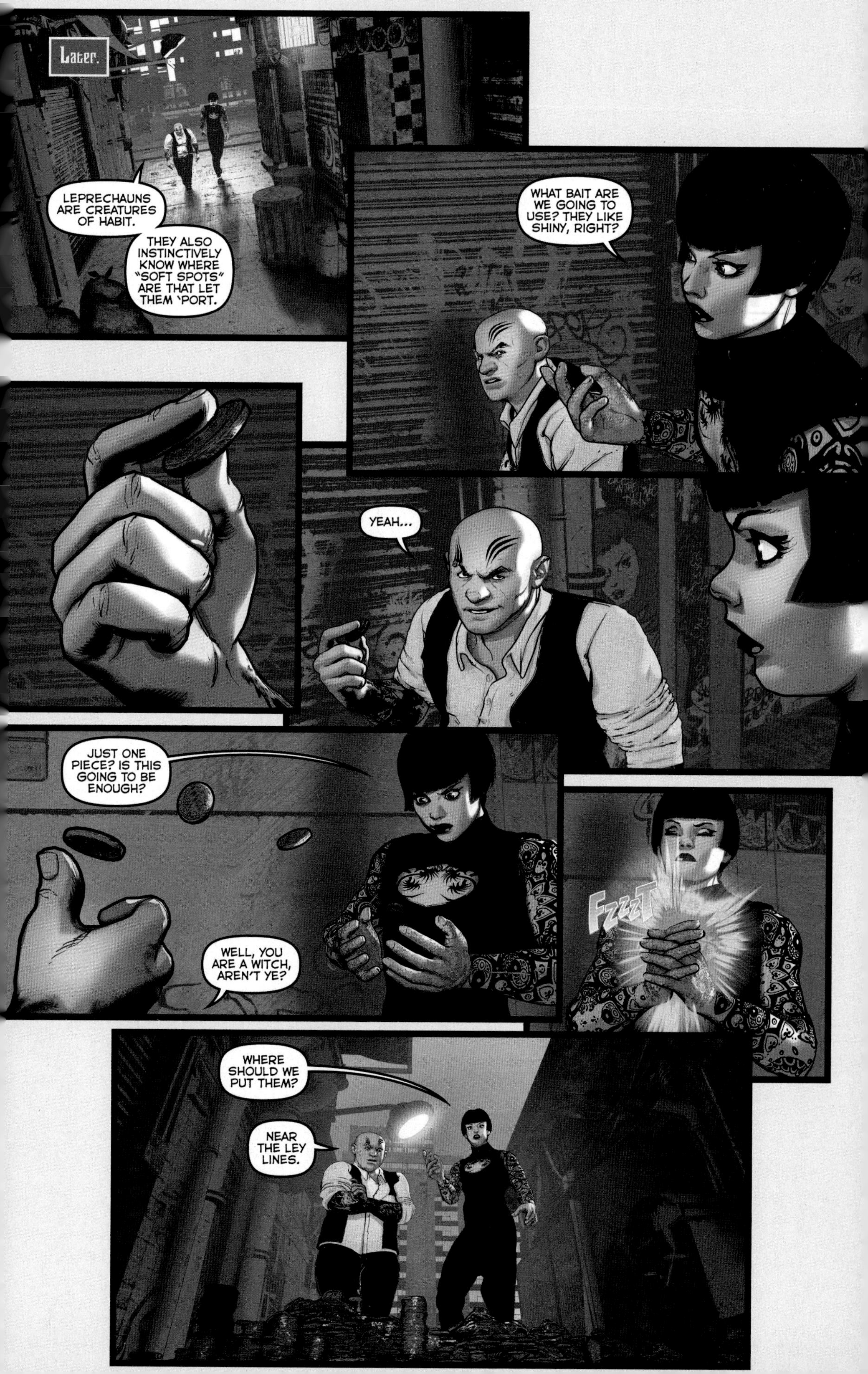
Later.
LEPRECHAUNS ARE CREATURES OF HABIT.
THEY ALSO INSTINCTIVELY KNOW WHERE "SOFT SPOTS" ARE THAT LET THEM 'PORT.
WHAT BAIT ARE WE GOING TO USE? THEY LIKE SHINY, RIGHT?
YEAH...
JUST ONE PIECE? IS THIS GOING TO BE ENOUGH?
WELL, YOU ARE A WITCH, AREN'T YE?
FZZZT
WHERE SHOULD WE PUT THEM?
NEAR THE LEY LINES.

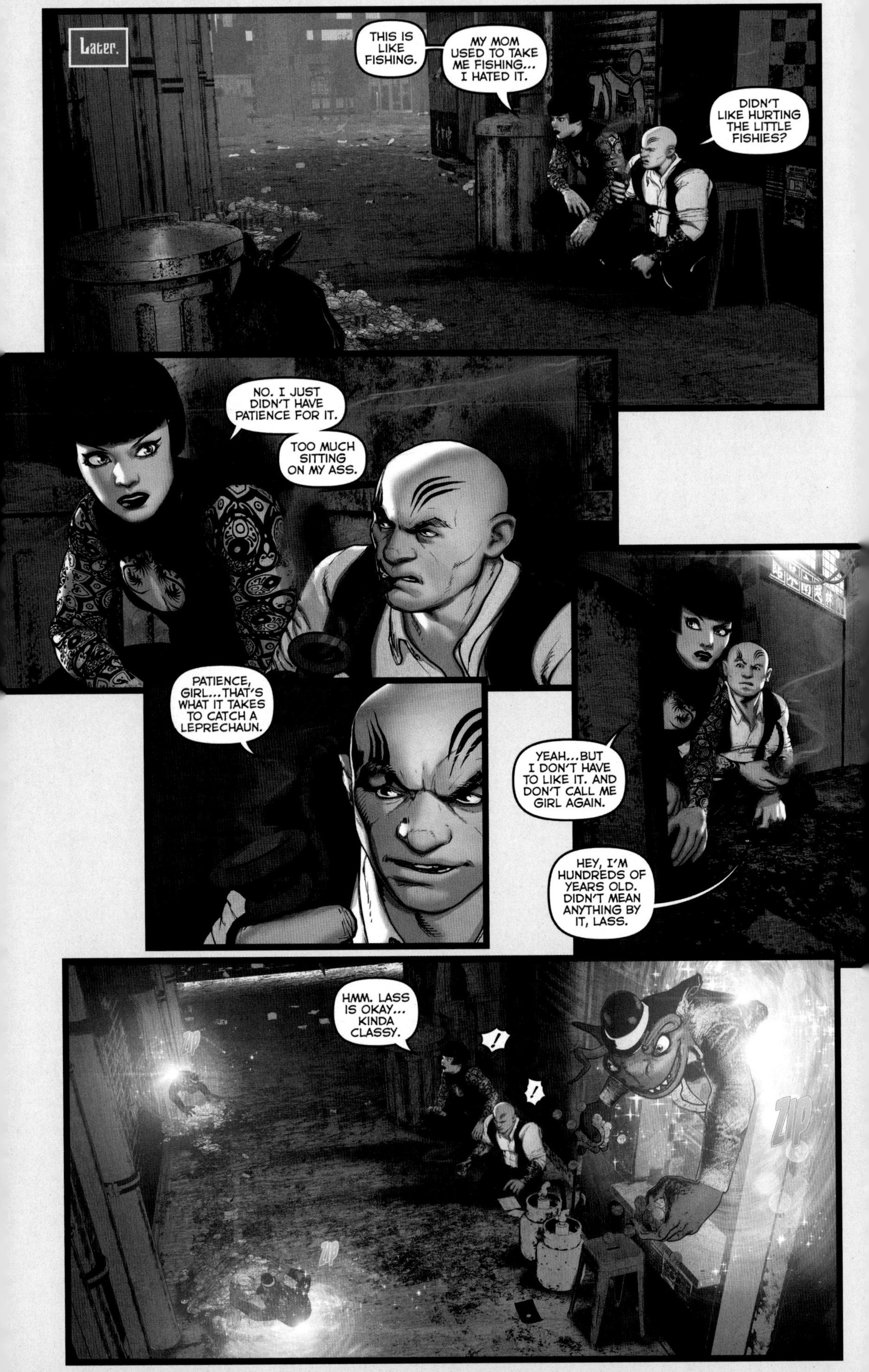
Later.
THIS IS LIKE FISHING.
MY MOM USED TO TAKE ME FISHING... I HATED IT.
DIDN'T LIKE HURTING THE LITTLE FISHIES?
NO. I JUST DIDN'T HAVE PATIENCE FOR IT.
TOO MUCH SITTING ON MY ASS.
PATIENCE, GIRL...THAT'S WHAT IT TAKES TO CATCH A LEPRECHAUN.
YEAH...BUT I DON'T HAVE TO LIKE IT. AND DON'T CALL ME GIRL AGAIN.
HEY, I'M HUNDREDS OF YEARS OLD. DIDN'T MEAN ANYTHING BY IT, LASS.
HMM. LASS IS OKAY... KINDA CLASSY.
!
!
ZIP
ZIP
ZIP

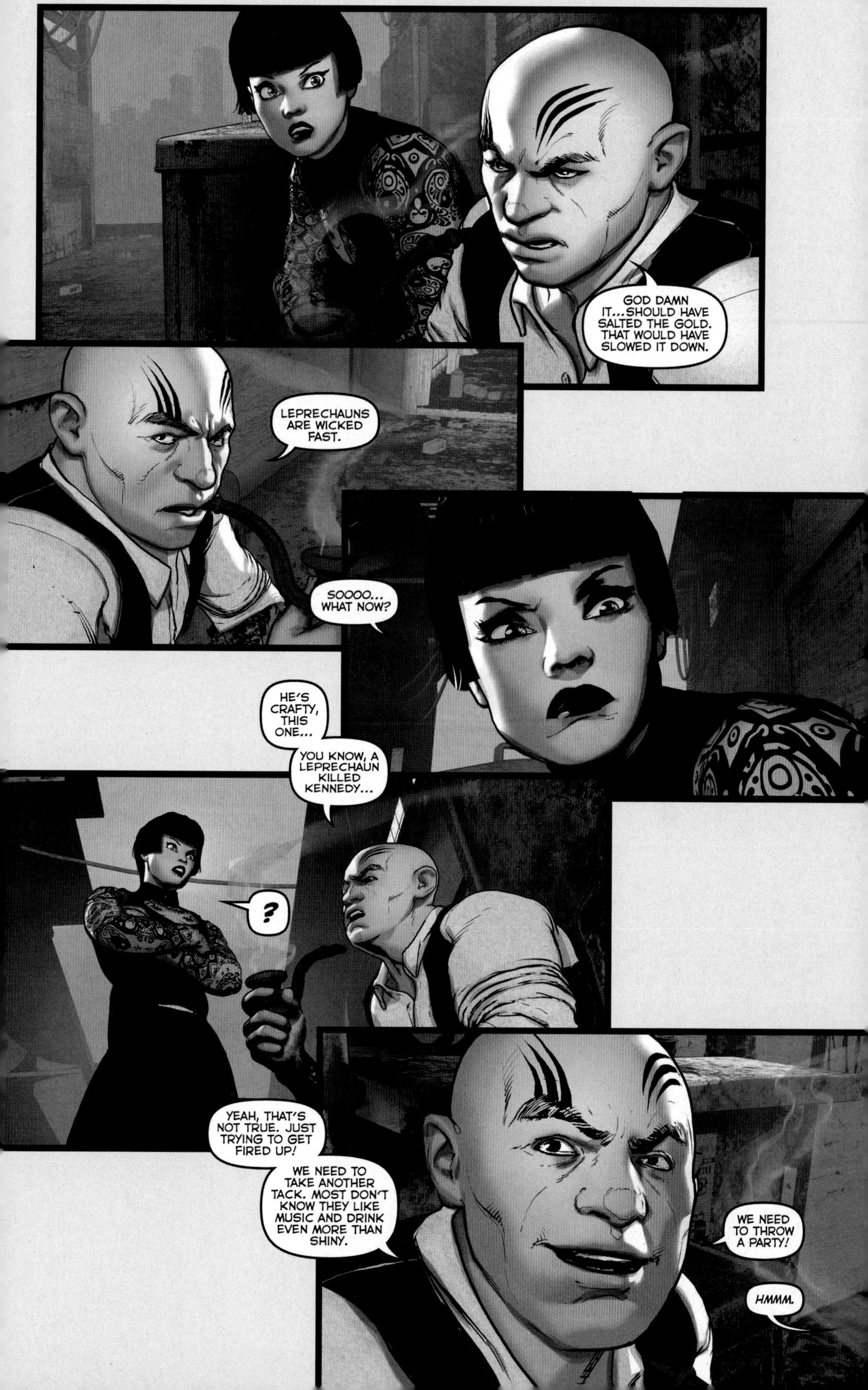
GOD DAMN IT... SHOULD HAVE SALTED THE GOLD. THAT WOULD HAVE SLOWED IT DOWN.
LEPRECHAUNS ARE WICKED FAST.
SOOOO... WHAT NOW?
HE'S CRAFTY, THIS ONE...
YOU KNOW, A LEPRECHAUN KILLED KENNEDY...
?
YEAH, THAT'S NOT TRUE. JUST TRYING TO GET FIRED UP!
WE NEED TO TAKE ANOTHER TACK. MOST DON'T KNOW THEY LIKE MUSIC AND DRINK EVEN MORE THAN SHINY.
WE NEED TO THROW A PARTY!
HMMM.

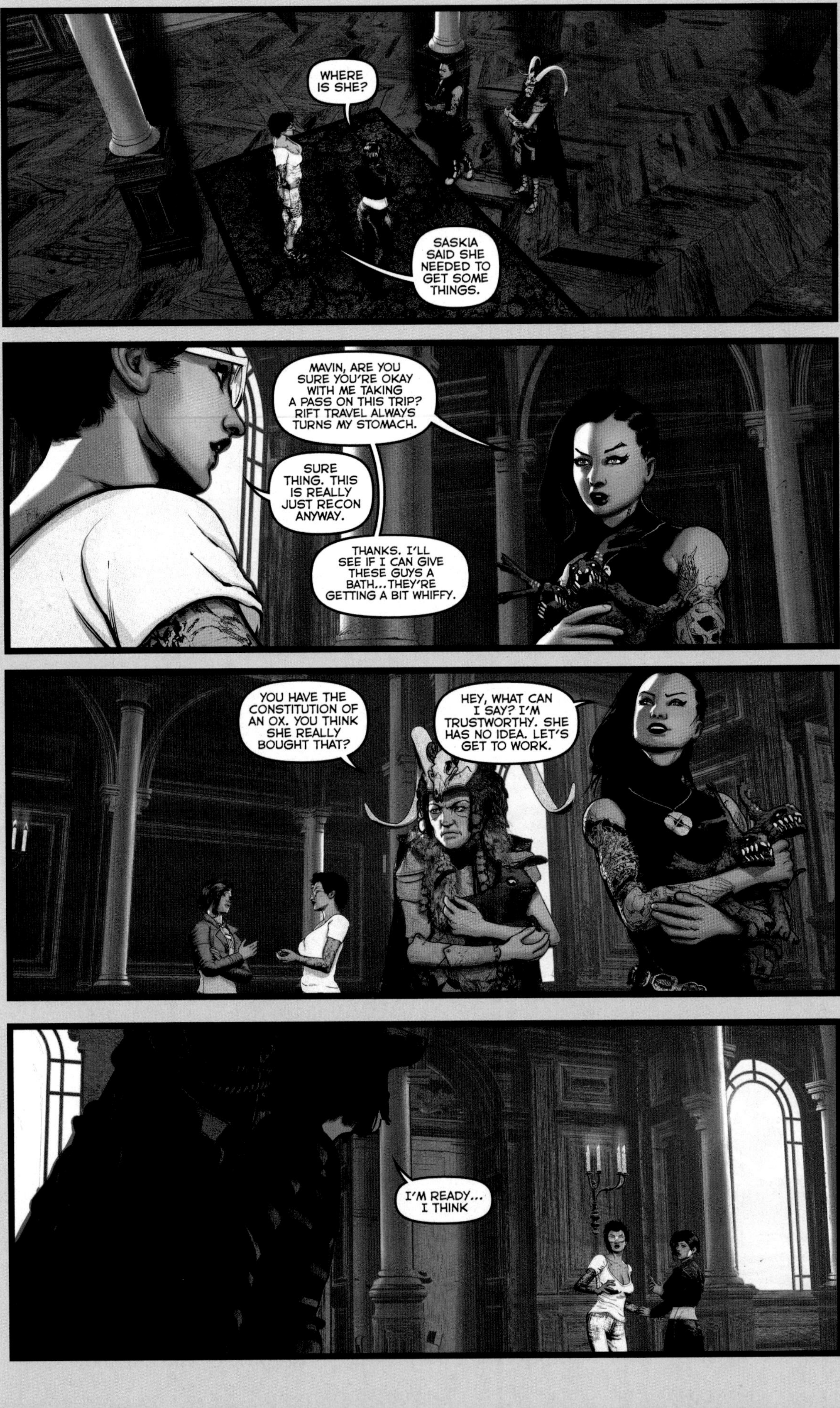
WHERE IS SHE?
SASKIA SAID SHE NEEDED TO GET SOME THINGS.
MAVIN, ARE YOU SURE YOU'RE OKAY WITH ME TAKING A PASS ON THIS TRIP? RIFT TRAVEL ALWAYS TURNS MY STOMACH.
SURE THING. THIS IS REALLY JUST RECON ANYWAY.
THANKS. I'LL SEE IF I CAN GIVE THESE GUYS A BATH...THEY'RE GETTING A BIT WHIFFY.
YOU HAVE THE CONSTITUTION OF AN OX. YOU THINK SHE REALLY BOUGHT THAT?
HEY, WHAT CAN I SAY? I'M TRUSTWORTHY. SHE HAS NO IDEA. LET'S GET TO WORK.
I'M READY... I THINK

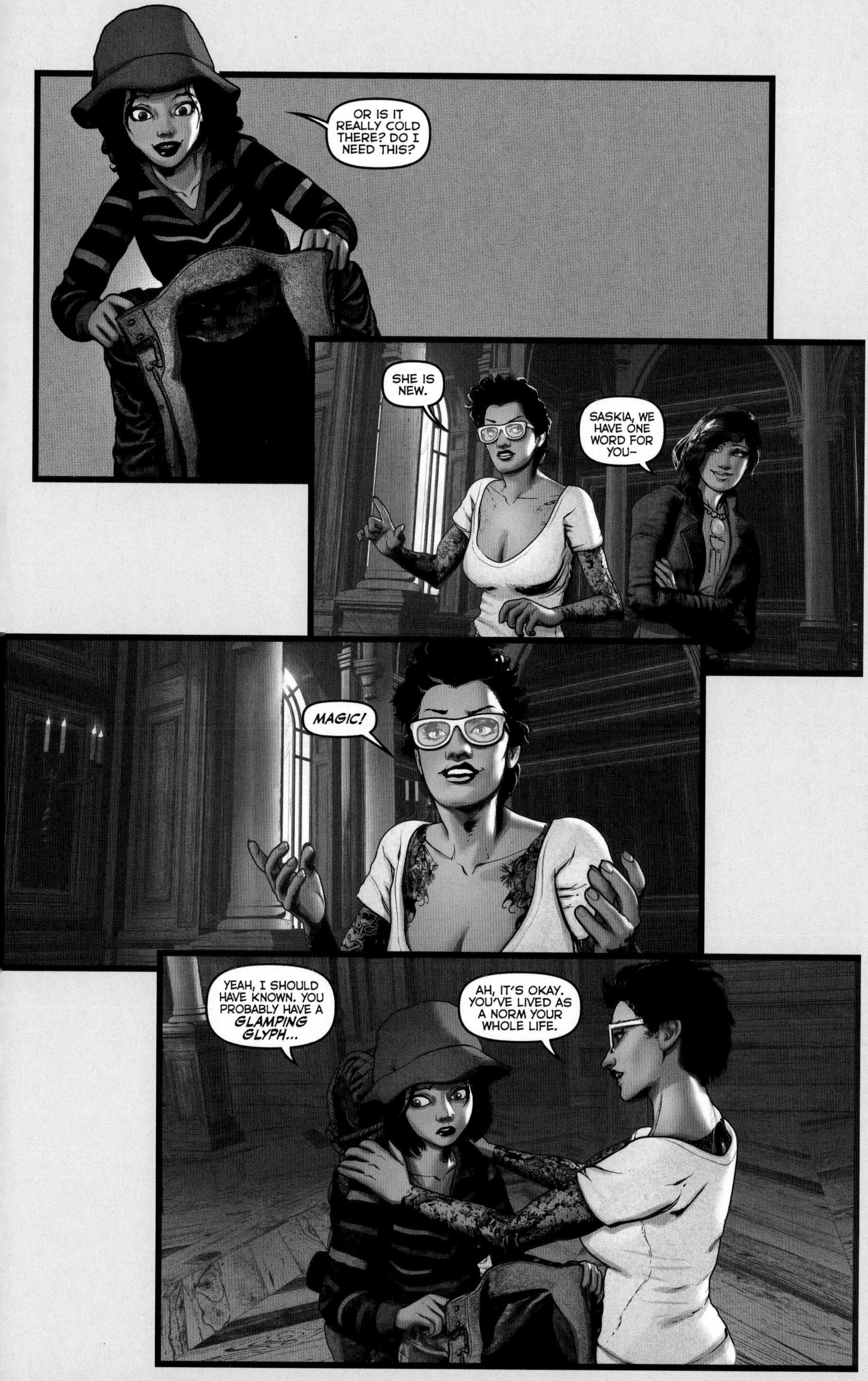
OR IS IT REALLY COLD THERE? DO I NEED THIS?
SHE IS NEW.
SASKIA, WE HAVE ONE WORD FOR YOU–
MAGIC!
YEAH, I SHOULD HAVE KNOWN. YOU PROBABLY HAVE A GLAMPING GLYPH...
AH, IT'S OKAY. YOU'VE LIVED AS A NORM YOUR WHOLE LIFE.

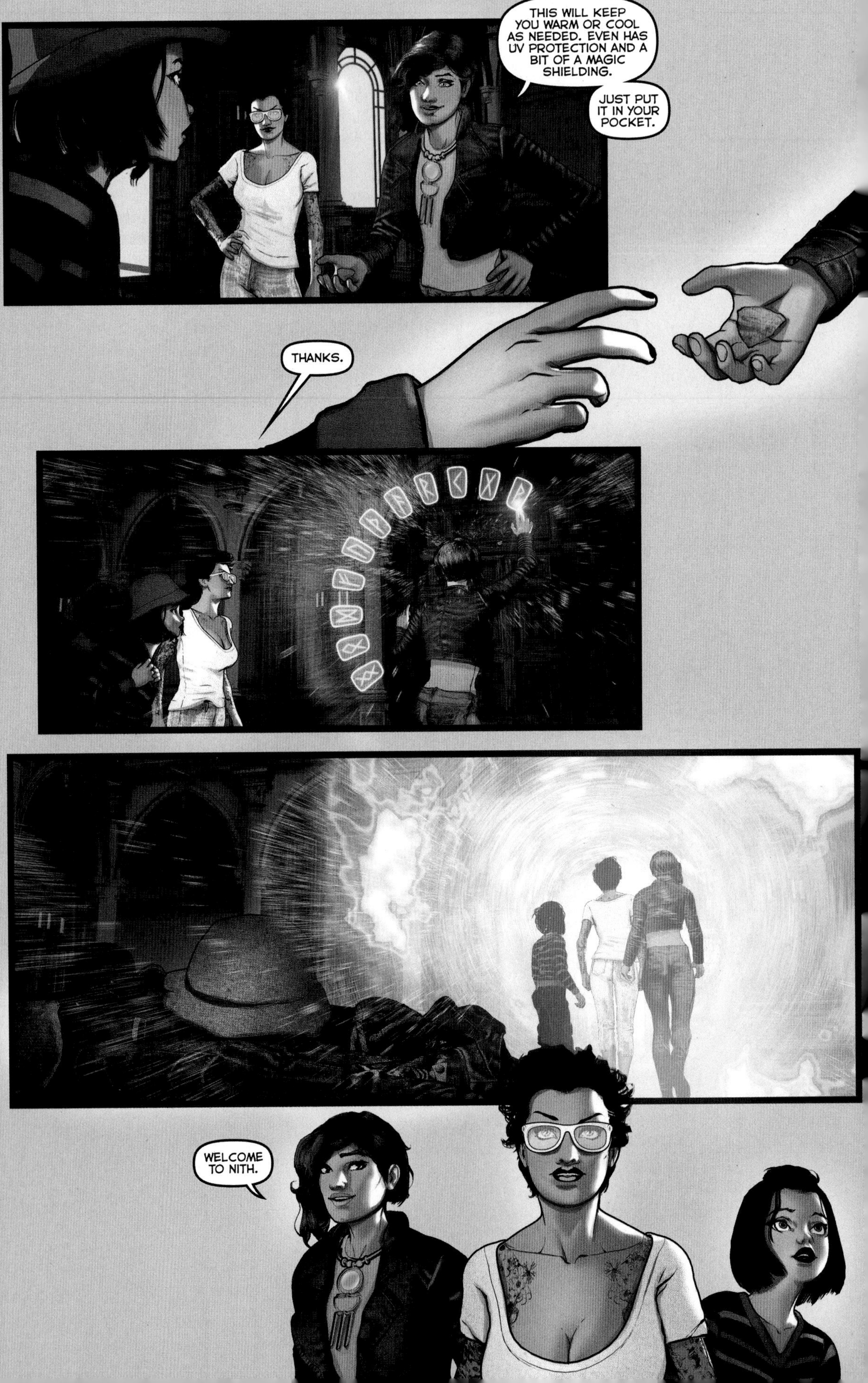
THIS WILL KEEP YOU WARM OR COOL AS NEEDED. EVEN HAS UV PROTECTION AND A BIT OF A MAGIC SHIELDING.
JUST PUT IT IN YOUR POCKET.
THANKS.
WELCOME TO NITH.

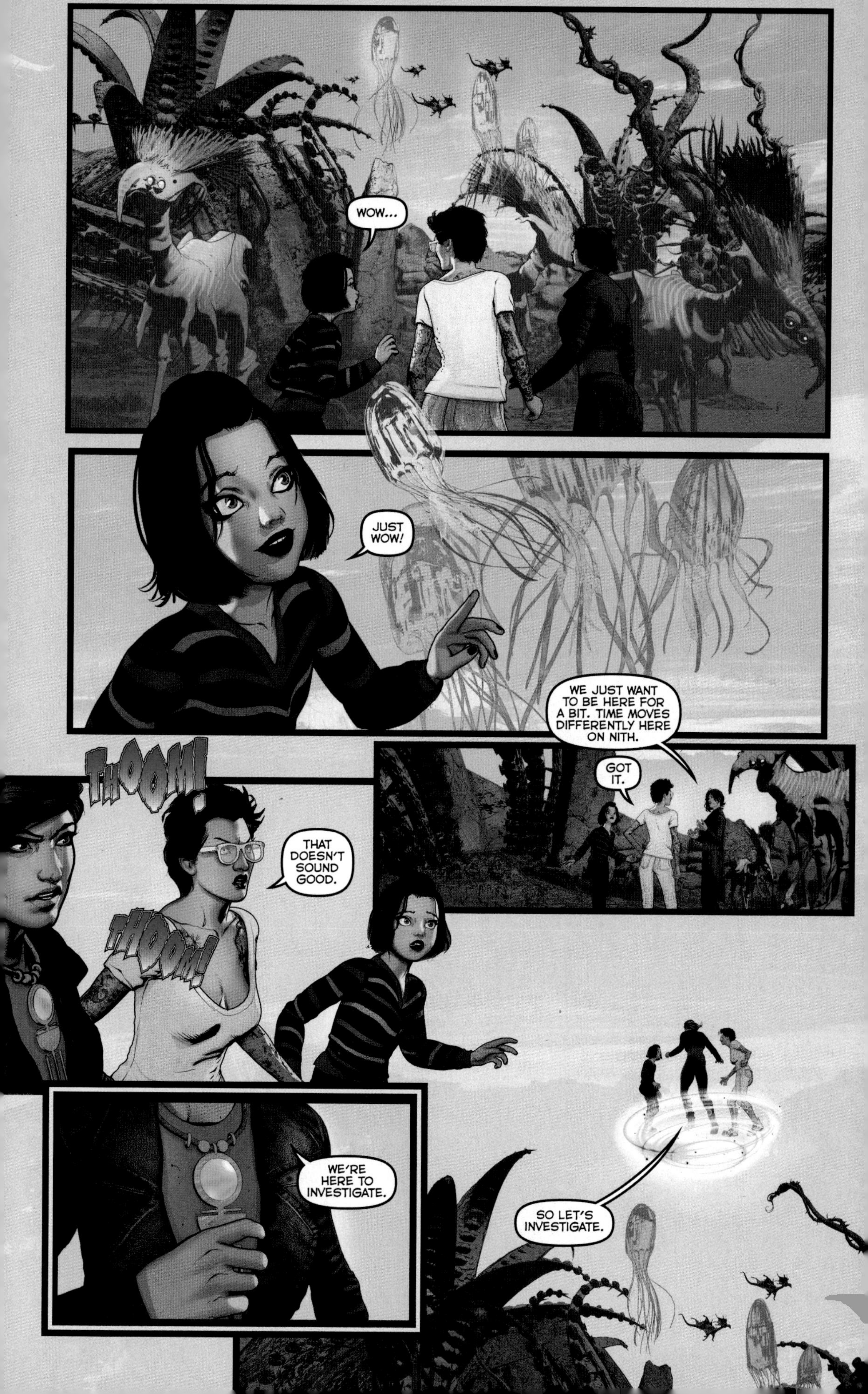
WOW...
JUST WOW!
WE JUST WANT TO BE HERE FOR A BIT. TIME MOVES DIFFERENTLY HERE ON NITH.
GOT IT.
THOOM!
THOOM!
THAT DOESN'T SOUND GOOD.
WE'RE HERE TO INVESTIGATE.
SO LET'S INVESTIGATE.

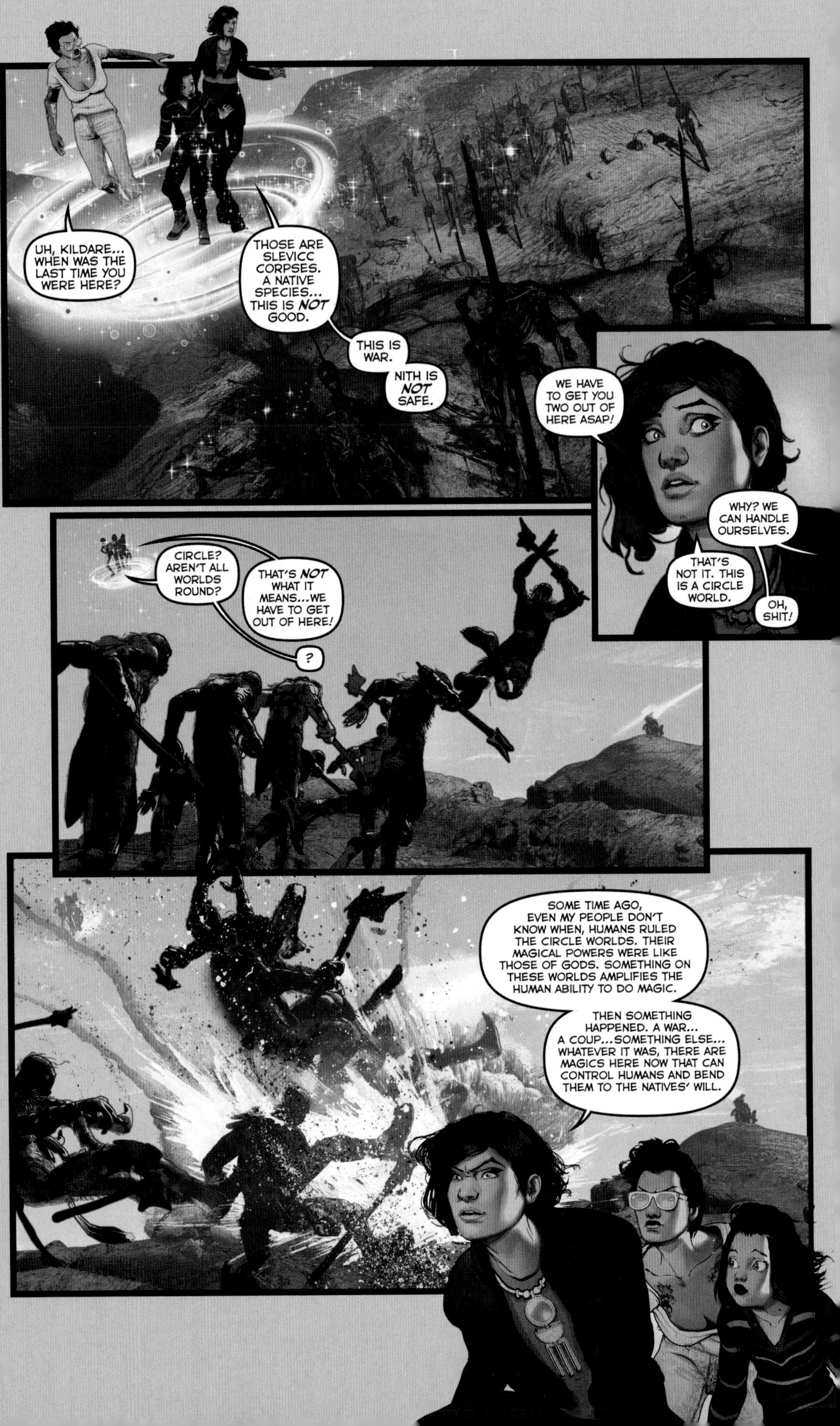
UH, KILDARE... WHEN WAS THE LAST TIME YOU WERE HERE?
THOSE ARE SLEVICC CORPSES. A NATIVE SPECIES... THIS IS *NOT* GOOD.
THIS IS WAR.
NITH IS *NOT* SAFE.
WE HAVE TO GET YOU TWO OUT OF HERE ASAP!
WHY? WE CAN HANDLE OURSELVES.
THAT'S NOT IT. THIS IS A CIRCLE WORLD.
OH, SHIT!
CIRCLE? AREN'T ALL WORLDS ROUND?
THAT'S *NOT* WHAT IT MEANS...WE HAVE TO GET OUT OF HERE!
?
SOME TIME AGO, EVEN MY PEOPLE DON'T KNOW WHEN, HUMANS RULED THE CIRCLE WORLDS. THEIR MAGICAL POWERS WERE LIKE THOSE OF GODS. SOMETHING ON THESE WORLDS AMPLIFIES THE HUMAN ABILITY TO DO MAGIC.
THEN SOMETHING HAPPENED. A WAR... A COUP...SOMETHING ELSE... WHATEVER IT WAS, THERE ARE MAGICS HERE NOW THAT CAN CONTROL HUMANS AND BEND THEM TO THE NATIVES' WILL.

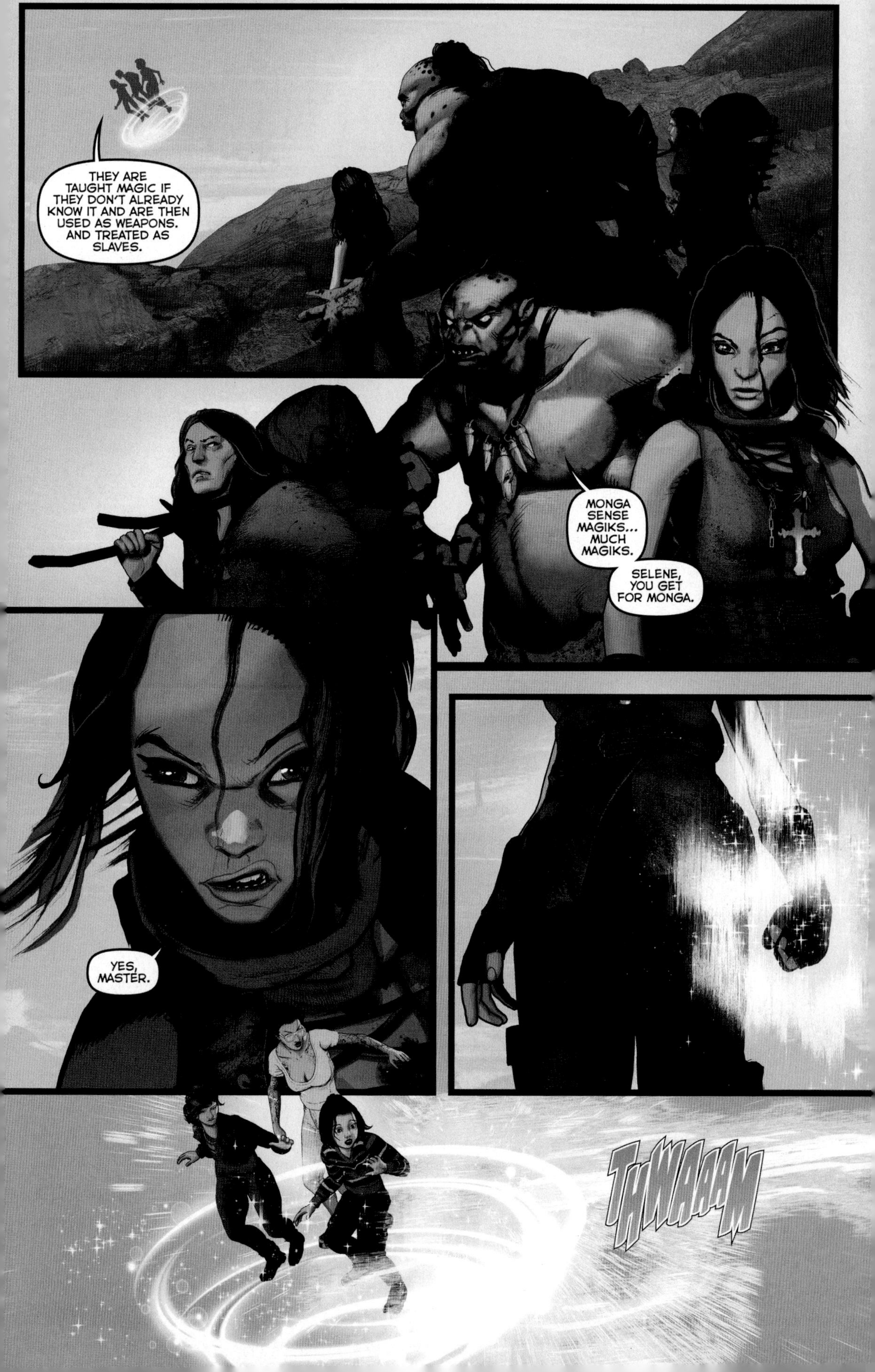
THEY ARE TAUGHT MAGIC IF THEY DON'T ALREADY KNOW IT AND ARE THEN USED AS WEAPONS. AND TREATED AS SLAVES.
MONGA SENSE MAGIKS... MUCH MAGIKS.
SELENE, YOU GET FOR MONGA.
YES, MASTER.
THWAAAM

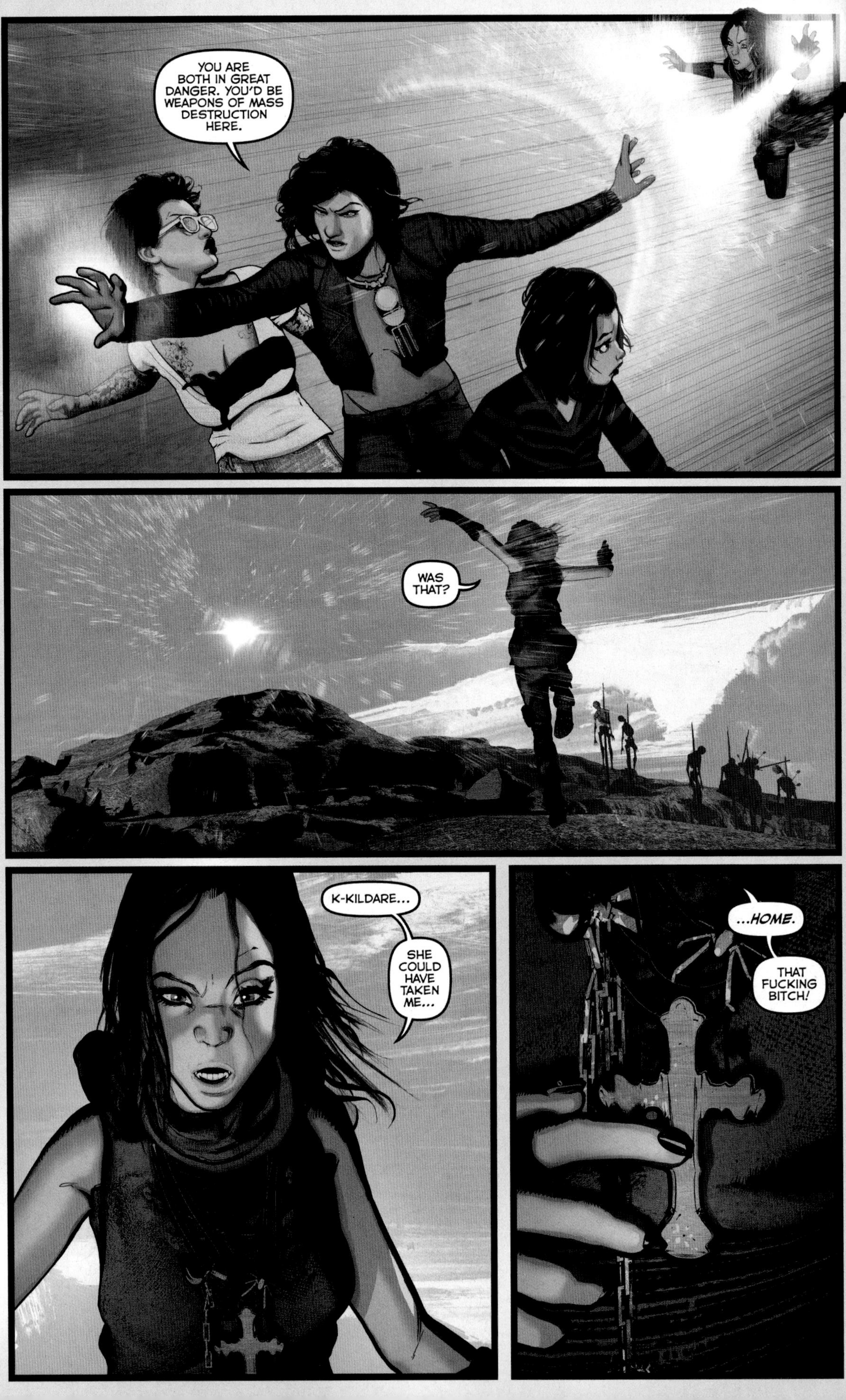

YOU ARE BOTH IN GREAT DANGER. YOU'D BE WEAPONS OF MASS DESTRUCTION HERE.
WAS THAT?
K-KILDARE...
SHE COULD HAVE TAKEN ME...
...HOME.
THAT FUCKING BITCH!

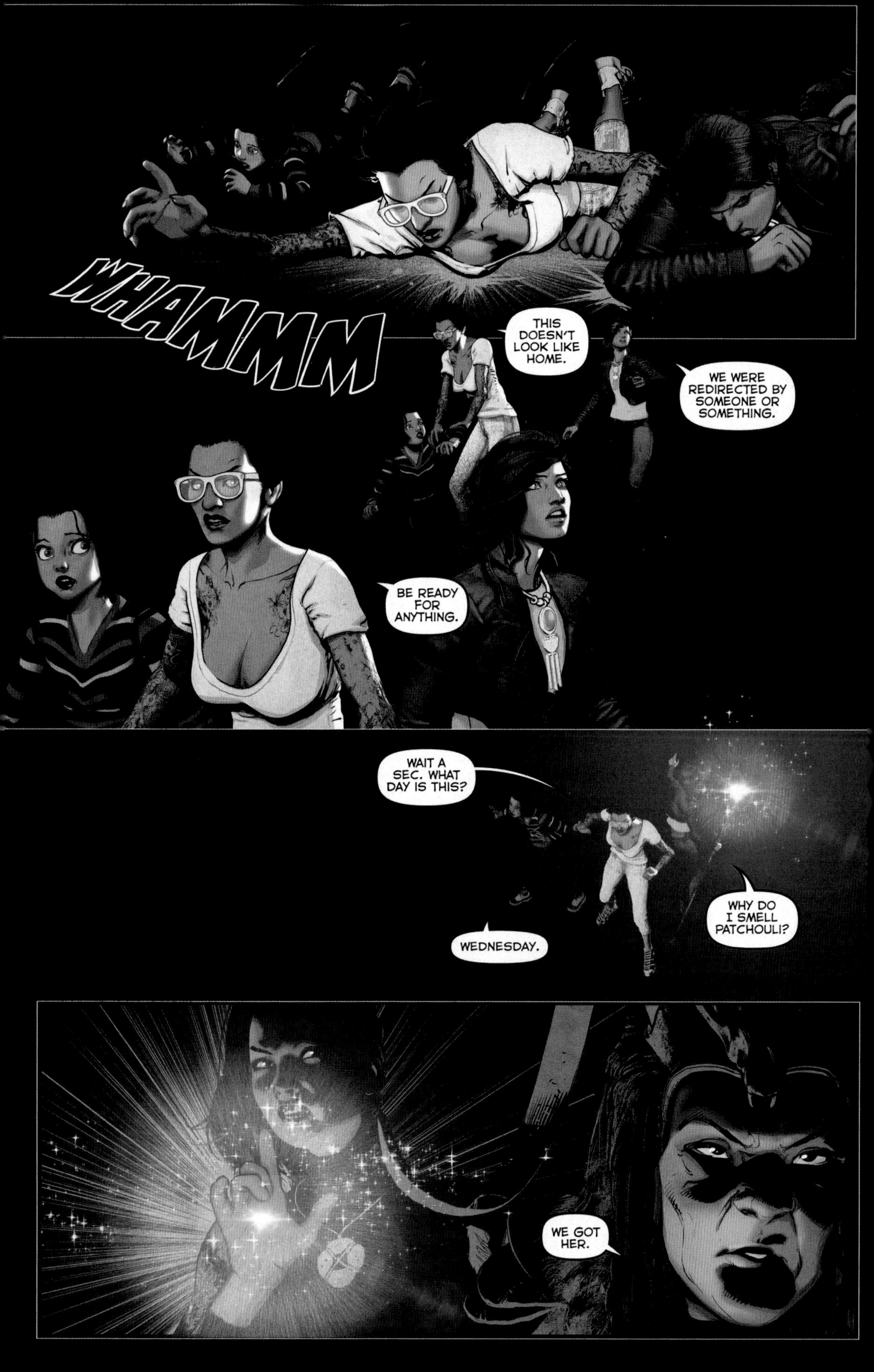
WHAMMM
THIS DOESN'T LOOK LIKE HOME.
WE WERE REDIRECTED BY SOMEONE OR SOMETHING.
BE READY FOR ANYTHING.
WAIT A SEC. WHAT DAY IS THIS?
WEDNESDAY.
WHY DO I SMELL PATCHOULI?
WE GOT HER.

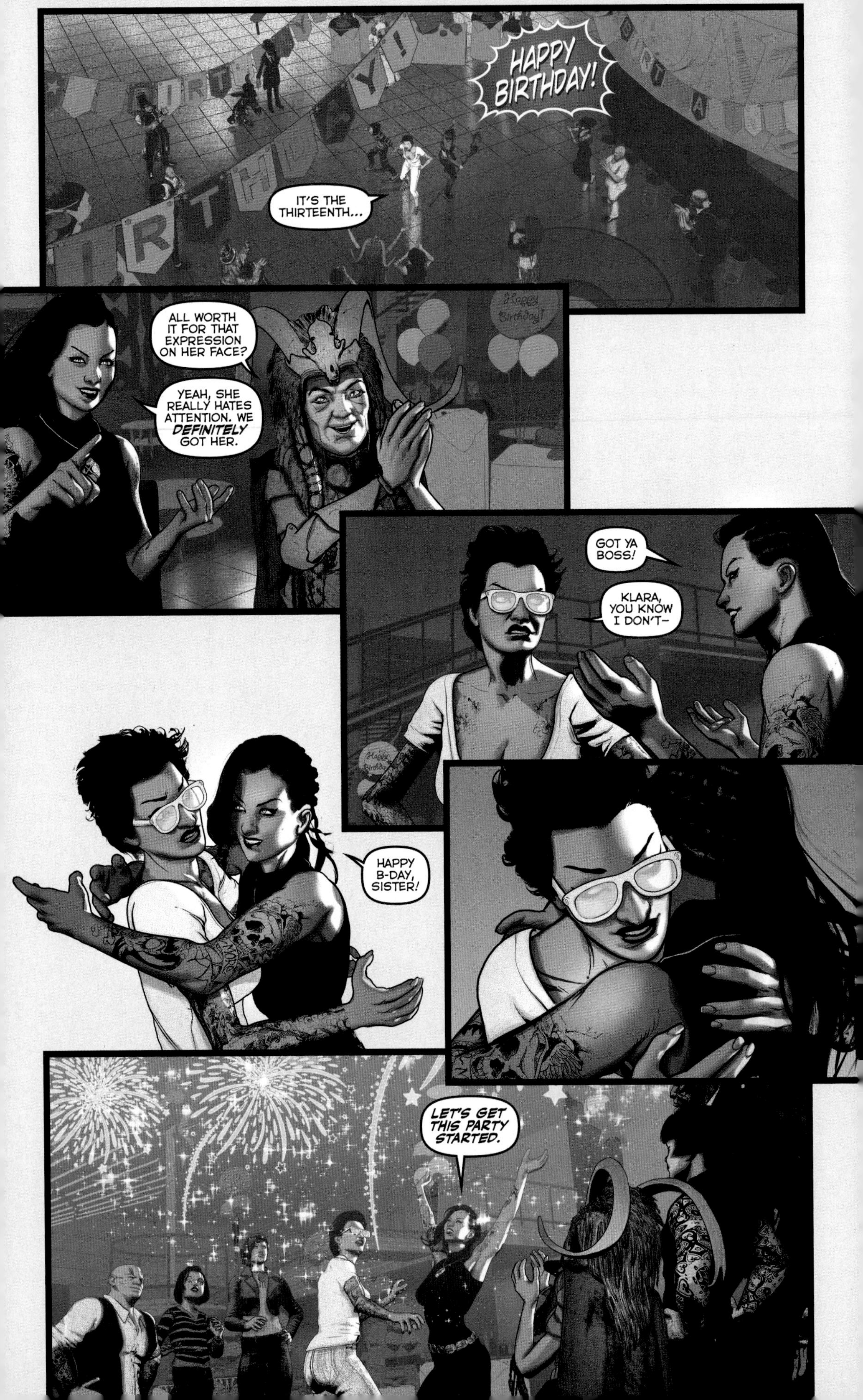
HAPPY BIRTHDAY!
IT'S THE THIRTEENTH...
ALL WORTH IT FOR THAT EXPRESSION ON HER FACE?
YEAH, SHE REALLY HATES ATTENTION. WE *DEFINITELY* GOT HER.
GOT YA BOSS!
KLARA, YOU KNOW I DON'T–
HAPPY B-DAY, SISTER!
LET'S GET THIS PARTY STARTED.

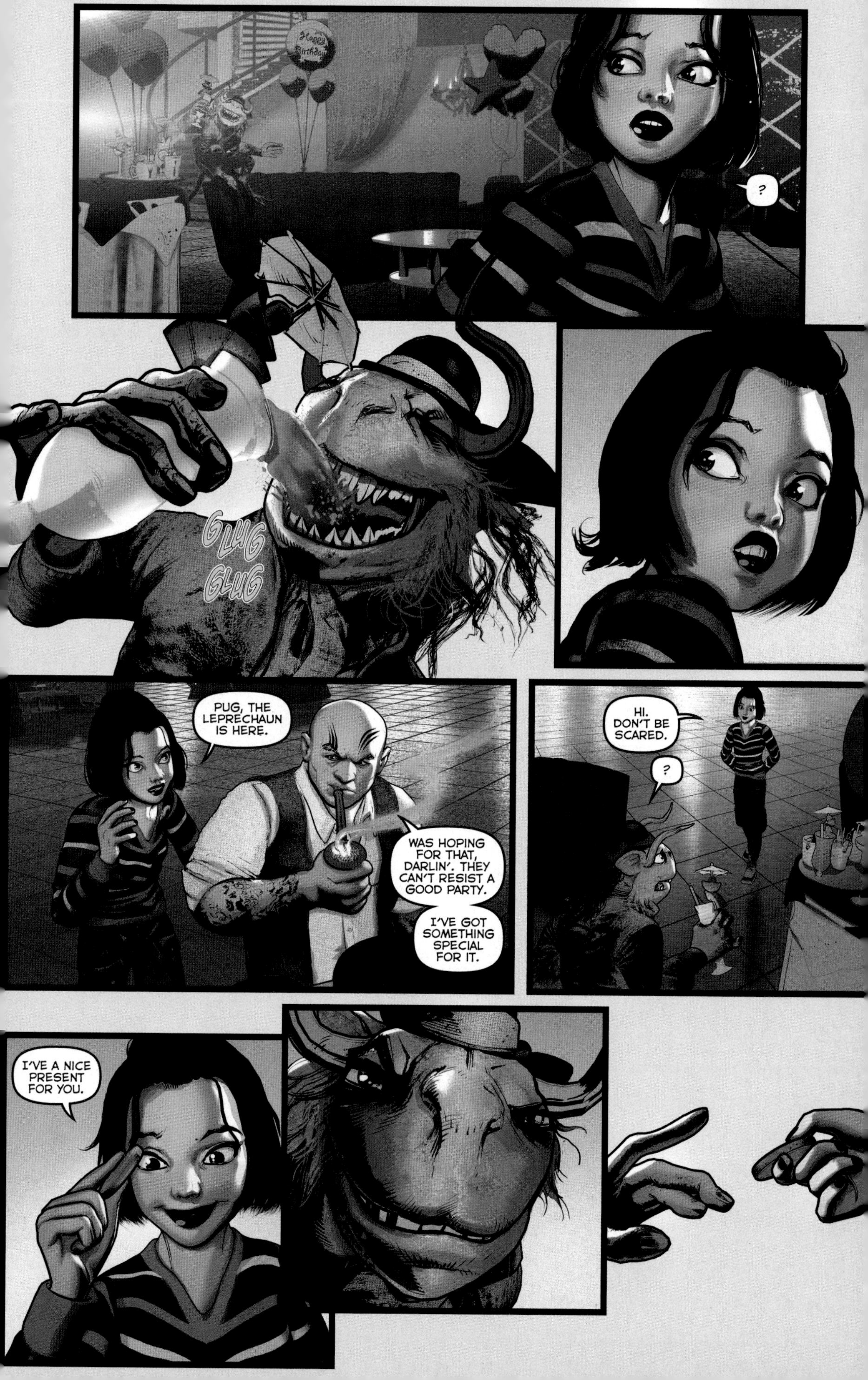
?
GLUG GLUG
PUG, THE LEPRECHAUN IS HERE.
WAS HOPING FOR THAT, DARLIN'. THEY CAN'T RESIST A GOOD PARTY.
I'VE GOT SOMETHING SPECIAL FOR IT.
HI. DON'T BE SCARED.
?
I'VE A NICE PRESENT FOR YOU.

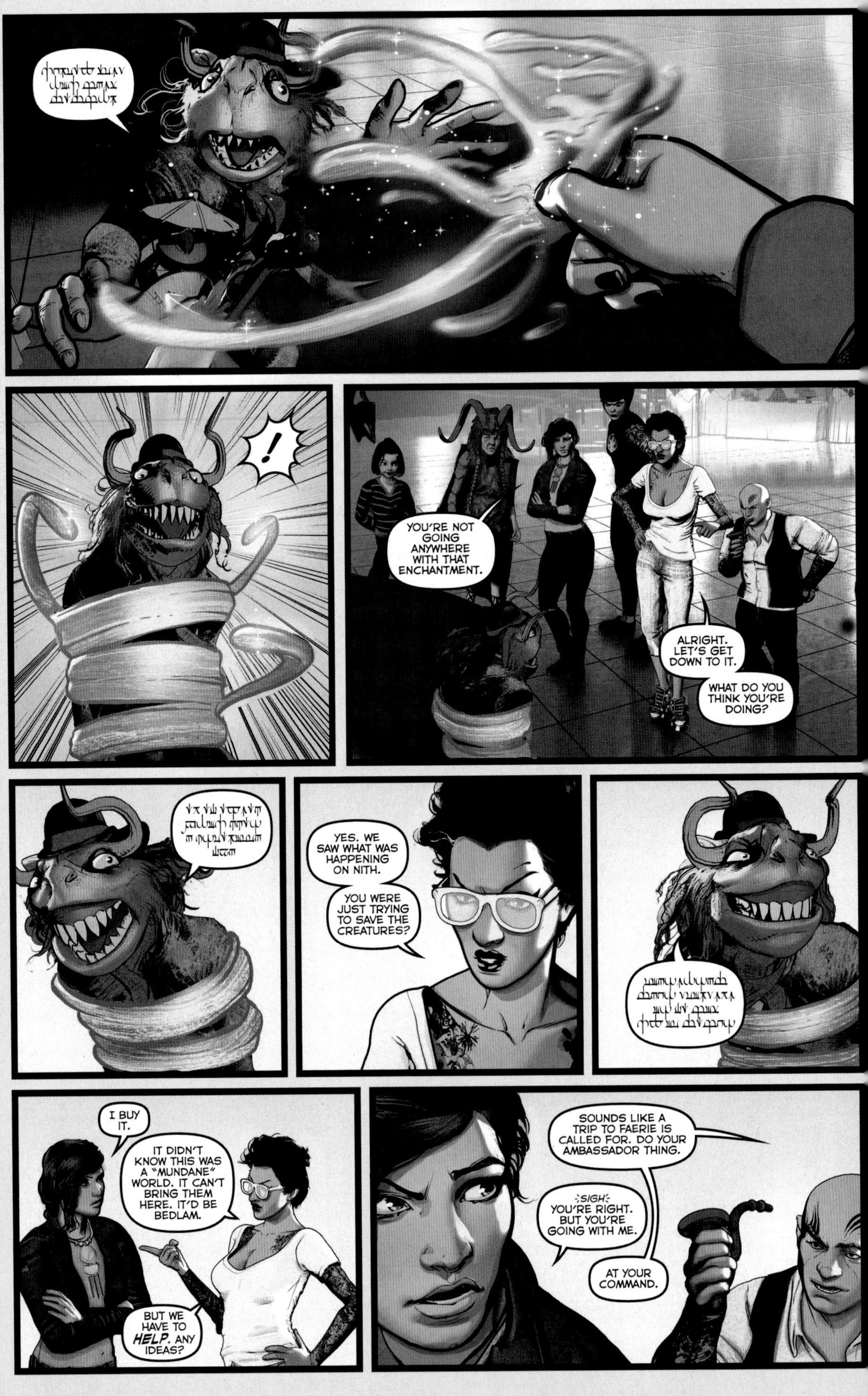
!
YOU'RE NOT GOING ANYWHERE WITH THAT ENCHANTMENT.
ALRIGHT. LET'S GET DOWN TO IT.
WHAT DO YOU THINK YOU'RE DOING?
YES. WE SAW WHAT WAS HAPPENING ON NITH.
YOU WERE JUST TRYING TO SAVE THE CREATURES?
I BUY IT.
IT DIDN'T KNOW THIS WAS A "MUNDANE" WORLD. IT CAN'T BRING THEM HERE. IT'D BE BEDLAM.
BUT WE HAVE TO HELP. ANY IDEAS?
SOUNDS LIKE A TRIP TO FAERIE IS CALLED FOR. DO YOUR AMBASSADOR THING.
SIGH
YOU'RE RIGHT. BUT YOU'RE GOING WITH ME.
AT YOUR COMMAND.

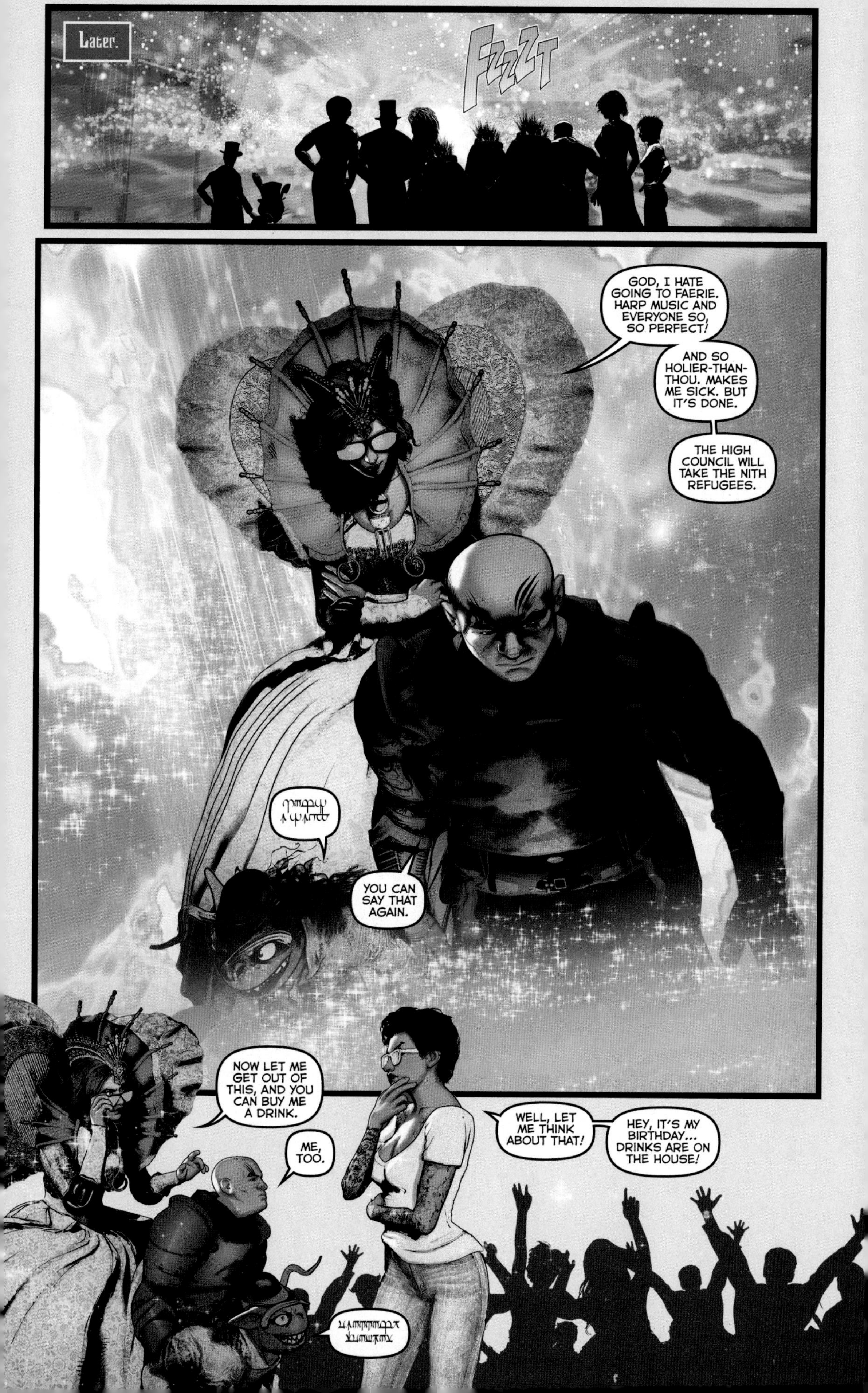
Later.
FZZZT
GOD, I HATE GOING TO FAERIE. HARP MUSIC AND EVERYONE SO, SO PERFECT!
AND SO HOLIER-THAN-THOU. MAKES ME SICK. BUT IT'S DONE.
THE HIGH COUNCIL WILL TAKE THE NITH REFUGEES.
YOU CAN SAY THAT AGAIN.
NOW LET ME GET OUT OF THIS, AND YOU CAN BUY ME A DRINK.
ME, TOO.
WELL, LET ME THINK ABOUT THAT!
HEY, IT'S MY BIRTHDAY... DRINKS ARE ON THE HOUSE!

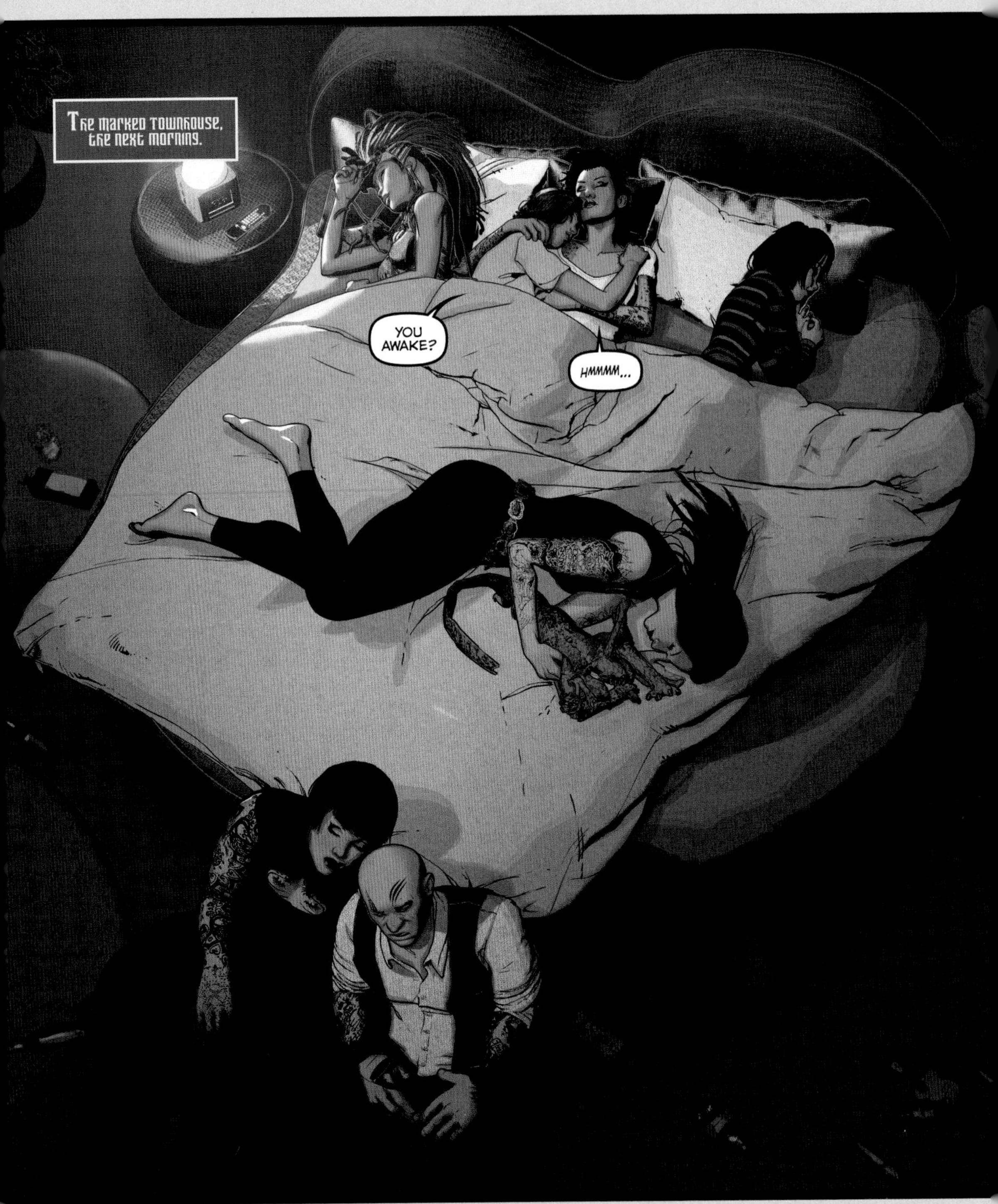
The marked townhouse, the next morning.
YOU AWAKE?
HMMMM...

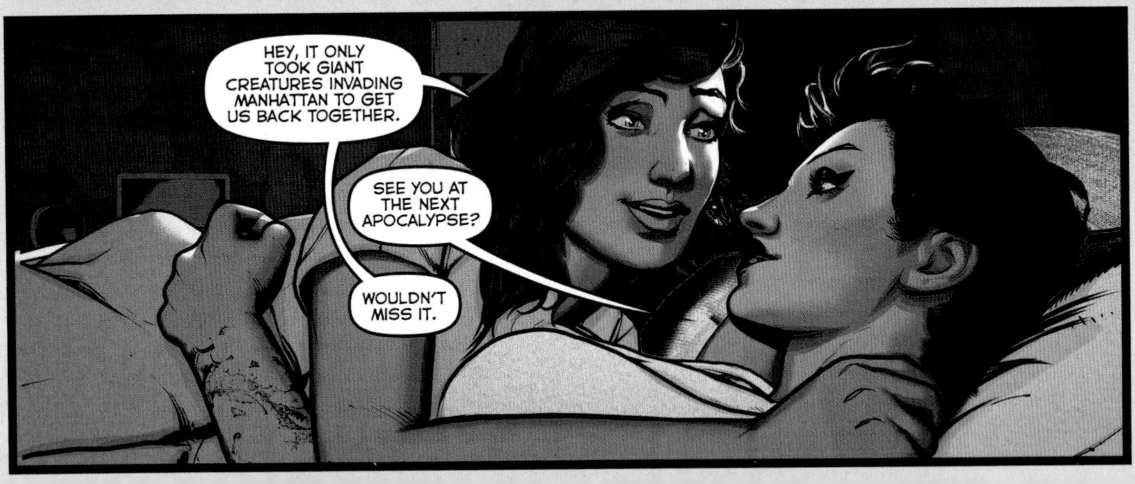
HEY, IT ONLY TOOK GIANT CREATURES INVADING MANHATTAN TO GET US BACK TOGETHER.
SEE YOU AT THE NEXT APOCALYPSE?
WOULDN'T MISS IT.

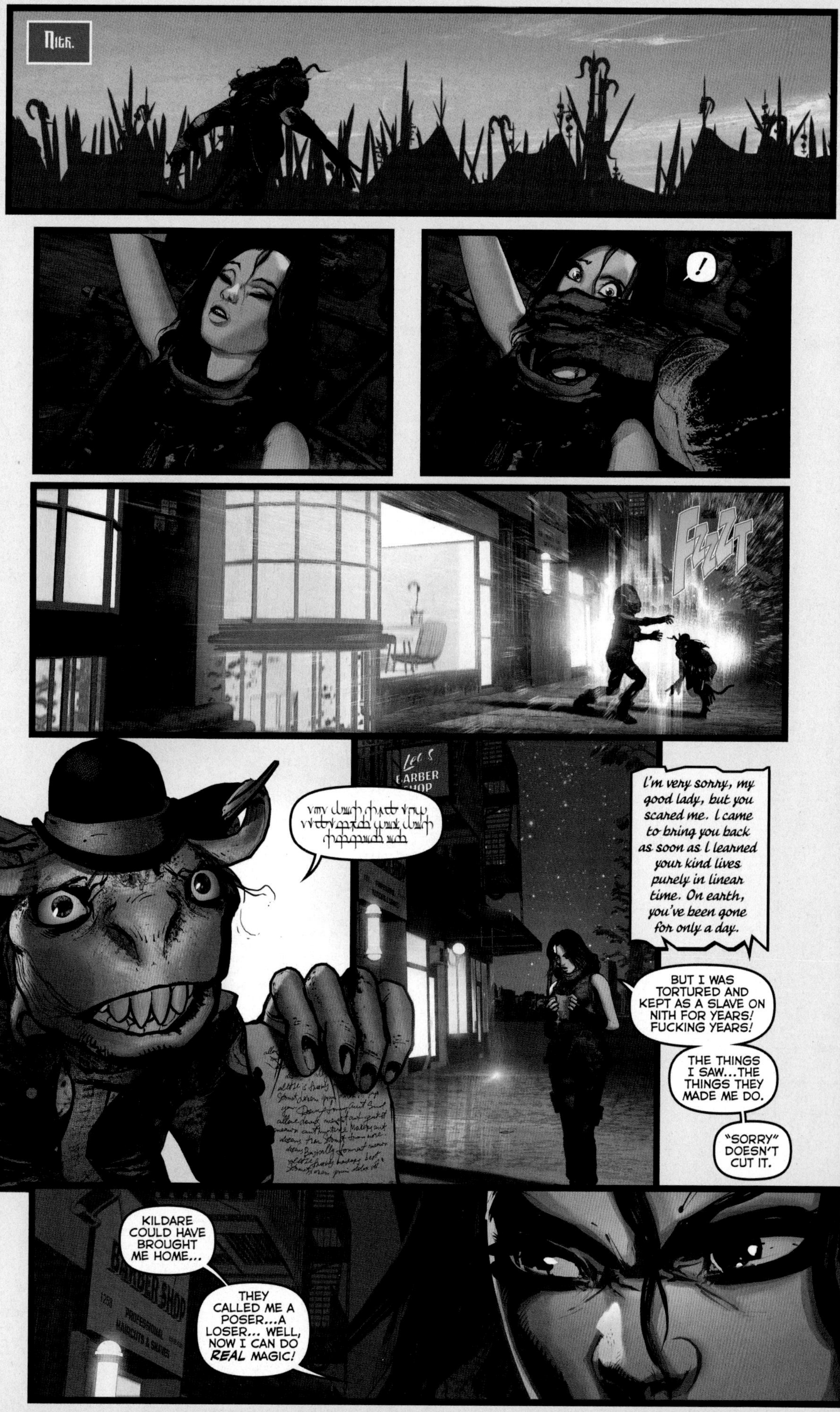
Nith.
!
I'm very sorry, my good lady, but you scared me. I came to bring you back as soon as I learned your kind lives purely in linear time. On earth, you've been gone for only a day.
BUT I WAS TORTURED AND KEPT AS A SLAVE ON NITH FOR YEARS! FUCKING YEARS!
THE THINGS I SAW... THE THINGS THEY MADE ME DO.
"SORRY" DOESN'T CUT IT.
KILDARE COULD HAVE BROUGHT ME HOME...
THEY CALLED ME A POSER... A LOSER... WELL, NOW I CAN DO REAL MAGIC!

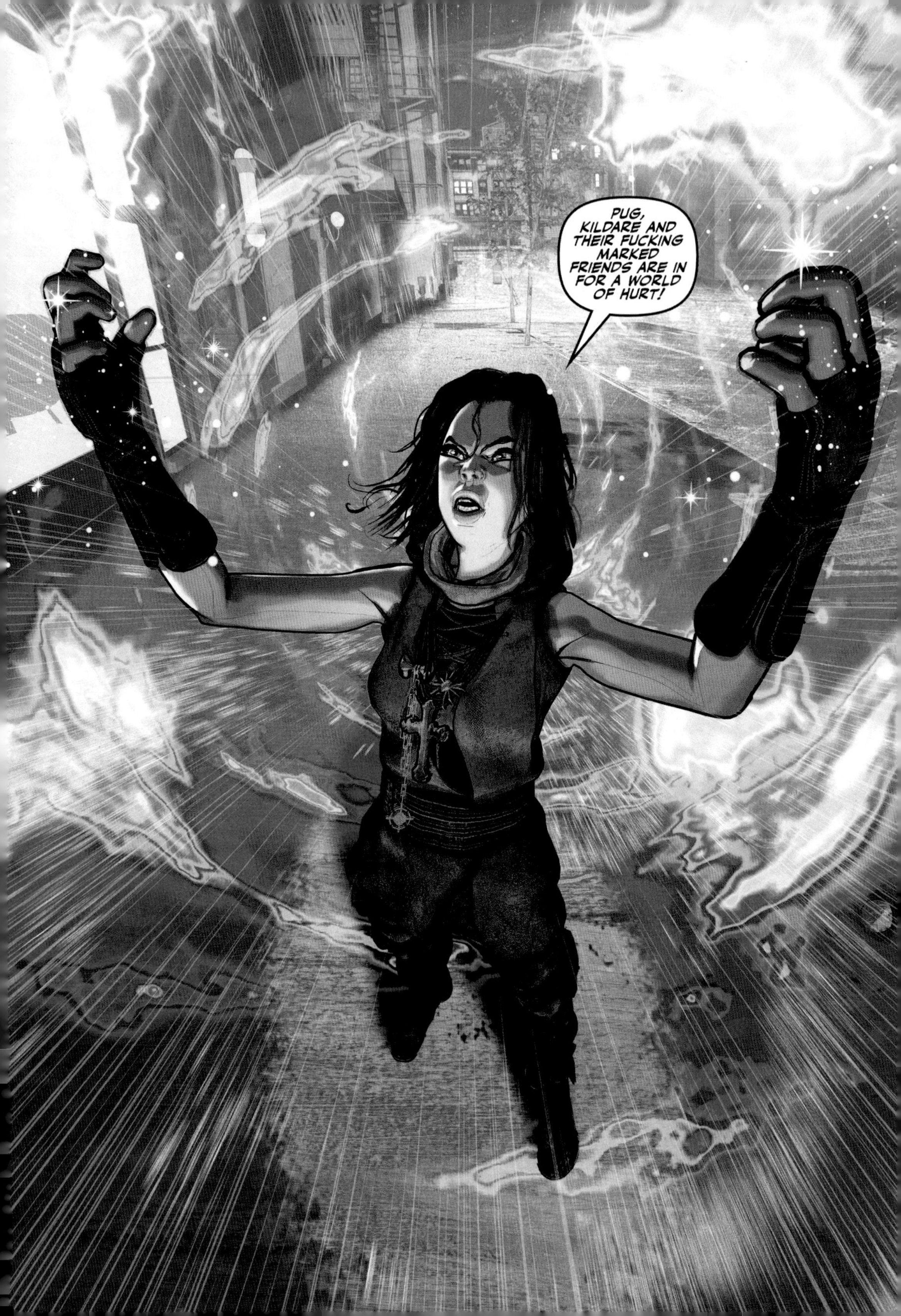
PUG, KILDARE AND THEIR FUCKING MARKED FRIENDS ARE IN FOR A WORLD OF HURT!

CHAPTER TEN

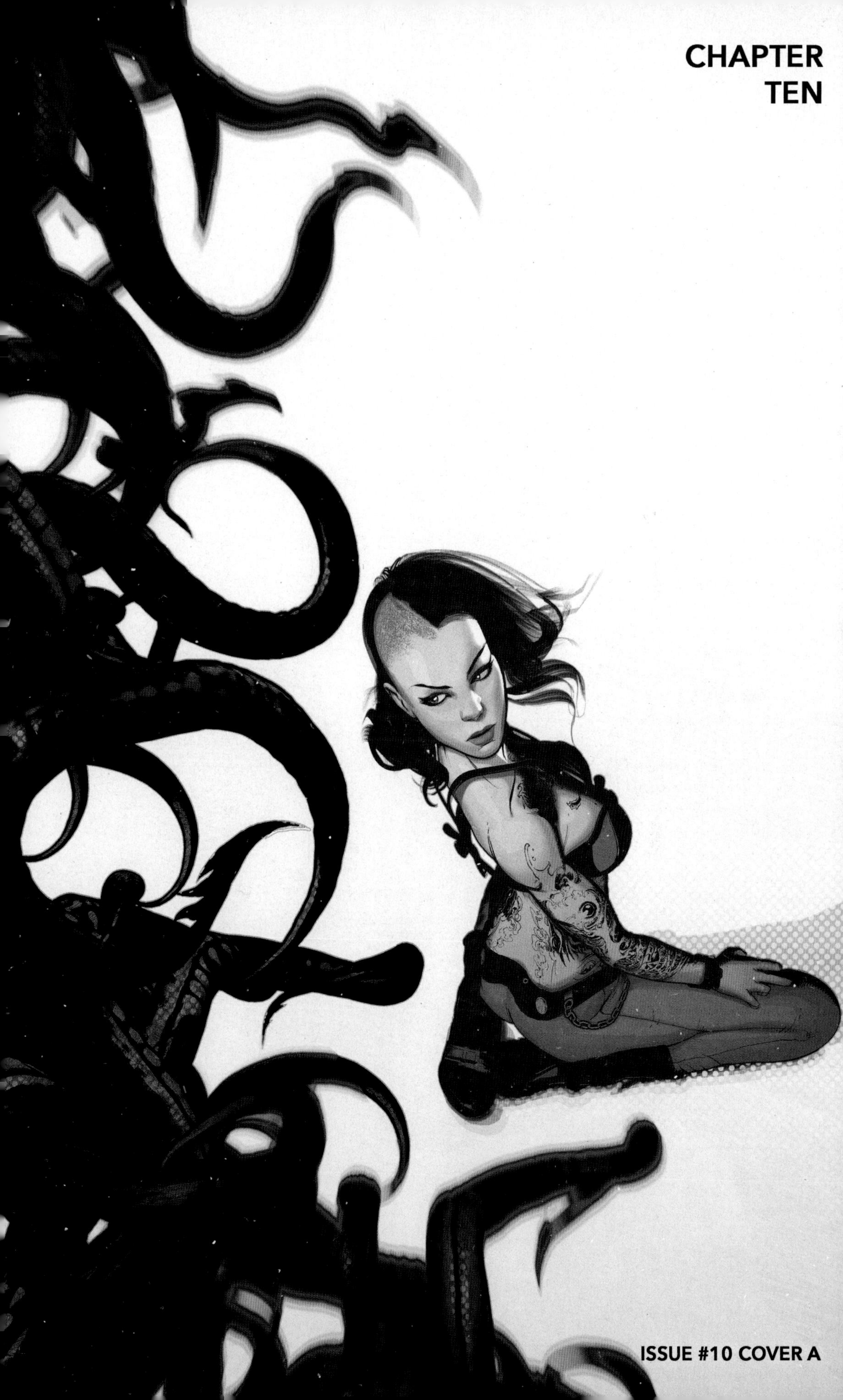

ISSUE #10 COVER A

ISSUE #10 COVER B

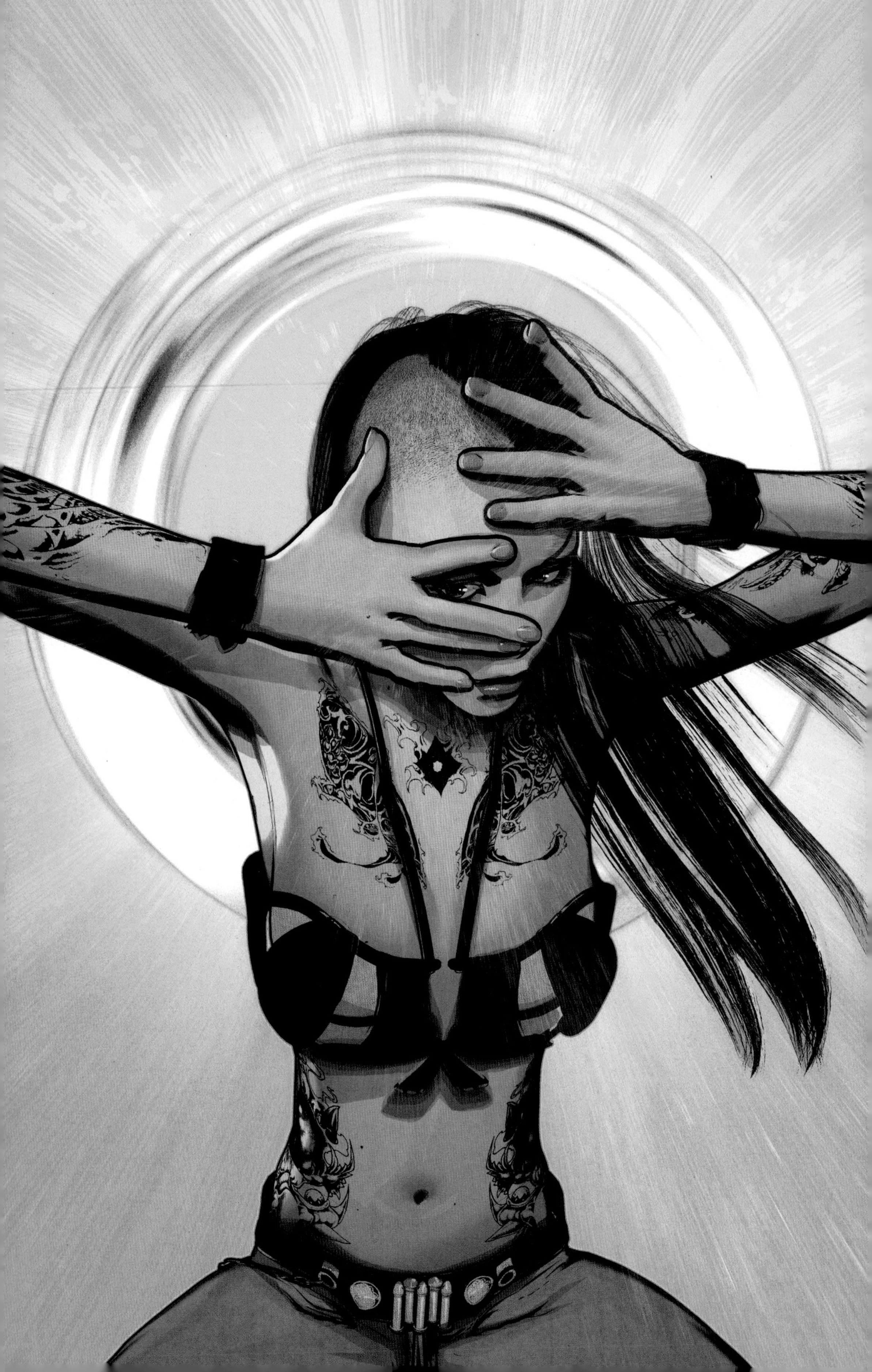

I'LL SHOW THEM.

NO YOU WON'T... YOU RUIN EVERYTHING.

SHUT UP!

Chapter I:
BACK in BLACK

LOST CAT

646-555-2953

Name: CAPTAIN AHAB
MISSING RIGHT EYE. Suffers epileptic seizures. He is not an outdoor cat and we are desperate to find him. Can be lured with cheese bits.
$500 REWARD FOR RETURN

WE'LL START WITH KILDARE'S PRECIOUS LITTLE STORE... LET'S GET RID OF THAT FIRST!

FzzZ444PP!

UMM...?

YOU MIGHT WANT TO WARN HER ABOUT THE *REPULSOR SPELL* ON YOUR STORE, KILDARE.

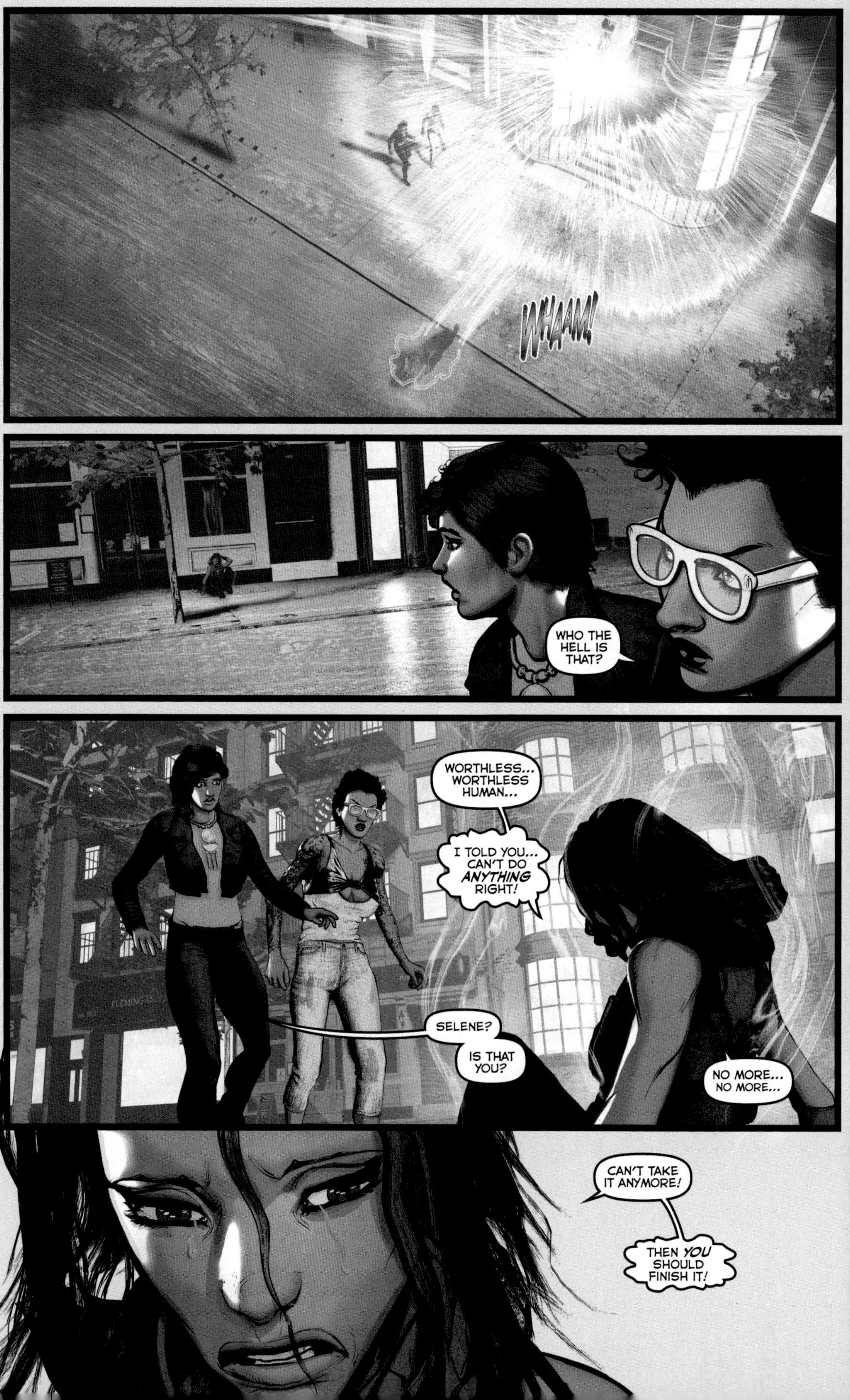
WHAAM!
WHO THE HELL IS THAT?
WORTHLESS... WORTHLESS HUMAN...
I TOLD YOU... CAN'T DO ANYTHING RIGHT!
SELENE?
IS THAT YOU?
NO MORE... NO MORE...
CAN'T TAKE IT ANYMORE!
THEN YOU SHOULD FINISH IT!

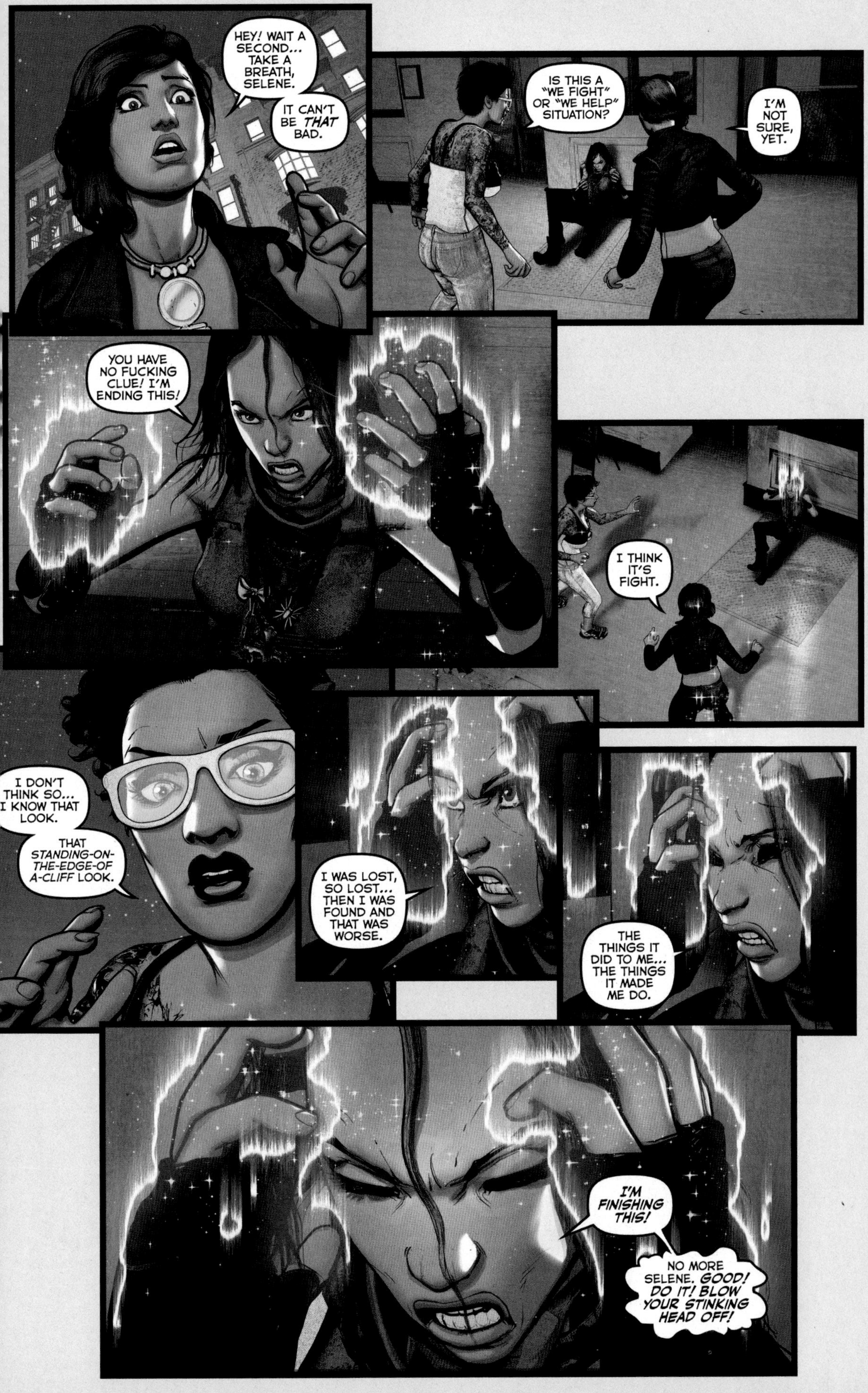
HEY! WAIT A SECOND... TAKE A BREATH, SELENE.
IT CAN'T BE *THAT* BAD.
IS THIS A "WE FIGHT" OR "WE HELP" SITUATION?
I'M NOT SURE, YET.
YOU HAVE NO FUCKING CLUE! I'M ENDING THIS!
I THINK IT'S FIGHT.
I DON'T THINK SO... I KNOW THAT LOOK.
THAT *STANDING-ON-THE-EDGE-OF A-CLIFF* LOOK.
I WAS LOST, SO LOST... THEN I WAS FOUND AND THAT WAS WORSE.
THE THINGS IT DID TO ME... THE THINGS IT MADE ME DO.
I'M FINISHING THIS!
NO MORE SELENE. *GOOD! DO IT! BLOW YOUR STINKING HEAD OFF!*

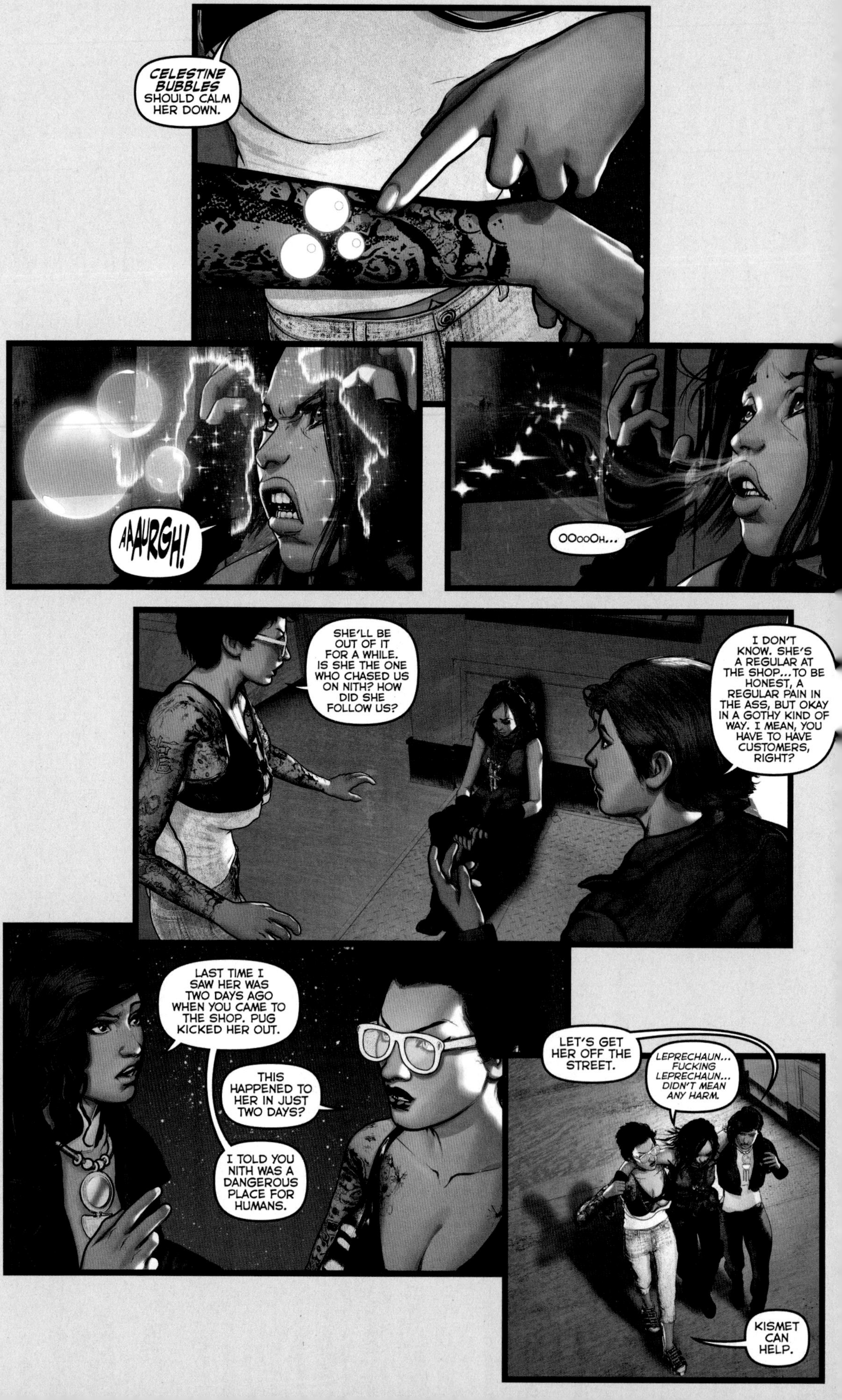

CELESTINE BUBBLES SHOULD CALM HER DOWN.
AAAURGH!
OOooOH...
SHE'LL BE OUT OF IT FOR A WHILE. IS SHE THE ONE WHO CHASED US ON NITH? HOW DID SHE FOLLOW US?
I DON'T KNOW. SHE'S A REGULAR AT THE SHOP...TO BE HONEST, A REGULAR PAIN IN THE ASS, BUT OKAY IN A GOTHY KIND OF WAY. I MEAN, YOU HAVE TO HAVE CUSTOMERS, RIGHT?
LAST TIME I SAW HER WAS TWO DAYS AGO WHEN YOU CAME TO THE SHOP. PUG KICKED HER OUT.
THIS HAPPENED TO HER IN JUST TWO DAYS?
I TOLD YOU NITH WAS A DANGEROUS PLACE FOR HUMANS.
LET'S GET HER OFF THE STREET.
LEPRECHAUN... FUCKING LEPRECHAUN... DIDN'T MEAN ANY HARM.
KISMET CAN HELP.

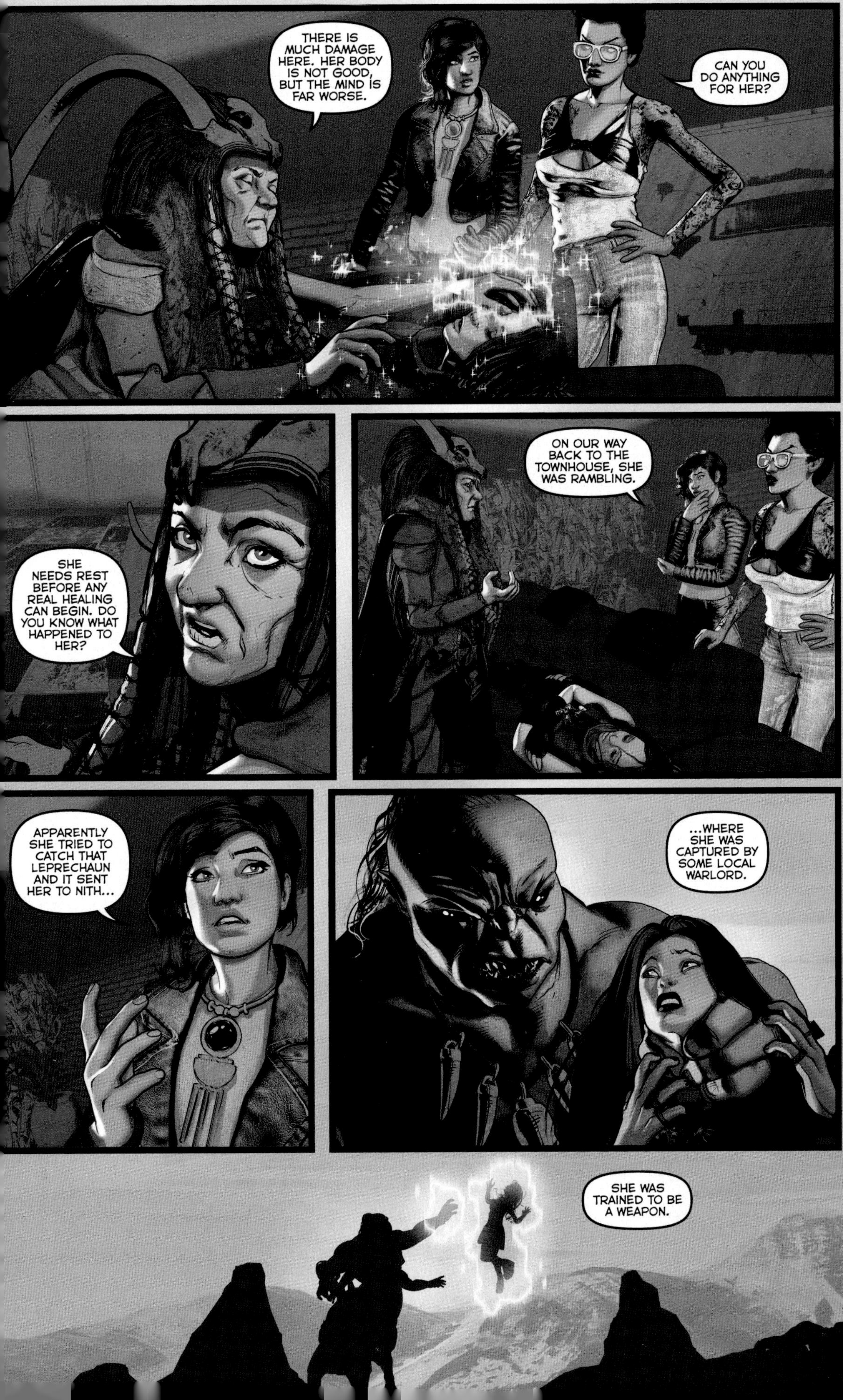
THERE IS MUCH DAMAGE HERE. HER BODY IS NOT GOOD, BUT THE MIND IS FAR WORSE.
CAN YOU DO ANYTHING FOR HER?
SHE NEEDS REST BEFORE ANY REAL HEALING CAN BEGIN. DO YOU KNOW WHAT HAPPENED TO HER?
ON OUR WAY BACK TO THE TOWNHOUSE, SHE WAS RAMBLING.
APPARENTLY SHE TRIED TO CATCH THAT LEPRECHAUN AND IT SENT HER TO NITH...
...WHERE SHE WAS CAPTURED BY SOME LOCAL WARLORD.
SHE WAS TRAINED TO BE A WEAPON.

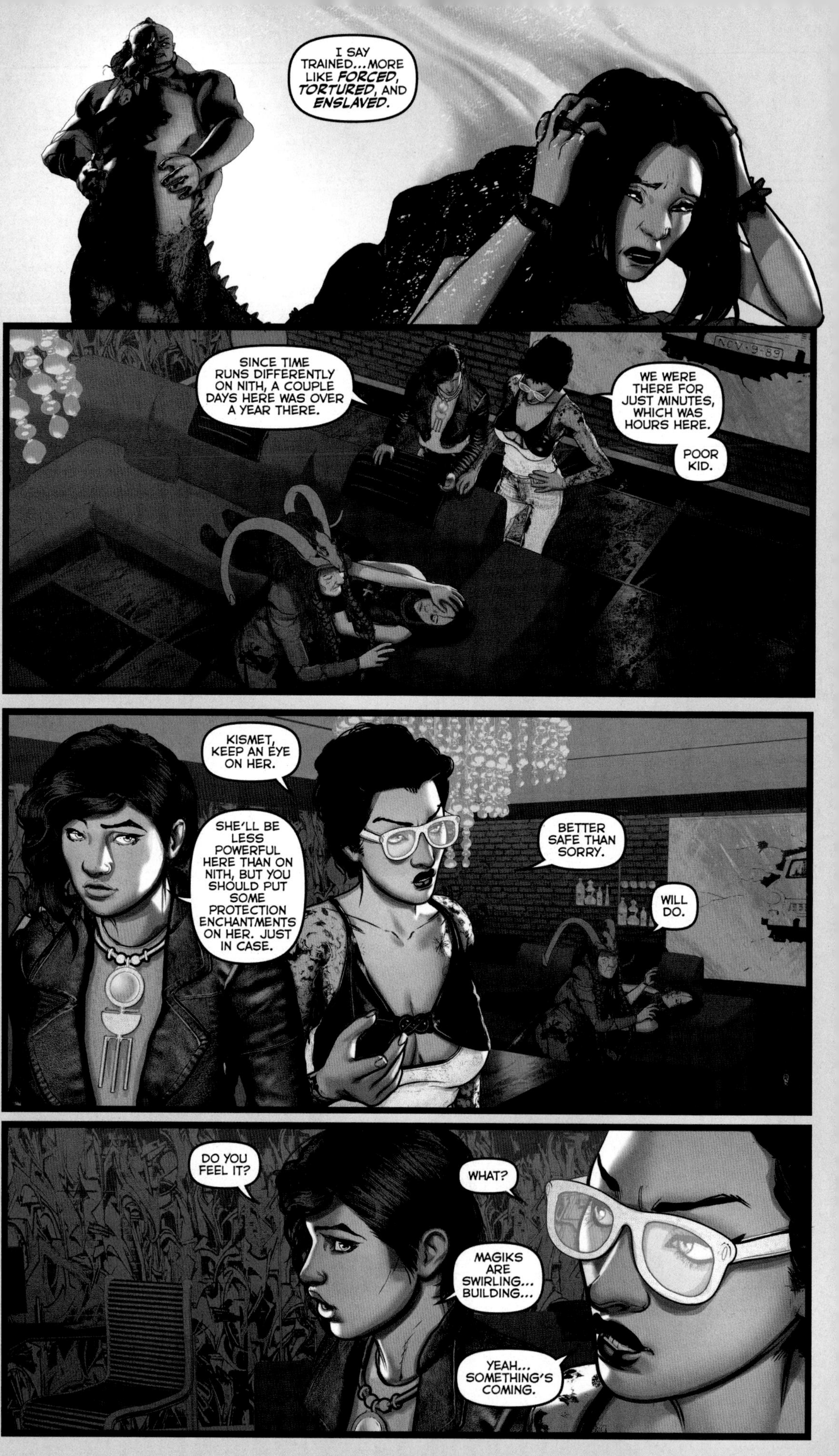
I SAY TRAINED...MORE LIKE *FORCED*, *TORTURED*, AND *ENSLAVED*.
SINCE TIME RUNS DIFFERENTLY ON NITH, A COUPLE DAYS HERE WAS OVER A YEAR THERE.
WE WERE THERE FOR JUST MINUTES, WHICH WAS HOURS HERE.
POOR KID.
KISMET, KEEP AN EYE ON HER.
SHE'LL BE LESS POWERFUL HERE THAN ON NITH, BUT YOU SHOULD PUT SOME PROTECTION ENCHANTMENTS ON HER. JUST IN CASE.
BETTER SAFE THAN SORRY.
WILL DO.
DO YOU FEEL IT?
WHAT?
MAGIKS ARE SWIRLING... BUILDING...
YEAH... SOMETHING'S COMING.

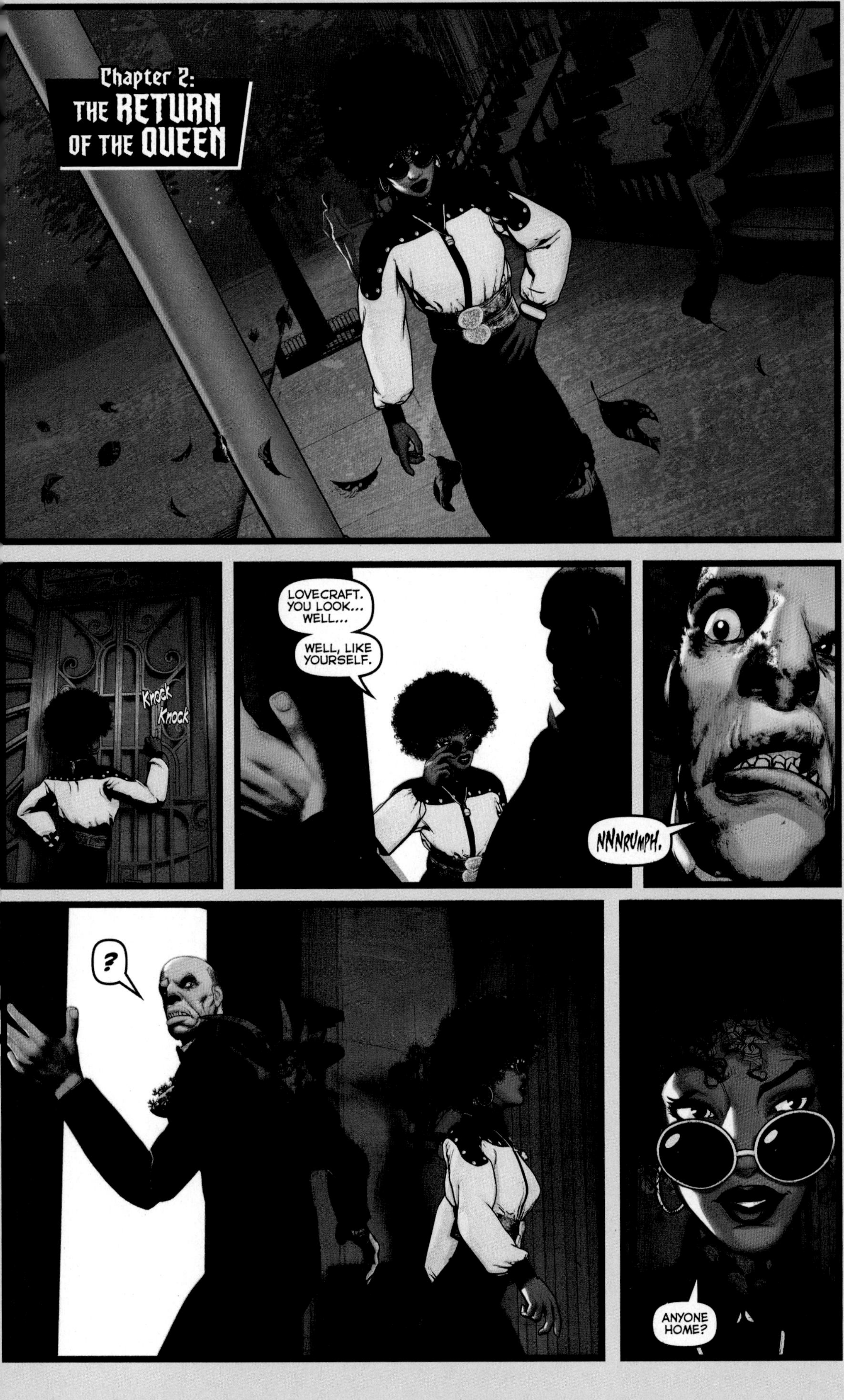
Chapter 2:
THE RETURN OF THE QUEEN
Knock
Knock
LOVECRAFT. YOU LOOK... WELL...
WELL, LIKE YOURSELF.
NNNRUMPH.
?
ANYONE HOME?

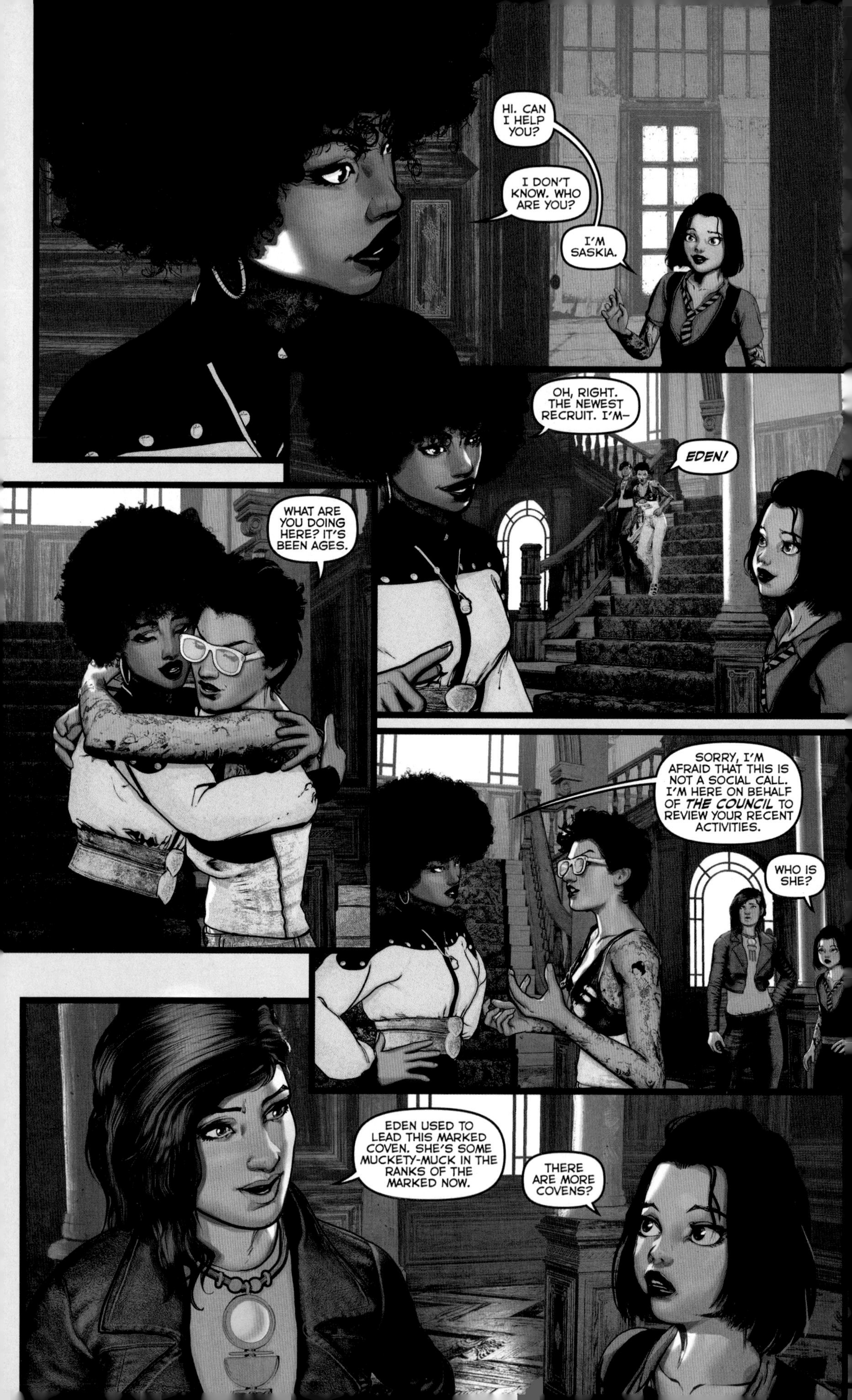
HI. CAN I HELP YOU?
I DON'T KNOW. WHO ARE YOU?
I'M SASKIA.
OH, RIGHT. THE NEWEST RECRUIT. I'M—
EDEN!
WHAT ARE YOU DOING HERE? IT'S BEEN AGES.
SORRY, I'M AFRAID THAT THIS IS NOT A SOCIAL CALL. I'M HERE ON BEHALF OF THE COUNCIL TO REVIEW YOUR RECENT ACTIVITIES.
WHO IS SHE?
EDEN USED TO LEAD THIS MARKED COVEN. SHE'S SOME MUCKETY-MUCK IN THE RANKS OF THE MARKED NOW.
THERE ARE MORE COVENS?

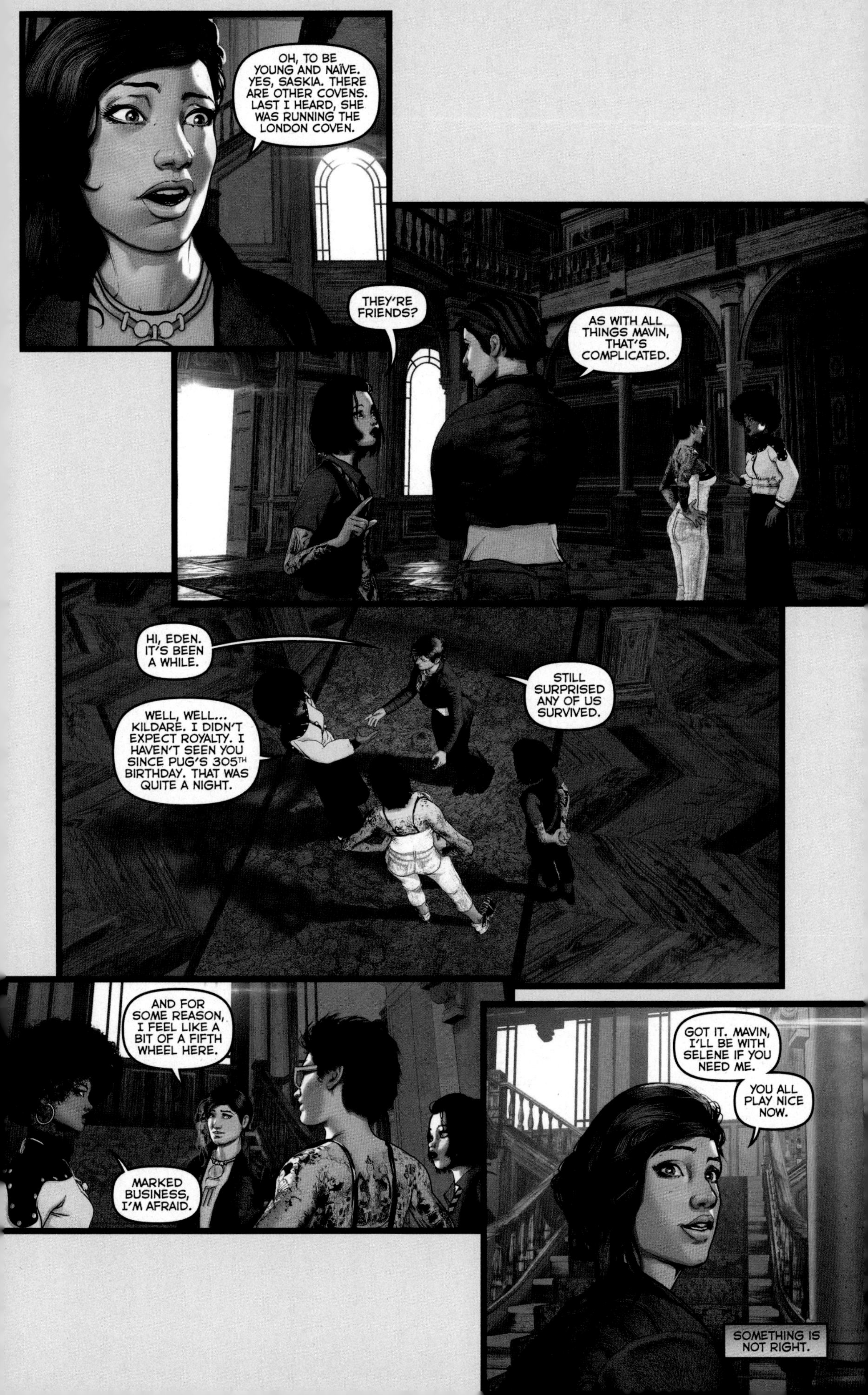
OH, TO BE YOUNG AND NAÏVE. YES, SASKIA. THERE ARE OTHER COVENS. LAST I HEARD, SHE WAS RUNNING THE LONDON COVEN.
THEY'RE FRIENDS?
AS WITH ALL THINGS MAVIN, THAT'S COMPLICATED.
HI, EDEN. IT'S BEEN A WHILE.
STILL SURPRISED ANY OF US SURVIVED.
WELL, WELL... KILDARE. I DIDN'T EXPECT ROYALTY. I HAVEN'T SEEN YOU SINCE PUG'S 305TH BIRTHDAY. THAT WAS QUITE A NIGHT.
AND FOR SOME REASON, I FEEL LIKE A BIT OF A FIFTH WHEEL HERE.
MARKED BUSINESS, I'M AFRAID.
GOT IT. MAVIN, I'LL BE WITH SELENE IF YOU NEED ME.
YOU ALL PLAY NICE NOW.
SOMETHING IS NOT RIGHT.

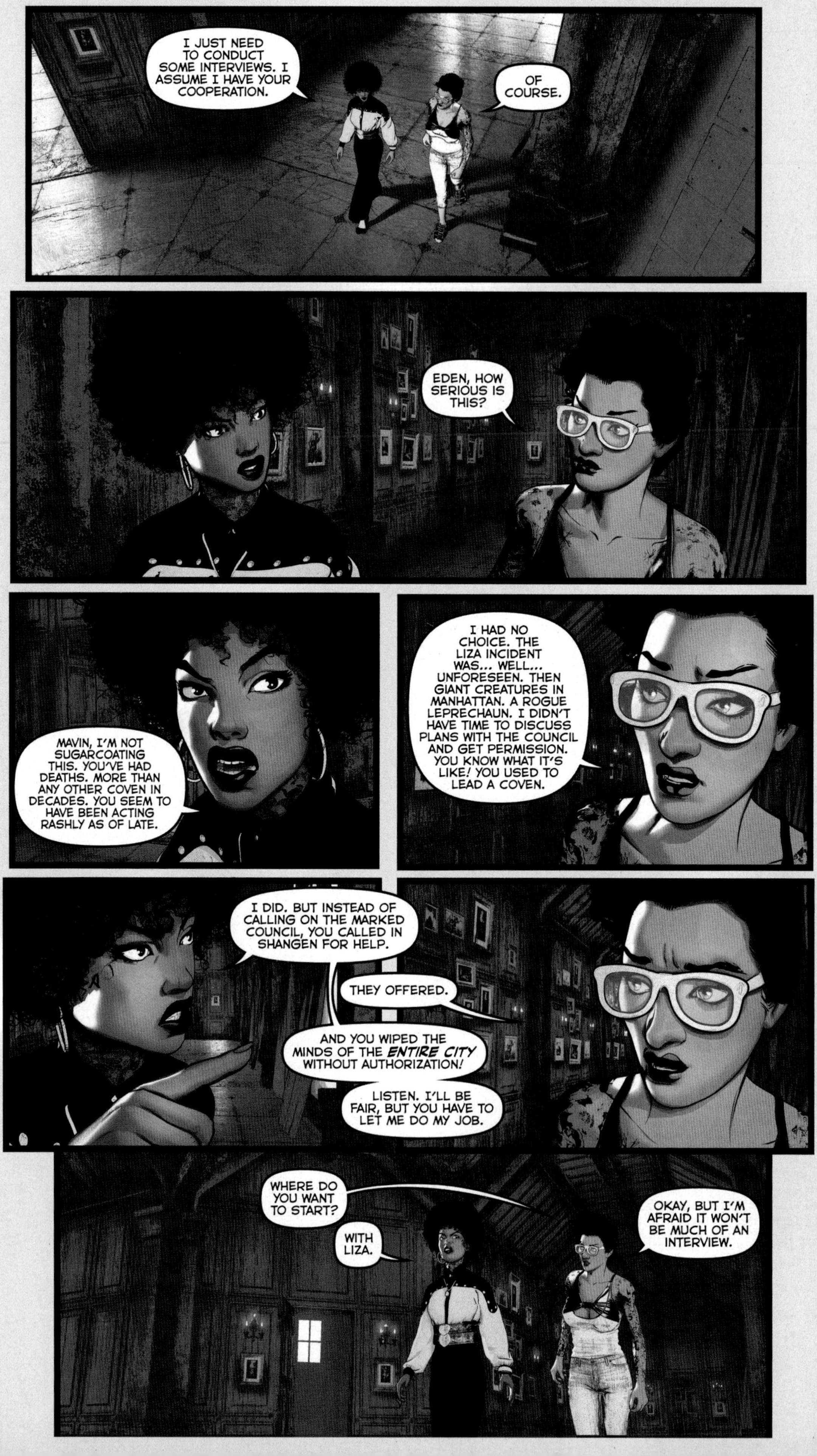
I JUST NEED TO CONDUCT SOME INTERVIEWS. I ASSUME I HAVE YOUR COOPERATION.
OF COURSE.
EDEN, HOW SERIOUS IS THIS?
MAVIN, I'M NOT SUGARCOATING THIS. YOU'VE HAD DEATHS. MORE THAN ANY OTHER COVEN IN DECADES. YOU SEEM TO HAVE BEEN ACTING RASHLY AS OF LATE.
I HAD NO CHOICE. THE LIZA INCIDENT WAS... WELL... UNFORESEEN. THEN GIANT CREATURES IN MANHATTAN. A ROGUE LEPRECHAUN. I DIDN'T HAVE TIME TO DISCUSS PLANS WITH THE COUNCIL AND GET PERMISSION. YOU KNOW WHAT IT'S LIKE! YOU USED TO LEAD A COVEN.
I DID. BUT INSTEAD OF CALLING ON THE MARKED COUNCIL, YOU CALLED IN SHANGEN FOR HELP.
THEY OFFERED.
AND YOU WIPED THE MINDS OF THE *ENTIRE CITY* WITHOUT AUTHORIZATION!
LISTEN. I'LL BE FAIR, BUT YOU HAVE TO LET ME DO MY JOB.
WHERE DO YOU WANT TO START?
WITH LIZA.
OKAY, BUT I'M AFRAID IT WON'T BE MUCH OF AN INTERVIEW.

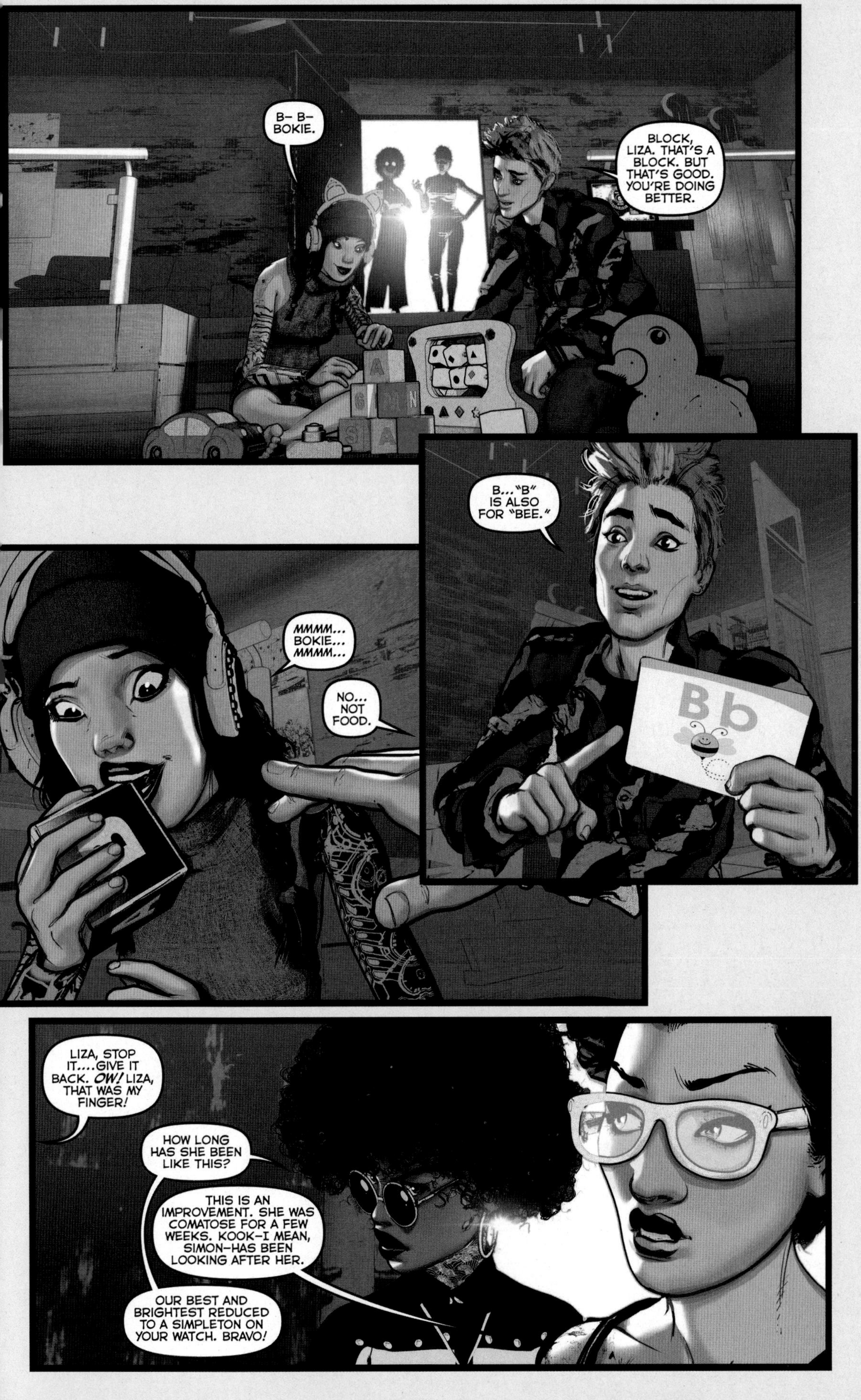

B– B–
BOKIE.
BLOCK, LIZA. THAT'S A BLOCK. BUT THAT'S GOOD. YOU'RE DOING BETTER.
B..."B" IS ALSO FOR "BEE."
Bb
MMMM... BOKIE... MMMM...
NO... NOT FOOD.
LIZA, STOP IT....GIVE IT BACK. OW! LIZA, THAT WAS MY FINGER!
HOW LONG HAS SHE BEEN LIKE THIS?
THIS IS AN IMPROVEMENT. SHE WAS COMATOSE FOR A FEW WEEKS. KOOK–I MEAN, SIMON–HAS BEEN LOOKING AFTER HER.
OUR BEST AND BRIGHTEST REDUCED TO A SIMPLETON ON YOUR WATCH. BRAVO!

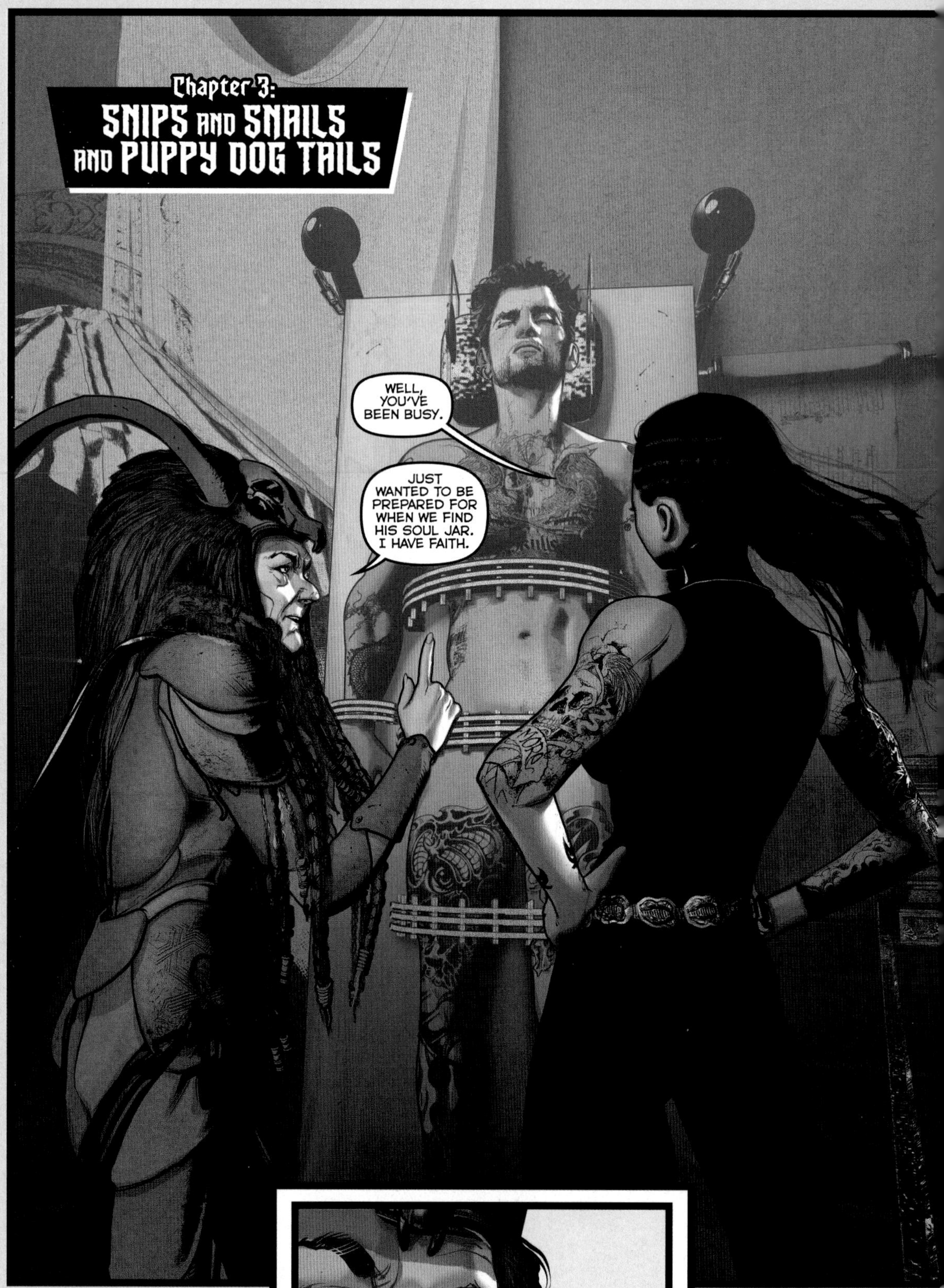
Chapter 3:
SNIPS AND SNAILS AND PUPPY DOG TAILS
WELL, YOU'VE BEEN BUSY.
JUST WANTED TO BE PREPARED FOR WHEN WE FIND HIS SOUL JAR. I HAVE FAITH.

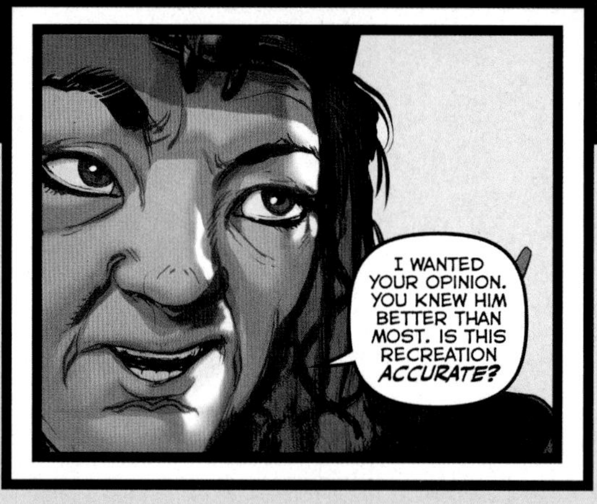
I WANTED YOUR OPINION. YOU KNEW HIM BETTER THAN MOST. IS THIS RECREATION *ACCURATE?*

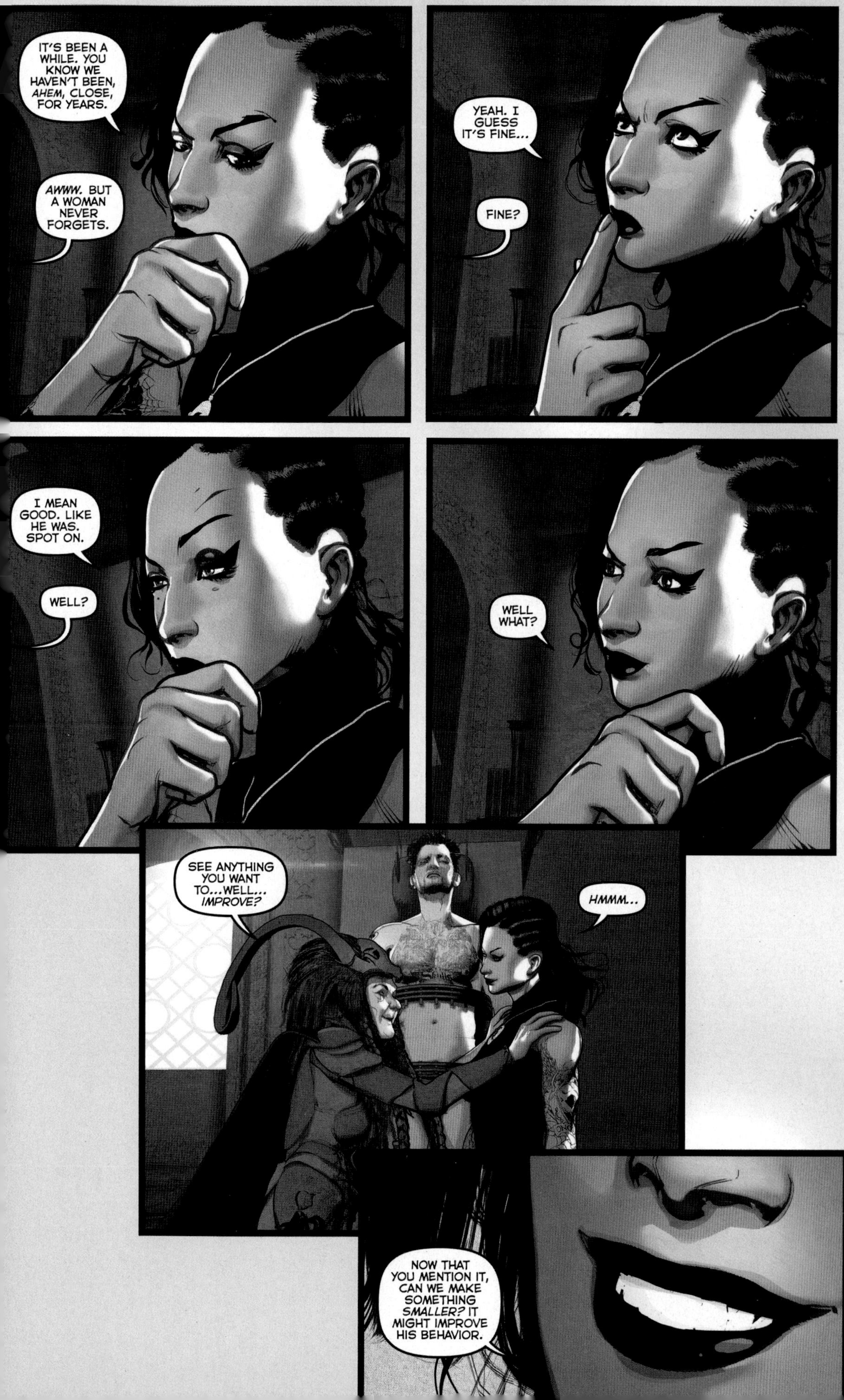
IT'S BEEN A WHILE. YOU KNOW WE HAVEN'T BEEN, *AHEM*, CLOSE, FOR YEARS.
AWWW. BUT A WOMAN NEVER FORGETS.
YEAH. I GUESS IT'S FINE...
FINE?
I MEAN GOOD. LIKE HE WAS. SPOT ON.
WELL?
WELL WHAT?
SEE ANYTHING YOU WANT TO...WELL... *IMPROVE?*
HMMM...
NOW THAT YOU MENTION IT, CAN WE MAKE SOMETHING *SMALLER?* IT MIGHT IMPROVE HIS BEHAVIOR.

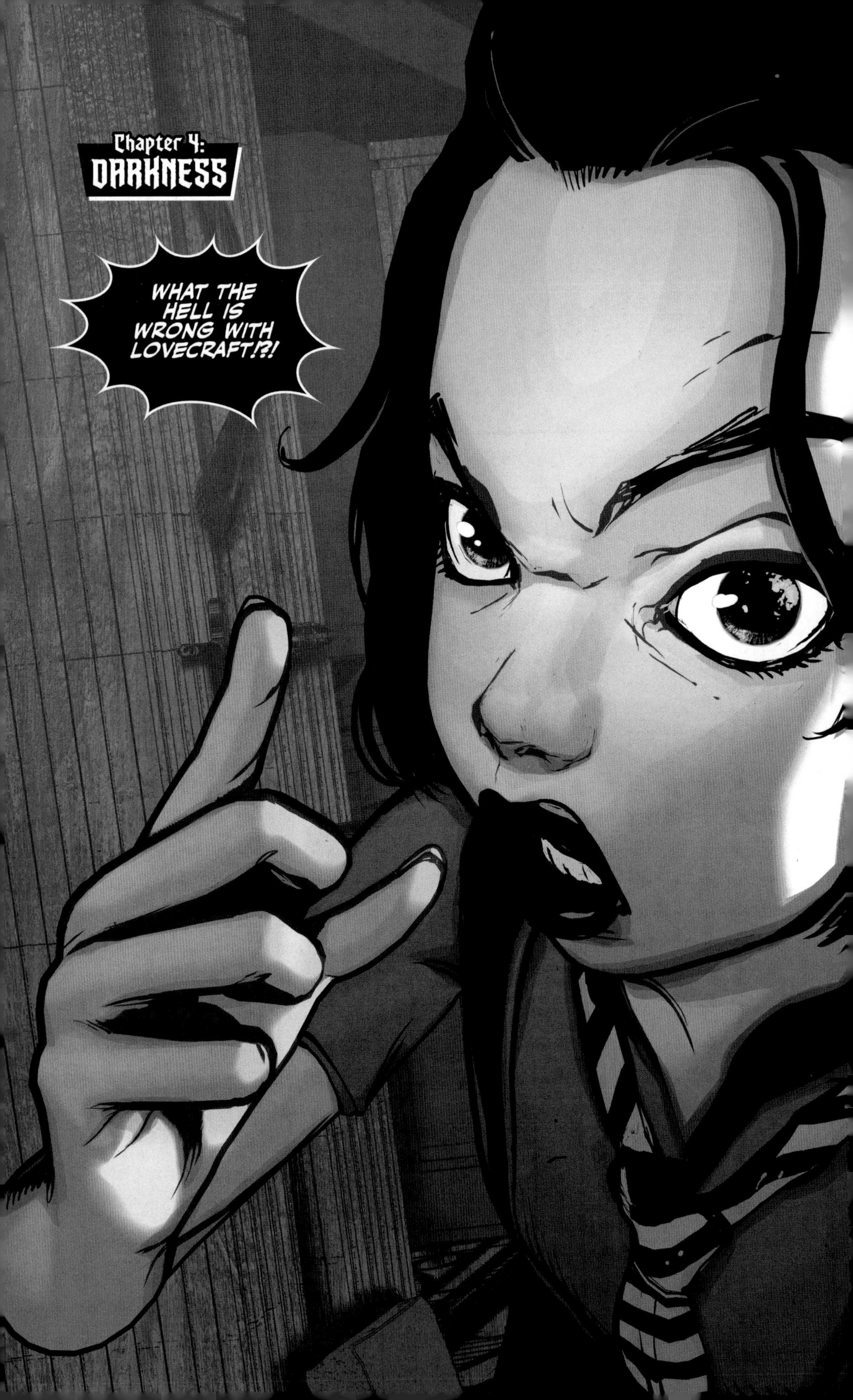
Chapter 4:
DARKNESS
WHAT THE HELL IS WRONG WITH LOVECRAFT!?!

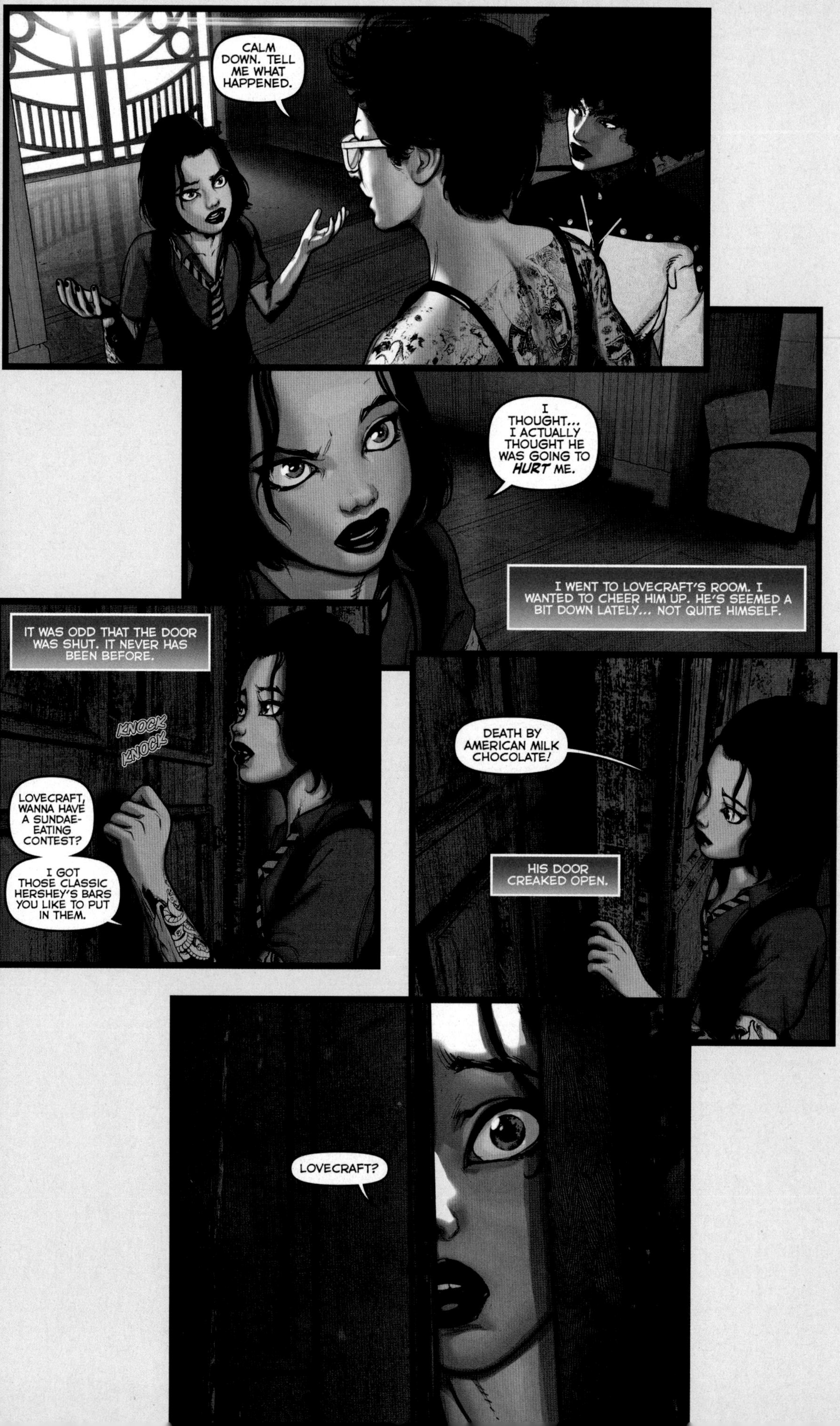
CALM DOWN. TELL ME WHAT HAPPENED.
I THOUGHT... I ACTUALLY THOUGHT HE WAS GOING TO *HURT* ME.
I WENT TO LOVECRAFT'S ROOM. I WANTED TO CHEER HIM UP. HE'S SEEMED A BIT DOWN LATELY... NOT QUITE HIMSELF.
IT WAS ODD THAT THE DOOR WAS SHUT. IT NEVER HAS BEEN BEFORE.
KNOCK KNOCK
LOVECRAFT, WANNA HAVE A SUNDAE-EATING CONTEST?
I GOT THOSE CLASSIC HERSHEY'S BARS YOU LIKE TO PUT IN THEM.
DEATH BY AMERICAN MILK CHOCOLATE!
HIS DOOR CREAKED OPEN.
LOVECRAFT?

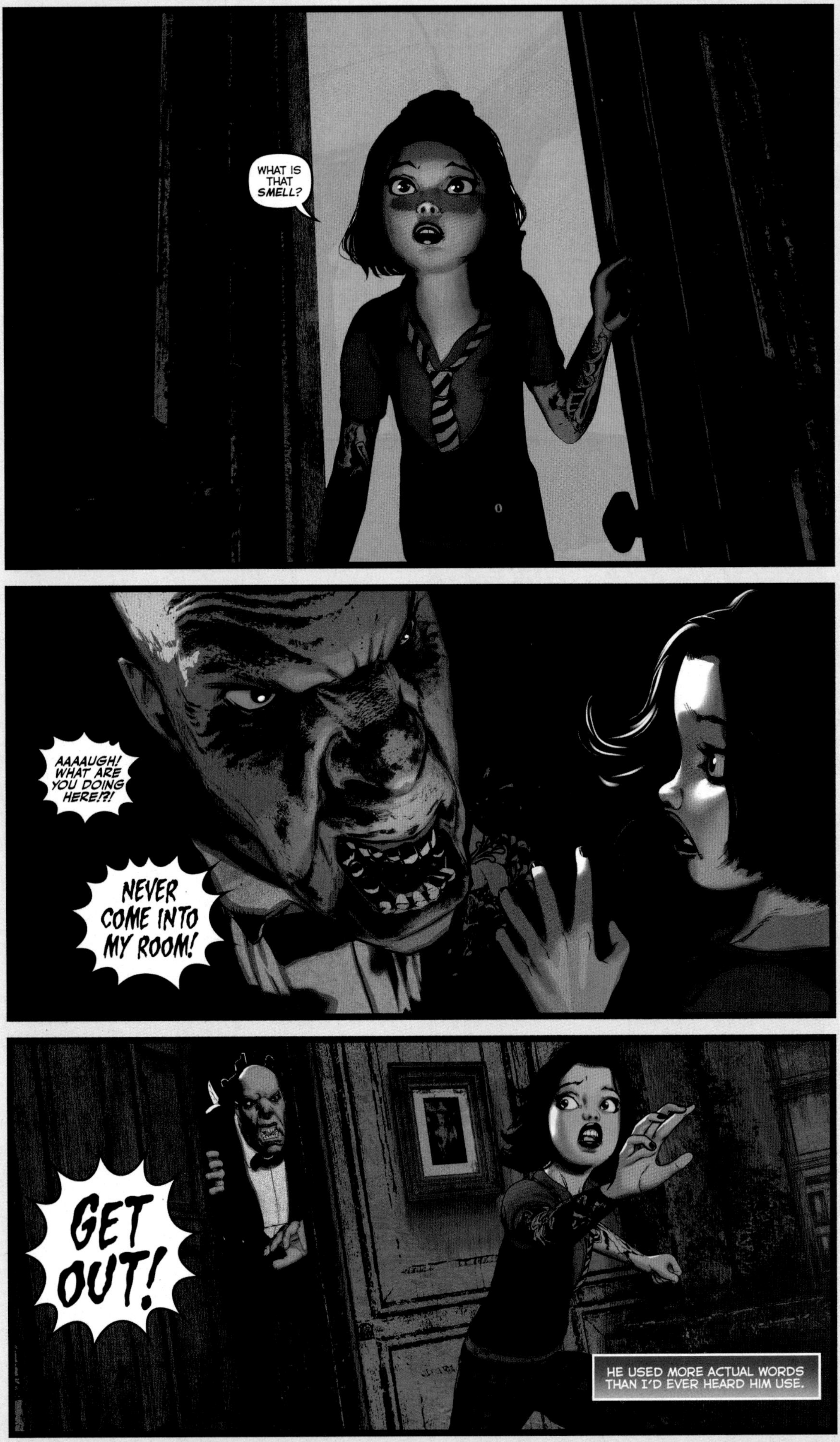
WHAT IS THAT SMELL?
AAAAUGH! WHAT ARE YOU DOING HERE!?!
NEVER COME INTO MY ROOM!
GET OUT!
HE USED MORE ACTUAL WORDS THAN I'D EVER HEARD HIM USE.

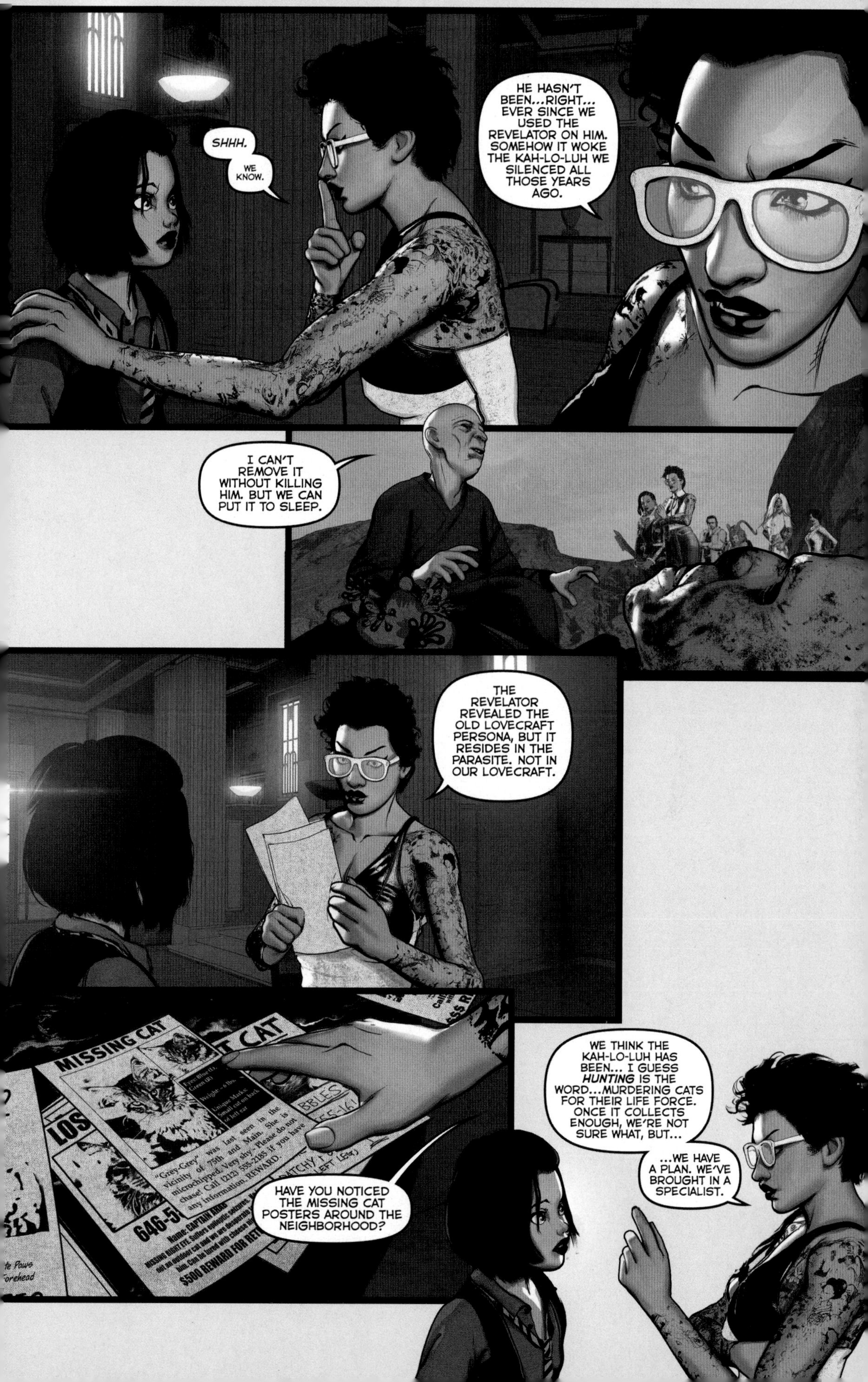
SHHH.
WE KNOW.
HE HASN'T BEEN...RIGHT... EVER SINCE WE USED THE REVELATOR ON HIM. SOMEHOW IT WOKE THE KAH-LO-LUH WE SILENCED ALL THOSE YEARS AGO.
I CAN'T REMOVE IT WITHOUT KILLING HIM. BUT WE CAN PUT IT TO SLEEP.
THE REVELATOR REVEALED THE OLD LOVECRAFT PERSONA, BUT IT RESIDES IN THE PARASITE. NOT IN OUR LOVECRAFT.
MISSING CAT
HAVE YOU NOTICED THE MISSING CAT POSTERS AROUND THE NEIGHBORHOOD?
WE THINK THE KAH-LO-LUH HAS BEEN... I GUESS *HUNTING* IS THE WORD...MURDERING CATS FOR THEIR LIFE FORCE. ONCE IT COLLECTS ENOUGH, WE'RE NOT SURE WHAT, BUT...
...WE HAVE A PLAN. WE'VE BROUGHT IN A SPECIALIST.

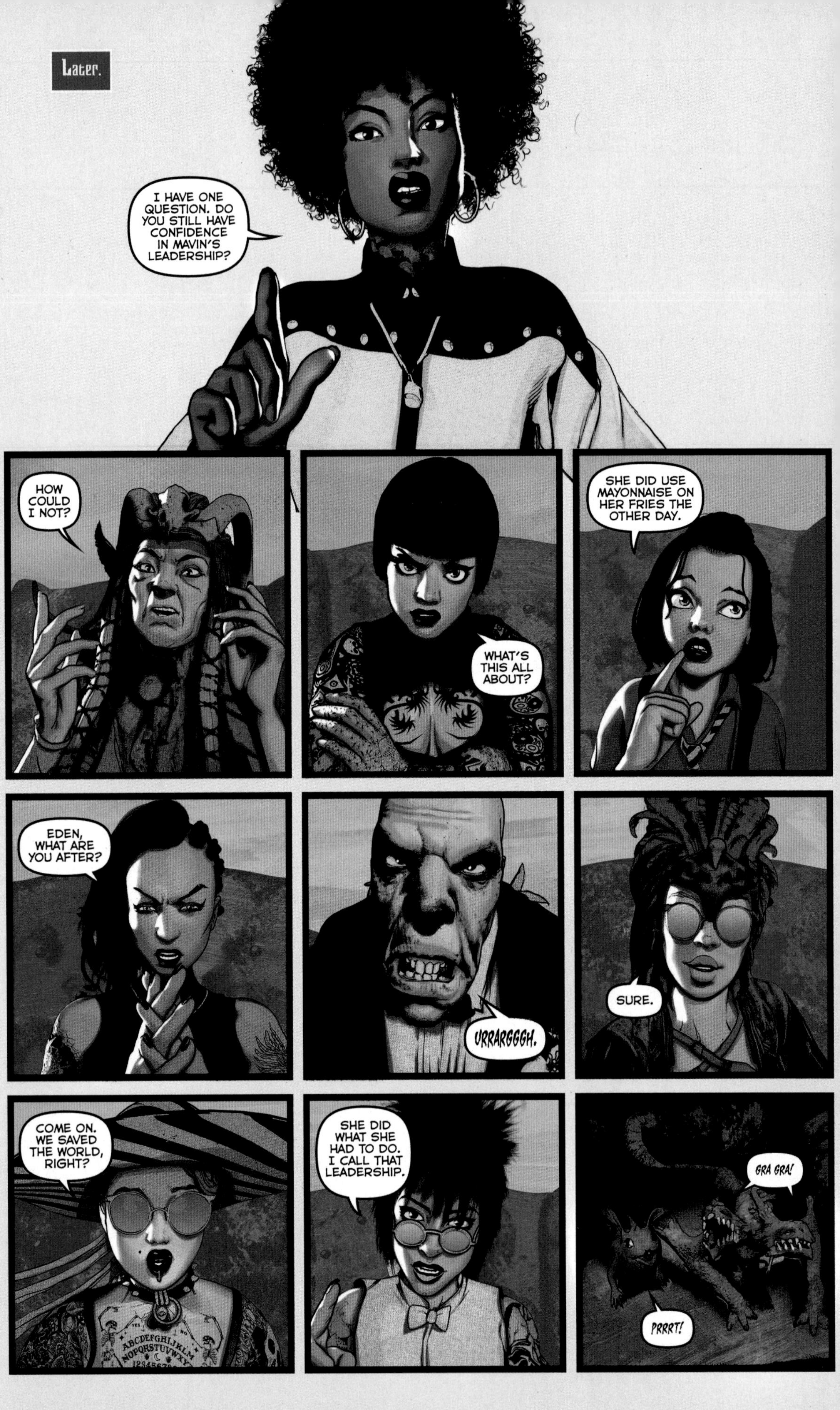
Later.
I HAVE ONE QUESTION. DO YOU STILL HAVE CONFIDENCE IN MAVIN'S LEADERSHIP?
HOW COULD I NOT?
WHAT'S THIS ALL ABOUT?
SHE DID USE MAYONNAISE ON HER FRIES THE OTHER DAY.
EDEN, WHAT ARE YOU AFTER?
URRARGGGH.
SURE.
COME ON. WE SAVED THE WORLD, RIGHT?
SHE DID WHAT SHE HAD TO DO. I CALL THAT LEADERSHIP.
GRA GRA!
PRRRT!

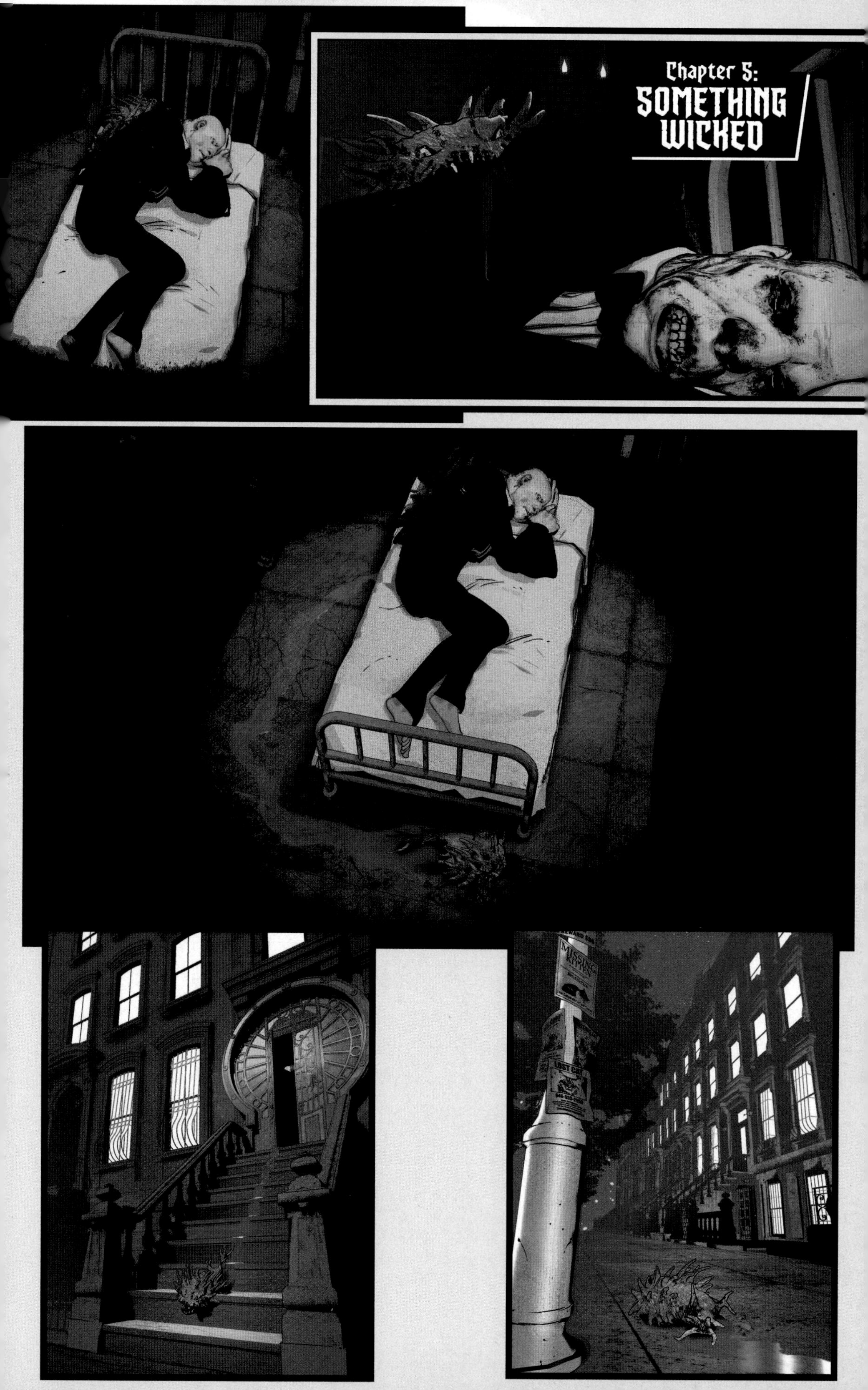
Chapter 5:
SOMETHING WICKED
MISSING KITTEN
LOST CAT

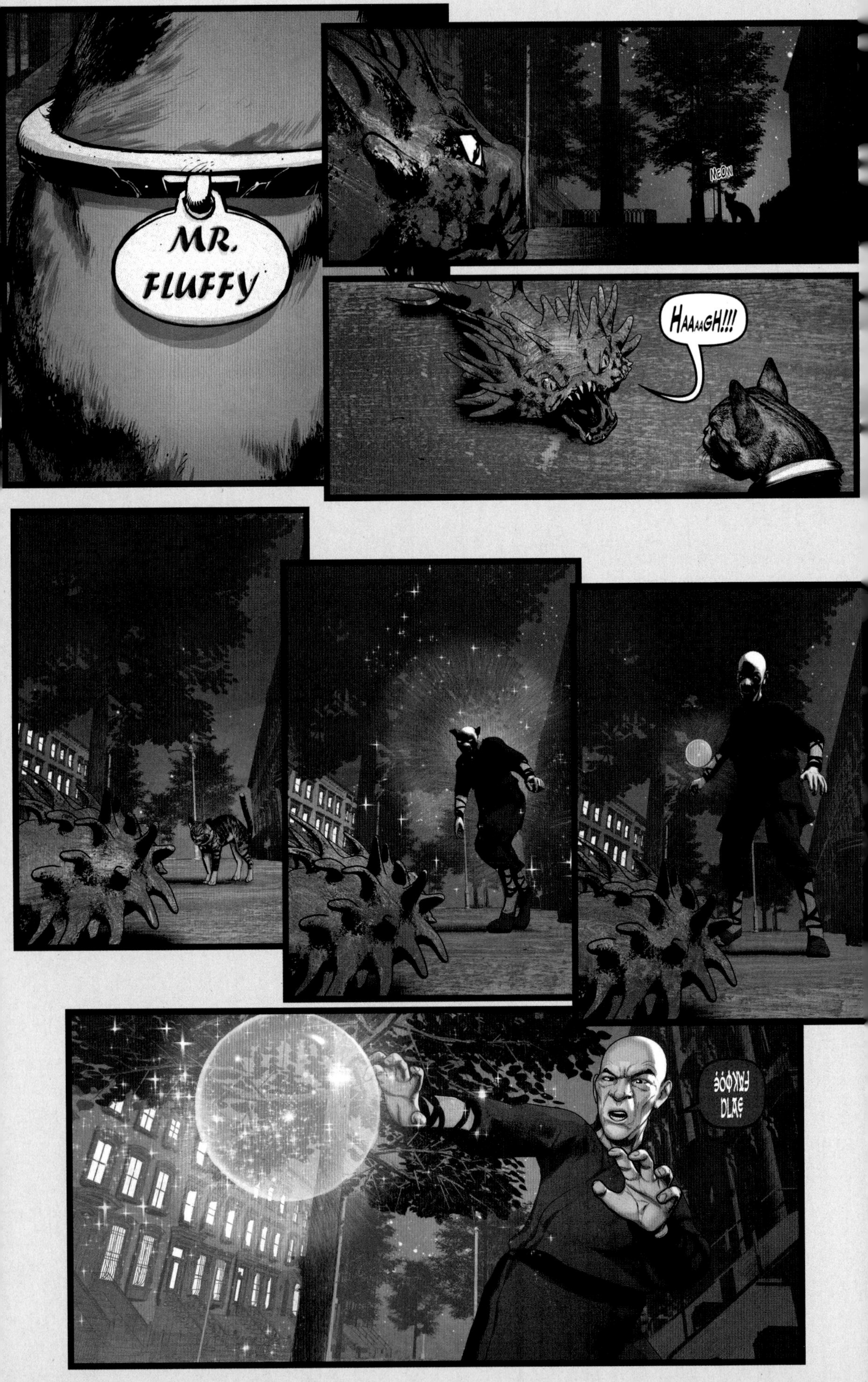
MR. FLUFFY
MEOW
HAAAAGH!!!

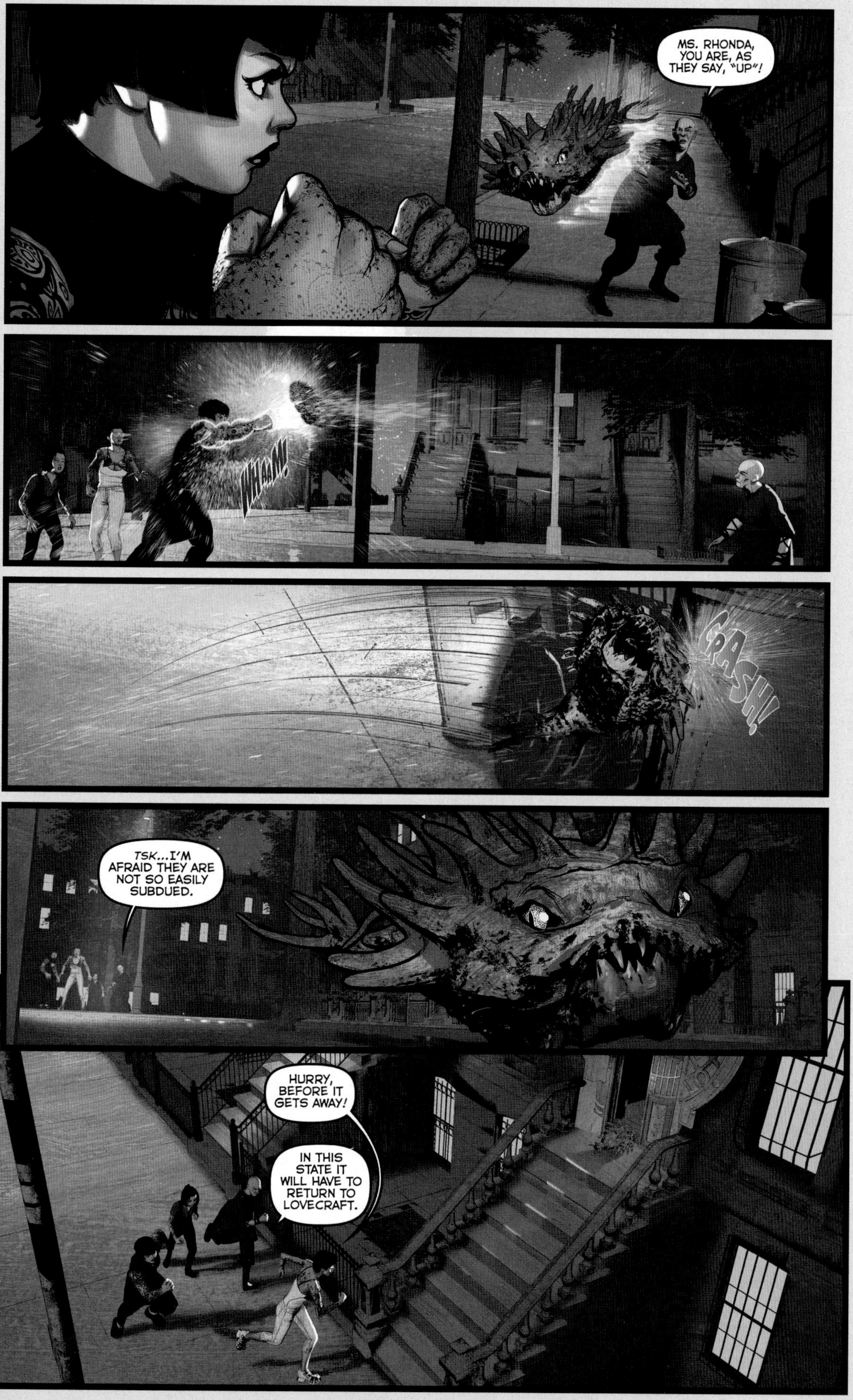
MS. RHONDA, YOU ARE, AS THEY SAY, "UP"!
WHAAM!
CRASH!
TSK...I'M AFRAID THEY ARE NOT SO EASILY SUBDUED.
HURRY, BEFORE IT GETS AWAY!
IN THIS STATE IT WILL HAVE TO RETURN TO LOVECRAFT.

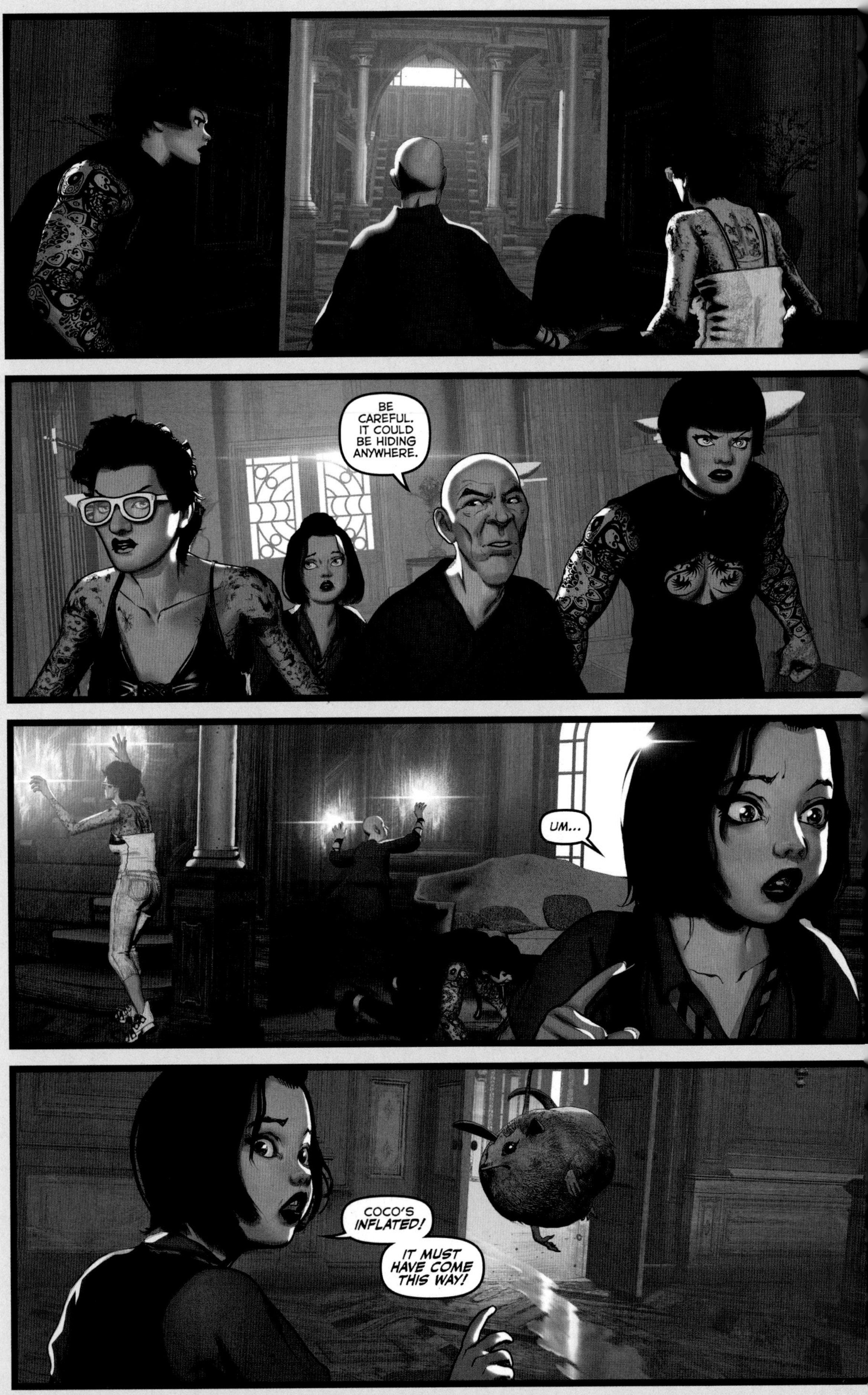
BE CAREFUL. IT COULD BE HIDING ANYWHERE.
UM...
COCO'S INFLATED!
IT MUST HAVE COME THIS WAY!

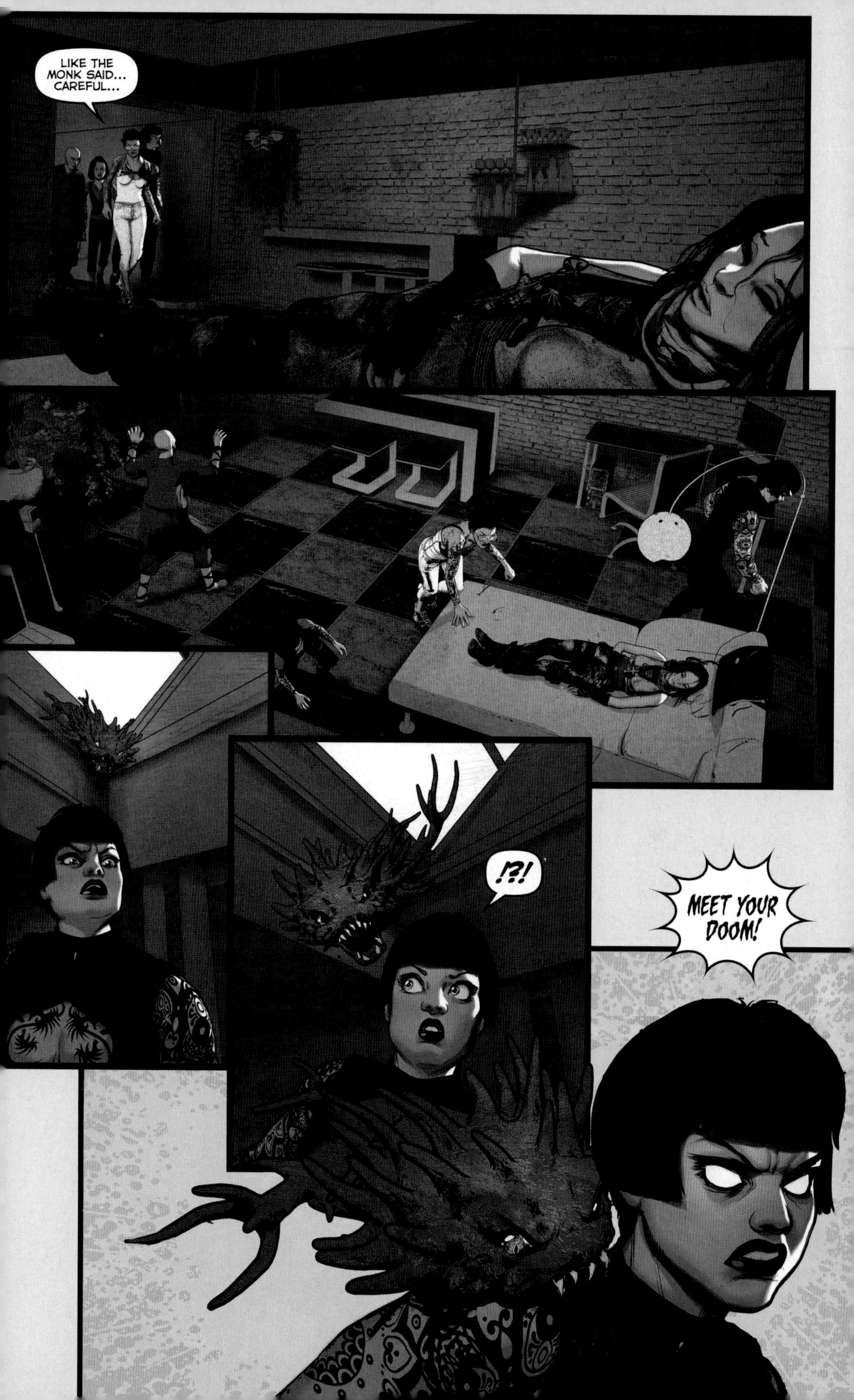
LIKE THE MONK SAID... CAREFUL...
!?!
MEET YOUR DOOM!

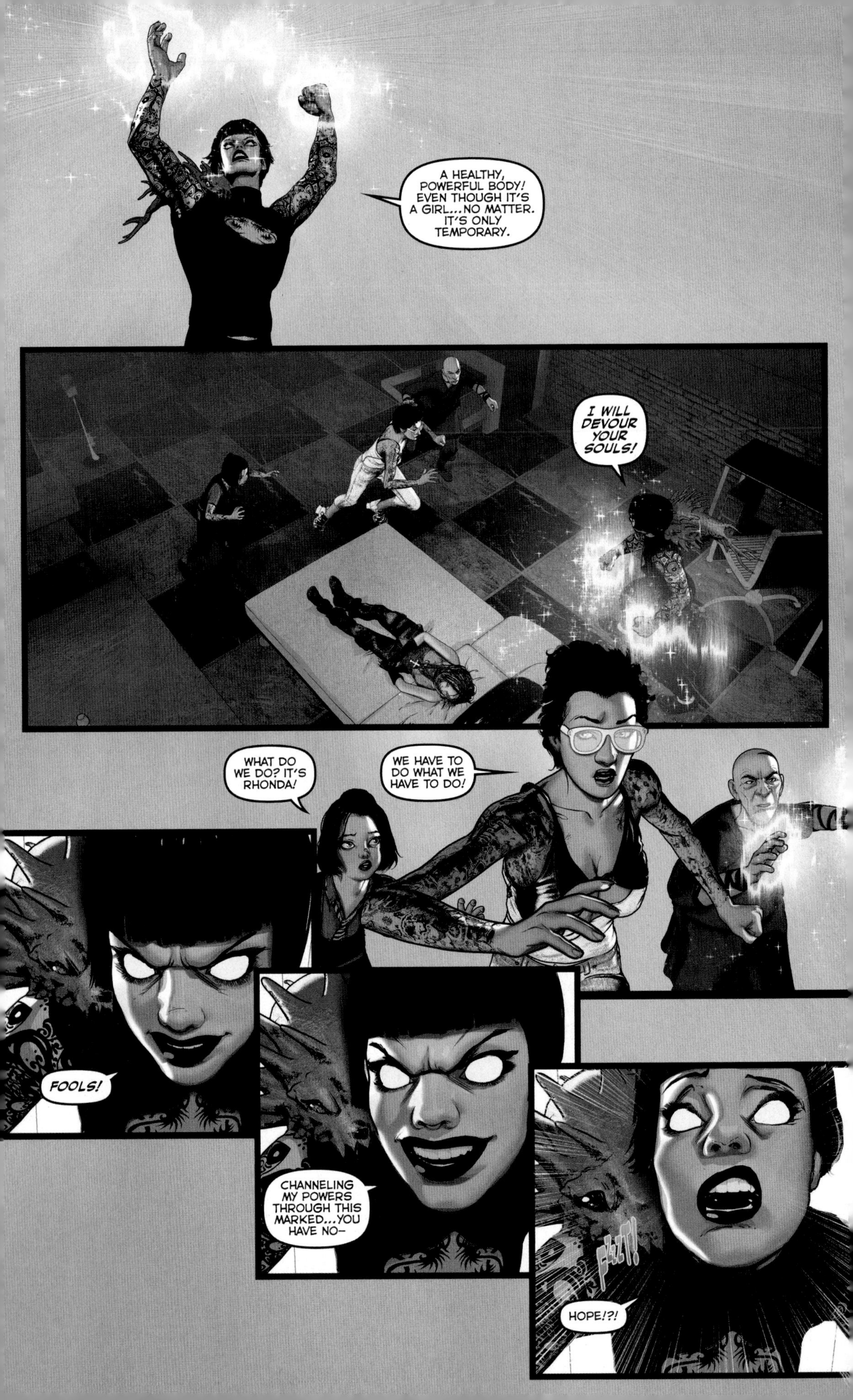
A HEALTHY, POWERFUL BODY! EVEN THOUGH IT'S A GIRL...NO MATTER. IT'S ONLY TEMPORARY.
I WILL DEVOUR YOUR SOULS!
WHAT DO WE DO? IT'S RHONDA!
WE HAVE TO DO WHAT WE HAVE TO DO!
FOOLS!
CHANNELING MY POWERS THROUGH THIS MARKED...YOU HAVE NO–
FZZZT!
HOPE!?!

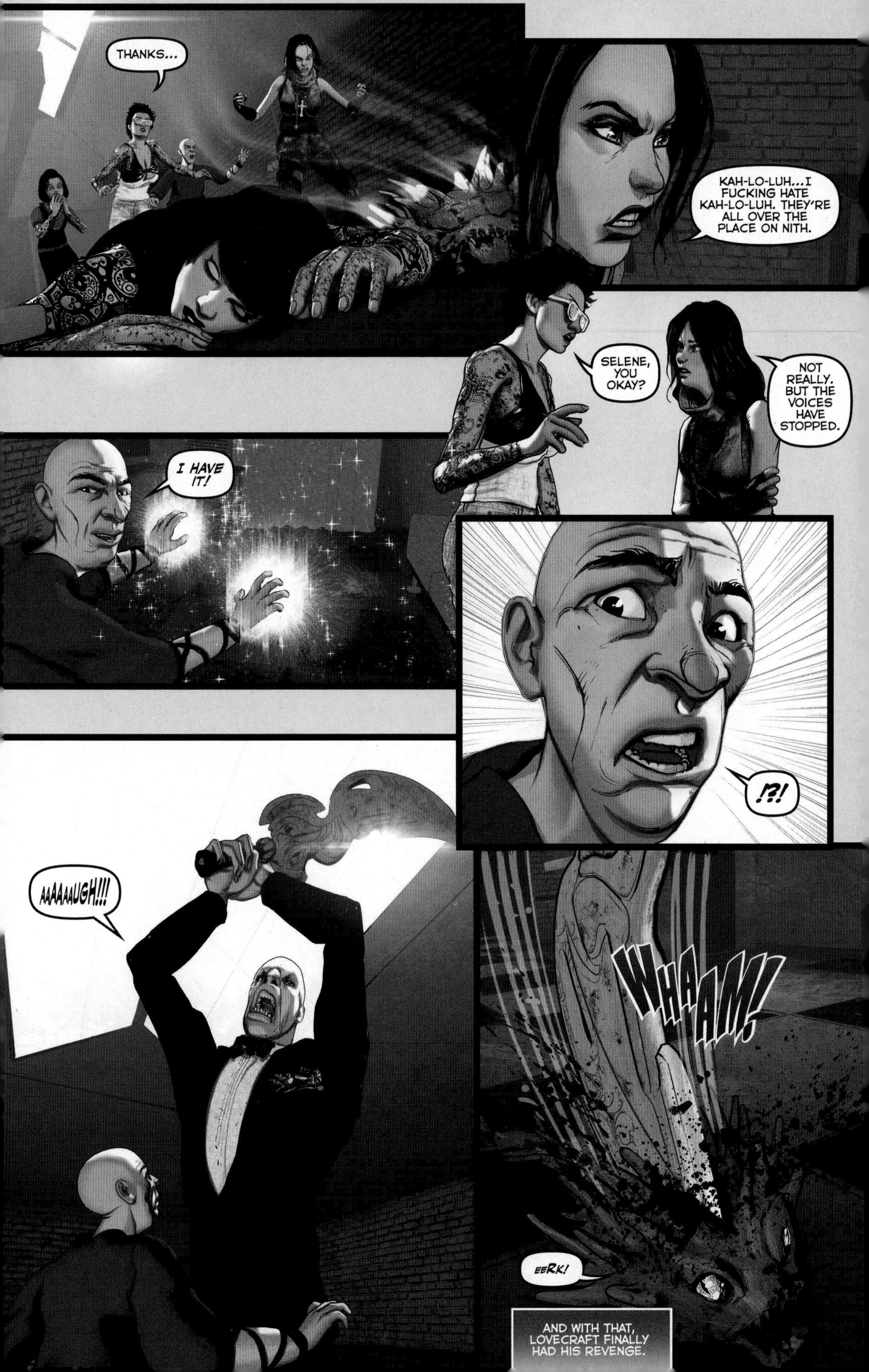
THANKS...
KAH-LO-LUH...I FUCKING HATE KAH-LO-LUH. THEY'RE ALL OVER THE PLACE ON NITH.
SELENE, YOU OKAY?
NOT REALLY. BUT THE VOICES HAVE STOPPED.
I HAVE IT!
!?!
AAAAAAUGH!!!
WHAAM!
EERK!
AND WITH THAT, LOVECRAFT FINALLY HAD HIS REVENGE.

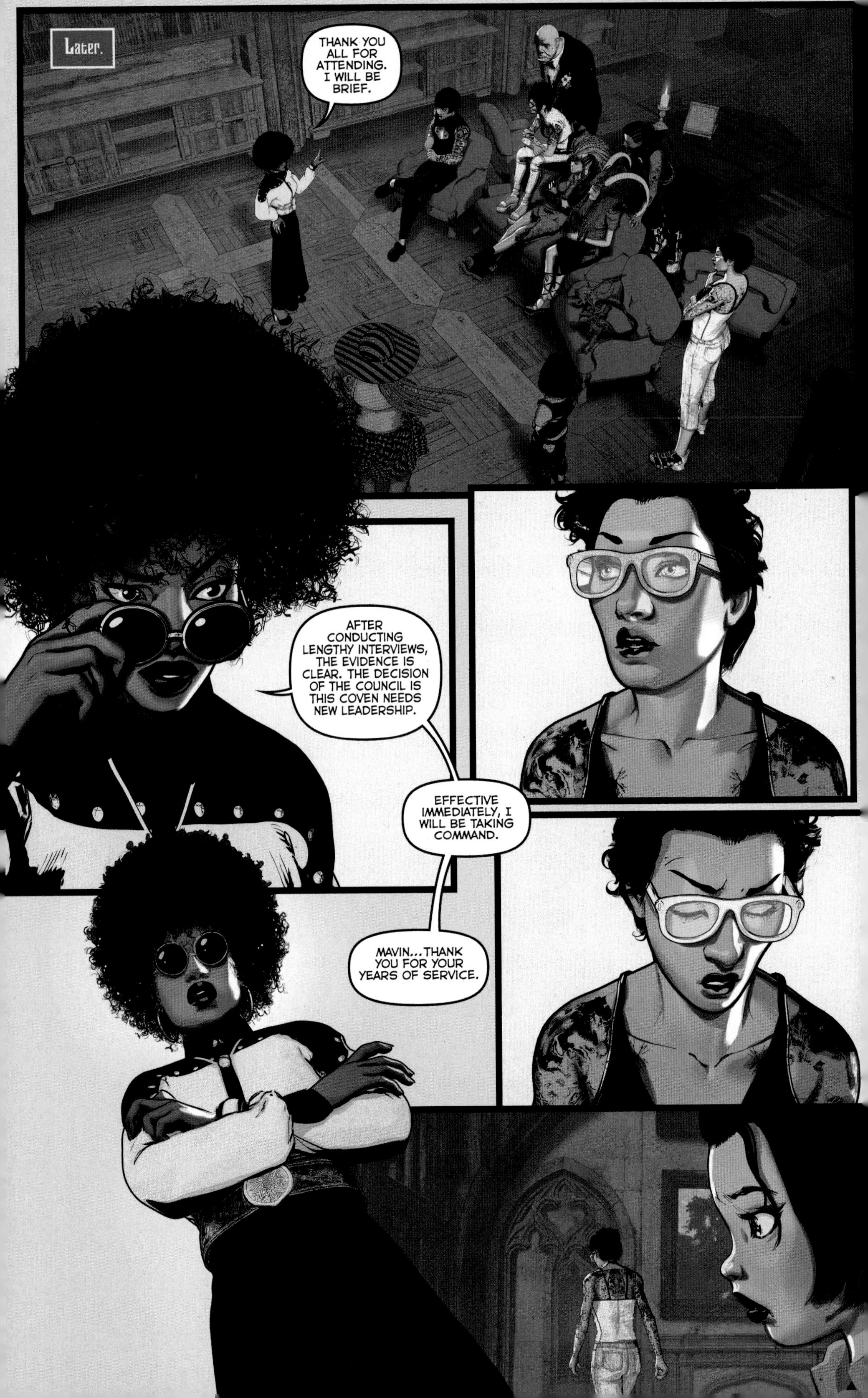
Later.
THANK YOU ALL FOR ATTENDING. I WILL BE BRIEF.
AFTER CONDUCTING LENGTHY INTERVIEWS, THE EVIDENCE IS CLEAR. THE DECISION OF THE COUNCIL IS THIS COVEN NEEDS NEW LEADERSHIP.
EFFECTIVE IMMEDIATELY, I WILL BE TAKING COMMAND.
MAVIN...THANK YOU FOR YOUR YEARS OF SERVICE.

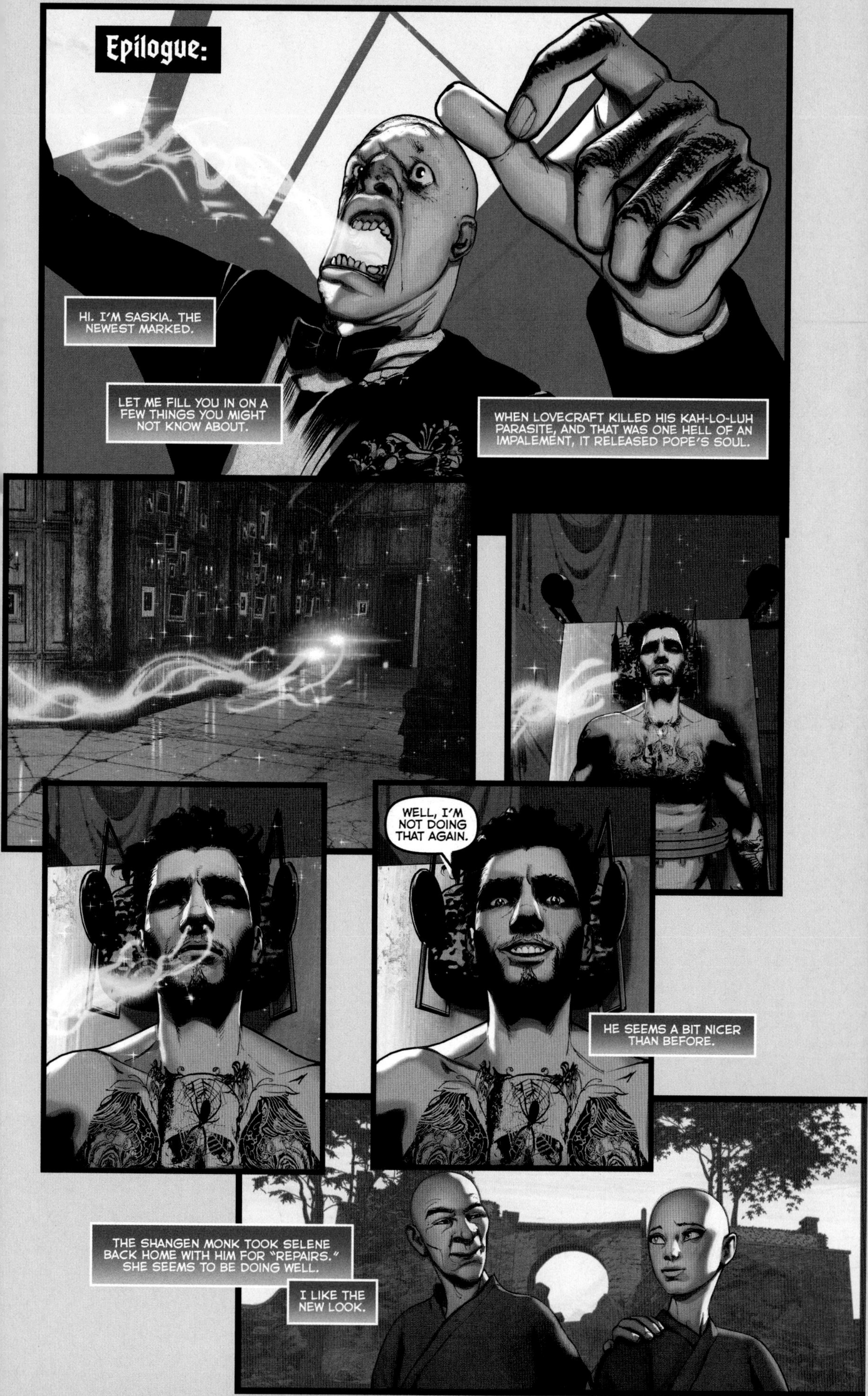
Epilogue:
HI. I'M SASKIA. THE NEWEST MARKED.
LET ME FILL YOU IN ON A FEW THINGS YOU MIGHT NOT KNOW ABOUT.
WHEN LOVECRAFT KILLED HIS KAH-LO-LUH PARASITE, AND THAT WAS ONE HELL OF AN IMPALEMENT, IT RELEASED POPE'S SOUL.
WELL, I'M NOT DOING THAT AGAIN.
HE SEEMS A BIT NICER THAN BEFORE.
THE SHANGEN MONK TOOK SELENE BACK HOME WITH HIM FOR "REPAIRS." SHE SEEMS TO BE DOING WELL.
I LIKE THE NEW LOOK.

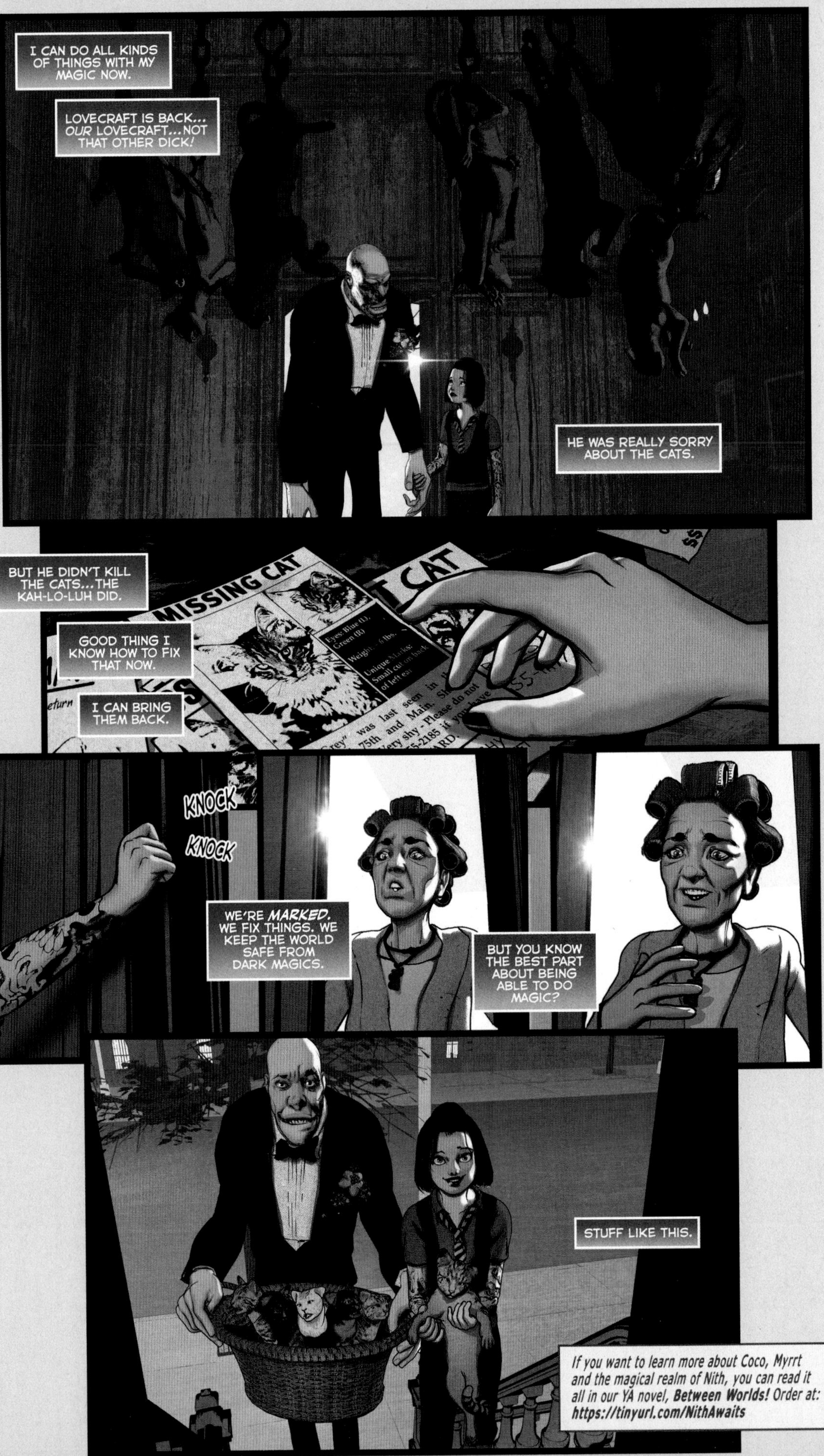
I CAN DO ALL KINDS OF THINGS WITH MY MAGIC NOW.
LOVECRAFT IS BACK... *OUR* LOVECRAFT...NOT THAT OTHER DICK!
HE WAS REALLY SORRY ABOUT THE CATS.
BUT HE DIDN'T KILL THE CATS...THE KAH-LO-LUH DID.
MISSING CAT
Eyes: Blue (L), Green (R)
Weight: 6 lbs.
Unique Marks: Small cut on back of left ear
GOOD THING I KNOW HOW TO FIX THAT NOW.
I CAN BRING THEM BACK.
KNOCK
KNOCK
WE'RE ***MARKED.*** WE FIX THINGS. WE KEEP THE WORLD SAFE FROM DARK MAGICS.
BUT YOU KNOW THE BEST PART ABOUT BEING ABLE TO DO MAGIC?
STUFF LIKE THIS.
If you want to learn more about Coco, Myrrt and the magical realm of Nith, you can read it all in our YA novel, ***Between Worlds!*** *Order at:* ***https://tinyurl.com/NithAwaits***

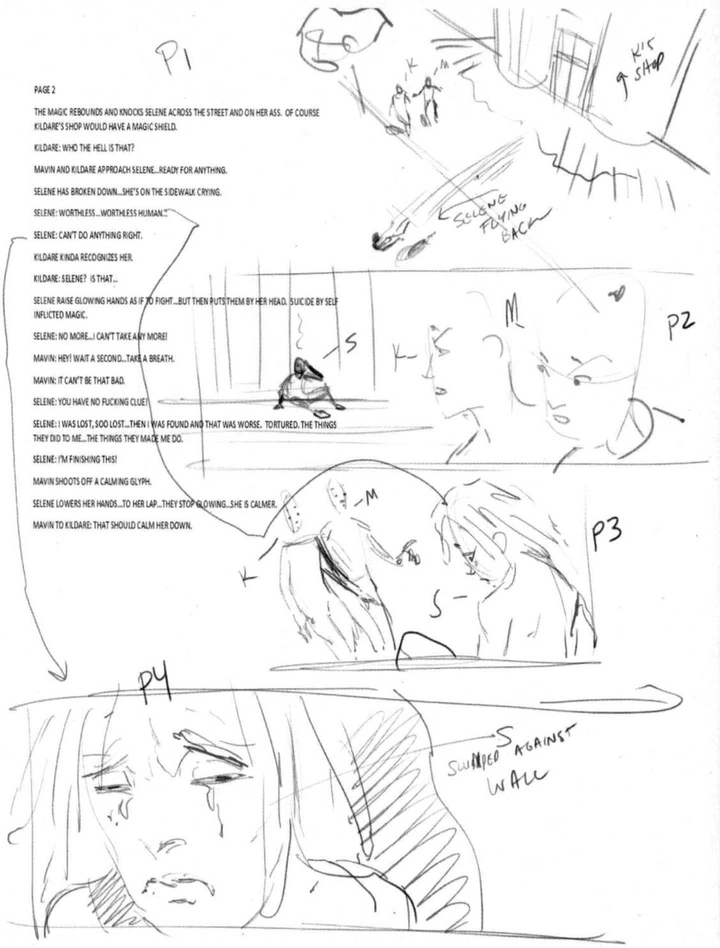
P1
PAGE 2
THE MAGIC REBOUNDS AND KNOCKS SELENE ACROSS THE STREET AND ON HER ASS. OF COURSE KILDARE'S SHOP WOULD HAVE A MAGIC SHIELD.
KILDARE: WHO THE HELL IS THAT?
MAVIN AND KILDARE APPROACH SELENE...READY FOR ANYTHING.
SELENE HAS BROKEN DOWN...SHE'S ON THE SIDEWALK CRYING.
SELENE: WORTHLESS...WORTHLESS HUMAN...
SELENE: CAN'T DO ANYTHING RIGHT.
KILDARE KINDA RECOGNIZES HER.
KILDARE: SELENE? IS THAT...
SELENE RAISE GLOWING HANDS AS IF TO FIGHT...BUT THEN PUTS THEM BY HER HEAD. SUICIDE BY SELF INFLICTED MAGIC.
SELENE: NO MORE...I CAN'T TAKE ANY MORE!
MAVIN: HEY! WAIT A SECOND...TAKE A BREATH.
MAVIN: IT CAN'T BE THAT BAD.
SELENE: YOU HAVE NO FUCKING CLUE!
SELENE: I WAS LOST, SOO LOST...THEN I WAS FOUND AND THAT WAS WORSE. TORTURED. THE THINGS THEY DID TO ME...THE THINGS THEY MADE ME DO.
SELENE: I'M FINISHING THIS!
MAVIN SHOOTS OFF A CALMING GLYPH.
SELENE LOWERS HER HANDS...TO HER LAP...THEY STOP GLOWING...SHE IS CALMER.
MAVIN TO KILDARE: THAT SHOULD CALM HER DOWN.
KIS SHOP
SELENE FLYING BACK
P2
P3
P4
S SLUMPED AGAINST WALL

Behind the Scenes:

LAYOUTS TO FINISH

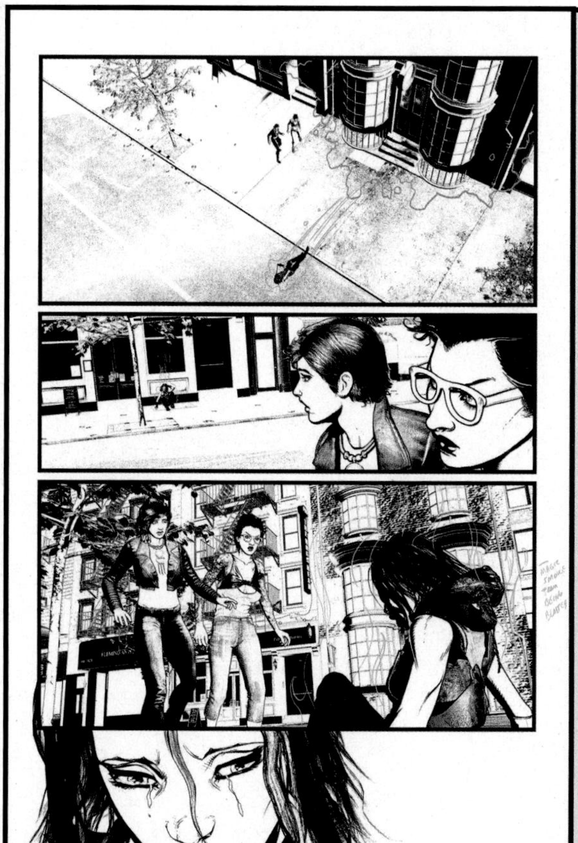

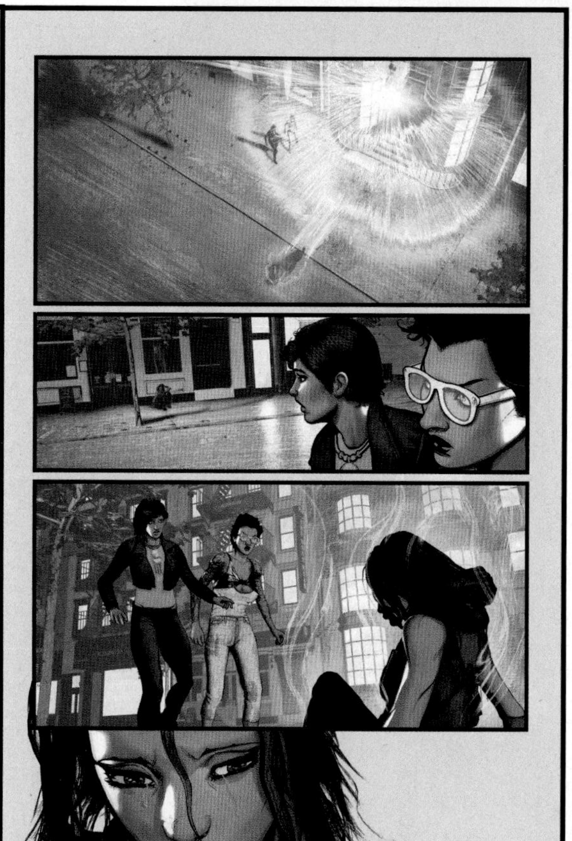

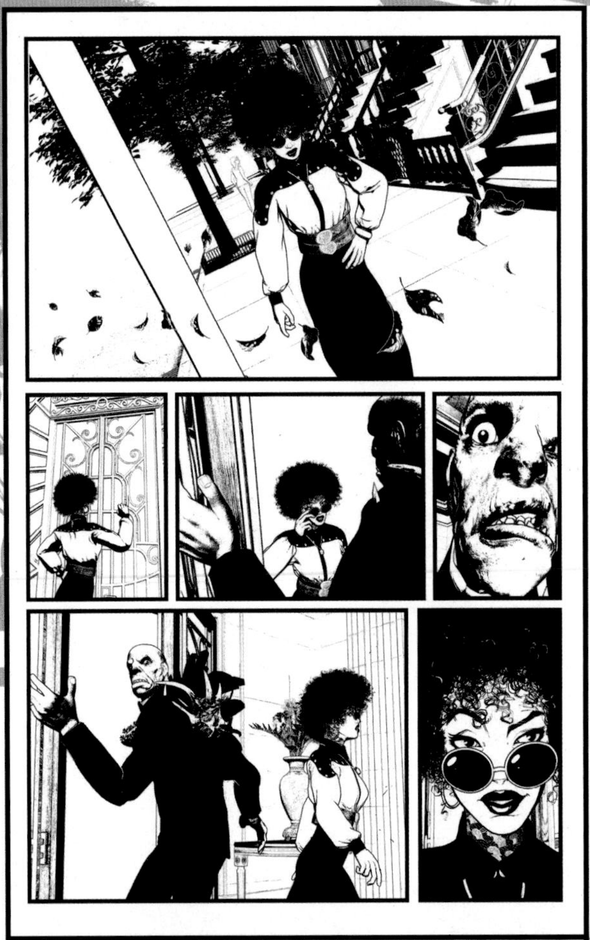

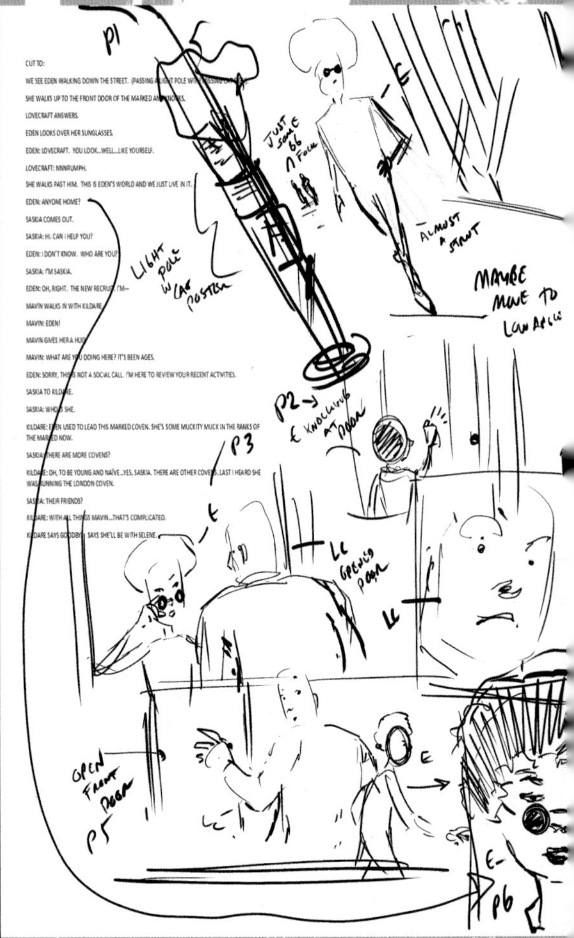
P1
CUT TO:
WE SEE EDEN WALKING DOWN THE STREET. (PASSING A
SHE WALKS UP TO THE FRONT DOOR OF THE MARKED AN KNOCKS.
LOVECRAFT ANSWERS.
EDEN LOOKS OVER HER SUNGLASSES.
EDEN: LOVECRAFT. YOU LOOK...WELL...LIKE YOURSELF.
LOVECRAFT: NNNRUMPH.
SHE WALKS PAST HIM. THIS IS EDEN'S WORLD AND WE JUST LIVE IN IT.
EDEN: ANYONE HOME?
SASKIA COMES OUT.
SASKIA: HI. CAN I HELP YOU?
EDEN: I DON'T KNOW. WHO ARE YOU?
SASKIA: I'M SASKIA.
EDEN: OH, RIGHT. THE NEW RECRU I'M—
MAVIN WALKS IN WITH KILDARE.
MAVIN: EDEN!
MAVIN GIVES HER A HUG
MAVIN: WHAT ARE Y U DOING HERE? IT'S BEEN AGES.
EDEN: SORRY, THI S NOT A SOCIAL CALL. I'M HERE TO REVIEW YOUR RECENT ACTIVITIES.
SASKIA TO KILD RE.
SASKIA: WHO S SHE.
KILDARE: E EN USED TO LEAD THIS MARKED COVEN. SHE'S SOME MUCKITY MUCK IN THE RANKS OF THE MAR ED NOW.
SASKIA: HERE ARE MORE COVENS?
KILDA E: OH, TO BE YOUNG AND NAÏVE...YES, SASKIA. THERE ARE OTHER COVE S. LAST I HEARD SHE WAS UNNING THE LONDON COVEN.
SAS IA: THEIR FRIENDS?
KIL ARE: WITH A L THI GS MAVIN...THAT'S COMPLICATED.
K DARE SAYS GO DBY SAYS SHE'LL BE WITH SELENE.
LIGHT POLE W CAR POSTER
JUST SOME 66 FOCUS
ALMOST A STRUT
MAYBE MOVE TO LOW ANGLE
P2 → E KNOCKING AT DOOR
P3
LC OPENS DOOR
OPEN FRONT DOOR
P5
P6

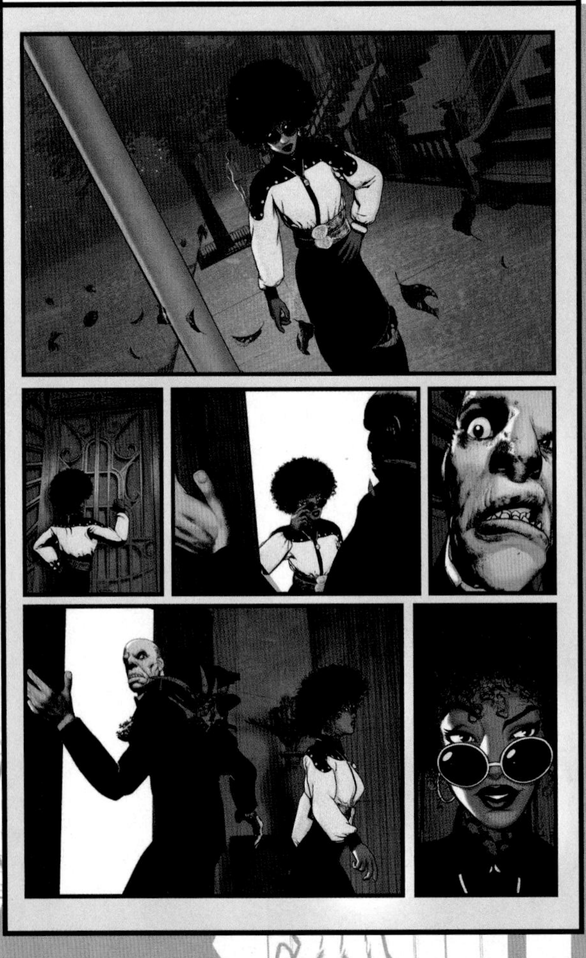

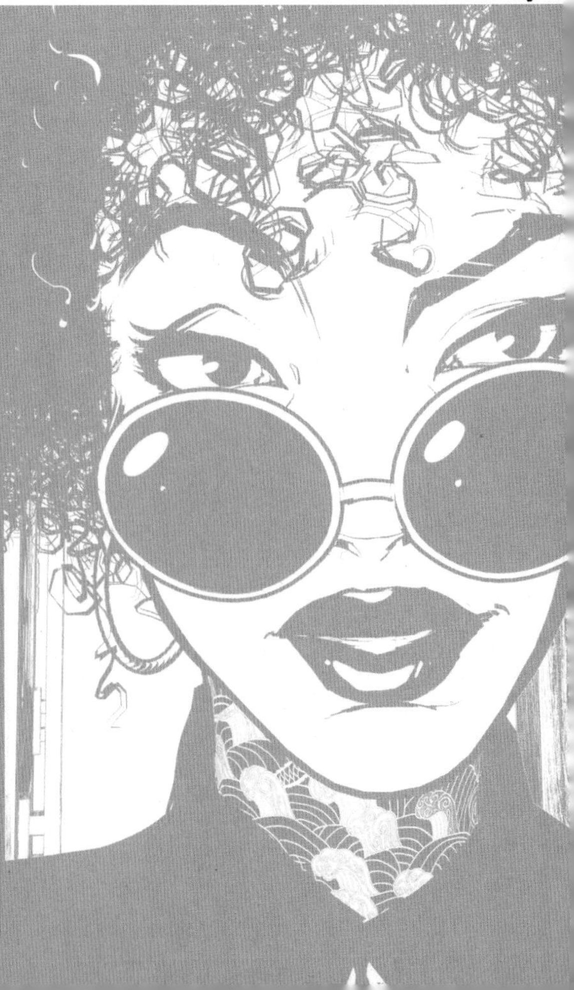

CUT TO:

LIZA'S ROOM.

MAVIN AND EDEN ARE SILHOUETTED IN THE BACKGROUND FRAMED BY DOOR WAY.

IN FOREGROUND IS LIZA SITTING CROSS LEGGED PLAYING WITH BLOCKS...CHILD LIKE. KOOK IS SITTING WITH HER SHOWING FLASH CARDS.

KOOK: B...B IS FOR BEE.

LIZA LAUGHS AND STARTS CHEWING ON A BLOCK.

KOOK: NO...BAD LIZA. (BETTER).

REVERSE ANGLE.

BOTH SERIOUS.

EDEN: HOW LONG HAS SHE BEEN LIKE THIS?

MAVIN: THIS IS AN IMPROVEMENT. SHE WAS COMATOSE FOR A FEW WEEKS. KOOK...I MEAN (HIS REAL NAME) HAS BEEN LOOKING AFTER HER.

EDEN: OUR BEST AND BRIGHTEST REDUCED TO A SIMPLETON ON YOUR WATCH. BRAVO!

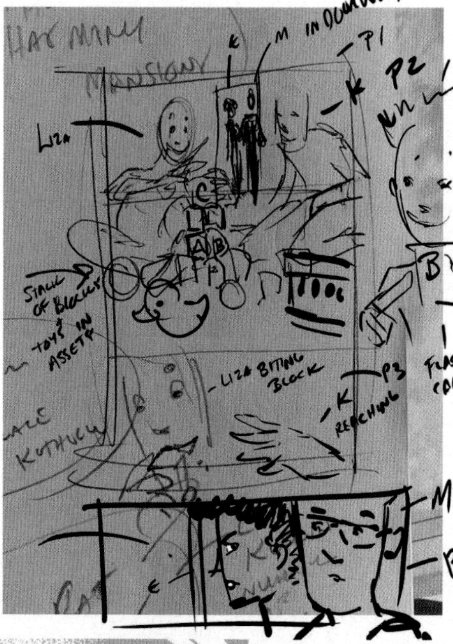

M IN DOORWAY
P1
K
P2
K
LIZA
STACK OF BLOCKS
TOYS IN ASSETS
B
LIZA BITING BLOCK
P3
FLASH CARD
K REACHING
M
P4

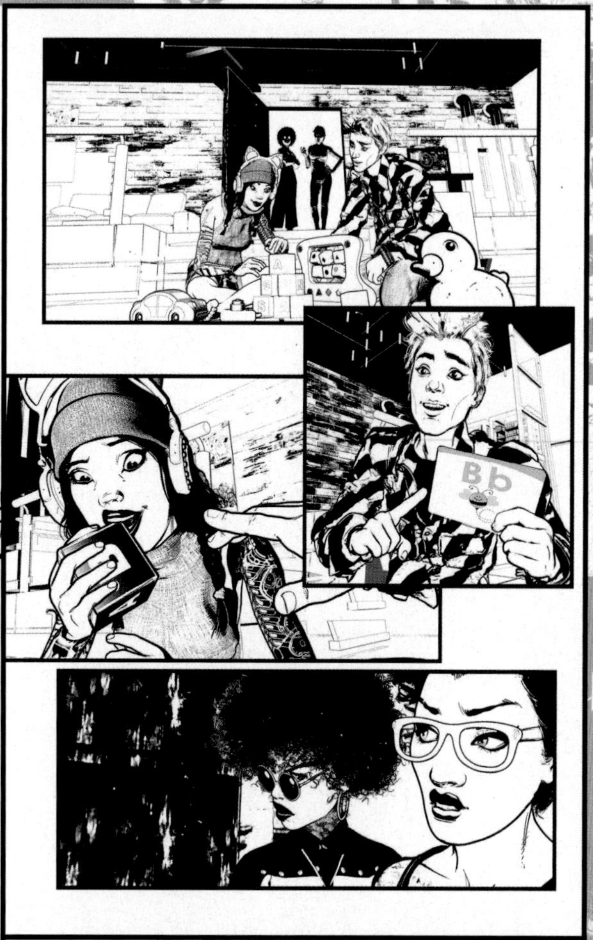

Bb

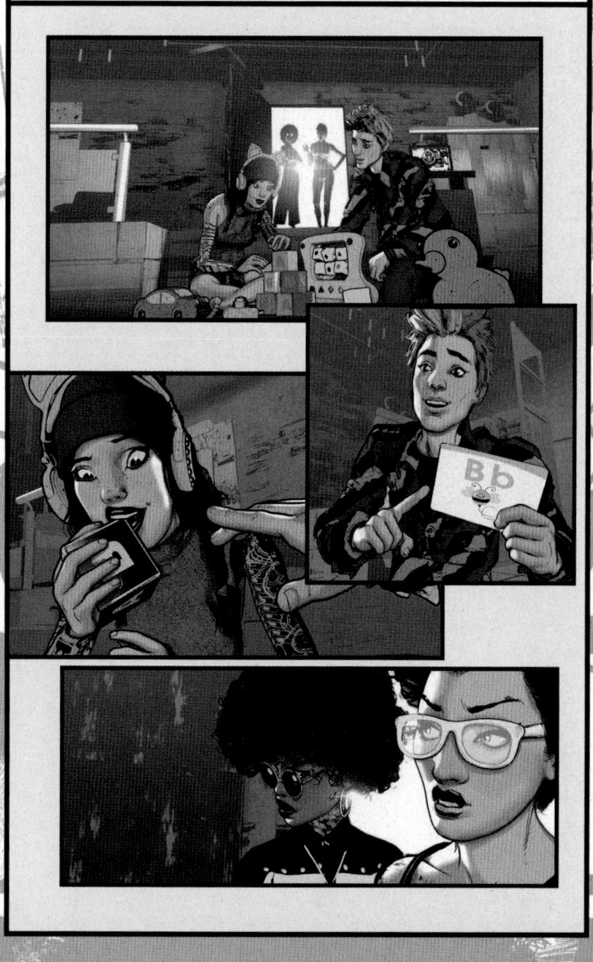

Bb

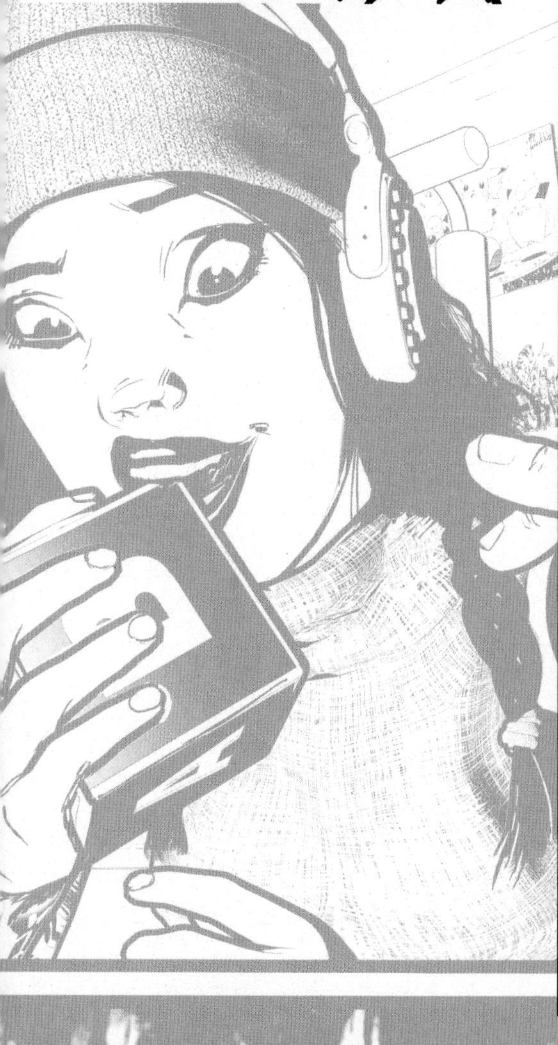

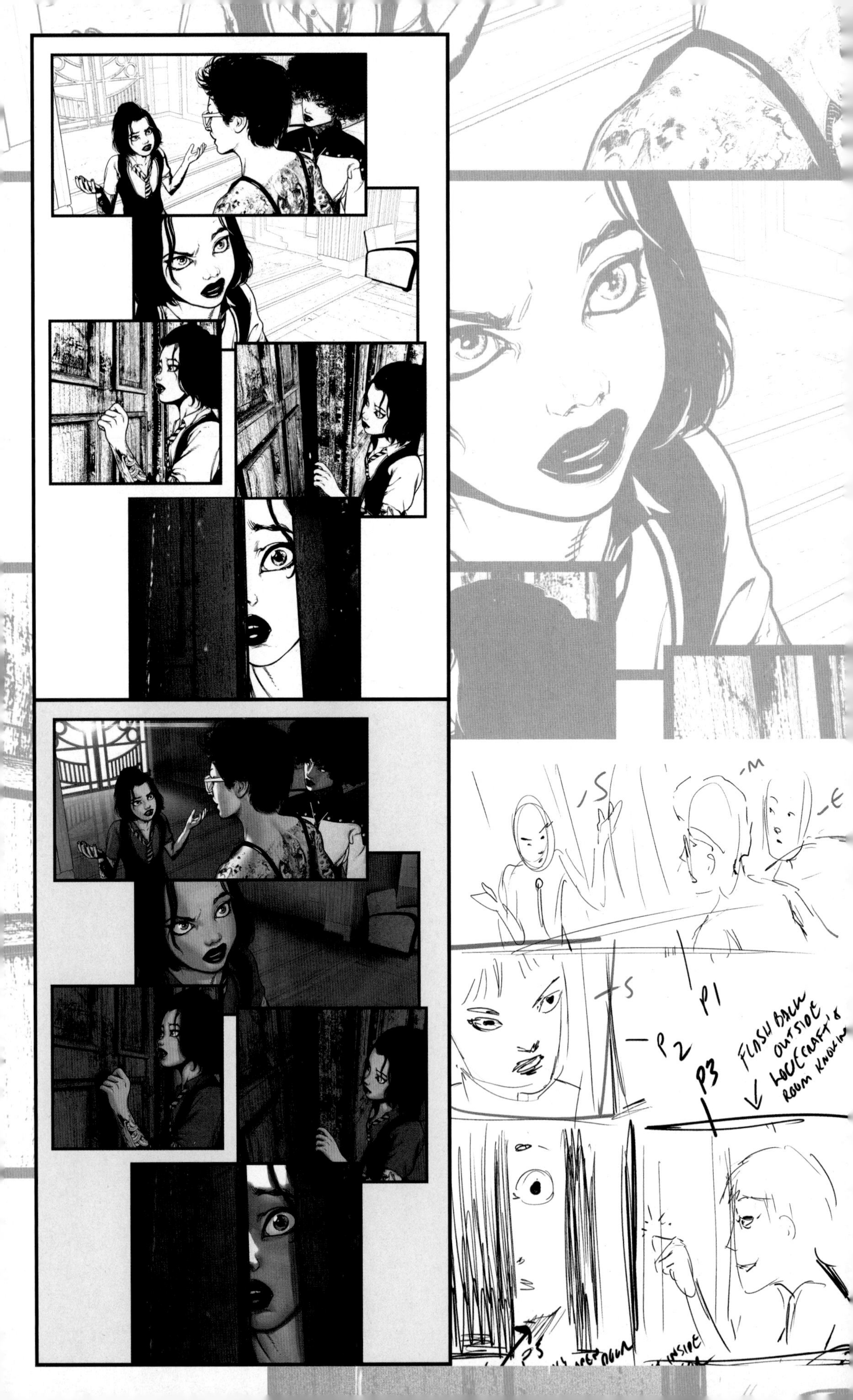
P1
P2
P3
FLASH BACK OUTSIDE LOVECRAFT'S ROOM KNOCKIN

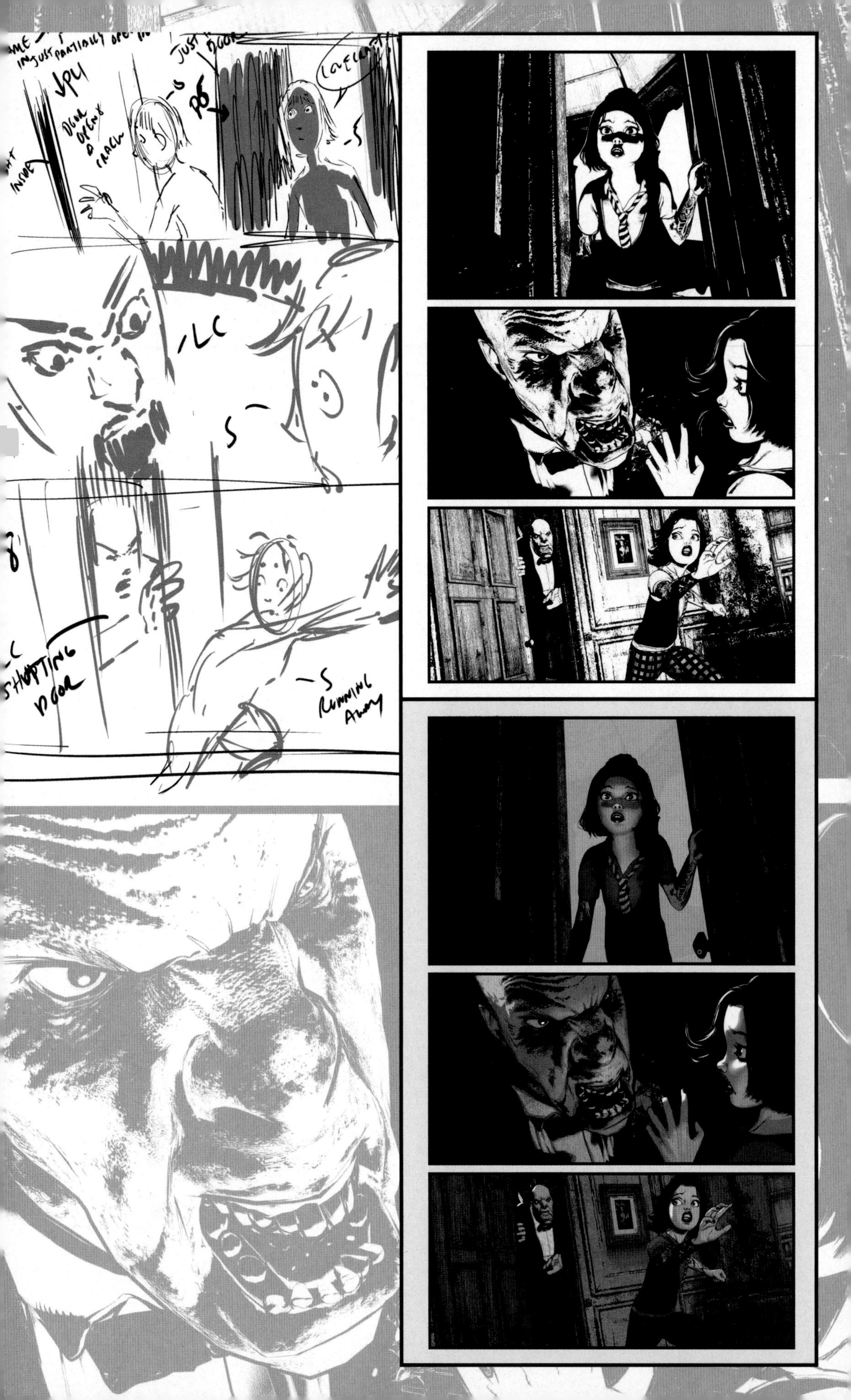

DOOR OPENS A CRACK
-LC
-S
SHUTTING DOOR
-S
RUNNING AWAY

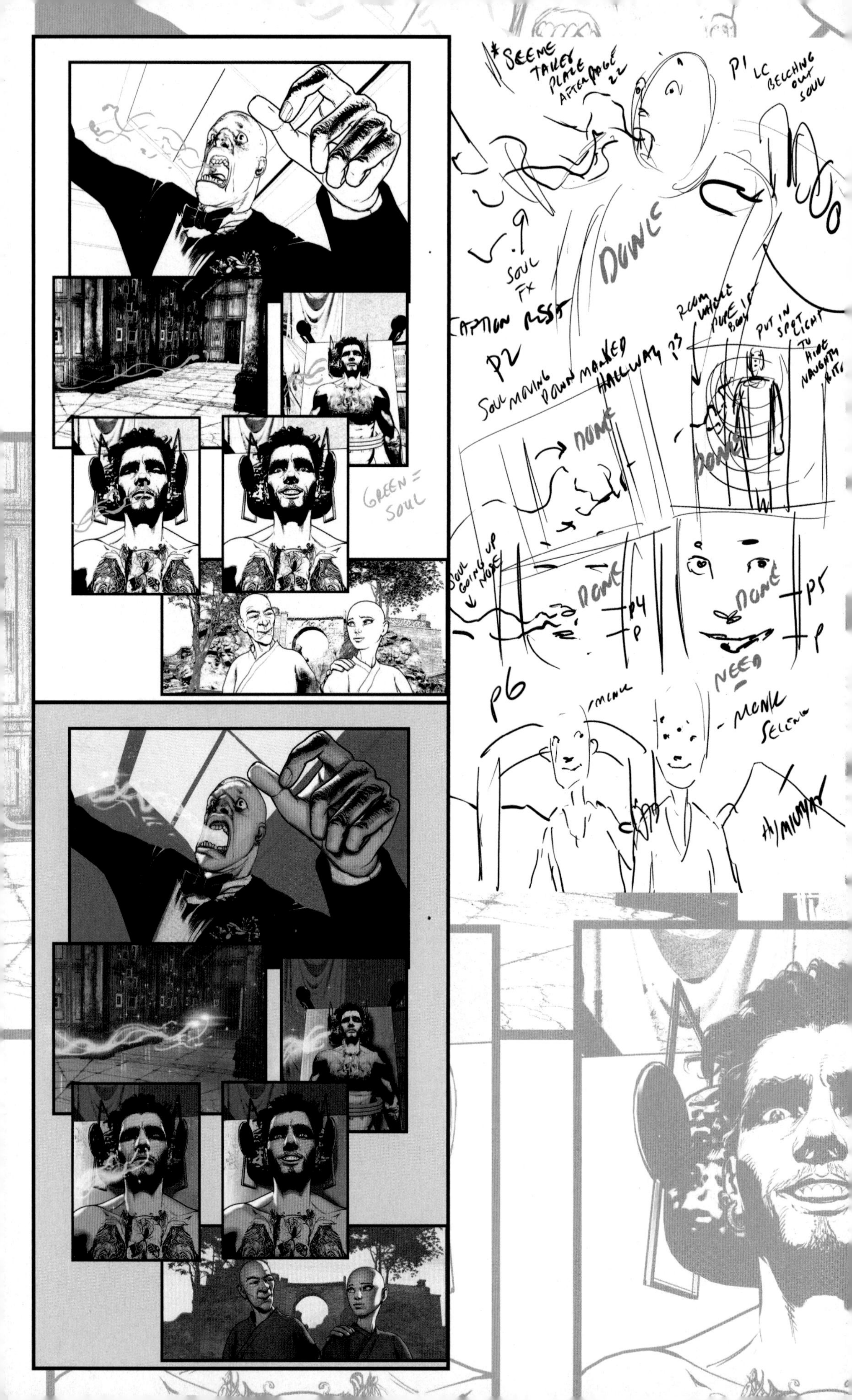

P1
LC BELCHING OUT SOUL
SOUL FX
DONE
P2
SOUL MOVING DOWN MASKED HALLWAY ??
PUT IN SPOT LIGHT TO HIDE NAUGHTY BITS
DONE
DONE
GREEN = SOUL
SOUL GOING UP NOSE
DONE
P4
DONE
P5
P6
MONK
NEED
MONK SELENE

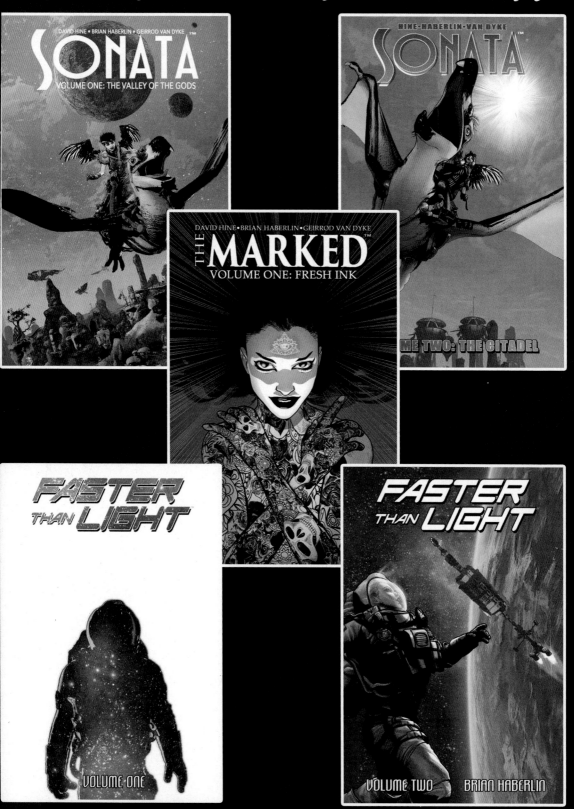

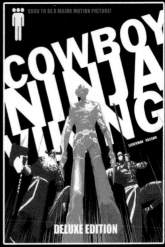
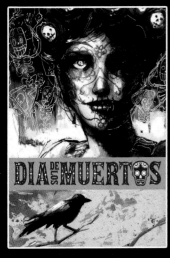
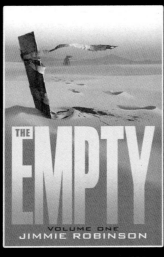